Arielle Immortal Resolve

*The Immortal
Rapture Series*
Volume 8

Lilian Roberts

Cover Design by Shari Ryan
Edited by Jacy Mackin

This is a work of fiction. Names, characters, places, brands, media, and incidents are either the product of the author's imagination or are used fictitiously. Any resemblance to similarly named places or to persons living or deceased is unintentional.

ISBN 978-1-945415-15-9

Library of Congress Control Number: 2015918638

 *Chapter 1*

SEBASTIAN PULLED ARIELLE into his arms, gave her a soft peck on the lips, and whispered in her ear, "I'll be right back baby, miss me..." Following Annabel's scent, he darted toward the corner of the country club.

Sebastian tracked Annabel carefully, trying to remain calm while anger and loathing filled his lungs. Tonight he was determined to kill her; he was committed to ending this part of his life and ridding Arielle of Annabel's relentless terror. He was willing to die if that's what it took to make sure Arielle was safe. He was responsible for pulling her into this frightening world of immortality. He was responsible for making her live in constant fear of a crazy immortal woman's unwavering desire to kill her for vengeance. Sebastian was ready to end it all, one way or another.

The skies were clear and the moon illuminated the night. Sebastian made his way across several miles of the club grounds at an inconceivable speed and when he reached the end of the property line his sharp immortal eyes caught a glimpse of two people in the distance. One of them was Annabel. The other was a man, but Sebastian couldn't see his face. His sense of smell became stronger as he drew closer to them; his nostrils filled with their immortal scent. They ran next to each other and paused for a moment, looking back, scanning the darkness. Sebastian crouched behind the wall that surrounded the property line and watched them intently. They seemed to be satisfied that they weren't being followed as they turned their heads and started to run at a slower pace.

They ran for quite a long time through the dark streets of Brighton and Sebastian followed at a safe distance, guzzling fresh air to help his thoughts remain on the right path. He wanted desperately to end this tonight; he didn't want her to slip away like she did back at the cemetery in St Jean De Luz. Suddenly they stopped and remained motionless. They'd reached the edge of a park that stretched for a couple of miles ahead and ended in a large square surrounded by beautiful homes. They scanned their surroundings again and then crossed the manicured lawns of the park toward the square in slow strides. When they arrived at the other side of the park, they stopped again, and seemed to carry on a short dialogue. Then the man turned and darted in the opposite direction. Sebastian never had a chance to get a good look at him, but he wasn't interested in the guy right now. Annabel was poised to step into the square when suddenly she paused at the curb and looked back, gaze piercing through the dark.

Sebastian held his breath, consumed by the uneasy feeling that Annabel knew she was being followed. He hid behind a large tree trunk on the other side of the park with teeth gritted, filled with resentment and loathing for this woman who had created total chaos in his life.

He waited patiently, in high hopes that tonight this part of Arielle's nightmare would be over. He wasn't going to let his anger guide his actions this time around. He needed to find out who she was working with and what they were plotting.

Annabel stood motionless for a moment, as if contemplating whether to move forward or abort reaching her destination. Sebastian took a long breath of relief when he saw her finally cross the square, take a little side street for a couple of blocks, and stop in front of a small house.

She again scanned the area around her carefully before she reached up and pressed the button at the gate twice. The lights came on and Sebastian's immortal hearing picked up a young female voice on the intercom asking the person's name. Annabel gave her name and immediately a tall, young girl came running out the door and across the garden, taking the padlock off the gate. Sebastian could hear their conversation while they were still outside.

"Are they here yet?" Annabel asked.

"No, not just yet, but I'm sure they'll be here shortly. They wouldn't break an agreement with you; they know better than that," the young girl replied, chuckling.

"Jane, I'll have to run out again for a short time. If I'm not back when they arrive, tell them to wait for me."

Together they walked up the few steps and crossed the threshold, shutting the door behind them. Sebastian moved swiftly and soundlessly across the cobblestoned square, reaching the corner of the dark street in a few strides. The street sign displayed the name York Street.

The house that Annabel had entered looked a bit run down and tall hedges surrounded the walls, preventing access or a view from the outside. Sebastian looked at the large metal chain and padlock that held the iron gate secure and chuckled under his breath. His immortal strength could crush the deadbolt to soft powder, but he chose to hurdle the tall fence and move quietly. He pushed carefully through the hedges and stood behind them, avoiding any unnecessary racket.

The night sky was dark and thick shadows surrounded the house. He stood in that darkness behind the hedges, right by a huge window that would give him a perfect view of the front room. The room was dark, so he waited patiently. Suddenly the light came on and his breath rushed through his lungs so fast that it made him a bit lightheaded.

He took a few deep breaths and inched closer. Peeking carefully through the sheer curtains, he saw Annabel and the girl she'd called Jane engaged in an animated conversation. Annabel was giving her directions about the people who were arriving to meet with her. Then she turned, walked toward the stairs that led to the upper floor, and started to scale the steps two at a time. She was almost at the top landing when Sebastian heard Jane's voice one more time.

"We installed the secret path you requested. Do you want to see it?" Jane inquired.

Annabel paused and, looking down at Jane, followed her finger that was pointing at the opposite wall. Sebastian saw Annabel's eyebrows narrow as a short smile crept across her ghastly face. She leaped down the stairs and dashed swiftly toward that wall. Sebastian saw Jane blink with a shocked look on her face, unable to follow Annabel's immortal speed. Jane crossed the floor in fast strides to keep up. Annabel had already reached the wall at the far end of the room and waited impatiently for Jane to catch up. Jane lifted her hand, and with her palm, pushed against an invisible spot on the wall. Sebastian watched, astonished, as the wall parted, revealing a secret entrance.

It wasn't so much the secret entrance that surprised Sebastian, but its location. This was a rundown, dilapidated house, not quite where anyone would expect to find secret passages. Annabel seemed to hesitate and then moved quickly through the gap in the wall with Jane by her side. They disappeared behind it, leaving no signs that would disclose what Sebastian had just witnessed. The opening had closed instantaneously, leaving what now seemed to be a normal wall.

Sebastian's thoughts whirled, trying to make sound decisions in a matter of milliseconds. His loathing for Annabel increased by the minute, but he decided to do the right thing. He pulled his mobile phone out of his pant pocket and pressed Troy's number. Troy picked up on the first ring.

"Troy," Sebastian said, his voice dropping to a whisper. "Where are you?"

"I'm on my way," Troy said. "Give me the exact location."

Sebastian gave him the address and added, "Listen, Troy, I'm going in. I want to deal with Annabel in a swift and conclusive way. Come find me in case I need help. There's something very peculiar about this run-down house. I saw Annabel and a human friend of hers go through a secret passage. The house is very small, so I'm thinking that this opening leads to some kind of secret cellar. The location of the switch is on the wall approximately one-point-five meters from the northeast corner and two-point-one meters high."

"I'll be right there."

"Thanks, Troy," he said, but didn't wait for his friend's reply. He ended the conversation and slipped his mobile back into his pocket.

The door was locked, but that wasn't an issue for Sebastian. He soon found himself standing in the middle of the front room, which was poorly furnished and silent as a tomb. Quickly he scaled the staircase to the upper floor. He was going to clear any obstacles and leave Annabel as his last and most revolting elimination. This was the best and most shrewd way to approach this attempt on Annabel's miserable life.

Four fully furnished bedrooms graced the upper floor and they all looked lived in. He was now sure that more people were in this house besides Annabel and Jane. Sebastian was standing in the last bedroom, one filled with Annabel's scent, ready to walk out, when he heard footsteps and froze. It was but a few minutes before Jane walked in carrying a laundry basket. Sebastian was standing behind the open door; he didn't want to hurt her, but he'd do what it took to carry out his mission.

Jane set the basket on the bed, started to take clothes out, and put them carefully in the dresser drawers. She was nearly done when Sebastian's phone went off and she spun around to face the angry immortal. Her jaw dropped and her eyes reflected intense fright.

Sebastian was stunned for a moment as silence stretched and he forgot about the phone when she suddenly darted toward the door. Her mouth opened as she prepared to scream. Sebastian moved with unfathomable speed, grabbed Jane by the throat, muting her scream forever. His strength broke her neck, and when he let her go, she dropped lifeless to the floor. Sebastian pulled her body into the small closet and shut the door. He felt dreadful for killing a human, but didn't regret his choice. She'd been ready to alert the other occupants that something was wrong and he couldn't allow that.

Leaving the room, he moved like a ghost along the upstairs corridor and descended the staircase carefully. He crossed the room on the main floor, walked down a small hallway, and noticed two doors, one on either side. He went into the door on his left and found himself in a small study full of books, boxes, and a foul odor that had to be a combination of several things. He backed off and shut the door behind him, shaking his head to rid his nostrils of that awful odor. He moved down the hall and opened the second door. Again, he was struck with the most god-awful smell. It was a sitting room connected to the kitchen area. Both rooms were poorly lit, giving Sebastian's perfect immortal eyes a sharp view of a disgustingly dirty area.

The smell came from the kitchen floor that was clogged with garbage bags, animal food, and feces, making the odor intolerable. Sebastian held his breath, moved quickly out into the hall, and shut the door behind him, shaking his head again in pure disgust. He headed back to the front room, where he stood in front of the wall through which he'd watched Annabel and Jane disappear. He looked for a noticeable gap, but there was none. He ran his palm across the wall, feeling every little bump and scrape until he encountered a small rise.

He pressed, holding his breath, and was delighted to see the wall part, exposing the opening. He listened for any sounds, contemplating his next move. Sebastian knew that Annabel was there, but was she alone? And if not, how many immortals would he be facing? Pulling his mobile from his pocket, he glanced at the screen. A smile spread across his face when he saw Arielle's text. *I'm worried to death. I love you more than life, please be careful.* His arms ached for her, but he had a serious issue to deal with, so he set the phone to vibrate and slipped it back in his pocket. Troy had to be getting close, so he decided to go for it.

Quickly he crossed the opening and forgot to breathe, consumed by total shock. He found himself on the landing of a steel staircase that spiraled down to a dark corridor. Taking a deep breath, he filled his lungs with the stale air and descended cautiously, one step at time, until he reached a damp floor. His immortal vision gave him a well-defined view of the place and he gasped in astonishment. How could a small house like this conceal such a large cellar? Sebastian scanned the area and noticed several doors on either side of the long corridor, but they all appeared dark and soundless except for the last two on the right. A thin streak of light escaped from a tiny crack at the first door.

Sebastian moved slowly, listening for any noise, but all he heard was his own footsteps. He exhaled as he reached the door, pausing to listen. Men's muted voices and low laughter reached him. Sebastian set his eyes on the crack and saw three men sitting around a small table playing cards. They seemed completely engrossed in their game, totally unaware of his presence.

Sebastian moved away quietly and approached the last door. His breath caught in his throat as the air thickened with Annabel's scent. He waited, motionless, while his mind assessed his position and his desperate wish to rid the world of Annabel for good. His nerves jumped and his breathing quickened as he turned the knob and pushed the door wide open.

Sebastian focused his startled eyes on Annabel, who was sitting in a large chair, watching him intently, a smug look on her face. She crossed her legs and clasped her hands in undisguised amusement.

"Welcome to your prison, my love," she said. Her laughter rang with clear pleasure. "I've been waiting patiently," she continued.

Sebastian was thunderstruck; her enthusiasm didn't surprise him, but the fact that she'd known he was coming was a complete shock. His stomach muscles tightened and his teeth clenched.

"Did you really think that I was that stupid?" she asked while Sebastian tried to regain his composure. "I wanted you to follow me; that was my plan all along and you fell in my trap like an amateur." Annabel laughed with disdain.

Sebastian looked straight ahead, avoiding her gaze and swallowed hard. His mind was spinning, trying to find a solution to a bad turn of events. He scanned the room, felt his skin crawl and icy fingers creep up his spine, when he realized that he was standing in the middle of a torture chamber.

He drew enough breath to utter in sheer revulsion: "What is it exactly that you want from me, Annabel?"

"Sebastian, why do you keep asking the same question over and over?" She studied him intently, waiting for an answer.

"I keep asking the same question because you seem to have a hard time understanding that you and I are never going to happen. I didn't want you in my life then and I don't want you now," he replied, grinding his teeth. "So again, what is it that you want from me?" Sebastian gave her a look full of venom.

Annabel crossed her arms looking totally unruffled and leaning back on the chair, smiled with clear amusement. "You...You are what I want and nobody else will ever have you in this century or any other. You're mine and you'll be mine for eternity." She smiled as she stood and approached him with a wanton smile. "You look scrumptious in that beautiful suit. Any special occasion?" she laughed spitefully.

"I hate you, Annabel, I've never been yours and I'd rather die, so let's end this right here, right now."

"What do you mean?" she asked smugly as she walked back toward the chair.

"I'm going to kill you, Annabel; I want you out of my life for good." He hoped his expression painted a clear picture of determination.

"Sebastian…let me bring up a few things that you might've overlooked." She was still smiling. "You came here alone with no weapons, and I know that you already saw the men in the next room, who are awaiting my signal to take you down. I know that you're strong, but one against four? How are you planning on killing me?" She seemed to be enjoying herself.

"I don't need weapons, Annabel, you know that, I'm a lot stronger that you and a better fighter, too." Sebastian shot toward her, catching Annabel off guard. He grabbed her by the throat and threw her across the room. She crashed against the far wall face first and buckled to the ground where she remained unmoving for several seconds. She finally regained her strength and stood slowly, a startled look on her bloody face. She shook her head, leaning against the wall for a moment. Sebastian was now fully alert; he knew she wouldn't give up that easy. He was still pondering her next move when she launched into the air and threw herself against him with so much force that they crashed to the hard floor with a loud thud and skidded across the room until the wall stopped them.

Annabel jumped to her feet and tried to run, but Sebastian was much faster. He reached up and grabbed the back of her jacket with one hand, making a hard fist with the other. Annabel span around to free her arms from her jacket and Sebastian's fist landed right between her eyes, sending her flying across the room to crash on the ground in a daze.

Sebastian crossed the room in a slow stride and looked down on Annabel's bloody face with satisfaction. He bent down, picked her up by the throat, and steadied her upright in front of him long enough to land another punch to her face that sent her crashing into the far wall with a loud bang. The sound of crushing bones was loud when Annabel's body came in contact with the wall, giving Sebastian pleasure. She let out a growl and crumpled to the floor.

Sebastian turned his attention to the door and stilled, listening carefully, his body tensed, but he didn't hear any footsteps and the door remained closed. Annabel stirred and moaned across the room; Sebastian turned to look at her. She was trying to shake off the confusion and clear her dazed head. She coughed and spat the blood that was dripping from her mouth onto the floor. She moaned again as she raised her hands slowly and touched her bloody face. She cursed with clenched teeth and, bringing her hands down, stared at the blood. She stood slowly, leaning against the wall and steadied herself. Sebastian knew she was going to heal extremely fast so he had to take advantage of her confusion and keep her in a state of haze.

He closed the distance between them watching her with fury in his heart and punched her one more time in the pit of her stomach. Blood gushed out of her nose and mouth and she crumpled to the ground with a snarl. She tried to grip his arm but he jerked free.

"I hate you, Annabel, more than you'll ever know." Sebastian's voice was full of venom. Annabel lifted her eyes to his.

"There's a thin line between love and hate, Sebastian, and that's exactly where you stand with me, right on that line." Her voice was barely audible, her face bruised, reflecting shock and repulsion and she closed her eyes, grinding her teeth.

"I want you out of my life," he whispered, voice full of revolt.

Annabel opened her eyes and stared at him in defiance, her voice scarcely audible. "I still love you," she sighed, grimacing.

Sebastian shoved her down one more time and walked over to sit on the chair, watching her intently and waiting to hear from Troy. He turned his head away from Annabel and closed his eyes, hoping to have this over with in a short time.

He was lost in his thoughts gazing at his feet when he was startled by a noise. He tried to keep the shock off his face when he saw Annabel leap toward the door and he reacted instantly. He practically ejected himself from the chair and dashed after her, catching her wrist and yanking her back. She swayed wildly back and forth and as her body turned toward Sebastian he lifted his free hand and slugged her between the eyes over and over again, dropping her to the floor, as she let out a blood-curdling scream. She was now a bloody mess and moaned in sheer agony.

"I want you to be looking at me when I kill you," he growled.

The next few minutes were a complete frenzy that drove a cold chill up Sebastian's spine. He felt the barrel of a gun pressing painfully into his back and several strong arms pulling him off of Annabel, throwing him face down on the ground. Sebastian broke from the restraint, spun around and hit the man with the gun hard, sending him flying against the opposite wall. The gun flew out of the man's hand, slid across the floor and landed in the corner on the opposite side of the room.

Sebastian took a quick scan and realized that he was in a lot of trouble. He was facing two more of Annabel's friends, or hired thugs, who were large, hard-muscled immortals. Soon Annabel and the third guy would be healed and back on their feet. He watched the anticipation cross their faces and knew they were ready to tear him apart. He pressed his lips together and hurled himself toward them, and in that millisecond he saw a balled fist coming fast toward him. He dodged the blow and taking careful aim, landed a rapid kick to the guy's midsection, sending him cursing to the ground.

Three down, one to go. From the corner of his eye he caught the flash of a blade swinging very close to his body. He spun and struck upward, throwing another vicious blow to the last guy, but not before the blade sliced through his shirt and into his chest. Sebastian gritted his teeth as his muscles clenched painfully and that was the last thing he remembered before a heavy object whacked him hard on the back of the head and he crumpled unconscious to the floor.

* * *

Annabel was still a bloody mess, but completely aware of her surroundings. Her face flaunted a strange mixture of emotions, victory and defeat simultaneously. Two of the three men dragged Sebastian's unconscious body across the floor and propped him upright against the wall. They stretched his arms and legs apart and secured his wrists and ankles with wide metal hooks that'd been drilled deep into the concrete wall. Sebastian was extremely strong but there would be absolutely no way to bust free unless he took the whole wall down. The hooks had been drilled twenty feet deep into the concrete. This was their world and they had complete knowledge of their extraordinary gifts.

"Paolo, get off the floor." Annabel's voice rang harsh in the quiet of the room.

Paolo flinched, shook his head and gave her a dry smile. He gathered himself and stumbled to his feet. He shook his head again and stiffened when his eyes fell on Sebastian's unconscious body. He sprinted to his gun on the other side of the room and headed toward Sebastian, seeking revenge. Annabel was remarkably fast despite her wounds; she hurled herself forward, grabbed Paolo's arm and pulled it back just before he thrashed Sebastian's head. Paolo spun in sheer astonishment to face Annabel with eyebrows raised. A cold warning flashed at him from her eyes.

"What?" he asked, trying to hold back his rage.

"Don't you dare touch him!" she screamed. "He's mine and I'll deal with him my way." Annabel glared at him to be sure he understood and he immediately backed off. She then turned and looked at Sebastian's bloody, limp body for a moment. Venom filled her eyes and averting her gaze to her goons she growled, "Get out!"

They instantly turned and walked out, shutting the door behind them. Annabel approached Sebastian's unconscious body with a wild look in her eyes and ran her fingers across his lips.

"Don't go anywhere pretty boy, I'll be right back." She turned and walked out, closing the door behind her.

*　*　*

Sebastian opened his eyes sluggishly and his gaze swept the room carefully. He shut his eyes again, thinking that he was hallucinating, overwhelmed with mixed emotions his mind couldn't separate out individually. His thoughts were muddled and exhaustion grasped him like a vise. He tried hard to remember and his immortal intuition told him that he was in some kind of trouble, but nothing tangible. His mouth was dry, his face tight and an unease crept over him. Shearing pain spread across his skin like waves of fire, burning every single muscle and ripping every fiber in his body. He trusted his insight to search through unknown paths in his mind and find the conscious awareness in his head that would clear his thoughts.

He opened his eyes again and suddenly the smell of dust, mildew, and blood drifted up his nostrils, setting his nerves on edge. He remembered immediately where he was and tried to move, astonished when he realized he was shackled to the wall. He tried to pull away to no avail. He looked over and noticed the thick metal staples that were driven into the concrete and cursed aloud in rage. Sebastian licked his dry lips and stared for what seemed to be eternity at the dry blood covering the front of his shirt. He tried to remember how he got hurt but was unable to recall.

The room was empty and his mind swirled wildly wondering, *Where's Annabel? And where's Troy?* He shook his head in anger and ran his tongue over his dried lips once again.

He was startled when his mobile vibrated in his pocket, but he had no way of answering. He cursed aloud, pulling hard at the shackles trying to get loose. He closed his eyes, despondent. His mind filled with dread. If he could cry he'd be crying right now, because he'd failed her again. If anything, he'd succeeded in loosing Arielle forever. He let out a deep sigh and slumped back against the wall.

He was startled to hear the door flung open. Annabel stepped in then let it slam shut behind her. He hoped his expression was a blank. He could see disaster racing toward him, but he wasn't going to give her the satisfaction to gloat.

"Darling…I'm happy to see that you're still here," she chuckled. Her disgusting laughter drove a dagger in his heart.

"Did you miss me?" she asked with clear gratification, as she closed the distance between them. Their faces were now only millimeters apart. Sebastian could see that she'd healed and had changed her bloody clothes.

"You…are…now…completely…mine," she said, pleasure accentuating each word.

"I'll never be yours, Annabel, my heart belongs to someone else," he replied with clenched teeth.

"I don't care about your heart, Sebastian," she said. She laughed again as she moved even closer, a seductive look in her eyes. She cupped his face in her hands, making him gaze in her eyes.

"I've always loved you, Sebastian," she whispered. She wrapped her arms around his neck and pressed her lips to his with pure hunger. Sebastian felt nausea settling in the pit of his stomach. He closed his eyes and remained completely still. Her touch didn't sear him; it just engulfed him with unbelievable fury. It didn't stimulate him; it triggered a suffocating feeling that was choking him, making it difficult to breathe.

"I hate you, Annabel," he snarled in a ragged voice. "You're the most ghastly woman I've ever met."

Where's Troy? He should be here by now.

"I am going to have you one way, or another, Sebastian, so try to enjoy yourself." She laughed again, reveling in her dominance over him. "You've been my life's long desire and I finally have you where I want you."

Her voice was making him sick; he closed his eyes, trying to endure. She leaned against him, pressing him against the wall, laughing with amusement. Sebastian tried to pull away but the shackles wouldn't budge. She lifted her hand and brushed her fingers over his lips and down his cheek, moaning with desire.

"What does this miserable, breakable human have, that I don't," she asked. Her eyes searched his face for an answer and, leaning in, her lips brushed his ear.

Sebastian recoiled, and lifting his head glared at her with repugnance. "Arielle is everything you're not. She's perfect," he said, his words choked with passion.

Rage flashed in Annabel's eyes. Jealousy shot across her face. "You're never going to see her again!" she shrieked. Her jaw stiffened, her eyes filled with anger. She pulled out a knife, grabbed his jacket and shredded it, laughing wildly. Next she gripped his shirt and tore it wide open, sending the buttons tumbling in every direction. She ran her hands over the planes of his chest, moaning, her eyes slit in passion.

The contact sent a repulsive jolt through his body. He sucked in a deep breath and looked in her eyes with pure loathing. "Listen Annabel and listen to me very carefully," Sebastian hissed, clenching his teeth.

"You can do whatever you want with me, because I don't care. My heart and my love will always belong to Arielle. She's my life, the girl who gave meaning to my miserable existence. You, on the other hand, will always be the most despicable nightmare I've ever come across during my 600 years on this earth. I despise you with every single fiber in my body and in case you didn't hear me before, your touch...makes my skin...crawl," he emphasized his last words.

Her next move left Sebastian speechless, but he quickly regained his composure. She pulled out a dagger, her eyes wild. She lifted the blade and held it close to his face. If she was trying to evoke terror, she failed miserably. Sebastian was calm. He wasn't going to give her the satisfaction of his fear.

She ripped his shirt completely away from his body and threw it to the floor. Her eyes roved over his muscular body. "Mmmm..." she snarled, "let's see if I can make your skin crawl with this touch."

In a lightning move, she slashed his bare chest with the blade. Sebastian moaned in agony as blood oozed out of the deep gash. Annabel laughed manically and raised the blade one more time, coming down harder this time, slicing his chest even deeper. Sebastian let out a low growl of anguish, as he felt his body crumpling, unable to stand. His arms strained in their bonds on the metal hooks that kept him from crashing to the floor. She moved with unbelievable speed and gashed deeper wounds in his upper arms. Annabel seemed to get a sick thrill from watching Sebastian suffering in a bloody mess.

She leaned close to his ear and whispered voice full of mockery, "Don't worry, Sebastian. I'm not going to let you die. I'm going to make you feel pain. I want you to suffer like I've suffered from your cruel rejections over the centuries." She ran her tongue over his earlobe and groaned in sick enjoyment.

"Despite everything you've said, I still love you," she moaned. "I'm going to finally have you and I don't care who you love, or who has your heart. I have you now." She moved her lips over his mouth and kissed him with passion. "I know you're going to heal fast," she said, utterly possessed, running her hands over his lacerations, holding the tip of the knife against his breastbone, as he was unable to defend himself.

"I'm going to drain some of this delicious blood from your gorgeous body until you surrender to me." She pressed the knife deep one more time and Sebastian's beautiful face twisted as he growled in pain. Annabel took a step back and threw her head back, letting out wild laughter with a face illuminated by thrilling satisfaction.

"How could you be so stupid? Here you are with no one to help you and no way to fight back." She broke out again into a hardy laugh, as she moved closer and ran her hand over his bare skin. Sebastian was barely breathing as blood gushed out of the deep cuts. His jeans were soaked and he could now see a small puddle shaping around his feet. His face was a clear mask of agony and even though he was getting weaker by the moment, deep in his gut he could still feel utter revulsion for this woman.

Weakness gripped him like a vise and he succumbed to his destiny as his heart sank and his last hope for rescue disappeared. His weak mind told him that something must've happened to Troy; otherwise he'd have been here by now. His breath weak and ragged, he tried to speak but the words faded on his lips. He looked straight in her eyes, summoned every bit of strength he had left, and spat on her face.

Annabel recoiled and screamed, as she raised her hand and wiped her face, consumed by fury and unmitigated rage. The door flew open and Annabel's thugs came running in. She spun around, her eyes glaring wildly. "Get out!" she screamed at them, pointing at the door. When the door closed behind them she glared back at Sebastian with clenched teeth.

"Are you willing to die for her?" she screeched.

"She's worth dying for," he whispered with a faint smile. He knew that he was on the brink of collapse when he felt Annabel's warm breath against his ear and her words drove the dagger deeper into his heart.

"Do you remember Gaston, my love? He was your best friend. He's here with one desire and one desire only; to conquer Arielle's heart with or without her consent."

Sebastian winced just before he was consumed by darkness and fell unconscious.

* * *

Annabel's frown deepened, hatred for Arielle clenched her chest with unbelievable pressure. She swallowed hard the lump forming in her throat and bit her lip in frustration. Arielle had taken the only man Annabel had ever truly wanted. Sebastian had been her sole quest for 600 years now. All she ever wanted was for him to love and desire her like no other. She closed her eyes, distressed at knowing that it was a futile attempt, but she wanted him all to herself and was determine to keep him prisoner until she decided otherwise.

She retreated to the chair and sat intently watching this stunning man. Even in his unconscious state he made Annabel's blood boil and stirred up every craving she'd ever possessed. Annabel knew how the immortal body worked. Sebastian would be able to satisfy her sexually even in his unconscious state. She darted out of the chair and shed her clothes, dropping them to the floor. With the dagger, she quickly shredded Sebastian's pants away from his body. She was determined to satisfy every single desire even though Sebastian was unconscious and unable to fight back.

If he were cognizant, the moments that followed would've been the worst nightmare of his immortal life. Annabel violated his body in every way possible. She finally pulled back, satisfied and staring at his naked, gorgeous body, laughed wildly.

"I told you I was going to have you one way or another, but you didn't believe me," she screamed and laughed again. She picked up her clothes and walked backward until she reached the wall behind the chair. She put her hand up and pressed against it, exposing a second secret passage.

"I'll be back, my love, so don't go anywhere," she promised, as she crossed the passage and let it close behind her.

 *Chapter 2*

WHEN TROY ANSWERED the phone he could sense in Sebastian's voice the excitement and resolve to end Annabel's life. Sebastian's zeal gripped Troy's attention, giving him a surge of commitment to run to his side. Troy slipped the mobile back in his pocket and paused for a moment to smile. He ran his tongue over his lips, savoring Gabrielle's kiss, and darted into the night after Sebastian.

He tracked his scent and soon arrived at the edge of the park Sebastian mentioned on the phone. He scanned each direction carefully before he crossed it in large strides. He reached the cobblestoned square, which was surrounded by average size homes. It was the typical European roundabout with five exits. He stood motionless before walking quietly in the night like a ghost until he located York St. He was to look for the second house on the left off of York St. The quiet was deafening as he stood behind a huge tree across from the two-story house.

His immortal gift gave him a clear view of the small rundown house and its tall fence with the large padlock at the gate. This wasn't going to be an issue for Troy and his immortal strength. The house appeared deserted but Sebastian was already in there. He paused again and after scanning deep in the dark he approached the house in slow, calculated movements like a panther after its prey, and hurdled the fence without any difficulty, landing inside the garden. He darted toward the tall hedge growing against the house and disappeared behind it. He noticed that the light was on in one of the rooms so he crept along the wall and stood underneath the window. He peeked inside but the room was empty. *Where's Sebastian; where is anybody in this house?* Troy's thoughts whirled like a windmill in a storm.

He decided to move but just before he emerged from the hedges he heard footsteps approaching from the far side of the dark street and caught a clear view of three men emerge from the shadows and stop short of the gate. Troy examined their faces and immediately knew that he was dealing with immortals. Their lips were moving but their conversation was soundless to a human ear; however Troy could hear every word. He paused and pulled back behind the hedges, waiting for their next move. The man who seemed to be the leader of the trio looked around as if he was waiting for someone.

"We must wait for Clair before we meet with Annabel," he said. His voice was loud and quite intense startling Troy.

"Jon, what if the price is ridiculously low?" one of the guys asked the man who wanted to wait for Clair.

"We don't have to take the job," he replied. "She did, however, promise that it'll be a hefty amount. I guess we have to wait and see." He continued looking around nervously.

A weird silence fell between them again, as Troy's body tensed. Sebastian was in there with Annabel and maybe a few more thugs and now there were three more guys and a woman who would be joining them shortly. The odds were stacking against him, how was he ever going to overcome this kind of obstacle? With jaw tightened and breath held in his throat his thoughts pulsed wildly, realizing that he needed more help.

He cursed silently, knowing that Ian and Eva had left for their honeymoon. He didn't have Loren's number but he could call Christian and Isabella as well as Nathan. Lost in thought, he started when he felt his phone vibrate.

He pulled it out of his pocket and upon gazing at the screen, his jaw dropped. How could that be possible? Antonius' name flashed across the screen like a rescue vessel throwing out a lifeline. He found himself smiling and a spurt of exuberance rushed through his body like lightning in the night. He answered the call with a text message.

I can't talk, but I need your help.

I'm heading your way with friends. Don't try to do anything stupid alone.

But how did you know?

Gabrielle called. She said you needed help.

Troy chuckled softly, relief engulfing him.

I have a strong feeling that Sebastian is in deep trouble. He's not picking up his phone or texting back.

Where are you?

Troy gave him the address, put away his mobile with a sigh of relief, and waited for his friends to show up.

With no clue as to where Antonius was coming from, he pulled further back into the hedges and waited. His eyes were locked on the three men, hoping they'd make their move soon; he needed to make sure that Sebastian was safe. Just as his patience was wearing thin, he caught a movement in his periphery. He spun around and was shocked to see four men creeping in the shadows across the street.

It couldn't have been more than a couple of minutes since he'd spoken with Antonius, but as he scanned their faces he recognized Antonius, Gerard, Giani, and Arturo. His friends seemed to be aware of the three thugs standing at the gate as well because they were watching them intently. He let out a deep breath of relief and his eyes turned back toward the gate. Troy studied the men again and frowned, his worry over Sebastian increasing; every minute that ticked away could bring Sebastian closer to disaster. He sought revenge in such a brutal way that he would've moved the Alps to get to Annabel and that could land him in deep trouble. Troy pursed his lips. Worrying wasn't helpful at the moment. He glanced again inside the room but it was still deserted.

"Clair, there you are…" An amused voice made Troy jump and turn his gaze back toward the gate. A young woman had approached the three men and they were exchanging friendly greetings. They pressed the button on the wall and the faint sound of a bell was heard from somewhere inside the house. At first there was silence and it was long enough to make Troy anxious but finally the door flew open and a large-built man step over the threshold. He glared at the gate with an assessing look and finally walked across the garden and unlocked the padlock. He didn't seem to know any of the newcomers but introduced himself as Raffaele with a dry smile. The woman stepped in front of the three men and her voice came out cold and firm.

"I'm Clair," and pointing at the others she continued. "These are Jon, Liam, and Oliver. We're here to meet Annabel at her request."

Raffaele nodded, moved aside, and let them in. He secured the padlock and headed back toward the house. There was no further dialog between them as they crossed the threshold and disappeared behind the front door.

As soon as the door closed behind them Troy's friends run across the street, scaled the fence and crossed the garden in large strides. They shook hands quietly, Troy's relief quite palpable. Words formed on their lips but no audible sounds were heard. They peeked through the window and watched the man who called himself Raffaele pause for a moment, then advance across the room. He stopped in front of the wall directly opposite the front door.

The newcomers looked around and finally rested their gaze on Raffaele. They watched him intently as Raffaele placed his hand flat on the wall, leaned in, and pressed. The wall gave in, revealing a secret passage. He stepped aside and, looking back at them, motioned for them to enter first. He followed at their heels, pressed his palm against the wall on the inside, and the opening disappeared.

Troy cursed with clenched fists and eyes narrowed to slits. His mind was whirling with wild thoughts.

"What is it?" Antonius asked.

"I'm worried about Sebastian and wondering how many immortals we have to face behind that wall." Troy's voice was full of concern.

"It doesn't matter how many they are. We can handle them." Antonius smiled wide and patted Troy on the back. The front door wasn't a challenge and soon enough they stood in the middle of the room.

Giani and Arturo climbed the steps soundlessly to eliminate any thugs on the upper floor while Gerard and Antonius moved down the hall to search the rooms on the main floor. Troy remained on guard to prevent any surprises from the outside or the secret passage. The upstairs rooms seemed to be empty and so were the filthy rooms on the first floor. They all assembled again in the front room and walked over to the wall to find the secret passage.

"Where in the hell is everybody?" Giani whispered. "Are they all behind that wall?"

"Most likely," Troy replied, glancing around the room.

Their eyes honed in on the wall that concealed the invisible door. Girard crept up to that wall and, leaning forward, placed his hand flat on the surface. His fingers traced around the area they'd seen the goon pressing a few minutes earlier. It wasn't long before he felt the small bump on the wall and, pressing it impatiently, exposed the opening. A faint smile of satisfaction crossed his face as he looked back at his friends and motioned them to follow.

They stepped inside the opening and came to a halt, adjusting to the intensified darkness, as the door closed behind them. They scanned the area, eyes darting from side-to-side. They were shocked to find themselves standing at the top landing of a long spiral metal staircase, leading down into a dark cellar. They could feel the coolness of the stone and the dampness of the air around them. A thick, musty odor filled their nostrils, making it hard to breath.

They exchanged brief glances, as anger intensified and silence filled the air. They made their way quietly down the spiral staircase, trying to pick up Sebastian's scent. That wasn't an easy task as the scent of immortality was everywhere. Their eyes focused on the dark corridor as they stepped down on the wet cold floor. They could clearly see slithers of light coming from two rooms at the very end of the corridor. As they moved further down the passageway they heard muffled sounds coming out of the room closest to them. They moved closer and peering through the cracks of the door, observed a small room dimly lit and poorly furnished. There was a large dirty sofa pushed against the concrete wall, a small fridge stained with mold and dirt and several chairs around a large old table. There were six men in that room and that included the man who called himself Raffaele; three were the newcomers Jon, Liam, and Oliver. The other two scums seemed to answer to Raffaele. To their surprise the female who called herself Clair seemed to be in her late teens. They were all seated around the table.

"Where in bloody hell is Annabel?" the man who called himself Jon asked with clear frustration.

"She had to run an errand that couldn't wait but should be back shortly," Raffaele replied.

The newcomer cursed in disapproval. "I told Annabel that I don't like to be kept waiting." The anger in his eyes deepened.

"Well you can either wait or just leave," said Raffaele, in a firm tone. "Annabel calls the shots," he explained.

Jon raised an eyebrow at Raffaele and, leaning back in his chair crossed his arms, a displeased look on his face.

Silence felt. Clair stood and started to pace anxiously.

"Sit down!" Jon growled looking up at her. "You're utterly annoying."

She looked stunned. Rage stained her face and she shot him a look full of anger. Jon's expression was cold and unruffled, so Clair slumped down on the dirty sofa.

"Is there anything to drink in this sticky place?" she spit at Raffaele.

"You don't have to stay if you don't like it here," Raffaele replied, his tone pissed. "There's Salve and beer in the fridge. If you want something to drink you can get up and get it yourself, there's nobody here to cater to you," Raffaele replied stiffly, glaring at Clair in annoyance. "Take it or leave it." His voice was harsh and icy.

"Thanks," she replied, seemingly undaunted by his rudeness.

Troy and the guys needed to locate Sebastian immediately. Dealing with Annabel's thugs came last. They were six immortals in that room almost equal to Troy and his friends. They could use the element of surprise, but the fact that Sebastian was in trouble was shifting the scale to the other side. To their relief the men decided to play cards to pass the time waiting for Annabel. Soon enough they were all involved in a lively game, including the girl. Their laughter and conversations became louder as Salve and beer were consumed. They were being energized and inebriated in equal measure, and that seemed to be a plus for the guys.

Troy turned his attention to the faint sliver of light coming from the cracks in the door at the end of the corridor. He crept closer and put his ear against the door, but all he could hear was silence. He peeked through the crack and his body stiffened as he gasped in shock.

"What is it?" Girard asked in a low voice, grabbing everyone's attention. Troy raised his hand for silence, turned the knob and threw the door wide. Sebastian's appearance made the guys gasp in horror, curses leaving their clenched teeth. Utter disbelief was their first reaction. The room was equipped with torture contraptions that included binds, metal frames designed to clamp over a body, metal cables with shackles at the end to restrain and hoist bodies on the concrete walls. Silence fell among the men as they looked in horror at Sebastian's naked body. Troy shut the door behind them and moved toward the wall.

Large metal shackles protruded from the concrete wall, restraining Sebastian's arms and legs. His body was slumped forward, the metal cuffs cutting off his circulation. Troy's lips twisted with rage as he gazed at the agony and excruciating pain filling Sebastian's face.

His eyes were closed but Troy was sure that Sebastian had focused all of his energy in resisting the pain. His torso had been sliced in three different places with a large blade leaving deep gashes across his bare chest. Thick globs of dried blood covered the wounds while his shirt and what used to be a suit were on the floor ripped to shreds and blood-drenched. The smell of blood was so thick in that room that they could actually taste the nauseating, rusty stench.

It wasn't surprising that he was still unconscious and looking extremely weak, as a fair amount of blood pooled the floor around him. Sebastian's naked body convinced the guys that something very strange had taken place in this room. They were sure that his body would heal fast, however he wasn't going to regain his energy without Salve after losing all that blood.

Moving fast, Giani and Gerard broke the shackles and lowered Sebastian's body to the floor.

"It sounds like Annabel will be returning shortly," Troy said with anxiety in his voice and clenched teeth.

"Sebastian's already healing, but he'll remain weak until we get some Salve into his veins," Antonius said tightly.

"I think the best thing to do will be to take Sebastian outside and make sure he's safe," Troy said voice firm, face hard.

"I agree." Antonius nodded at Troy's suggestion.

"If we can get out of here without a fight it'll be great, but if they try to prevent our escape it'll make things a little more difficult. Let's take Sebastian out so he doesn't become a victim while unable to defend himself."

"Giani, go ahead and take him outside," Troy insisted.

"But...I should stay in case something goes wrong. There are seven thugs in there, not to mention the girl, and if Annabel returns that'll make it eight against five," Giani argued. "Not very good odds."

"True, but our priority is to make sure Sebastian is safe." Troy remained persistent.

"He's right, Giani. We need to protect Sebastian, so get going," Antonius said in a firm voice.

Giani shrugged, and lugging Sebastian over his shoulder in a fireman's carry, opened the door and darted like a tiger toward the staircase, scaling the steps two at a time. When he reached the top of the landing he pressed the lever on the wall and opened the secret passage. He never looked back; he dashed across the room and out the front door in a matter of seconds.

Troy picked up Sebastian's shredded clothes from the floor and dashed out the door like a cat after prey, Gerard, Arturo, and Antonius right on his heels. They reached the spiral staircase that was now illuminated by light that was spilling down from the front room through the passage opening.

They were getting ready to mount the steps when a door swung open with a loud noise and a bottle shattered on the stone floor. They spun around and their eyes locked on the man who stepped out into the corridor, clutching something in his hand. Shock crossed his face at the sight of the four men; he tilted his head in disbelief and backed off toward the door, staring at them in horror. His harsh voice made them brace for the unexpected.

"Hey! Who are you? What are you doing here?" he roared, alerting the rest of the thugs to their presence. They hadn't time to mute his scream. For a moment it looked as if they would have to defend themselves right then and there but Troy made a decision to take the fight upstairs. They spun around and started climbing the steps, while a powerful voice bellowed, "STOP!" But they didn't stop until they crossed the wall and into the front room. They could hear the heavy footsteps of their pursuers climbing the metal staircase. Troy motioned for the other guys to step to either side of the opening to get out of their enemy's immediate line of sight. That would give them the element of surprise. They didn't have to wait long and six guys stormed out of the passage with the girl right behind them.

Giani heard a large commotion inside the house but he didn't stop. He lowered Sebastian's weak body to the ground and made sure he was safe behind the hedges. He immediately turned and headed back inside.

He stopped as soon as he crossed the threshold and assessed the situation. Seven thugs were in the middle of the room with their backs to him, facing his four friends who were standing on either side of the opening with their backs to the wall. Giani scanned the faces of his friends and saw their determination to get this over quickly. They paused for moment and then jumped into action and the fight started.

The man who called himself Raffaele was the first to jump on Antonius and with a tight fist he aimed for Antonius' face. Antonius jerked back avoiding the hit and with lips drawn back, hurtled on Raffaele, knocking him flat to the ground. Raffaele sprang up with supernatural speed and jumped at Antonius attempting to slug him again right between the eyes. Antonius ducked, avoiding the hit and caught Raffaele by the throat, twisting hard, separating Raffaele's head from his body with an awful sound.

There were hard hits and painful moans coming from each direction.

Troy grabbed one of Annabel's thugs by the throat and with a swift kick sent him flying across the room to land against the wall with a loud impact. He growled in agony as his body collapsed to the floor. Troy didn't give him time to recover as he launched toward the goon and, bending, pulled him up, grabbed his head between his hands like a clamp and twisted hard, severing it from his body in a matter of seconds.

He immediately turned to avoid the girl who was sprinting toward him screaming in anger. She flung her full weight on him. Making contact with him was like hitting a concrete wall; Troy moved slightly but never budged. He stared as she spun around, a dagger gleaming in her hand. She sank the knife deep into Troy's chest. He collapsed to the floor and she was on him like a wild animal. Antonius was right behind her. He leaned down, and putting his arms around her throat, lifted her completely off of Troy and threw her across the room into Arturo's strong headlock. She let out a stifled cry and it was over within milliseconds. Antonius reached over Troy and grabbing the hilt of the dagger yanked it out of his chest. Troy was alert and they both knew that he would heal fast.

Antonius turned to face Raffaele, who was much taller and quite husky. Raffaele's face was dark and his eyes narrowed to slits watching Antonius carefully. He gave Antonius a cold smile that said he would crash Antonius to dust. He obviously didn't know Antonius' reputation among immortals as an accomplished warrior who enjoyed a good fight.

Raffaele threw the first blow, hitting Antonius in the middle of his chest, sending him back a few feet. Antonius stumbled but kept his balance. He launched across the room and caught Raffaele with his open fist right in the middle of the face. Blood sputtered from the guy's nose and mouth, hitting Antonius in the face, but that didn't stop him.

His next blow caught Raffaele again in the middle of his face, blinding him. Raffaele shook his head and put his hands up, trying to brush the blood away from his eyes, but it was too late. Antonius flung himself with amazing speed, landing simultaneously one fist into the middle of Raffaele's face and the other into his throat.

Raffaele sank to his knees, choking and moaning with rage, grasping his chest, trying frantically to take a breath.

Antonius didn't give him any time to recover. He reached down and, lifting this huge man, slammed his fist repeatedly into his face and chest with enormous force. Raffaele groaned with every blow and finally he crumpled to the ground coughing mouthfuls of blood, unable to breathe. Antonius finally had enough; he pulled Raffaele into a tight grip and finished him off.

Giani and Gerard stood back-to-back taking on two thugs, teamwork and technique allowing them to immobilize and finish their opponents. They stood and assessed the damage; five guys and the girl all dead.

Arturo was fighting the one remaining thug, but it didn't look like he needed any help. He decked the guy right between the eyes, sending him flying across the floor, stunned. The thug moaned in pain when his body crashed against the wall. Since he landed by Gerard's feet, Gerard bent down and finished him off.

The guys looked around the room; it looked like a war zone. Troy was already healed. He pulled himself upright and rubbed his temples, mumbling to himself.

Antonius walked over and put his hand on Troy's shoulder. "What is it Troy?"

"What happened to Annabel? She was to meet with these thugs." Rage flickered through Troy's eyes.

Antonius shrugged his shoulders and cursed aloud. "There has to be another secret passage," he said. "I've a feeling the bitch saw what was going on. The odds were against her, so she chose to disappear."

Troy shook his head in disappointment and thanked Antonius for saving his life.

"I think we better get to Sebastian," he said. Giani ran out the front door and through the hedges, motioning the others to follow.

Sebastian was sitting up, leaning against the wall. He seemed to be completely healed but extremely sluggish and disoriented. The lacerations were almost closed and a few, faint lines remained across his chest. His whole body was a bloody mess, but they knew those wounds would disappear as well.

Sebastian's eyelids blinked as he struggled to clear his vision. His eyes were filled with confusion as he scanned around him with intensity trying to adjust to his surroundings, still very weak, moving in and out of consciousness. His gaze fell on the guys and he smiled as he recognized his friends.

"What happened?" he muttered.

Troy kneeled next to him. "Let's get you back to normal and then we can talk."

"Troy," Arturo called out. "I'm going down to the cellar to get the Salve out of the fridge."

Without waiting for a reply he turned and sprinted back into the house.

"Wait...wait...I'm coming with you," Giani called, darting after Arturo. They were gone but a few seconds, when they returned with two large containers of Salve.

Antonius put his arm around Sebastian's shoulders and held him up, while Troy forced the Salve down Sebastian's throat slowly, making sure he ingested a large amount.

They stood in silence, waiting patiently for the Salve to surge through Sebastian's veins and revitalize him.

 *Chapter 3*

THE AIR WAS COOL. Sebastian took a deep breath and with extra effort drew himself upright. Scorching pain blasted through the back of his head and his face twisted in anguish. His hand moved fast to touch the back of his head. He leaned against the wall, pursing his lips while an excruciating look crossed his eyes. He looked at Troy incredulously and his face hardened.

Troy reached out and put his hand on Sebastian's shoulder. "What is it?"

"All I can remember is a hard blow on the back of my head sending me to the floor," Sebastian replied, through clenched teeth. Hesitating, he stared out somewhere in the dark, and finally gazed down at his body in utter disbelief.

"What in bloody hell happened to me?" he asked in shock. "Where are my clothes?"

"It looks like someone cut you really bad," Antonius grinned ruefully.

Troy gazed at Sebastian with a smile, motioned toward his naked body. "I think you better manifested a pair of jeans for yourself," he said. "We don't want to have to look at your ugly naked self for much longer," he added, chuckling.

Sebastian gave a faint smile and soon enough he was standing there in a new pair of jeans. He took his last sip of Salve in gloomy silence, his mind in turmoil. He drifted away again, trying to recall the details of his awful experience. Suddenly his body went rigid, his mind overwhelmed by the icy grip of realism. He rubbed his wrists forcefully, agonizing over the uncertainty of what took place in that room. Sebastian took a deep breath and stared at Troy, perplexed and alarmed.

"What is it?" Troy asked.

"I remember being alone with Annabel in that awful room," Sebastian murmured. He shook his head in frustration, voice strained, lips quivering. "I can't remember what happened, but I have this strange feeling that my life changed utterly and irreversibly," he murmured.

His face reflected the emptiness, as awareness swept over him recalling the torture chamber. He cursed aloud and pursed his lips again, visualizing the failure of his attempt to get rid of Annabel. He gazed down at his partly naked body now and swallowed hard, face shuddered by mixed emotions.

"How did you end up in that room? Do you remember?" Troy asked.

"It was a trap, Annabel had it all planned out. I walked right into her trap like a two-year-old. I saw the men in the next room, but didn't bother with them. I wanted to find Annabel, deal with her quickly and get out before her thugs were alerted. It turned out to be a trap. She was waiting for me, how stupid could I be?" he pursed his lips and cursed. "God! I hate that bitch so much! She makes my skin crawl..." his frustration showed and he took a few steps away from the wall.

Sebastian's mind was now swirling wildly and his body tensed, remembering that his eagerness to kill Annabel had nearly destroyed him this time around. He couldn't remember any other occasion in his long immortal life that'd brought him so close to what could've been the end of his life. He ran his hand through his hair as a cold shiver went up his spine. He was so weak he slid back down to lean against the wall.

"Do you want to head home?" Troy asked, watching Sebastian intently. He was sure that he would need a couple of hours to get back to his normal self. In the meantime he would need a lot of help.

"Do you want me to manifest a car?" Antonius asked Troy.

"No...no..." Sebastian interrupted. "I need to walk and think things through. I need the time to recover a bit before we get home," he murmured anxiously.

"All right then, we'll walk, lad," Antonius said with a smile.

"Thanks," Sebastian replied in a barely audible voice. He was still sitting on the ground, leaning against the wall, taking deep breaths.

"But...what happened to you?" Sebastian asked Troy. "I thought you were on your way when I went into the house."

"I ran into unforeseen roadblocks," Troy said, tension straining his voice.

"Like what?"

"When I arrived at the house there were three thugs at the gate preventing me from going inside. They wasted a large amount of time waiting for a fourth person to join them. They were meeting with Annabel to receive a large amount of money to carry out some kind of contract." Troy looked at Sebastian steadily.

"What kind of contract?"

"I don't know; they didn't discuss any details at the gate. As it turned out we didn't get to hear much of anything, since the meeting never took place," Troy groaned.

"What in the hell happened in that room with Annabel?" Antonius asked gazing at Sebastian. His voice was filled with apprehension at the memory of Sebastian bound naked against the wall in that icy and dreadful room.

Sebastian closed his eyes, face twisted in torment, trying to remember but he remained silent. The silence dragged out.

Sebastian manifested a shirt to cover his aching torso. Troy and Antonius pulled him to his feet carefully and started to walk away from the house, supporting him on either side. He was still pretty sluggish and the gashes quite obvious and bloody. They wouldn't go away for a couple more hours. They moved away from the house in short strides.

"How did you guys know that Troy and I were in trouble?" Sebastian asked quietly. "Did Troy call you?" Sebastian stopped walking and watched Antonius with a gratifying look.

"No, as a matter of fact, it was Gabrielle who called," he said. "The girls were extremely worried about you two and they thought you might need help. I asked Gerard, Giani and Arturo if they wanted to come along and you know how much they love action," Antonius said smiling.

"First, let me say that I'm sincerely grateful for your help," Sebastian said, gazing between the guys. "But what happened with the thugs?"

"Oh...there was a short fight and it was all over," Troy laughed.

"How many are we talking about?"

"Seven of them; six men and one woman against five of us. It was a great fight, trust me; sorry you missed it." Antonius chuckled in amusement.

Sebastian smiled. "And how did I end up out here?"

"Giani carried you out here to make sure you were safe, because you were still unconscious." Gerard replied.

"I'm sorry about that," Sebastian said, swallowing back his grief.

"Let's go home," Troy insisted.

As they started to walk again, Arturo paused and, turning, looked back at the house with a puzzled look on his face.

"What is it?" Antonius asked. There was an unusual stillness in the air.

"Well...I was thinking that since we're here, why don't I stay back and wait, in case Annabel comes back. If she does, I can finish this for Sebastian," he said. His smile was sinister.

"Oh...I think I like your idea," said Antonius, with pleasure.

"I'll stay with him," Gerard offered.

"All right then. You guys stay here and we'll take Sebastian home," Antonius said. "He's still pretty weak."

"Are you going to Troy's or Sebastian's?" Gerard asked.

"We're going to my house," Troy replied. "Arielle went home with Gabrielle. They're at my house together."

Antonius, Sebastian, Giani, and Troy disappeared in the dark. Sebastian's body tensed at the sound of Arielle's name. His need for her was intensified and he let out a sigh of relief, knowing that he would be with her in a very short time. He suddenly stopped walking again, looking extremely troubled.

"What is it, Sebastian?" Troy asked.

"There's something that really bothers me," he said, watching his friends carefully. They remained silent, waiting for him to continue.

They were standing in front of poorly-lit café, which was empty except for a man sitting behind the counter reading a book, and he never looked up.

"Can we sit for a minute out here?" Sebastian requested.

"Do you want me to manifest a car?" Troy asked.

"No, like I said before, I want to walk, I need the time," Sebastian, replied.

Troy nodded and they sat around a small outside table. The table was located at the very far corner of the establishment. The poor lighting from the inside didn't reach that table. They didn't want anyone to be able to see Sebastian's bloody mess.

"I have to clear some things before we get home," Sebastian murmured. "I'm starting to remember things and I'm not feeling very good about it. I've this horrible impression that something happened with Annabel while I was going in and out of consciousness. I have now a vivid picture in my mind of Annabel shredding her clothes off and I do remember feeling her hands touching me in a wild way making my skin crawl." The dark shadows that crossed his friend's eyes didn't escape Sebastian. He noticed Antonius and Giani's jaw muscles tense but they remained quiet.

"All right, what is it? I had a bad feeling before, but now I'm convinced looking at your faces that something is terribly wrong." Sebastian drew a deep breath as he waited for an answer.

"You're right, Sebastian, it seemed that a lot more than torture went down in that room." Troy murmured, avoiding Sebastian's gaze.

"Well...go on, what are you trying to say?" Sebastian was looking at Troy closely. Troy started to say something, but stopped. The young man had left the counter inside the café and was approaching the group with a smile.

"Good evening or good morning," he said. "Can I take your orders please?" The guys knew they had to order something while occupying the table so they ordered a round of beers and the man walked back into the cafe.

"Well?" Sebastian was still watching Troy like a hawk.

"When we came into the room, you were unconscious and completely naked," Troy said.

"What are you saying?" Sebastian asked.

"We're pretty sure that Annabel did a lot more with you than slice your chest and arms. There was plenty of evidence for us to make that assumption," Troy replied, his face serious.

Sebastian recoiled and his body stiffened, as Annabel's words flashed in front of his mind. *"I'll have you one way or another,"* that was the last thing he remembered just before he lost consciousness.

Sebastian looked into his friend's eyes but they remained quiet. Sebastian felt bile climbing up his throat and cursed aloud with clear fury.

"You can't be serious," Sebastian's eyes now narrowed to slits.

"I am afraid it's true," Troy said watching Sebastian's face attentively.

Sebastian stood still, pale with disbelief. He was having a hard time breathing. He pinched the tip of his nose and took several deep breaths, trying to regain his composure. He cursed aloud with extreme resentment, making his friends quite concerned.

He started mumbling with fury, "It's my fault...it's my fault...my big mistake was prolonging the punishment to enjoy seeing Annabel suffer before she died. I should've finished her when I had the chance. Why didn't I do that? When am I ever going to learn? What in the world am I going to do now?" He stopped talking and sat.

He finally looked across the table at his friends and said through clenched teeth, distraught, "What am I going to do now?"

"There's nothing *to* do," Antonius said thoughtfully. "You must forget about it and move on with your life until we meet Annabel again."

He stood, walked around the table to Sebastian, and patted his back genially. "You must go on and wipe this from your mind," he added.

"I've decided to begin remembering Annabel as a lifeless object. That'll make it easier for me to think or talk about her without using her name," Sebastian said, teeth clenched.

"Sebastian, there's a girl at home waiting for you. She's madly in love with you. She's looking forward to your wedding. You've got to forget about tonight—as if it never happened," Antonius said emphatically. His voice was firm and he continued watching Sebastian, who was looking bewildered. He made a sudden move for his pocket and a deep frown creased his forehead.

"Bloody hell! She has my mobile," Sebastian said, obviously annoyed.

"No Sebastian, I have your mobile," Giani said. "I picked it up off the floor." Giani reached in his pocket, pulled out Sebastian's mobile, and handed it to him.

"Thanks Giani," Sebastian said, relief in his voice. He leaned closer and setting his hands on the table, held his mobile tightly. He stared at the black screen for a moment and then pressed the start button.

His screensaver came on and a pair of beautiful sapphire eyes brightened the screen. A smile tagged the corners of his mouth and sheer warmth surged through his body like a tidal wave at the sight of Arielle's face.

He saw two text messages. The first was from Arielle. He'd received that while standing in the middle of the bedroom facing the girl just before he killed her.

He clicked on the second text and a strong jolt made him quiver. He stared at the screen silently, expression overwhelmed with contempt and revulsion. He finally swallowed hard and his head slumped on the table. The phone dropped from his hands with a crackling noise, sliding across the surface and stopping at the edge, just before crashing to the ground. Sebastian was growling in utter despair.

Troy picked up the phone and looked at the screen. His face twisted with anger and hatred flickered in his eyes.

"What?" Antonius and Giani asked at the same time. Troy handed them the phone and they gazed at the screen in complete shock. It was a text message from Annabel.

Hello, my love. I thought you might want to know that our marriage is now consummated. We're bonded together forever. You belong to me.

Sebastian raised his head and gazed into his friends' worried eyes. He knew intuitively the meaning of Annabel's text message. He was feeling hollow and his eyes were full of hate. Annabel had devastated his life in a matter of minutes.

"I can't face Arielle," he said. Face submersed with despair. "She wouldn't want me after—"

"You're dead wrong," Antonius interrupted.

"You don't understand, Antonius," Sebastian said, gazing at the screensaver. "I made a promise to Arielle that she would be the only one for eternity. My love is still pure, however my body's been tainted. In good consciousness, I couldn't touch Arielle because she's wholesome, loving, sensual, and good. Annabel has put her dirty mark on me and I've no rights to be with someone like Arielle. I feel nauseated," Sebastian muttered. What made it worse was the fact that he didn't believe that he could exist without her.

"Sebastian!" Troy said, clearly frustrated. "You're the same good man Arielle fell in love with, the same man who loves her, with every fiber in your body. This doesn't change a thing." He emphasized his last words.

"Why then do I feel so different? Why do I feel that I just can't lay in the same bed with Arielle any longer?" Sebastian's voice was filled with anxiety.

Troy got to his feet. "Don't be ridiculous!" he yelled, staring down at Sebastian, unable to hold back. "You must stop this, I beg of you as a friend. You can't do that to Arielle."

"Troy, I've never been scared of anything, but I'm scared to death to face Arielle," he murmured. He looked on the brink of a breakdown.

"Sebastian, can I ask you a question?" Giani chimed in. Sebastian turned, his gaze rested on Giani's face without replying. Giani ignored the silence and continued. "What if Arielle was raped?" he asked softly.

Sebastian recoiled; a horrified sigh escaped his lip. He stared out in the distance, transfixed by his tense thoughts. He was startled again by Giani's firm voice.

"Would you leave her? Would you refuse to touch her again for something she had no control over?"

Sebastian remained silent. He pressed the button on his mobile and Arielle's picture filled the screen. He stood still, engulfed by the irresistible appeal of her face. He thought he smelled freesia and smiled.

"Well? Would you?" Giani insisted.

"No—no I wouldn't, I love her too much," Sebastian whispered.

"So what's the difference here? Annabel took something from you without your knowledge; you had no part in it, so how can you say that you're dirty? Do you understand where I'm going with this?" Giani asked, but this time he waited for a reply.

Troy and Antonius nodded their agreement.

Sebastian looked panicked. "But why do I feel so bad?" he murmured.

"Because you were violated," Troy said. "You had nothing to say about Annabel's actions and that's why you feel bad. Don't let Arielle get involved in this mess. Let it go...let it go..." he repeated.

"I'll try," Sebastian promised. His face was lined with wretched sadness. "Maybe we should head home now," he said, standing.

"Maybe we should wait a little while longer. You need to get over the unpleasant letdown, and face your up-coming wedding and future with Arielle."

Sebastian agreed and sat back down. Troy moved to sit next to him.

"Remember, Sebastian, Arielle's a very sensitive girl and she'll notice changes in you, so make sure you don't dwell on this. Don't let the best thing in your life slip away. Don't let Annabel succeeded in destroying your relationship. I'm not going to say anything more except that you must let the past remain in the past." Troy watched him attentively.

"Of course, I know you're right. She's my life and I couldn't breathe if she wasn't in it. I just couldn't touch her right now, not until I scrub myself down and wash away Annabel's stench." He smiled and breathed deeply. They were getting ready to get up and leave when Antonius phone went off. He flipped the phone and listened intently for a while and finally put the phone back in his jean pocket, cursing explicitly.

"What's going on?" Sebastian asked watching Antonius intently.

"Bitch…" he cried out.

"What happened?" Giani asked.

"That bitch is gone again!!! She tricked us! Gerard and Arturo waited across the street for her return. She didn't come through the front door, but they saw her for a brief moment standing in the front room. She looked around with a shocked look on her face and disappeared quickly, turning the lights off, bringing the house into complete darkness. They ran inside, but she disappeared just as fast as she appeared. They did a methodical search throughout the cellar and found a couple more passages in the cellar. One was under the staircase and the other in the torture room behind the large chair that was pushed against the wall. Both lead out to several blocks away from the house. She was gone," Antonius said. He pursed his lips one more time and cursed aloud.

"This is my life story, invariably," Sebastian chuckled bitterly.

"This woman is either really good or just very lucky," Giani said and they all agreed.

"I'd rather go home first, and clean up, but that may be even more suspicious to Arielle." Sebastian was thinking aloud.

"You're absolutely right, you're still sluggish and you need time to heal completely; I'm sure Arielle will understand," Troy said.

Sebastian nodded in agreement and they were on their way. He'd lost a lot of blood and needed more energy, more Salve. His head still ached from the hard hit he'd received from Annabel's thugs.

 *Chapter 4*

GABRIELLE AND ARIELLE sprang from the sofa anxiously at the sound of voices. Arielle's arms were aching for Sebastian. She ran full speed with the sole purpose of falling into his splendid embrace. The guys were walking in as the girls reached the foyer. Antonius stepped in front of Sebastian in attempt to help him to the sofa and Arielle ran right into him, unable to stop her forward momentum. She staggered for a moment, trying to regain her balance. Antonius spun around and, putting his arms around her, held her steady to her feet. Arielle stood still, a little disoriented and staring into Antonius' eyes. Running into Antonius' body felt like hitting a brick wall.

"Excuse me," she muttered, embarrassed.

"Are you all right?" Antonius asked.

"Yes, thank you," she replied, with a soft smile. Antonius step aside and Sebastian came into Arielle's full view. She froze, shocked at his bloody appearance. Stunned silence fell, as their eyes met. Sebastian's face lit up as a soft smile tagged the corners of his mouth. Her heart started hammering in her chest making it painful to breathe. Her exultation evaporated and her face fell at the sight of him.

His face was shattered and pale. His lips twisted in agony, his expression distorted. The exposed parts of his skin were covered in dry blood, his body weak and unbalanced between Troy and Giani. She approached slowly and stood in front of him, gazing deep into his emerald eyes, but he seemed to be looking vacantly somewhere in the distance. Arielle's heart sank and tears came to her eyes.

"Sebastian!" she cried out unable to hold back. He was more than startled and seemed to snap out of his blankness. He took several deep breaths before he could speak.

"Hey baby!" he whispered softly. That sweet velvety voice didn't reflect the way he looked. "Did you miss me?" he asked, and the corners of his mouth lifted into the smile he held only for her.

"Sebastian, what happened?" she murmured, and carefully wrapped her arms around him overwhelmed with the need to hold him. To her utter astonishment he didn't encircled her in his arms as she anticipated. Her heart was now beating franticly. Something had changed in Sebastian and the path she'd set for her life back in St Jean De Luz was in jeopardy.

Sebastian's mind was in turmoil. Arielle's touch practically set him on fire, and his desire for her was making him crazy, but he had no right to touch her. The stench of Annabel was still all over his body and he felt nauseated. How was he ever going to get over this ghastly part of his life? He looked at Arielle's beautiful face and felt her shudder. She stepped away from him, expression filled with hurt and disappointment, visibly shaken. Sebastian couldn't believe he was the cause of the awful look that painted the face he lived for. God! What was happening to him? He couldn't make any sense of it. Sebastian took a deep breath and gazed at Arielle anxiously.

"I love you, Arielle," he murmured.

She gazed into his eyes again and lifting herself up on her tiptoes pressed his lips with hers softly. The intensity of the kiss wasn't what she'd hoped for. It was a bit of a letdown but she still moaned breathlessly, as warmth spread across every fiber of her body. She pulled back slowly and gazed at him a little closer.

"Oh...my...God...is that dried blood all over your arms?" she exclaimed, and before anyone could comment any further she continued. "What happened? Are you hurt?"

"I'm fine, baby, just need a little time to completely recover."

"Recover from what? What happened?" Arielle had a bad feeling about this.

"He's fine, Arielle," Antonius interrupted, putting his arm around her shoulders and pulling her away from Sebastian. "He needs his energy back and a little more time to heal completely."

She was silent and a bit stunned as they all walked into the study and helped Sebastian to the sofa. Troy dashed out and came back with a glass of Salve. Arielle watched as if she was seeing a movie unfold. Her mind was in turmoil. She found it extremely strange that he had on jeans and a shirt, rather than the nice suit he'd on when he dashed after Annabel. *Why? What happened to his suit? Why does he look so filthy and dipped in blood?*

Sebastian lifted his hand to take the glass from Troy and his shirt fell open in the front, revealing three awful looking long lacerations and a lot of dried blood all over his chest. They were much better than the deep gashes he received from Annabel's dagger earlier that evening, and would eventually disappear, but they still looked horrific. Arielle gasped and placed her hands over her mouth to mute the scream that rose to her lips. Cold hands of horror spread across every fiber of her body making her quiver. She knew something terrible had happened but she was afraid to ask. Tears filled her eyes and she froze.

Troy looked up at her with a soft smile. "He'll be fine, Arielle, I promise. Give him time to regain his strength. He'll be back to normal soon and you'll never be able to tell the difference. He'll be the same ugly guy we all love." Troy chuckled.

She lifted her eyes to meet his gaze, hoping he could see her gratitude.

He wiped her tears away. "There's no need to cry; he's fine. Remember that we're immortals; we heal, and there are no scars left to remind us of our bad episodes."

Troy was smiling but she saw a dark shadow cross his eyes, making her wonder if there was more to the episode that just a fight.

"Arielle—" Sebastian's voice jolted her to reality.

"Sebastian," she whispered with tremendous concern, as she walked and sat next to him. She reached over and pulled his shirt together covering his exposed chest.

"Did you miss me?" he whispered, his voice pained.

"Oh...My...God...Sebastian, I couldn't breathe," she murmured. She laid her head gently against his chest and he held her lightly. She felt a surge of exhilaration. He took another sip of Salve and she noticed warmth in those beautiful emerald eyes and the corners of his lovely bowed lips curved up. Her breath held in her throat as a surge of adoration for this man swept through her body. It was a few minutes later when he stood, still looking pretty tired, and taking her hand, announced that they were going home. Just before they walked out the door he thanked all the guys by shaking their hands. He walked to Gabrielle, took her in his arms, and smiled gratefully.

"Thank you, Gabrielle, you're an exceptional woman. Troy's a very a lucky guy." He gave her a peck on the cheek while she held a wide smile on her face.

Sebastian averted his gaze to Arielle and their eyes locked. A declaration of desire sent a wave of heat through Arielle's body, as he placed his arm around her waist and pulling her a little closer, nuzzled her hair.

"You're my world," he whispered, and they walked out the door. Arielle drove home but Sebastian didn't seem to want to talk about the incident at all and she didn't press for answers. She was hoping to get the chance to find out the details when they were home alone. She was lost in her thoughts when his musical voice made her look at his amazing face and she felt peaceful. He was the sanctuary of her existence. There was nothing that could hurt her when he was next to her. She reached over and, taking his hand, pressed it softly.

"Are you okay, baby?" she murmured.

"Yes, I'm fine," he whispered. Arielle could tell he was a bit different compared to when he left her standing at the club parking lot. His touch, his kiss, and his manner around her, had changed. Stony silence fell between them again. She finally took a deep breath and said.

"I'm really worried about you. What happened?"

"I don't want you to worry about me," he replied without looking at her. "I'll always be by your side and I'm here now."

She tried to feel the warmth and the security he always provided for her but something in his voice was missing. She smiled solemnly. "Are you feeling any better?"

"Yes, I just need to take a shower and I'll feel much better," he replied.

Arielle turned to look at him and the dark shadow that crossed his eyes didn't escape her. It was the same shadow she'd see in Troy's eyes when she'd asked him for details. Something happened tonight; she could feel it, but she didn't want to push him right now. She thought it might have something to do with an immortal healing process. She pulled into the garage and just as she prepared to shut the engine off she watched, astonished, as Sebastian literally dashed out of the car and in the house without looking back.

She was completely dumbfounded, unable to explain what in bloody hell was going on. Stress and anxiety filled her. She took her time getting out of the car and entered the house with measured steps.

Sebastian was already in the shower with the bathroom door closed. She stood in the middle of the bedroom, upset, as this was not a typical occurrence in their relationship. Any other day he would've taken her in his arms and walked into the shower with her, but not tonight. Something happened with Annabel and she had to find out. This wasn't the Sebastian she knew.

Arielle pulled her mobile out of her pocket, walked out of the bedroom and called Troy.

"Hello, Arielle," Troy's voice came across the wire softly. Her name must've shown up on his mobile screen.

"Troy, you must tell me what happened tonight. Sebastian's acting very strange and I'm a little lost and hurt. He's avoiding me as if he's afraid to touch me." She was desperate for information.

"Arielle, you have to be patient, Sebastian will come clean when he's ready. Give him time and most of all trust in him. I can tell you one thing that's completely true; he's irrevocably in love with you." Troy stopped talking and there was a long silence across the wire.

"Okay, Troy, thanks for talking to me," her voice broke.

"Trust him," were Troy's last words before the phone went dead.

Arielle got ready for bed and waited for Sebastian to come out of the shower for what seemed to be an eternity. She laid back, put her hands behind her head, and closed her eyes. Her head was filled with wild and crazy thoughts. It was clear to her that Sebastian was avoiding any type of physical touch with her. Tears filled her eyes and her heart was breaking; rejection by Sebastian was like death. She must've been completely worn out because she dozed off and didn't wake until 3:00 in the morning.

The bedroom was dark and quiet and Sebastian wasn't in bed. She wanted to get out of bed and go looking for him, but decided to give him time to resolve whatever the problem was.

At 4:00 in the morning, she just couldn't wait any longer. She jumped out of bed and walked in the dark from one room to the next looking for him but he wasn't in the house. She looked in the garage and his car was still there, so she hoped he was outside in the back sitting in the garden as he liked to do when something bothered him.

Her heart was breaking; she wished he'd share with her the details that were keeping him so distant. She put on a jacket and stepped outside, pulling the door shut behind her. The air was crisp, making her shiver and button up the jacket. He wasn't in the garden either and she pursed her lips, her mind whirling wildly, trying to understand what was happening in their lives. She was now standing at the end of the property, looking out toward the ocean, feeling utterly distraught.

It was the end of twilight and the beginning of dawn. The sky was beginning to lighten, the sun still below the horizon. She heard waves crashing against the beach and the smell of the ocean filled her nostrils. Any other time it would be a heavenly experience but this morning she was filled with anguish and pain. She turned her gaze toward the beach, giving her eyes time to adjust between the twilight and the dawn. Her breath caught when her eyes fell on Sebastian. He was breathtaking in a white shirt and jeans. He was stretched full length on the sandy beach, hands behind his head.

She took the trail towards the steps and descended while pressing her lips together to keep her body from trembling. She stepped on the cool sand and walked slowly toward him, halting at by his side. She looked down at his face into those amazing emerald eyes and all she could see was despondency in the intensity of his gaze. His body was motionless and the cold stillness in the air made her reach up to her neck and grab her necklace. Her mind raced, as she felt a sharp pain in her chest and, taking a tight breath, whispered.

"Don't you want to be with me anymore?" her voice was breaking her eyes were tearing. He turned and watched her carefully as the same dark shadow crossed his eyes, making it hard for her to understand what he was thinking.

"Hey, baby." His lips curved to that awesome smile and she fell apart. She collapsed down on the sand next to him and, putting her hands over her face, began to sob. She wasn't sure how long she sat there and suddenly she felt his hands pulling hers away from her face and as she looked up found him sitting upright across from her. His hands cupped her face and with his thumbs he wiped the tears away.

"Don't cry, baby, I love you so much, it breaks my heart to see you sad." He watched her closely, and lifting her head, pressed his lips softly on hers. She threw herself at him and wrapping her arms around him pulled him to her and kissed him with hunger, with desire, with want.

"I miss you," she whispered without breaking the kiss, overwhelmed when Sebastian pressed her down in the sand and crushed her lips beneath his with passion that send scorching heat across her body. She was still savoring the taste of his immortal scent when he suddenly pulled back and drifted away again.

She'd found the old Sebastian and lost him again in a matter of seconds, leaving her completely out of breath and dazed. He'd never done that before, if anything she was the one trying to stop a scorching encounter on the beach. Something was wrong and she wasn't moving an inch until she found out what was going on.

The more he pulled back the more obsessed she became with uncovering the truth. She sucked in a deep breath and putting her hand at his nape she held his gaze to hers. She opened her mouth and shut it again, trying to find the strength to continue with her thought and finally she came out with it. She started to talk without taking a breath and didn't stop until she'd said all she wanted to say.

"Sebastian, you have to tell me what's going on because I'm going out of my mind. Don't tell me nothing's wrong, because I'm not a fool. I know you much better than you think I do. I'm in love with you, don't you understand that?" she said in desperation. "We're going to be married in another month. Does that mean anything to you? You and I are going to sit here until we clear the air." Her voice quivered and tears streamed down her face, but she was determined to have it all out.

She saw a trace of torment in his emerald eyes and he exhaled slowly as if pleading with her to understand. She had absolutely no clue as to what he was about to say, so reaching out she touched his hand slightly and smiled softly.

"I love you, Sebastian," she murmured. His eyes searched hers and she could see he was attempting to regain control of his thoughts. Suddenly he leaned in and spoke anxiously.

"Arielle, my life was shattered in just a few moments by that dreadful wicked entity of evil."

Disillusionment engulfed him and she now knew that whatever he was about to say had something to do with Annabel. She wasn't sure what to expect but the fact that Annabel was involved caused nausea to intensify inside of her and she tried hard to fight it back.

He regained his composure quickly and without hesitation added, "Our happiness is stained with smut," he enunciated the word with clenched teeth.

She was at a loss with all the weird images in her head that seemed worse than dreams. She knew that her life had been set on a new and strange path two years ago when she'd set eyes on this beautiful man and fell irrevocably in love with him. She had to find out what happened between him and Annabel that was torturing him so severely. She took his hands in hers. They gazed in each other's eyes and she could see they both feared these emotions were affecting them immeasurably.

"Please talk to me," she whispered.

He started to say something and stopped again, looking almost uncomfortable to discuss whatever this nightmare was, but she waited patiently and suddenly he started to talk. The more he talked the more relaxed he became. He stopped several times and exhaled and every time Annabel's name came up his face twisted in rage. Arielle's eyes widened in shock as he delved deeper and deeper into the incident; she still couldn't find one thing that would excuse his rejection.

It was a few moments later that things started to make sense for her; it was the point of the physical assault. Pain flashed across his face and she tasted bile, making her eyes burn and her body recoiled. Her mind whirled and she racked her brain, and finally she was transported to another place and time.

Mat's face flashed before her eyes and memories rushed in, bringing back the hours she spent in the shower trying to scrub his filthy touch away from her skin. She recoiled at the thought of anyone touching her and remembered anxiety taking over her, knowing that if Sebastian were home she'd have pushed him away.

She was now leaning away from Sebastian, and she suddenly drew herself further back, pursing her lips against the bitter taste in her mouth. She winced and flinched, finally understanding why Sebastian had spent all that time in the shower and why he didn't come to bed. Everything was becoming crystal clear. He was going through the same emotions she had with Mat. She shivered and pulled her jacket tighter around her. Suddenly she realized that he'd stopped talking and was watching her carefully. She looked at him, waiting for him to continue but he smiled bitterly and looked the opposite way.

"I can't go on," he murmured and his lips quivered. She could see that his mind was in turmoil. Her head was spinning; she'd never expected sexual assault and never even considered it to be a scenario in this whole event. She pursed her lips again and, reaching out, placed her hand on his. He turned and looked at her with warmth, with love and she fell apart.

"Sebastian, I'm here and I'll remain by your side every step of the way," she murmured. "I don't care how long it takes, I'll wait..." her voice trailed. She ran her finger gently over his lip line, making him smile softly.

"We're not going to talk about this anymore, not now, not ever," she said, firmly. She stopped talking and waited. He lay back on the sand, pulled her down and she laid her head on his shoulder. He held her tight against his body this time and she felt him relaxing.

"I'm sorry, Arielle," he murmured, nuzzling her hair.

"For what? You're not responsible for an evil woman being misled by her sick mind." Her voice was warm and understanding. She lifted her eyes to meet his gaze. He was watching her with that amazing smile that made her love him even more.

"You have absolutely no clue as to how much I love you," he whispered and she smiled with all the love she felt for this gorgeous man.

The gashes on Sebastian's chest were almost gone and his body was returning to its perfect form. She ran her fingers over the lines that were barely visible now, kissing each of them. His emerald eyes rested on her face and his smile made her stomach flutter as if a thousand butterflies had invaded her body.

There were no more words spoken as they sat up and gazed across the ocean. His arms encircled her and she rested her head against his shoulder. The sight of the cloudless sky was breathtaking, weak sunlight from below the horizon announced the breaking dawn and the sky became a beautiful mix of oranges and yellows. They remained unmoved until the leading edge of the sun appeared above the horizon. Arielle gasped at the unspeakable beauty of the miracle transpiring right in front of her eyes.

They sat on the beach for a long time before finally deciding to head home. They walked holding each other in silence. He was now completely healed and there were no signs that he'd ever been wounded on the beautiful planes of his chest. He was back to the physically perfect specimen she'd fallen in love with.

Once in bed she was happy to be in his arms again. He pulled her tight against his body and they drifted to sleep.

 *Chapter 5*

SEBASTIAN AND ARIELLE never discussed the unfortunate incident again. It'd been two weeks since their conversation on the beach and her emotions were pretty similar to a rollercoaster ride. Every morning she woke up wishing that some of the recent events were just a dream, but reality would kick in and she'd find herself heartbroken again. Sebastian spent most of his time with Troy at the office, while she spent most of her time helping Gabrielle, whose wedding day was fast approaching.

Arielle spent quality time with her parents and took long walks with her father in the garden. This was something they hadn't done for a very long time and her father was delighted. Sebastian was warm and loving but he wouldn't allow his affection to go any further than a soft kiss or a tight embrace. Each and every night he followed the same routine; stayed up quite late either reading a book or watching the telly, and wouldn't go to bed until he thought Arielle was asleep, at which time he would slip quietly under the covers.

Arielle felt distraught and ashamed at pretending to be asleep, but she wasn't going to bring it up. All she could do was remain quiet, her eyes filled with tears. In the morning he was gone before she woke, leaving freesia on her pillow and his usual note, *Miss me.*

Every day she rose with the same lingering frustration and the overwhelming desire to talk with Sebastian. She was determined to explain her madness, but instead would bury her head in her pillow and cry. She missed his warm embrace and she was having a hard time sleeping.

Gabrielle must've noticed that she didn't have much interest in the wedding preparations and that her mind was somewhere else consistently. Arielle was sure Gabrielle had already heard every ghastly detail from Troy and she didn't want to add any more fuel to the fire by discussing it with Arielle. Gabrielle was sweet and understanding, and Arielle's best friend. She would wait until Arielle was good and ready to talk, and not a minute before that.

It'd been almost three weeks since the incident. Gabrielle and Arielle made plans to drive to the Lanes and do some shopping. Arielle didn't know how to hold back her frustration any longer. She dreaded the subject, but had to get it out of her system...TODAY. Eva and Ian were coming home soon and she desperately needed to get her life back in order.

Gabrielle showed up around 11:00 to pick up Arielle. She slipped into the passenger seat and pretended to look nonchalant.

"Hey there," Gabby greeted cheerfully.

"Hi, Gabby." Tension dominated Arielle's vocal cords. She tried to hide her nervousness, resisting the need to gaze toward Gabby.

"Are you all right?" Gabrielle asked, with a tentative smile. She knew her best friend was deeply troubled because Troy had discussed the miserable details about Sebastian's incident. Arielle looked lost in her thoughts and Gabrielle felt a wave of compassion. She fumbled with the steering wheel, waiting for Arielle to say something.

"Gabby, I'm going out of my mind," she finally mumbled.

"Do you want to talk?" Gabby's green eyes assessed Arielle, giving her time to make a decision.

Arielle put her hands to her face and began to sob.

Gabrielle hesitated for a moment then pulled Arielle's hand away from her face and turned her gently towards her.

"Arielle, I'm here, talk to me," Gabby whispered.

Arielle pressed her lips together and wiped her eyes with the back of her hands. She dropped her hands to her lap and sighed, but remained silent. Gabrielle started the car and they drove to the mall in silence.

When they arrived at the Lanes, Gabrielle pulled into a remote parking spot and stopped. She didn't have to wait long before Arielle unleashed her frustration.

"I—I'm miserable," she said in a quivering voice, tears pouring down her face.

"What is it?" Gabby's voice was warm and sympathetic.

"He doesn't want to touch me anymore," she whimpered, her voice breaking. "We haven't made love in over three weeks. He's tormenting me and he doesn't have a clue as to how I feel."

"What do you mean?" Gabby asked disbelievingly.

"Gabby, this is how it works almost every night. He comes to bed; he takes me in his arms and kisses me. He strokes my body through the kiss and spreads heat throughout every fiber of my existence. He then lets me run my hands over the planes of his back. I feel his hard muscles and caress his beautiful skin thinking that he might be coming back to me, and just about that moment without any warning he pulls back pushing me softly away. 'I can't,' he says, completely out of breath."

She gasped, in sheer exasperation. "He then kisses me softly, just before he gets out of bed and walks to the other room."

Arielle started to sob again and Gabrielle put her arm around her shoulders trying to calm her. "Arielle, he's going through a very difficult time," Gabby said.

Arielle shook her head bitterly. She searched through the clatter in her mind in a futile attempt to find sensible words. "I understand what he's going through," she finally said.

"How could you possibly understand what he's going through?" Gabrielle exclaimed making Arielle blink.

"Gabby, I do understand. Are you forgetting about Mat?" she asked, watching Gabrielle intensely. "Did you forget what I went through last year?" she asked.

"Oh—My—Gosh...are you serious?" Gabrielle's tone startled her.

"What?" Arielle asked, incredulously.

"These two events are completely different," she said. There was an edge to her voice and immediately her defiance went up.

"How do you mean?" Arielle demanded, trying keeping her expression inquisitive.

"I mean, you were almost violated, and if I remember right, it took a long time for you to get over that. He was actually violated while being unconscious. Can't you see the difference here?" Gabrielle was watching her carefully.

Arielle's heart sank, and she pursed her lips, realizing that Gabrielle was absolutely right.

"I know and I've been trying to understand the turmoil he's going through, but, Gabrielle, I miss him terribly," she swallowed back her misery, and groaned in defeat, overcome with guilt.

"I know. I do understand, but he did say something to Troy that might answer your questions."

"What's that?" Arielle lifted her eyes and met her friend's gaze.

"He told Troy that he feels dirty and not worthy of you anymore."

Arielle gazed at Gabby in astonishment.

The smile was gone from Gabby's face.

"Where you eavesdropping?" Arielle asked.

"Yes." She smiled, sounding rather sheepish.

"God," Arielle sighed and shut her eyes, more confused now than before.

"Arielle, I think he just needs time to sort things out," Gabrielle insisted.

Arielle gave Gabrielle a thoughtful look while she pressed on.

"Besides it's hard to see his point of view if you've never had the same experience. He also did say to Troy that he couldn't live if he couldn't be with you. Knowing that alone should make you feel delighted." Arielle was watching Gabrielle's face and she was smiling gently, making her feel better and less anxious. Gabby was right and Arielle needed to suck it up and let things unravel like they should.

She knew Sebastian loved her and she also knew he was trying hard to resolve his nightmare. She nodded, smiling, and pushed the car door open. The air was warm but the sky was cloudy, it was a typical Brighton day. They made their way down the ancient winding narrow cobblestone streets. Shopping at the Lanes was like stepping back in time. The buildings were old and beautiful, not showing their 400-year-old age. They spend a good part of the day shopping until they got tired of walking and decided to head home.

*   *   *

Eva and Ian called on Sunday to let them know they were home.

"How about coming over, we'd love to see you." Ian's voice was happy and relaxed.

Sebastian and Arielle went over around 2:00 in the afternoon; Troy and Gabrielle were already there. Arielle was so pleased to see them back; she'd truly missed their friends.

Eva and Ian's happiness illuminated their beautiful faces. Arielle gazed at them and marveled at their presence. She was sure she would never get over their flawless immortal splendor. She was sure that beauty was the empire in which all immortals dwelled. She smiled with wonder.

They'd brought wonderful gifts and the story behind them was even more incredible. Two wonderful, large, wooden bowls were called *tanoa*.

"They're hand-carved from a single piece of Vesi (hardwood) called Yaqona," Eva explained. "Yaqona comes from the root of a pepper tree. In times long gone, the Yaqona was prepared by the young girls (virgins) of a village, who chewed pieces of the root into a pulpy mass before adding water. After water was added the gritty pieces were strained through a bundle of vegetable fiber, usually the shredded bark of the Vau tree." Eva finished her story, her eyes glimmering.

Gabrielle and Arielle were filled with wonder listening to the story behind these beautiful pieces of art. The three girls beamed with excitement. They were together again, and decided to take a walk out in the garden, talking nonstop. Gabrielle and Arielle wanted to know all about Eva's honeymoon and look at the amazing photos of their trip. Eva went on and on about the wonderful time they spent in the amazing beach house they'd manifested in Nadi, a small island in Fiji, with serenity and the most beautiful beaches she'd ever seen.

"How was the honeymoon?" Arielle asked, chuckling.

"Unbelievable…" Eva replied with a long sigh, a sparkle in her eyes.

"What do you mean?" Gabrielle grinned.

"I mean that Ian and I will never have enough of each other. I could never explain to you in simple words how amazing is to be an immortal, how it's changed our lives."

Gabrielle and Arielle knew that immortality would have to remain a mystery for them.

"What else did you manifest?" Arielle asked, curious.

"A yacht," Eva replied in a very calm voice.

"You manifested a yacht?" Arielle exclaimed.

"Sure, why not?"

"I guess no reason at all; I'm just so amazed how you do that."

"Well Sebastian and Troy can do the same thing so it's nothing unusual for immortals. We were determined to visit some of the islands of Fiji and enjoy everything we could as long as we were there."

"Any encounters on the yacht?" Gabrielle asked in amusement looking at her intently. Her eyes glittered, lips quivered, as a wide smile made her face glow.

"I never had encounters like that with Ian. It was almost like they were out-of-body experiences. The intensity, the desire, the wonder of it all was nothing I ever dreamed growing up." She was smiling and gazing away, looking mesmerized. Arielle closed her eyes as the memories of her encounters with Sebastian rushed in. She felt a sting behind her eyes while intense sadness spread across every fiber of her body.

"We're really happy for you, Eva; the wedding was incredible and it sounds like your honeymoon was even more so." Gabrielle's voice made Arielle open her eyes and she saw Eva studying her intently. She knew her distraction didn't escape Eva's notice. She touched Arielle's shoulder.

"What's up Arielle?" her gaze puzzled.

"Bloody hell," she muttered, grinding her teeth. She didn't want to ruin the moment with her personal issues.

"What's going on?" Eva repeated and Arielle wished she had a bit more control over her emotions.

"There've been a few snags in my relationship with Sebastian," she said through clinched teeth.

"Are you going to explain or do you plan to make this a guessing game?" Eva was now frustrated, glancing between Gabrielle and Arielle.

"Something happened at your wedding," Arielle said, anxiously trying to suppress all the details her head was summoning against her will.

"At my wedding?" Eva exclaimed unable to keep the surprise off her face.

"Yes. Annabel showed up," Arielle said through clenched teeth. Eva stiffened.

"Annabel?" she shrieked.

"Yes; we don't know exactly how long she'd been there but I noticed her at the end of your reception," she murmured, rubbing her hands together nervously.

"What happened?" Eva demanded.

"We were on our way to the parking lot and had stopped to talk before we went our separate ways, when I noticed her and a man standing inside the Club entrance glass doors." Arielle was now a little nervous reliving Annabel's loathsome arrival all over again.

"What did you do?" Eva asked again while a strange frigid sensation swept through her body.

"I fell apart, totally horrified and Sebastian took after her like a wild animal. She has to be pure evil, otherwise I just can't understand the magnitude of hate she's been carrying for centuries now against Sebastian," she muttered, as Annabel's face took over her mind and made her shiver.

"She doesn't hate him, Arielle. She loves him and she doesn't want any other woman to have him. She's trying to hurt him through you because she knows that this time Sebastian's really in love." Eva was grinding her teeth, fists pressed against her body.

"I can't wait to get my hands on her miserable body. I'll rip her to shreds. I'll never forget that cold disgusting laughter outside the locked door in St Jean De Luz. She left us in that room to die and she'll pay." Her voice shocked Arielle to the core; she'd never heard Eva talk that way before.

"You haven't heard the best of it!" Gabrielle chimed in.

"There's more?" Eva's eyes widened as she watched Arielle's face darkened. She braced herself expecting the worse but Arielle was unable to withhold her emotions, and as she started to talk she choked on her words and broke into sobs. Eva glanced at Gabrielle first then put her arm around Arielle.

Eva started to talk then paused, looking for the right words.

"Arielle, we don't have to talk about this right now," she said softly. She had a strong feeling she already knew that recalling the details was extremely painful for Arielle. Eva turned her attention to Gabrielle and casually changed the subject giving Arielle time to regain her composure.

"How are you doing with the wedding plans?" Eva asked Gabrielle.

"I'm completely ready," she replied and chuckled in excitement.

"All that's left is to walk down that aisle and marry that beautiful man." Her eyes were brilliant, filled with eagerness and desire.

"Did your gowns come in?" Eva asked, glancing between the other two women.

"They were delivered last week and it all seems like a dream," Arielle murmured, gazing at the deep blue waters. They'd walked to the end of the property, admiring the ocean that stretched in front of them like a huge mirror as far as their eyes could see. The waves rolled to the shore and retreated, forming multicolor ripples as the ocean was bathed in the sunlight. The smell of salt filled the air. They watched the seagulls gracefully circle above the water waiting for a chance to feed on unsuspected fish.

"Gosh, what a sight!" Arielle murmured, not sure if she thought it or said it aloud.

"Yes, I was thinking the same thing," Eva whispered, answering her unspoken question.

"We're so fortunate to live by the ocean," Gabrielle muttered, contented.

A comfortable silence fell between them and Arielle took a deep breath, trying to imagine what it would be like, to be married to the man she wanted more than anything in the world.

"I'm not going to believe we're getting married until the moment I stand next to Sebastian at the altar," Arielle said aloud with a sigh.

"Arielle, Look at me!! Look at my life!!" Eva said. "The last two years of my life have been literally unbelievable. I actually died, brought back as an immortal. Who would ever believe that? It all seems like a dream but it's utterly and amazingly factual." She exhaled and smiled.

"If I were given a chance again I'm sure I wouldn't change even one second of the last two years. My life is utopia and Ian is my knight in shining armor," she murmured in her musical voice.

"I'm so happy for you," Arielle said, with a soft smile.

Sebastian's rejection flooded her thoughts and she tried to hide the ache. Eva noticed her expression because nothing escaped her immortal friend.

"Are you ready to talk about it now?" she asked a warm smile on her beautiful face. She rested her hand on Arielle's arm.

Arielle glanced cautiously at her watch and sighed as the smiled faded from her face.

"Are you in a hurry?" Eva asked, with amusement

"No," she replied with a soft chuckle. As soon as she decided to talk and the words came out, she reassessed and remained tight-lipped.

"Oh, come on!" Eva exclaimed, "Since when do we have secrets between us?" she pressed on.

"It's not that at all, I'm just a little nervous bringing back the whole story," she pursed, and taking a deep breath, recapped Sebastian's ordeal in extreme detail. When she got to the point of the physical assault, Eva's body stiffened as she unsuccessfully tried to hold back a cry of dismay.

"That's inconceivable!" Eva exclaimed. "How's Sebastian taking it?" she asked watching her carefully.

"Not very well." Arielle continued the dramatic story of the outcome and how the guys went to help both Troy and Sebastian, seeking vengeance only to fail again.

There was silence for quite a while as the three women stared out towards the ocean, listening to the waves break with a soft murmur over and over again.

"What's the issue with you and Sebastian?" Eva asked, knowing that there was something more tormenting Arielle.

"He feels dirty and doesn't touch me anymore," Arielle said, sadly. Eva's eyes widen in shock.

"I'm having a hard time believing that he doesn't want to touch you," she said, her face compassionate, surprise in her eyes.

"Well it's true. He's rejected me for three weeks now." She bit her lip so hard that she tasted blood and winced.

Eva frowned and proceeded to take up for Sebastian. Unfortunately there was very little she could say that would make Arielle feel wanted. Eventually she gave up and instead stood, gazed down at Arielle for a moment, and then she turned around and gazed out toward the ocean.

Arielle's emotions surged and she was fighting off tears but knew she had to talk to Eva.

 *Chapter 6*

EVA WAS THE PERSON to whom Gabrielle and Arielle had poured their hearts out all through their youth. She was the one who could see their future and warn them of bad things ahead. Arielle needed that kind of support right now.

"Eva, I need you, I'm desperate and don't know what to do," Arielle said. They exchanged looks and just before either one of them could utter a single word Gabrielle exhaled loud in frustration, making them look at her.

"Arielle, can't you understand that this isn't about you. This is about Sebastian and the horrible ordeal he had to endure. You have to trust him. He needs time to figure things out and he'll come around before you know it. He's in love with you. How many times does he have to tell you?"

Arielle was hurt by her friend's tone, but deep inside knew she was right. *What in the world is wrong with me?* Why couldn't she trust the man who fit the blueprint of her existence? His words came back to her with unexpected clarity, *"When are you going to start trusting me?"*

Eva's gentle voice brought her back to reality. "All I can see between you and Sebastian is great! He loves you more than his own life and you're never going to be apart," Eva said.

Arielle stared at her intense gaze and felt warmth that made her smile. Arielle knew that Eva could see right through her, just as Eva's lips quirked into a gentle smile.

"Are you feeling better?" she asked.

"Yes, thanks, Eva, I do feel much better." Arielle smiled.

"Do you want to walk down to the beach for a little while?" Gabrielle asked, and without another word they made their way down the path and descended the wooden steps that lead to the secluded beach. They took off their shoes just before they stepped onto the soft, cool sand.

"Are Troy's friends coming for the wedding?" Eva asked and Gabrielle was happy to go on and on about the four guys responsible for saving Troy and Sebastian's lives a few weeks back. And yes, she informed her friends, they would be part of the wedding.

"So when are they coming back?"

"They should be here in a couple of week," Gabrielle said, smiling. On that note Arielle decided to talk about Gaston.

"Eva, I think Gaston was standing next to Annabel at your reception," she said. Eva stopped walking and turned to face her, dumbfounded.

"Gaston from Calais?" she exclaimed with a high-pitched tone in her voice. Arielle pursed her lips and nodded.

"Are you sure?" she asked again.

"No, I'm not completely sure but there was a man standing next to Annabel and somehow when I looked at him I knew he had striking blue eyes," she said softly.

"And...." Eva prompted.

"Well, it was dark and they were a few hundred feet away so there wasn't any bloody way for Arielle to see the color of his eyes," Gabrielle chimed in.

"How did you know?" Eva asked Arielle, watching her carefully.

"I've no idea, but I had this feeling that it might've been Gaston," she said. She was now rubbing her hands together in nervousness; she could close her eyes and see his face and those striking blue eyes piercing through her very soul, making her shake. She felt her heart beat in a low monotonous rhythm. Suddenly she felt sick to her stomach and sank to the sand.

"I think I'm going to throw up," she whispered and Eva moved fast to her side. They sat and Gabrielle handed her a bottle of water. Arielle took a sip and closed her eyes, trying to slow her breathing.

"Hey there!" Troy's voice came from up the hill. They saw Ian and Sebastian standing next to him, looking down at them. Arielle never saw them move but before she could blink they were standing next to them. She'd never get over their speed.

"What were you talking about?" Sebastian asked, glancing between the three of them judiciously. Arielle thought he could see that she was a little anxious.

"Something about going back to Calais but nothing specific," Eva replied, trying to play the whole thing down. Everyone seemed to turn their attention to Arielle, who was now breathing a little better. The guys exchanged looks and Sebastian moved slowly and sat on the sand next to her, putting his arm around her, making her shiver.

"What is it, baby, are you okay?" he asked tenderly. She forced a smile, winding her fingers through his.

"I'm fine," she whispered. She closed her eyes, trying to wipe the thought of Gaston away from her mind and suddenly fright took over her again, as she bit hard down on her lower lip. The rusty taste of blood told her that she broke through a few layers of skin. A very beautiful face with striking blue eyes appeared again in front of her. She felt Sebastian's arms pulling her closer and turning her head to face him. Their faces were a breath apart and she heard his soft voice.

"What's...going...on in there?" he asked pointing at her head anxiously. Arielle was silent for a moment. She exhaled a long breath trying to hold back the nausea.

"It was Gaston," she murmured.

Sebastian lowered his eyes scanning her face in alarm. "Gaston!" Sebastian exclaimed. "Gaston Bartaud!" He looked at her, thunderstruck.

"I'm sure he was the man standing next to Annabel the night of Eva's wedding," she said softly and Sebastian winced.

"What I don't understand is what he was doing here with Annabel. He never liked her, I even remember many occasions that they came to blows right after Annabel and I were married." He shook his head and swallowed hard.

"I wonder what he's doing here?" he murmured. Arielle wrapped her arms around his neck pulling him close.

"I remember something he told me just before he left the ball that morning in Calais," she said, gazing in his eyes.

"What was that?" he asked.

"He said that he always gets what he wants and I was what he wanted. I remember the fear that took over me because the last person who told me the same thing was Mat Winston just before he tried to rape me."

Sebastian mumbled a curse under his breath as he pulled her tighter. "It all makes sense now," he said looking at her, extremely worried.

"What makes sense?" she asked.

"Annabel told me that Gaston was here to claim you for himself. I didn't put much significance on those words until now. I'm sure that you saw Gaston, and Annabel is using him to try and destroy what we have." He kept gazing in her eyes and she saw darkness cross those beautiful emerald eyes.

"We know that Annabel is unpredictable but I'm sure that sooner or later we'll figure out her sick game," Troy said. His musical voice had a resolved tone.

Sebastian nodded, grimly.

"Right now let's all concentrate on the wedding coming up, and our friends arriving for the festivities."

Troy pulled Gabrielle into his arms, pressed his lips on hers and groaned with pleasure. "I hate to think about a whole week without you," he said frowning. "Can't you just stay with your parents for one day?" He was pleading with that miserable voice of his, and even though Arielle was still pretty upset, she broke out laughing. The atmosphere became lighter and more relaxed after Troy's short statement.

"When are the guys flying in?" Sebastian asked.

"Two weeks from today and that includes Jon, Pierre, and Jacques," Troy said with a satisfied smile.

"We invited Nathan and Christian as well, and I hope they'll make it, however, they haven't replied as of yet," Gabrielle added.

"I'm sure they will," Sebastian said, looking around. "I guess there'll be a lot of partying since Gabrielle won't be home."

Troy chuckled at Sebastian's remark and gazed at Gabrielle sheepishly. Ian smiled as he remembered the good old days in Saint Jean De Luz. He was sure that being an immortal himself, partying would be much better this time around with all these guys.

"Let's go home, baby," Sebastian said to Arielle as he pulled her up gently. They all walked back up the steps holding hands. They thanked Ian and Eva for their wonderful gift and walked out the door, Troy and Gabrielle right behind them.

"Three more weeks!" Gabrielle exclaimed, and they waved as they got into the cars and drove away.

Sebastian took Arielle's hand and held it tight all the way home. Arielle fell quiet. Passion was thick in that small space but no words were spoken. When he pulled in the garage he turned the engine off and turned to face her.

"I don't want you to worry about anything. I can't imagine Gaston conspiring with Annabel to hurt you. He severed our longtime friendship over you, so I'm sure he would never agree to harm you." He helped her out of the car and put his arm around her as they walked into the house.

"What if he's trying to hurt you?" Arielle pressed her lips together, trying not to hyperventilate over that thought.

"I can take care of myself, Arielle, don't worry. I will never walk into a trap again. This was a grand lesson for me and I have our nightmare to thank." He smiled softly, looking totally unruffled. Arielle understood that by their nightmare he meant Annabel. She reached up and their lips met. He took her in his arms and held her tight, making her quiver as her lips moved feverishly beneath his. He gently broke away and she understood that tonight would be exactly like every other night since his unfortunate incident with Annabel.

She took a deep breath and ran her tongue over her lips, savoring the sweet taste of his immortal kiss. He gave her a peck on the forehead before he walked into the shower and pulled the door closed. A strong ache shot right though her body and tears welled up blurring her vision. She walked quietly into the bathroom to wash her face, brush her teeth and change into her little camisole. Disappointed, she slipped under the covers, consumed with sadness. Her desire for Sebastian was overwhelming. She missed his seductive ways, his never-ending cravings, and the way he made love. How long was he going to reject her? How long would she have to wait? Her pulse throbbed as she tried to hold back tears. She lay still as the ache for him increased. She closed her eyes, overcome by a numb coldness and tears poured down her face, drenching her pillow. Sleep claimed her before Sebastian came to bed.

Sebastian finished his shower and walked into a dark silent bedroom. He was sure that Arielle was asleep and that made things a lot easier. He slipped under the covers and moved closer, gathering her in his arms, spooning around her. She didn't try to get any deeper into his embrace, so he was sure she was asleep. Sebastian moved even closer as her breathing slowed. He buried his face in her hair and the smell of freesia made him smile. He was madly in love with her. His desire to be with her was something he'd never be able to understand. He wanted to love her every moment of every day but he felt unclean and dirty. Not good enough to touch or claim her beautiful wholesome body. Hurting Arielle was the last thing he wanted to do but that was exactly what he was doing. He cursed under his breath and squeezed her softly. *Oh, God,* he thought, the torture was unbelievable. Her body was so soft, her skin felt like silk, and her scent was sweet as honey. Sleep took a long time that night to claim him.

Arielle woke tightly encircled in his embrace. The room was dark and the clock on the end table showed 2:30 a.m. Sebastian was sleeping quietly with his face against her nape. The feel of his naked body against hers and his erection pressing against her buttocks sent a crashing wave of heat across every fiber in her body. Anticipation aroused every muscle and every craving she'd held for the last three weeks. Then reality hit her and she squashed those feeling just as fast as they'd come. She swallowed hard and sobbed quietly until sleep claimed her again.

The phone startled her and she fell out of bed trying to answer it. She looked around the room and her heart sank. Sebastian was already gone to the office and even though she knew that this was his new routine, she felt extreme disappointment. Her eyes welled up again and she answered the phone in a barely audible voice.

"Hello."

"Arielle," Gabrielle said, voice filled with joy. "What are you doing?"

"I just woke up," she murmured, and yawned.

"Did I wake you? Sorry!" she said.

"No...No...I needed to get out of bed," she said.

"Do you want to come over? The weather's beautiful and there are a lot of people at the beach just enjoying the day."

"Sure, I'd love that." She put the phone away and got in the shower still upset from the night before. She put on her bathing suit and was on her way. The weather was cool so there would be no swimming, however the sun was bright and warm and it would be wonderful to just lay out and get some sun. Gabrielle was ready when she arrived. They took a couple of beach towels and grabbed bottled waters from the fridge then crossed the short distance from the garden to the steps that separated the house from the beach. Brighton's beaches have a rare natural beauty and are always very sought after.

The sun was absolutely breathtaking, shining brilliantly in the clear blue sky. A large crowd had invaded the beach at this early morning hour. Some people ignored the cold long enough to enjoy the ocean waters, and others simply relaxed and sunbathed.

They descended the long brown wooden steps and stepped onto the soft white sand. Arielle felt stress and anxiety as people's thoughts and concerns invaded her head. The two women picked up pace and walked among all these people, trying to get to a private spot. Arielle pursed her lips in concentration as she focused on compartmentalizing the information she was getting, away from her own thoughts. Gabrielle understood what was happening to her so she remained silent while heading for their private spot. Soon they were at the familiar quiet cove away from all the commotion.

"Is this all right with you?" Gabrielle asked, her eyes fixed on Arielle.

"It's great," said Arielle softly.

They spread the beach towels on the soft sand and took their clothes off. Arielle looked over at Gabrielle and smiled wide.

"What's so funny?" Gabrielle

"Look at me and look at you," she said, waving her hand between the two of them.

"What do you mean?" Gabby said guardedly.

"Gabby, you have to most beautiful tanned body. Why can't I get a decent tan?" she said gloomily. "I love the sun and have spent countless hours trying to get tanned. Well look at me, just as pale as ever."

"Arielle, I can assure you that you'd have an awesome suntan, if you'd stop using so much of that sunblock."

"Do you really think so?"

"Well think about it this way, there's no way for the sun to penetrate that thick sunblock armor you put on every time you go to the beach. Try to just lay here without using any sunblock. Spread on some of this tanning lotion and you may be surprised," she said, and giggling handed Arielle a bottle of dark tanning oil.

"I guess you're right," Arielle agreed.

"I know that it's a lot healthier to use sunblock," Gabby said. "However my priority has always been a nice dark tan, so sunblock hasn't ever been on my shopping list."

"Healthier or not, you look so much better than I do," Arielle said, shaking her head in frustration.

"Is Sebastian complaining about your tan?"

"Of course not, he never complains. He thinks I'm perfect." She chuckled nervously.

"What's bothering you, Arielle?" Gabby asked, gazing at her intently.

Arielle winced and bit her lip. "He doesn't touch me anymore. We haven't made love in over three weeks and I'm going out of my mind." Her voice broke. She firmed her lips and ran her hand through her hair with sheer exasperation.

"Arielle, I thought we talked about that before. You have to be patient. He'll come around before you know it," Gabby said, and smiled soothingly.

"That's a lot easier said than done." She sighed.

"He is in love with you, Arielle."

Arielle smiled, staring at the sand as she kneaded it with her toes. She spread a healthy amount of tanning oil all over her body then lay back on the towel and closed her eyes, letting the sun's warmth embrace her. She was dozing off when Gabrielle's voice startled her.

"Arielle, do you ever wonder how men like Sebastian and Troy, who are faultless in every way, amazingly beautiful, and could have any gorgeous immortal woman in their world, can be satisfied with us?"

"Oh…My…God…" Arielle replied on an exhale. "I wonder about that every time I set my eyes on Sebastian's stunning face. I can't explain it and he certainly can't enlighten me. I'm starting to think that he's doesn't want me anymore," she said and growled with anger.

Silence fell between them. Arielle succumbed to her thoughts that were now spilling over with his beautiful existence and his rejection. He kept telling her that she was his life and he couldn't live without her. She started to hyperventilate when the thoughts about their wedding invaded her mind. What if he didn't want to touch her even then? Would they get married? How could they have a honeymoon? How would this work?

She sat up because she couldn't breathe. Her heart was hammering her chest and her head felt like it was going to explode. She swallowed back the bile that was climbing up her throat and dug her heels hard in the sand.

"Arielle! Where are you?" Gabby called out.

Arielle blinked, snapping out of her thoughts and tipping her head to the side to look at her and smiled thinly.

"What do you mean?" she asked apprehensively.

"You've been somewhere else for a while and you haven't uttered a single word."

"I just drifted off for a moment."

She knew she had to stop dwelling on the same thing over and over, but it was so hard to stop thinking about Sebastian's rejection.

Gabrielle rolled her eyes and nudged her with a smile.

"Well you were gone for a while. If there's something you want to talk about, I'm here. I'm your best friend do you remember that?"

"Yes," said Arielle, a faint smile on her face.

"So, what's really on your mind?" Gabrielle pressed.

"Gabrielle, I'm so in love with Sebastian that I'm sure I would die if I couldn't be with him. I'm willing to live with the constant fear of Annabel trying to kill me. I never know when she'll show up and what she's plotting and now I have Gaston and the Russian Mafia added to the equation. If I had any sense at all I'd have stopped this from the very beginning, but I let my heart make all the decisions for me and now it's way too late, because I can't breathe without him," she muttered.

"I feel the same way about Troy, Arielle," Gabrielle murmured, her sigh filled with bliss.

"Do you think Sebastian will come around before our wedding?" Arielle asked. "Otherwise I just don't see how this is going to work," she continued, eyes filled with tears. Gabrielle reached over and took her hands in hers.

"I promise you, Arielle, that Sebastian will come around very soon. That's what Troy told me and I trust in him unequivocally. He talks with Sebastian about everything. They're best friends like you and me," she said, voice filled with pleasure.

Arielle embraced Gabrielle and smiled gratefully.

"Thank you, Gabby. I feel a lot better. I do love you and thank my lucky stars that you're my best friend."

Soon they were talking about their youth and laughed over some of the dumb things they did while growing up. They talked about the wedding coming up. Gabby seemed to have everything in place. The wedding planner had made all the proper arrangements and they'd placed a checkmark next to every item on her wedding list. It'd been a whirlwind of planning and they were shocked to discover how many details could've been overlooked if they hadn't made that list and looked at every little item over and over again.

 *Chapter 7*

EVA'S WEDDING HAD BEEN perfect, so they were sure Gabrielle was ready for her big day. All she had to do was show up and marry the man who'd become one of Arielle's best friends. The man who was responsible for saving Arielle's life at least five times in the last year. It wasn't long before the conversation drifted to Eva and Ian. Gabrielle was pretty animated, making Arielle laugh as she kept on about their hot encounters.

"I know how scorching sexual encounters can be with one immortal in the relationship but can you imagine two immortals in love and away from each other for a whole week before the honeymoon? Eva looked so happy when they got back."

Gabrielle paused for a moment then let out a long sigh full of yearning and Arielle was sure she was thinking of Troy.

Arielle broke the silence. "I remember how extraordinary my encounters were with Sebastian so I can easily imagine, even comprehend the intensity between two immortals."

"I'm sure it would feel like standing in the middle of a tornado or a lightning storm," Gabrielle said, amused and they broke out into hearty laughs.

Quiet descended and Arielle was sure they were both thinking about their upcoming weddings and honeymoons.

"Do you know where you're going on your honeymoon?" Arielle asked.

"No, Troy wants it to be a surprise and I'm perfectly fine with that. He's amazing and I love his surprises." Gabrielle chuckled with glee.

Arielle wasn't sure how long they lay there, but when she opened her eyes the sun was going down and she was sure they'd dowsed off in the middle of their conversation.

"Gabrielle," she said, nudging her friend.

Gabrielle opened her eyes then widened them in shock when she realized they'd been there for several hours and had fallen asleep.

"What time is it? Troy must be home by now."

"I've no idea but I think we'd better head home," Arielle said, as they stood up and picked up the towels. She turned to face Gabrielle, saw her startled look and a wide smile spreading across her face.

"Look at you!!" she exclaimed as she pointed at Arielle.

"What is it?" Arielle looked down and gasped, overjoyed. Her white bikini looked even whiter against a wonderful dark tan. She was speechless as she stared back at Gabrielle who looked pleased with Arielle's tan.

"I told you," she said with a big smile on her face.

"All these years I was unable to get a great tan and all I had to do was use this little bottle of dark tanning oil," she said. "Imagine that! I can't wait to get home and show Sebastian. I've complained about my pale skin a million times and look at me now. I'm not sure this is going to change anything about his rejection toward me but still, I'm happy with the results." Arielle was beaming and they hugged in joy.

"I had a real nice time," Gabrielle said, "And I'm happy about your beautiful tan."

"I always have a good time when we're together," Arielle replied.

When they walked back and reached the wooden steps, they saw Troy standing at the top watching them. They were sure he'd seen them lying on the beach, as the immortal eyesight was perfect and far-reaching. He smiled as Gabrielle climbed the steps two at a time and fell in his arms. He locked them into a warm kiss and Arielle smiled as she saw how similar their lives were. Troy gave her a hug and walked her to the car.

"Nice tan!!!" he complimented. Arielle felt happy.

"I'm sure Sebastian is anxious for you to get home." He chuckled.

She didn't know what he meant.

"I hope he'll be happy with my tan," she said, smiling. She threw her bag and clothes in the trunk and slipped in the driver seat with just her bathing suit on. She couldn't wait for Sebastian to see her nice tan. By the time she got home it was getting to be dusk.

"Hey baby?" she heard his musical voice as soon as she walked in the door.

"Hi," she called out, as she threw her bag on the chair, picked up a bottle of water from the fridge and walked into the library.

"We fell a...." she stopped mid-sentence, as her eyes zeroed on this awesome sight of a man who was sprawled in the big chair wearing only a pair of jeans. She could see the fine lines of his muscular chest and excitement trickled from her head to her toes, overwhelming every inch of her body. Her lips quivered and she forgot what she was about to say. Her emotions took complete control, and her eyes roved over every inch of that stunning man, drinking him in. Suddenly, her heart sank remembering that he kept his distance and she felt anxiety taking over. He looked up at her and she noticed his eyes widen. His lips curved up to that amazing smile that made her writhe, exposing his perfect white teeth.

"Wow...look at you...great tan!" His eyes sparkled with desire.

"Do you like it?" she asked.

"Mmmm...come here and let me look at you up close." He motioned for her to sit on his lap, and she wasn't sure if he was serious or joking. She decided to play it safe, so she leaned against the doorframe and smiled, trying hard to hide her lust; throwing her head back she chuckled softly, closing her eyes. She was startled when her feet left the floor and her eyes snapped open. She was cradled in his arms, his face a couple of inches away from her face. She was in absolute shock, but took advantage of the situation, leaned in and met his lips in a hungry kiss. She was used to his tireless encounters but what she couldn't get used to was the immortal speed.

"What are you doing to me...?" she heard his gasping voice without breaking the kiss.

Arielle's heart pulsated as extreme heat saturated her. She'd missed that expression so much! She chuckled and moaned without breaking the kiss. She had to be dreaming, and if she was, she didn't want to wake up. She lowered her head and pressed softly the hollow at the bottom of his throat and he growled in clear exhilaration. She brushed his lips with the tip of her tongue and pressed them open, so she could taste his splendid scent. He tasted like honey and she licked her lips, trying to inhale every drop.

"I missed you so much!" he murmured without leaving the kiss. His hands unclipped her bikini top and dropped it to the floor just before he laid her on the bed, lust in his eyes.

Oh my God, is this really happening or am I dreaming?

She shivered with pleasure, thinking that this couldn't be happening. She looked up and gazed in his emerald eyes with bliss. He was now out of his jeans and next to her, pulling her closer. She swallowed hard, unable to hold back her desire for him. Dream or real she was going to enjoy this encounter.

"I missed you," she murmured. Her voice broke and she started to sob from pleasure.

"Please don't cry!" he said, voice filled with anguish. He cradled her face and kissed away the tears. "I'm sorry, baby," he murmured. "I was selfish, only thinking of myself, forgetting what this was doing to you. I love you so much, I can't breathe if I'm not with you."

"Oh Sebastian, I've been dying inside unable to help you, and make you feel better," she whispered. Her lips pressed his in a hot kiss. Sebastian chuckled when she gasped as his hands closed around her breasts. Waves of ecstasy travelled like wild fire through her. Their lips remained locked as her hands caressed the muscled planes of his back.

"I want you…." he murmured, and she gasped again.

His hand stroked her breasts, awakening every fiber in her body. His mouth claimed hers with wild demand. She moaned through the kiss and pulled him closer. He bent down and set his mouth on her breast as her body bowed toward him and his lips closed around her hard bud. His breath was hot and her body surrendered with exhalation and expectation.

"What in the world was I thinking?" he murmured, as his lips found hers again and held her to a fevered kiss. She exhaled with eagerness, as she was sure of what was about to come.

God! Will I ever stop wanting this man? I don't think I'll ever have enough of him!

Sebastian hauled in a deep breath, and bending one more time, he crashed her lips beneath his. Arielle set her hand on the back of his neck and held him to her, moving into him in a demanding way. His hands moved restlessly, claiming every part of her body and she moaned, intoxicated by his very existence. His arms were now firm around her body and with a swift move he pulled her underneath him and stretched his body on top of her. She gasped as she felt his erection brushing her thighs and she muted a scream of elation.

"I want you," she murmured, and their eyes locked as their lips remained together in a ferocious kiss. The heat intensified to a painful point of want, and eagerness, and lust. He wasn't going to prolong this intense need, and without holding back he pressed into her, every muscle locked with a frantic hunger. Their lips were still locked and they both were panting hard through the explosion of emotions that swept over them while their bodies were merging into this amazing love dance.

Arielle's breath held in her throat, as her body arched upward and her nerves tightened. She was afraid she was going to shatter every nerve, every muscle, and every fiber swirling in this crashing wave of ecstasy. Sebastian groaned and dragging in a deep breath gripped her buttocks and pressed in one more time imploding, taking Arielle with him into an intoxicating climax. The sensation was so powerful that it was enough to make her scream in frenzy. She wrapped her arms around him and held him to her as his body relaxed and his head lay against her chest.

Sebastian exhaled deeply and smiled wide at the feel of her heartbeat. "I love you," he whispered.

She sighed, overwhelmed with incredible fulfillment. All she ever wanted was to give him pleasure. He finally lay back, closed his eyes, and exhaled deeply as his arms pulled her closer and held her tight.

"My desire for you is something I'll never understand," he murmured as he nuzzled her hair.

"I couldn't face your rejection another day," she whispered.

"I'm sorry, baby, please forgive me," he murmured. "I love you and will for eternity." His lips found hers and held her to a passionate kiss. She pressed herself closer to him and smiled, content.

"Did you have a nice time with Gabrielle?" he asked.

"Yes, it was wonderful, the water was a bit cool but the sun was warm. We've always loved spending time together."

"Did you talk to any guys?" he asked with a chuckle.

"You've got to be joking?" she said, gazing into his beautiful emerald eyes. Her eyes roamed his perfect body. He looked like a Greek God, a specimen of perfection and unbelievably he was hers to love and to have anytime she wanted. She chuckled with extreme pleasure.

"I'm a very jealous and selfish man when it comes to you," he murmured.

"I don't look at other men," she said in a very firm voice.

"Even if they're good-looking?"

"Better looking than you?"

"Yes," he replied.

She couldn't believe her ears. "Sebastian, you couldn't possibly believe that there are humans out there who possess your flawless immortal looks."

"Is that what you love about me? The immortal looks?" he was watching her carefully.

"Certainly not!" she protested. "I love you, Sebastian, but having met some of the women in your immortal world, your attraction to me is a puzzle," she murmured.

He looked concerned as his arms pulled her fast on top of him and his eyes rested on her face, looking like he was reading her very essence.

"You're the core of my very soul; you give meaning to my miserable life." He pulled her down and his tongue thrust into her mouth, giving her ecstasy. She kissed him feverishly and rolling off to her side, let her hands caress tenderly every part of his body. He moaned as she watched a hot volcano infusing his eyes.

"What are you doing to me?" he gasped and she laughed aloud. He was aroused again.

"You'll be the death of me," he said, and she knew that she had her old Sebastian back.

"I've never heard of anyone dying from pleasure," she chuckled.

"In the last two years I've not been able to explain the constant frustration that surrounds my very existence," he said. His voice was doused in pure desire.

"I don't understand," she said, confused by his statement.

"Arielle, you're like an invariable need that I can't elucidate. When we're apart I ache for you and when we're together that ache actually intensifies. How do you explain that?" he seemed desperate for an explanation, as he gazed at her in complete wonder. He fell silent for a few moments.

"I feel the same way," she broke the silence, as she bent down and claimed his lips with hers.

"Arielle," he groaned as his hands moved, touching, caressing, enjoying, taking over every inch of her body.

Sebastian had been sure that after two years he knew everything about this beautiful girl who'd turn his world upside down. He was shocked to find that every day there was something new driving his need for her to implausible heights. His hands moved fast enclosing her and pulling her tight against his body as he rolled over taking her with him and landing on top of her again. He heard her gasp with anticipation and he lost it. His need was so extreme that he had to be careful not to hurt her. Soon they were moving to the soft rhythm of pleasure and he heard her moan, gasp, and cry out in pure ecstasy and that took his body to a higher level. She was warm, soft, and the fragrance of freesia filled his nostrils, making him smile in bliss. His desire drove him to an ultimate stage when she arched her hips up, wanting more. Fire shot through every layer of his body and he was now burning up. He thrust his tongue in her mouth to devour her as he tightened his hold on her and heard her soft whisper.

"I love you, don't ever leave me," she murmured, and he felt her body shudder as his muscled clenched and he imploded. She lay totally exhausted and he collapsed next to her in utter bliss.

Why would she ever have to ask me not to leave her? That would be like choosing to stop living. He rolled over and, lifting up on one elbow, gazed down into her beautiful sapphire eyes as his lips curved up to the smile he held only for her.

"I'll never leave you, Arielle, I've told you over and over again that I can't live without you. I'm here to stay until you don't want me anymore."

His amazingly faultless face was but an inch away as she wrapped her arms around his neck and pulled him down to feel his beautiful luscious lips against hers. She smiled, completely satisfied that this man loved her and would be hers for as long as she lived. She closed her eyes and pressed her lips in frustration. The painful reminder of Sebastian remaining on this earth after she would be gone surged through her mind. She felt his soft lips on her forehead and his musical voice caressed her ears.

"What's bothering you, baby?"

"I was just remembering how jealous I get when I think about you remaining on this earth after I'm gone," she chuckled, sulkily.

"You're not going anywhere." His arms were pulling her up against his body and his mouth was searching for hers, as she heard him murmuring.

"I'll make sure you remain on this earth with me for eternity. Can't you just trust me?" She felt the warmth of his body and she was content. She felt exhausted, as she lay back down and he encircled her in his arms, settling in for the night. Sebastian was back and what a comeback! She smiled blissfully and drifted off to sleep.

*　*　*

The week before the wedding Troy and Sebastian's friends flew in, this time ready to party hard. They showed their support for Ian and Eva's new identities and welcomed them in their secret immortal world, while Gabrielle and Arielle still couldn't wrap their brains around the idea of immortality. Troy kept up his complaining about Gabrielle being away from him for a whole week and the guys were amused. Arielle spent quite a long time with Gabrielle, Eva, and Loren while the guys partied nonstop.

Paul and Ian educated the immortal boys in the English stag weekend's version and the mini-holiday before the wedding, as they called it. The girls knew that immortals loved to spend time together, boating, skydiving, golfing, and horseback riding. These guys could go to the end of the earth and back since they had no restrictions and no limitations. They could tell that they were into the party mode and ready to indulge.

Sebastian asked Eva to stay with Arielle. He was worried about Gaston showing up while he was away. Arielle understood his concern but she wasn't going to live her life afraid of breathing each and every day. She was sure Annabel knew that she created a frightful environment for Arielle and she must've been extremely happy about that.

*   *   *

It was the Monday before the wedding and Gabrielle had already moved in with her parents for the week. Troy's friends stayed at the house, while Jon, Pierre, and Jacques stayed with Sebastian and Arielle. Troy moaned and complained every single moment about Gabrielle staying with her parents. Eva and Arielle were stunned about Troy's relentlessness and how much he complained about Gabrielle being away from him for a whole week. On one hand they thought it was cute, but on the other, that he was absolutely ridiculous. On Tuesday, Arielle got ready to move in with her parents so the guys could have the house and party without any girls around. Sebastian asked her to take a walk down to the beach so they can talk.

"I want you to stay with Eva, I don't want you being home alone," Sebastian said. Arielle heard anxiety in his voice.

"Nonsense," she said defiantly.

"I don't want to worry about you," he said, low-voiced. "Arielle, I don't like the fact that Gaston showed up," he continued, with a sterile voice, as they made eye contact and he looked alarmed.

"Gaston? Why would you worry about Gaston? I thought you'd worry about Annabel," she said, shaking her head in surprise. He looked deep into her eyes and she saw a muscle twitch in his jaw.

"Annabel told me that Gaston was here for you," he said with an anxious voice and she recoiled.

"That's just crazy, I don't believe a word of it. She's just trying to get you upset and frighten me." Arielle gazed in his anxious eyes and pursed her lips.

"He was my best friend, we did everything together. We never had a single fight over anyone or anything until you. He severed a friendship that was solid, built in concrete, because of you. I never knew he was an immortal and I've no idea when he became one, however I can think of a thousand reasons why he'd keep something like that a secret." He cleared his throat awkwardly and pressed on.

"One thing I know for sure is that he goes after what he wants with no hesitation or concern for anything or anyone until he satisfies his desire. You. Are. What. He. Desires." He emphasized each word. Her jaw dropped and she felt a lump climbing up her throat. His arms pulled her against his body and held her tight.

"I'm not going anywhere if you stay here alone." He was unyielding.

"Do you really think he's here for me?" she asked with a trembling voice.

"Yes, I'm sure, because I know how he thinks. The morning after you left Calais he came looking for you. I told him to leave you alone. He was furious with me and walked out, but not before saying, 'I'll look for her no matter how long it takes and she'll be mine.' I brushed it off, as I thought it was just his bad temper," he said with a soft smile. "He usually got over girl tantrums fast, but this time he was serious. I didn't know he was an immortal; I didn't know any immortals in those days. I knew they were sought out by the government and when found they were murdered. I'm sure that's one of the reasons he kept it quiet. One thing I know for sure, he was in love with you because to my astonishment he severed our friendship for good. I saw him a few times after that, but we never had the same relationship. I never saw him or heard anything about him again, until you brought his name up when you returned from Calais."

"Sebastian, I'll go and spend a couple of nights with my parents. They keep asking me and I just never have the time."

"But you're going to spend a week with them before the wedding."

"I know, but you can go and have fun and I'll be all right."

"I don't like to come home and not find you here," he said anxiously.

"You can't be with me every moment of every day," she replied, quite amused.

"Yes I can. I've made a commitment to do that for eternity."

"Be serious; that's quite impossible," she said rolling her eyes.

"I guess you don't know me very well." His voice was immovable.

"I think this'll give you time to think and maybe work out the things that are bothering you," she said looking at her feet.

He put his finger under her chin and lifted her face to meet his gaze. "What are you saying?" he asked with concern.

"I missed you, Sebastian, and even though our encounters are back to normal, I know you need to work a few things out." She felt a sting in the back of her eyes and saw a shadow cross his. She continued without waiting for him to reply. "I was looking forward to spending some time with my father, and you won't have to worry if you don't make it home one night."

"All right, if that's what you want," he said, pulling her into his arms and holding her tightly.

"I love you," she murmured and their lips locked in a glorious kiss. They walked back to the house with their arms wrapped around each other.

"I didn't get the chance to tell you how I felt at Eva's wedding," he said.

"What do you mean?" she asked.

His lips curved up to that wonderful smile and gazing in her eyes he murmured, "Watching you walk down that aisle was excruciating. You were so beautiful and so amazing that I struggled to keep myself from running to you, picking you up and taking you home."

"I'm sure glad you didn't do something like that. It would've been utterly embarrassing for all of us." She laughed in pleasure.

"I'll try to control myself at Gabrielle's wedding," he said, a smile lifting the corner of his mouth.

 *Chapter 8*

A WEEK BEFORE Eva's wedding, Gaston attended an immortal gathering in Italy with a close friend, Cinzia Salerno. Cinzia was quite the socialite and very well-known in immortal private circles. She was in love with Gaston, but knew he was the untamable type. Girls loved him and he wasn't willing to give his love to just one girl. Cinzia called and pleaded with him to be her date for the night. He accepted even though he didn't know the host, but he did like Cinzia, and was always passionate about fun.

When they arrived, the party was already in full swing, champagne flowing in abundance. He recognized a few faces, but most of the guests were strangers to him. Somewhere in the mist of all the drinking, dancing, and loud conversations, he noticed a lot of racket coming from a small group of men. They seemed to be chatting enthusiastically among themselves and passing around several photos. Their dialog was loud enough for everyone in the room to hear. They were looking at the pictures and talking about their holiday at St Jean De Luz, in France. He looked again but didn't recognize any of them.

He wasn't the least bit interested at their conversation, or their photos. He wandered slowly through the rooms with a drink in his hand and chatted casually with a few people. Eventually he ended up back into the main room, and carried on a boring conversation with a few girls who approached him, eager for his attention. He looked over in Cinzia's direction and saw that she was lost in a dialogue with a friend. He sighed, brushing his hand across his hair in sheer boredom. He was ready to walk outside for a smoke when he felt a nudge at his side. He braced himself for another boring chat as he turned and came face-to-face with a beautiful girl in her mid-twenties. She hesitated as her honey-colored eyes scanned his face and she seemed to forget what she was about to say. Gaston held her gaze and smiled. He finally broke the silence.

"Can I help you?" he asked softly.

"Um…" she seemed to be in a haze. She coughed a couple of times to clear her throat. "Could you please pass this photo to the girl over to your right?" she said bashfully and handed him a photograph.

He took it absentmindedly and kept his eyes on her.

"Um…thank you," she murmured delicately. She tried to keep her composure, but her body language told Gaston otherwise.

"Sure," he chuckled. He averted his gaze from the girl to the photo and glanced at it in passing. It reflected a few happy guys and girls on a beautiful beach. His hand with the photo was moving slowly to his right when suddenly, something resonated in the back of his mind. He realized that two of the faces looked quite familiar. He pulled his hand back and scanned the photo carefully. His eyes narrowed and focused on the two faces in the middle. He swallowed hard and drew a breath, eyes fixed on those two faces. He gasped and took an even closer look.

"No…" he stammered, "that's impossible!" he shook his head in disbelief. One of the faces was that of Sebastian, his best friend from centuries ago. The other was that of a beautiful girl in a white bikini with amazing sapphire eyes. He was unreservedly astonished. "Arielle," he gasped in a barely audible voice, his jaw clenched. Her name was etched in his very soul. He inhaled deeply in absolute shock. His mind swirled wildly trying to understand the significance of this moment. He and Sebastian had been best friends, actually more like brothers. Sebastian's family was like his own and he was sure they were all mortals. How could Sebastian emerge in this photograph that was taken over 500 years later?

His thoughts ran wild again. After their friendship severed, he saw Sebastian a few times while he was married, *if you could call it that*, to Annabel. Their meetings were cordial, but never friendly. But after Sebastian finally walked out on Annabel, he never saw or heard from him again. Gaston was sure that after all these centuries, Sebastian was long dead and gone. So, who turned Sebastian to an immortal and when?

And what about Arielle? How can she be here after 500 plus years? Was she an immortal when they met? Where was she all this time? He skimmed his finger over Arielle's reflection and his lips trembled with emotion. He remembered how he kept his own immortality purposely secret from everyone around him. Keeping his identity from Sebastian was the most difficult decision he'd ever made. He just couldn't take the chance. He didn't want to be discovered and turned in to the authorities. Immortals were hunted with incredible animosity during those days. He grimaced at the thought and tried to wipe the memories away.

Someone shifted next to him and he snapped out of his deep thoughts. He turned and glanced at the girl who was watching him intently. She had a wide smile on her face and her arm was extended toward him. A perplexed expression was spread across his face and he looked a bit confused.

"May I have the photo," she said softly. He blinked and immediately released it in her hand.

"Sorry," he stammered, apologetically. "I thought I knew one of the people in the photograph, but I was mistaken."

"That's quite all right," she replied, amused.

Gaston felt apprehension and found it difficult to breath. He excused himself and walked outside for some fresh air. The night air was cool and the moon obscured by thick clouds. There were two lamps mounted on the wall on either side of the door dimly illuminating the entrance. He lit a cigarette and walked a few feet away and stood in the dark alone with his thoughts. He tried to flip through the piles of the painful pages in his memory book. He'd blocked out everything that created anxiety and discomfort. He winced at the ache that Arielle's memory sparked in him. He never got the chance to spend time with her. Her rejection was vivid in his mind and he groaned painfully, as he drew in a deep breath. He'd never believed in love at first sight until their eyes met. He lapsed into stillness as he assessed the bitter feelings stored in the back of his mind, following the severance of a treasured friendship between him and Sebastian. He'd loved Sebastian like a brother, but his decision to take Arielle from him was something he was never going to forgive.

So, Arielle was an immortal...what a shock! He was determined to find her. His mind still astounded, told him that Annabel would be the perfect person to locate first. The intensity of the thought made his chest hurt. He closed his eyes and hauled in a deep breath. He recalled that Annabel was filled with rage and hatred when Sebastian walked out, and she'd sworn revenge until one of them was dead. He was sure that not even centuries would defuse Annabel's rage.

He recalled clearly that many of their friends didn't trust Annabel. Following her separation from Sebastian she became unstable, cruel, and unreliable. Annabel seemed to be a person who spent most of her time conceiving cruel schemes to be used against her enemies. She did, however, love Gaston, and always wanted to spend time with him. It didn't take long for Gaston to get tired of Annabel's nasty outbursts that only worsened as time passed. He decided to distance himself, and so left France on a long quest for something more interesting that would satisfy his long immortal existence on this planet.

He was now determined to look for the one person who would get him close to Sebastian; Annabel. Her visage emerged out of the dusty memories in his head and he smiled wide. *What a wonderful surprise!* After all these centuries, he'd found the girl who'd etched her name in his soul. The girl who'd turned his life upside down. The girl who'd disappeared from his life in one short evening never to return. He was filled with exhilaration and unbelievable desire. He was willing to break every immortal code in his power to make Arielle his own. Compulsion was forbidden by the strict immortal code. He wasn't sure he could obey that code if Arielle refused to be with him. Vengeance was the only thought he had for Sebastian. He threw the cigarette away with a sudden move and walked back inside to find Cinzia. She was still chatting away and having fun. He waited until they were alone in the car, before he asked his question.

"Cinzia, do you know Annabel Draper?" the question came awkwardly to his lips. She turned and her eyes lingered on his face. She tried to get a feel for his thoughts. He didn't wait for an answer.

"She was once married to Sebastian Gaulle," he said, holding his breath anxiously. Cinzia held his gaze to hers, and recognizing Gaston's suspense, chuckled with amusement.

"I don't know Sebastian Gaulle, but everybody knows Annabel," she said, and gave an insinuating chuckle.

"Do you know how to get ahold of her?" he asked obsessively. There was some hesitation on her part.

"No, not exactly, but I know people who do, but why are you asking about someone like Annabel?" she asked wryly.

"She and I used to be quite close back in the late 1500s, and then I lost track of her. Her name came up the other day, and I thought I'd ask around. I'd like to see her again if I could," he said.

"Gaston!" Cinzia muttered, and pressed her lips together. "Annabel has a very dark reputation..." her voice trailed off.

"What are you saying?" he asked, probing.

"I don't know what type of person she was back then, but today she's known for being a nasty bitch completely out of control. I do believe she's psychotic."

Gaston chuckled. Annabel didn't sound much different today than what he remembered.

"It's not funny," Cinzia frowned. "Rumor has it that she's insane. She was madly in love with that Sebastian you mentioned who left her after a two-year marriage and she was utterly humiliated."

Gaston flinched at the sound of Sebastian's name.

Cinzia continued, oblivious to Gaston's thoughts. "The hurt and disgrace were so deep, that even after all these centuries, she's still seeking revenge. I personally think she'll succeed in killing this poor Sebastian. However, until she finds him, she seems to have the urge to punish every new man in her life, as if he was Sebastian," she murmured. Her lips tightened and she took a deep breath.

"What else have you heard?" Gaston asked, amused.

"She and her best friend, Giovanna, dated a lot of young foolish men, and when they got bored with them, the guys would disappear into thin air. Then, new guys would come in the picture, and the cycle would start over again. I couldn't even begin to visualize what happened to those poor young men." Her voice lowered almost to a whisper. "The rumors about that would drive chills through your bones. It's said that they had those poor boys murdered and their body parts spread across the land for animals to feed on." She shook in fright, wrapping her arms around her body, and pressed her lips together.

"Who's Giovanna?" he asked curiously.

"She was another sick bitch but nobody's seen her for over a year now. Maybe she's dead and maybe she's moved somewhere else to torture other poor souls. Gaston, you need to keep away from Annabel. She's a sick, disgusting bitch, and needs help, however nobody has the guts to tell her. She's very rich and very vicious. She has a lot of scums who do her dirty work and she pays them very well."

Gaston stared at Cinzia and caution flickered in his eyes. A long silence fell between them.

He remembered extremely well the moment Sebastian walked out of Annabel's life and never came back. Gaston was Annabel's friend and confidant at the time, because they shared the secret of immortality. He recalled Annabel confiding in him that Sebastian never shared her bed in the two years they were married. Their marriage was never consummated. She told him that she never thought Sebastian would leave her the way he did. She was never going to forgive the humiliation he bestowed upon her. Shame enveloped her like a heavy metal blanket that she had to carry for the rest of her life. She was overwhelmed with rage and vowed revenge on Sebastian for centuries to come. Gaston and Annabel parted ways a couple of years later, and lost track of each other.

Gaston evoked the magical night he met Arielle and the feel of her soft luscious lips. He'd looked for her everywhere to no avail, and he gave in to the only thing left, the struggle to forget her. He failed to succeed in scraping off the etching of her name from his very core. The thought of Arielle made Gaston anxious again and his mouth tightened. He ran his tongue over dry lips. Now he needed to find Annabel. He was sure she knew Sebastian's whereabouts. If he found Sebastian he was certain to find Arielle. He smiled wide filled with eagerness and desire.

Cinzia was now watching Gaston. She was sure by the expression on his face that he was evoking past times. He finally shook his head feeling hopeful.

"Will you spend the night with me?" Cinzia asked softly. She reached over, took his hand, and placed it on her breasts. Gaston chuckled and, gazing in her beautiful green eyes, leaned in and pressed his lips on hers fondly. Any other night he would've said yes, but tonight his mind and soul were filled with Arielle.

"Maybe another night," he murmured, pulling his hand back and holding her to that kiss. "I've a prior commitment. I hope you'll forgive me," he said. Cinzia pouted for a moment and then smiled softly. She was crazy about Gaston, but she wasn't going to confess her feelings. He was a stunning man, six feet tall with clear beautiful blue eyes, perfect features, and a muscular body to kill for. She sighed, wishing he was hers, but Gaston was a well-known playboy with many women in his life who were more than happy to be on his beck and call.

"Will you get Annabel's number for me?" he asked, just before he dropped her off at her house.

"Yes, I'll call you tomorrow," she said as she stepped out of the car. She turned and, leaning over the seat, asked for another kiss. She kissed him with hunger this time and he responded to her kiss with a chuckle.

The next day he anxiously waited for Cinzia's call. It didn't come until late that afternoon and he was going out of his mind. He thanked her and told her he'd call her soon. Eagerly he dialed Annabel's mobile. He thought his chest would burst from sheer excitement. He was getting closer to his quest for Arielle.

"Hello?" he heard a soft voice on the other end.

"Is this Annabel?" he asked.

"Who wants to know?" Her voice was quite abrupt.

"It's Gaston."

"Gaston!" she exclaimed. "Where are you?" Her voice was filled with excitement.

"I'm in Salerno for the summer. Where are you?"

"So am I!" she cried in sheer bliss. "When can I see you?" she asked eagerly. His instinct urged him to have this meeting as soon as possible.

"Can we meet today?" he asked.

"Right now would be just fine with me," she replied.

"Tell me exactly where you are and I'll come over." She gave him her location, and they hung up. The drive wasn't long and soon he was knocking at her door. He was startled as she threw the door wide open and fell in his arms in pure pleasure.

"Oh, Gaston, you look just as stunning as ever!"

"And you're just a beautiful as ever, Annabel, how have you been? I heard you're still breaking hearts left and right." She looked delighted with his comment and laughed aloud in joy.

"Well, you know me. More men more fun. How about you? Is there a permanent girl in your life? Or are you still looking?"

"Still looking," he chuckled. "Do you see any of our old acquaintances?" he asked and noticed a dark flash that crossed her eyes.

"Yes," she murmured, her eyes narrowed to slits. "Many of the people we knew back then are still around. A few have moved to other countries and some were killed in stupid fights."

Gaston nodded. His heart pounded while trying to find a way to get around to Sebastian. He pulled his gaze away from Annabel's and looked around.

"This is a beautiful home," he complimented. She followed his gaze around the room.

"It's just a place for the summer," she replied.

"Do you spent a lot of time in Italy?" he asked.

"No, not really. I move around a lot."

"Why is that?"

"I guess I like to change the view every now and then," she chuckled, bitterly. "But enough about me. What've you been doing? I haven't seen you for nearly 500 years," she said, watching him intently. Gaston could tell she was troubled and avoiding his question.

"What do you want to know?" he asked softly.

"I want to know where you've been for all this time. What have you been doing with your life?" She kept a pleasant look on her face.

"Well..." his voice trailed. "You don't want to hear my boring life story." He gave her a quick glance and looked away. Annabel moved closer and sat right across from him.

"Why would you think that?" she asked in surprise. "I care about you Gaston, you were always trustworthy." Her eyes scanned his face. Silence fell between them. Gaston closed his eyes and all he could think about was Arielle. How was he going to find a way back to her? He shook his head, opened his eyes, and forced a smile.

"Would you like a drink?" Annabel's voice broke into his thoughts. There was quiet concern in her voice.

"Sure, that would be nice."

She rose and walked over to the bar. "Scotch all right?"

"Fine."

She poured a class and walked back with a smile. "That should hit the spot," she chuckled, as if she knew something was bothering him.

Gaston took a sip and his voice came out soft and calm. "I moved around this boring planet for a long while. When I left France, I moved to Brazil where I found a great bunch of friends and spent approximately a century there. Then a few of us ventured out to the Far East where I spend nearly 300 years. That has to be the most amazing place I've ever lived. The women are fascinating and their way of life peaceful and graceful." He took another sip of his drink and continued. "Later I met a young lady in Singapore and we dated for a few years. I followed her to her native Russia, where we lived together for a while and when I got bored I moved to Spain." Gaston looked over at Annabel. "Spanish women are hot!" he chuckled again and she laughed with him. "I spent a reasonable amount of time in Spain but still hadn't found what I was looking for," he said bitterly.

"What is it exactly that you're looking for?" she asked, watching him with extreme curiosity.

"I'm not sure, Annabel, but I seem to be in quest of something." He stared at his glass and swirled his drink around. "I have a gut feeling that I might be getting close," he said, and bit his lip.

"Well, I hope you find what you're looking for," she said, with a kind smile. "Gaston, if you need my help, remember that I'm here." Her voice was firm. Reaching over, she gave him a soft pat on the hand.

"Right," he said, absentminded.

"So how did you end up here in Italy?" she asked softly.

"I tired eventually of being away from home, and returned to France when I connected with the old bunch and we're here for vacation. But I've always known that I would end up back in France or Italy. They're two of my most favorite places on this planet." Gaston focused his attention somewhere in the distance. He remained silent for a long time, as memories flooded his mind like a huge title wave and he stopped breathing. Annabel cannon-balled him a stunned look.

"Gaston," she called out. "What's wrong?" His blue eyes looked up at her a bit shocked.

"Oh...I'm sorry Annabel, I just got carried away." He smiled softly before he came out with his next question. "Why don't you tell me a bit about what you've been doing with your life?" he asked.

"Gaston...Gaston..." she said, shaking her head disappointedly. "My life has been a real roller coaster. Not that I would admit that to anyone else," she gazed at him intently. "I've roamed this globe for over 500 years and accomplished very little." She smiled resentfully. "I'm completely aware that I've screwed up most of the great opportunities that could've improved my miserable existence."

She tapped her fingers on the armchair and kept silent for a short while. She finally shot out of her chair and started to pace the floor nervously. Gaston was hoping that while she was in a rant, she would come around to talking about Sebastian. He was sure there was a lot to say and it didn't take long.

"I wish I could get rid of the awfully powerful animosity I've been carrying around for so very long..." her voice trailed and more silence. She finally looked at Gaston and her face went still. Her fists balled by her side and her voice turned cold, freezing cold. "I want to hurt him, I want to hurt him so bad!" her voice was filled with passion, her teeth clenched.

"Whom are you talking about?" Gaston asked, in sheer shock with Annabel's inconceivable fury.

"Sebastian!" she screamed and ran her hands through her hair, utterly frustrated.

Gaston flinched at his former best friend's name and tried hard to hide his excitement. He wasn't going to say anything to Annabel about the photo he'd seen and his theories.

"Sebastian?" he said acting astonished. "I thought Sebastian would be dead and gone by now. "

Annabel's pacing came to an abrupt halt. "Oh, Gaston, I made a big mistake. I turned Sebastian to an immortal a long time ago.

"What are you saying Annabel?" Gaston drew in an anxious breath.

"Sebastian's an immortal now because of me," she said. She laughed and it was a laughter of loathing and contempt. Then she sighed deeply but remained silent.

"What is it?" he finally asked breaking the silence.

"Gaston, the line between hatred and love is very thin, actually barely visible. I didn't want him to die. I wanted to make sure that I could punish him for centuries to come. I wanted my revenge to be long and painful," she said, and her eyes looked wild, filled with revulsion. "I was never going to let him be happy with another woman. I'd make sure I killed whoever he loved, just to deliver pain and misery in his life."

"So what's going on? Where is he?" he asked, pretending nonchalance.

"Gaston…"

"What?" he asked.

"I never really cared about his unimportant escapades with different women throughout the centuries. However this time around he's given a ring to a miserable human and planning to get married," she grimaced and cursed out loud. "I hate them both," she shrieked and pounded on the table. "I'll never let this marriage take place."

"Whom is he marrying?"

"I told you, some miserable human." Her lips pressed in a thin line.

"Who is she?" he persisted.

"Her name is Arielle and I loathe her," she murmured, and cursed again. However she didn't go into details about how many times she'd already tried to actually get rid of her for good. Her thoughts were interrupted by Gaston's thoughtful voice.

"I met a girl by that name and her two sisters, back in Calais."

"When?" she asked a bit curious.

"Oh, way back, when Sebastian and I were in our twenties."

"Then, I'm sure she's not the same girl. The name is just a coincidence."

"Are you sure?" he asked and hauled in a deep breath.

"Yes, I'm very sure. This girl is definitely human."

"Do you happen to have a photo of her?" he asked.

"Why?" She was now searching his face.

"Well do you? I need to see the girl's face."

"Yes, as a matter of fact I do. I've used the photos when I need to locate her whereabouts." She laughed contemptuously. She walked over to an end table and pulled a photo out of the drawer. She handed him the photo and watched him carefully. Gaston gasped in utter shock. It was Arielle, his Arielle.

"Annabel," he said, in a husky voice. "I met this Arielle girl back in the 1500s. Back when Sebastian and I were in our twenties. Way before he met you. She and her sisters were at a gala his parents gave in Calais. She couldn't possibly be human and still here after more than 500 years." He stopped talking and hauled in a deep breath. He ran his hand irritably through his hair in sheer frustration.

"I don't know anything about the Arielle you met," she said. "But there's nothing in this world that I'm more sure of, than the fact the marriage between this Arielle and Sebastian is never going to take place.

"But..." his voice trailed off. His expression was that of complete confusion. Annabel understood there was a lot more going on in his mind. Gaston appeared unable to separate his meeting with Arielle back in Calais and Annabel's testimony.

"But what? What's so upsetting to you?" she was now sitting next to him watching him extremely close.

"Annabel," he said, and exhaled deeply. He gazed in her eyes looking for answers.

"Are you sure this is the same girl?" she asked and pointed at the picture.

"Yes, I'm positive," he murmured, and silence fell between them. She looked totally mystified but soon enough she broke the silence.

"Well I'm not sure what all this means. I can tell you that I've met the girl and she's human." Her reply was stern, her eyes fixed on his face.

"Annabel, I'd like to see her again. Can you arrange that?"

"Why are you interested in this girl?" she asked, looking at him with extreme curiosity. Gaston shifted uncomfortably, as he couldn't help the odd feeling that traveled like a heat current through his body. *Arielle a human! How strange,* he thought to himself. He hesitated for a moment.

"How long have they been together?" he asked in a low voice.

"Almost two years, but, Gaston, why do you care about Arielle?" she asked again giving him a serious look. He gazed deep into Annabel's eyes, as emotion poured out of his mouth.

"I'm in love with her," he murmured.

Annabel shot out of her seat, as if she was on fire. Her body was locked in a shocked position.

"What?" Her shocked green gaze swept over his face. "What?" she asked again extra forcefully this time.

"I'm in love with Arielle," he said again and watched Annabel's mouth drop in sheer astonishment.

"You love her?" she cried out. "When did you meet her?" she tried not to get to excited before having all the details.

"I told you, Annabel, I met her in Calais. I can't explain how she can be human and here after 500 years, but I can assure you that this is the same girl." He pressed the back of his hands to his eyes and cursed quietly in total frustration. "I'm going out of my mind. She's the reason I severed my friendship with Sebastian," he said, his voice fierce with emotion.

"What do you mean?" Annabel asked, puzzled. Gaston swept her face with painful eyes and chuckled inconsolably.

"I told Sebastian back in Calais that I liked the girl and I didn't want him to interfere. Sebastian and I never argued over girls. If I liked someone, but he really wanted to be with her, I stepped back, and he did the same for me. This time was different. I fell in love with this girl from the moment I set eyes on her. To my astonishment Sebastian moved in on Arielle and wouldn't let go. I told him I felt strongly about her and that he needed to back off, but he dismissed me, as if I was a stranger."

"What happened then?"

"We argued, and I ended up leaving his house upset. I went back the next morning to find out if things had calm down between us. At first he was as joyous as always, but when I brought Arielle's name up he got extremely angry. Bitter words were exchanged between us and that was the end of our friendship. I must admit that I was devastated. Both of my worlds collapsed." Gaston growled, pain and longing flashed across his eyes.

"Both worlds?" Annabel whispered inquisitively.

"Yes, both worlds," he repeated. "The feeling of being in love for the first time and a long and treasured friendship. Both crashed and gone." He pressed his lips together as anxiety spread across his beautiful face.

A long stony silence fell between them. Finally Annabel rose and walking across the room where she poured another drink for both of them. She walked back and, handing him the glass, broke the silence.

"Maybe I can help," she said, a sinister smile painting her lips. He raised his eyes to hers.

"How?"

She didn't reply immediately. Gaston watched her intently. He was jolted by her suddenly hearty laugh. He tried to interpret her reaction. Excitement wasn't the word for it. It was pure elation. It felt like time stopped and everything went still. It took a little while before Annabel came out of her jovial mood and now she was smiling wide.

"Gaston! If I could cry from joy, I'd be crying right now," she said blissfully.

"I don't understand," he murmured.

Amusement flashed in her eyes. "This just couldn't be any more perfect," she whispered.

"Annabel, what in bloody hell are you muttering?"

"Gaston, you're the answer to my long-lingering desire to destroy Sebastian," she said filled with joy.

"Me?" he asked, astonished.

"Yes, can't you see the picture? You and I are a match made in heaven."

"How is that?"

"Gaston—Gaston—I—I want Arielle the hell away from Sebastian, and you—you want Arielle for yourself," she said, and laughed again. "Now, do you see what I'm trying to say?" An evil smile lingered at the corner of her mouth. Their eyes met, his thoughtful. He eventually nodded in agreement.

"I would like to see her. Do you know where she is?"

"Funny you ask. My informers have told me that a wedding will take place next Saturday. One of her best friends, Eva, is getting married, and Arielle is in the wedding.

"Eva! That's right," he said anxiously. "Eva was one of her sisters and the other girl was Gabrielle."

"That's very peculiar, but both those miserable girls are her best friends, not her sisters," she said.

"That's strange," he murmured.

"I plan to show up at that wedding for a couple of reasons," Annabel said, breaking his train of thought. "The first is to light a little fire under their feet and let them know that I'm here to stay. The second reason is a little more complicated."

"What do you mean?"

"Gaston you're welcome to come with me. I'm sure your presence will provide a strong distraction for your little human," she said, a menacing smile on her face. "However, I have some unusual plans arranged for Sebastian. It's my private issue with him, and I'll handle that alone."

"I don't want to upset Arielle and I definitely don't want to hurt her," he said.

Annabel stood and walked back toward the bar rolling her eyes. Irritation enveloped her as she recalled all the times she'd tried to kill Arielle and failed. She wasn't going to talk about that with Gaston. She was still doubtful that Arielle was the same person Gaston met in Calais, but if by some weird chance, she were, it would fit perfectly in her evil scam to destroy Sebastian. She could almost see her horrible scam coming to a close.

# *Chapter 9*

A WEEK LATER Gaston followed Annabel to Brighton and crept into Eva's wedding totally unnoticed. Hidden behind a large column, Gaston swallowed hard at the sight of Sebastian. It'd been centuries since he last saw him and Gaston was now overwhelmed with the unpleasant memories of their last conflict. Somewhere in the depths of his soul he really did miss their friendship. He was still lost in thought when his eyes were filled with the most awe-striking vision.

Arielle walked down the aisle with a bouquet of flowers resting against her chest, an astonishing smile on her beautiful face. His breath caught in his throat and his jaw tightened. He didn't breath and didn't blink, terrified that she was just a dream that would disappear. Waves of heat and desire grew bigger and bigger, as the time clicked away. When the ceremony was over he watched her walk out on Sebastian's arm and jealousy ripped right through him. He zeroed on her beautiful bright blue eyes and he was sure this was the girl he fell in love with 500 plus years ago.

He and Annabel stood by the side of the large entrance doors and watched their little group stand in the parking lot and chat cheerfully. They looked so happy and he was drawn into deeper sadness. Suddenly she looked up as if she sensed their presence and he saw a terrified look on her face. Why would she be so terrified? He never did anything to hurt her or even give her the idea that he wanted to hurt her. Gaston stepped to the side and hid himself from her direct view. He was startled when Annabel grabbed his hand tightly.

"We've got to go now." She didn't look like she was expecting a reply. She moved in that immortal speed of hers and he followed. They ran for a long while and Annabel stopped a couple of times to scan around them to make sure they weren't being followed. When they reached a large park she stopped him and pressing his hand made him face her.

"What happened?" he asked, hauling in a deep breath.

"They saw us and Sebastian is coming after me," she said. "Here's where the second part of my plan starts, and I need to do this alone. Gaston, you need to go and stay with my friend Andrew; he's expecting you. I'll come and see you tomorrow.

"Will you be all right?"

"Sure, I've everything arranged. Don't worry about me," she smiled, an unforgiving, meaningful flash in her eyes. Gaston was sure all of her anger was directed toward Sebastian.

*　*　*

It was a couple of weeks before Gabrielle's wedding and a warm beautiful July day. Arielle had agreed to meet Gabrielle and Loren at the Lanes. Sebastian left for the office very early, but not before waking her up and claiming, to her delight, what he knew was his, and only his for centuries to come. While driving to the mall, the vivid memory of their morning encounter flashed back in her mind. She felt heat spreading across her body and smiled wide, trying to concentrate on the road. She chuckled aloud, realizing the wild effect Sebastian had over every aspect of her life.

When she arrived, she scanned the parking lot for a vacant spot, but to her disappointment it appeared quite full. She drove around hoping to find an empty spot that wasn't so obvious at first look. She really wanted to be a little closer to the shops, but she was a bit frustrated, there were no parking spaces available. She decided to drive toward the very end of the lot and to her surprise found the perfect spot wedged between the wall and a large van. The car would be parked under a huge tree that would keep the inside cool while she was shopping. She smiled, pleased, even though she was a bit further from the shops, but today she was happy to walk. She turned the engine off, and twisting grabbed her purse from the back seat. She pulled the strap over her shoulder, and shutting the door, pressed the lock button on her key fob. She chuckled when she heard the familiar click of the lock. She took a deep breath, filling her nostrils with the salty scent of the ocean, and started to walk.

The walk from the parking lot to the stores was a hike, but the weather was wonderful. She looked around and smiled. Huge trees full of green leaves surrounded the parking lot, creating an amazing contrast against the clear blue sky. The sun's brilliant surface nestled in the middle of that smooth unending space, giving Arielle an amazing warm feeling. She marveled at the sight and picked up her pace. The plan was to shop for a couple of hours at their favorite shops and then have lunch. Loren was going to indulge them by pretending to have lunch. Arielle chuckled at the thought of the immortal world she was living in.

She was utterly lost in joyous thoughts about Sebastian, when a voice penetrated her mind.

"Arielle!" She froze mid-stride and gasped. The voice was very familiar, familiar enough to send fright down her spine. The air suddenly changed from warm and comfortable to icy cold. She shivered and started to hyperventilate; her heart started to pound in her chest, spreading searing pain through every fiber of her body. She couldn't breathe; she gulped a mouthful of air and felt faint. Suddenly she knew he was standing right behind her.

"Arielle!" the voice was now soft. This time she spun around and froze in place as the most stunning crystal blue eyes met hers. Chill was an instant reaction to his presence and her voice came out quivery but clear.

"Gaston!" she stammered. "What are you doing here?" she immediately knew it was a stupid question. The uncomfortable sensation continued, leaving her profoundly apprehensive. His last statement to her flickered in her mind like a neon sign. *I always get what I want, and you're what I want.* She pressed her lips together and tried to ignore him *as if that was possible* by staring at the ground.

Without another word she turned and started to walk again picking up pace. He kept pace with her. She was trying to avoid any conversation with him, hoping to get to the location where she was to meet Loren and Gabrielle. She felt the weight of his gaze on her, but didn't turn to look at him.

Gaston was watching her carefully, a smile spreading across his face.

"Arielle," he said again. His voice carried a demanding tone. "I need to talk to you. Can we please sit somewhere and have some tea?" he asked. She stopped walking and turned to face him. He reached out for her hand, but she stepped back, putting a little more distance between them.

"Gaston, I'm completely aware that you aren't interesting in eating or drinking any type of human foods, so please don't insult my intelligence." She felt a rush of vivid recollections from Calais and paused feeling awkward. She inhaled deeply and looked up at him, avoiding direct eye contact.

"What do you want, Gaston?" she asked through clenched teeth.

"I want to know about the link between the Arielle in Calais and the Arielle in this century," he said as he inched closer.

"Calais was a long time ago," she said and noticed Gaston's mouth stiffen.

"That's exactly why I'm here," he said. His voice troubled, his eyes filled with wonder. "I don't understand the correlation between you in Calais, and you right here, in the 21st century, knowing you're human," he said, accentuating his question. "How can that be possible? You're here, and I just don't understand." He ran his hands through his hair and mumbled something inaudible. He paused for a moment as his gaze swept over her face. "You have to say something, because I'm going out of my mind." His eyes hardened and his jaw clenched. He waited for a reply. Finally, unable to bear the silence, he said slowly, "Arielle, I'm not going anywhere, so you better start talking." He pinched the tip of his nose, tilted his head to the side and gazed at her, his expression inscrutable.

Anxiety stirred Arielle's emotions mixing with a sick feeling in the pit of her stomach. She turned her head to avoid a direct gaze into his eyes.

"It was time-travel," she replied quietly, her voice slicing through the silence.

"Time-travel!" he exclaimed. He looked shocked.

Strangely enough, Arielle thought she owed him an explanation.

"Yes, time-travel," she said again. "I met Sebastian a year ago in St Jean De Luz while on holiday with my family and we fell in love. One of my immortal friends has this special gift. The time-travel to Calais was my birthday present. I wanted to meet Sebastian before he became an immortal. That's how you and I met. Gaston, I was already in love and engaged to Sebastian for over a year. And even though you're amazing, my heart is already with Sebastian. Do you understand now?" She was trying to make sense out of a very weird situation.

He looked at her at a loss for words. "That's impossible," he murmured, "that's impossible."

Silence fell between them again, and she watched him run his hand through his hair, pressing his lips together and looking utterly confused. He finally looked up at her.

"Why did you lie about Gabrielle and Eva being your sisters?"

"How do you know about that?"

"I know everything about you."

"Well, they're my best friends and we've been like sisters ever since we were kids. Saying that we're sisters, it's truer than a lie. The time-travel was exciting and something that doesn't happen every day, especially to mortal people like us."

"Who's your immortal friend?" his voice raised in question.

"Eva."

"I don't believe you," he said.

"Well, it's true, whether you believe me or not," she replied stubbornly.

"I'm still confused, how can she be an immortal?"

"That's a different story and I don't feel like talking about that. Again, please try to understand. I was in love with Sebastian way before I met you, and he with me. That's why you and I are never going to happen. I don't know how else to explain my situation."

"Arielle, I don't care about Sebastian and I don't care about your love affair with him. I promised you that I was going to look for you no matter how long it would take," he said firmly. "I never expected that it would take a little over 500 years," he added, and burst into a hearty laugh.

Arielle wasn't amused. Her senses were alert, and she knew that whatever Gaston was up to, it wasn't good. She turned to look at him. His smile was sinister.

"I want to sit somewhere with you alone and just talk. Let's have a cup of tea. We must talk," he said firmly.

Arielle tried hard to suppress the desire to scream from pure frustration.

"Gaston, please! I need to go," she murmured, clenching her fists.

"Hm…this isn't going as well as I expected," he muttered, irritated. His voice was icy cold. Rage spreading across his face. She tried hard to remain composed but she was failing miserably.

"I'm sorry, but I'm meeting a couple of my friends, so this isn't a good time," she said civilly, voice quivering. She didn't want to make him angry, knowing his immortal power. He frowned and looked up toward the trees exhaling deeply. She took the chance, and turning around started to walk again.

"Hm…" she heard his voice behind her. She was startled when her body slammed right into him. He'd moved quickly in his immortal speed and blocked her path. The exquisite sensation of her body against his made him gasp in intense anticipation. His nerves flexed painfully and he stood completely still. The next moments brought chaos in Arielle's mind and body. Gaston reacted the only way his mind was directing. His arms wrapped around her and his mouth found hers in a greedy and powerful kiss.

Arielle was stunned. Lost for words, eyes wide open in shock, frozen in place. Gaston pulled back from the kiss and stepped back, intoxicated by her mere presence, thunderstruck by the aftermath of the kiss. He finally shook his head to clear the fog and gazed into those amazing blue eyes. He wanted her so badly he actually hurt at the mere thought. He shoved his hands into his pant pockets and smiled wide. His voice came out low but suggestive.

"When can we have that cup of tea?" He didn't move, waiting for an answer. Arielle was still in shock trying to grasp the sudden lust she felt when Gaston's mouth found hers.

I must be out of my mind, she thought. *What in bloody hell am I thinking?* She pursed her lips in anxiety.

"I'm not sure; I'm quite busy," she whispered. "So I've no idea when that could be."

"You'll have to pick a time, otherwise I'll pick the time for you right now." His voice wasn't soft anymore; it was rigid and demanding.

Fear spread across her body as she remembered now that Gaston wanted to destroy her relationship with Sebastian. She was having a hard time trying to keep her composure. She shut her eyes, trying to think fast on how she could get out of this situation without any problems. She looked around again and saw several people walking nearby, however she was smart enough to know that an army of humans couldn't help her if he wanted to hurt her.

"Gaston, I need to go, my friends are waiting and they'll come looking for me if I don't show up," she said, with a quivery voice. She wasn't sure this was going to have an effect on him but she had to try.

"Only if you promise to meet me and give me a chance to talk with you for a little while," his voice was firm, eyes hard.

"There's nothing to talk about," she replied defiantly, and knew that was a stupid statement. "I'm getting married and I'm sure Sebastian wouldn't appreciate this demand of yours."

He now stopped talking and chuckled, shaking his head in amusement.

"So, you're going to marry Sebastian," he said, and laughed bitterly.

His words came out like poison and she saw him shifting nervously. He pinched the tip of his nose and Arielle got panicky. knowing that immortal sign of frustration. Sebastian did that every time he was angry. Gaston stood frozen in place. He felt jealousy infecting every part of his body, every fiber, every vein. He was suffocating and he wasn't going to allow Sebastian to take Arielle away from him. He was here now and he would do everything in his power to persuade her to choose him. She looked up at him but not directly in his eyes and saw an angry look on his face.

"Well...you aren't married yet, so there's plenty of time for us to talk," he said wrathfully. He was now standing much closer and she felt his warm breath against her face, while his finger ran across her cheek and around her lip line. She recoiled and he noticed, because she saw a dark shadow cross his blue eyes as he pursed his lips.

"Arielle, you don't have a say in this matter, since I'll make it happen one way or another," he continued now completely unruffled.

"Stop!" she screamed. He backed off in shock. She was sure he didn't expect that kind of outburst.

"Well," he laughed, in pleasure, "There's fight in you and I love that. It makes the hunt much more desirable."

"I don't understand what you're saying, what hunt?"

"You, of course. I'm here for you, Arielle. Do you really think that after all these years, I'll just walk away, just because you said 'no'? I guess you don't know me very well." He chuckled, a sadistic smile on his face.

"Gaston, I'm in love with Sebastian, can't you understand that? There's nothing you can say, nothing you can do to make me change my mind," she said. Her voice was crackling and she felt a knot in the pit of her stomach. Gaston watched her carefully. His bright blue eyes narrowed thoughtfully. She could try and imagine the thoughts that were whirling around his head, but she was afraid to even take a guess. He took a deep breath, his voice now velvety soft.

"Arielle, I fell in love with you the moment I set eyes on you. Your name has been etched in my very soul. I've learned to live without you, but never did I forget about you. Standing here today is like someone bestowed upon me the most incredible gift; I've never received anything that made me feel as good as you do, in my whole miserable immortal life. Against all odds, I've found you after 500 years, and if you think for a moment that I'll just walk away, then you're deeply mistaken," he murmured. "Sebastian and I shared many girls and many things, but you're never going to be someone that I'll share. I'm not going to walk away. I'll destroy Sebastian if I have to." He laughed harshly and the tone in his voice made her back up a few steps in terror.

She tried to control her breathing as she felt anger creeping up and taking over her senses. She could see that fighting an immortal was futile, but she wasn't sensible right now. He was threatening Sebastian and she stopped caring about her own safety.

"Leave Sebastian out of this!" she shouted, shocked at the sound of her voice. He didn't flinch at her angry outburst. "I don't want you, Gaston, I'm in love with Sebastian, and nothing can change my feelings!" she yelled, and backed away from him a little further.

Gaston had a dark look on his face that terrified her. His jaw tightened and he shrieked through clenched teeth.

"Sebastian is never going to have you."

Arielle took a moment to gaze from Gaston toward the shops and swallowed hard.

"Gaston, you can't control my life," Arielle said, making sure he understood the intensity in her statement. She was breathing hard, her heart thrashing against the walls of her chest.

"Annabel told me about your wedding plans and neither one of us is going to let this happen. Arielle—I'm here to stay, and I'll have you whether you go along with this or not."

"Are you conspiring with Annabel!" she shrieked, appalled.

"I'm not conspiring with anyone. Annabel is a psycho; she's uncontrollable and completely unpredictable. I would've never gotten involved with someone like her, but..." his voice trailed.

"But what?" she asked, disgusted. "Why are you doing this, Gaston?" Her voice elevated in sheer exasperation.

"That's easy to explain," he said, chuckling in amusement. "She wants Sebastian and I want you. See how perfectly well that works for Annabel and myself?"

Arielle was startled by how much his words hurt. She was so angry that tears welled up. She gritted her teeth.

"Go away!" she screamed. "You and me are never going to happen." She took a few steps back, moving even further away, trying to put a larger distance between their bodies. Gaston's eyebrows lifted and his eyes went hard. A dark shadow crossed his clear blue gaze.

"Arielle, please don't make me do what is against immortal code." His voice was low but rigid. She watched him carefully; avoid looking directly into his eyes.

"I don't understand, what code?" she replied inquisitively.

Gaston paused, a soft smile tugged the corner of his mouth. He remained silent for a moment. Suddenly he shook his head, chuckled, and, moving in his immortal speed, was right in front of her once again. Arielle stiffened and every muscle in her body clenched tightly. His hands cradled her face and his touch sent her nerves on edge. She tried to pull away but his hold was firm. He tilted her head toward him forcing her gaze directly into his eyes. He was burning with desire for this human girl and he was ready to put his passionate desire to work. As soon as their eyes met he smiled and bored right through her gaze. It was but a few minutes later and he felt her relaxing. He smiled, pleased, and bending down, landed his mouth on hers with hunger and passion beyond any expectation. He was filled with exhilaration when he felt her arms wrap around his neck and surrender to his lust. Their tongues thrust against each other and the kiss deepened, leaving them gasping. She moaned, filled with anticipation that was infusing every single fiber of his body. Gaston moaned out loud.

"Arielle, you've been my sole quest for over 500 years. I love you," he murmured eyes still locked.

She sighed. She tasted that sweet scent in his kiss that was so familiar and felt heat that intoxicated her mind.

Gaston smiled, pleased to know that she was completely under his control. He put his arm around her waist and pulled her away from curious eyes. He stopped when he reached her car. They were completely alone with no person in sight. His arms were tightly wrapped around her and she succumbed to his touch and hot mouth. His arms were underneath her shirt and slid down to her hips slowly. His mouth was still on hers; the kiss deepened and she was totally unresisting. Arielle closed her eyes feeling warmth and excitement toward this beautiful man, a feeling that replaced the animosity she felt a few minutes earlier.

"Love me," he murmured, breathlessly. His mind was floating into a sea of lust. He was so absorbed in his conquest that he forgot about the temporary control of compel he imposed on her. It would wear off in a short time. He'd have to bore into her eyes again to keep it effective. Arielle kept her eyes tightly shut, feeling like she was having an out of body experience. She was now struggling to understand where she was and what she was doing. She was being pressed against her car by a strong body and warm hands were claiming sensitive parts of her, making her eager for more.

"Mm…you taste delicious," he murmured panting hard.

"Oh, Sebastian!" she murmured, moving into him sifting her body to feel more of him. She felt him go still and relax his pressure against her body. She was getting ready to protest when suddenly a loud curse snapped her into reality.

"Son of a bitch!" The voice was hard, hateful, dripping with venom. Her eyes flew open in shock and fright traveled down her spine. She and Gaston were still tightly intertwined in each other's embrace. She gasped and, dropping her hands, tried to pull back, but the car behind her stopped her movement. She put her hands up against his chest and tried to push him away, but it was like she was pushing against a concrete wall.

"What are you doing?" she screamed, her fists now pounding on his chest, looking horrified. She was puzzled as to why her necklace wasn't preventing him from whatever he was trying to do.

"Stop fighting me," he said through clenched teeth. He grabbed her hands and pressed them against her sides. She looked around in disbelief. Her mind swirled with tons of questions. What in the world happened to her? What was she doing in his arms in this remote corner of the parking lot? How did she get there? What time was it?

All these questions filled her mind and rage took over every single muscle of her body. Mat's face flushed before her eyes and she wasn't going to let this happen again.

She turned and looked at him, avoiding his direct gaze, and fire was burning her eyes. She was trying hard to swallow the bile searing her chest, trying to climb to her throat.

"Did you compel me into doing this?" she shouted, tears now running down her face. She was trying hard to clear her foggy mind, but he was now pressing her against the car, unwilling to let her go. His lips curved into a disturbing smile, eyes filled with rage.

"Calm down. I don't want to hurt you, I love you," he said furiously.

"I thought you said you wouldn't break the immortal code and look what you did," she said angrily.

"I didn't break any code. The code says that you aren't to compel someone to love you for eternity. I didn't do that. I just wanted to spend a short time with you and take you in my arms," he said amused. "You wouldn't let me do that if I hadn't compel you, would you?" An intimidating look painted his lips. Arielle flinched and tried to pull away.

"Gaston, please let me go, my friends are waiting, they'll be worried about me."

"I don't care about your friends right now, but you," he said firmly. "You're going to listen to me or you aren't going anywhere."

She stopped pushing and looked at him, totally alarmed.

"All right, I'm listening," she said quietly, voice quivering.

"I haven't been able to get you out of my mind since I saw your photograph at a party in Italy," he said.

"I don't follow you. What photograph and who had that photograph?"

"It was a guy attending the same party I did. He was showing his friends photographs from a holiday trip to St Jean De Luz."

Arielle stiffened and set her hand to her mouth, heart pounding. She was sure it was one of Troy's friends.

Gaston seemed oblivious to her reaction and continued. "I happened to gaze at one photo in passing, and there you were..." his voice trailed and he chuckled bitterly. "You and Sebastian wrapped around each other's arms. How sweet..." His jaw tightened as he spit the words out. "I'm sure you can understand my shock. It had to be a huge mistake. But there you both were. I spent countless hours thinking about you and Sebastian, trying to find out who and when you both turned immortal. I finally spoke with Annabel and she explained to me that she was the one who turned Sebastian."

He bit his lower lip and remained silent for a moment. Arielle bit back the impulse to say something that might anger him further so, lifting her arms, she ran her hands through her hair, trying to think of something smart to say.

"Well there you are," she finally murmured. "My worst nightmare answered your question so you don't have to wonder anymore."

She dropped her hands and took a few steps towards the shops, trying to regain her contentment level. Gaston bolted forward and grabbed her wrist, holding her back. Arielle tensed and her heart was pounding in her chest, creating enormous pain.

"No she didn't clear my concern." His voice was icy cold. "I was more confused by that time than before I spoke with her."

Arielle turned and looked at him uncomfortably.

"Why, I know that immortals have the power to turn a human. Isn't that true? So, why are you so confused about Sebastian?" she asked.

"No...no...no," he shook his head. "Sebastian wasn't the one who confused me. You were my biggest challenge."

"What do you mean?"

"Arielle, when we first met you were a mortal, and 500 years plus later I see you in photograph with Sebastian. My thoughts were that you and Sebastian were now immortals. How? I had no idea, however that was the only logical assumption. When I spoke to Annabel, she told me all about you and Sebastian. She didn't believe that you were the same girl I met back in Calais. She assured me that the girl with Sebastian now is a mortal. Can you see how confusing that can be to someone like me who doesn't know anything about time travel?" Arielle remained silent.

"My troublesome puzzle has been solved by you, so now, all I want, is you and me— together—," his lips curved up to an exultant smile.

"Gaston, I'm not going to be with you now or ever. If you're going to kill me, then go ahead and get it over with," she said.

"Kill you? Why would I ever want to do that?" he muttered totally shocked.

"I'm tired of being afraid each and every day that one of you is going to show up and torment me." She struggled to keep her voice steady.

Gaston's eyes narrowed to slits.

"What do you mean by saying 'one of you'? Who else is after you?"

"Oh...my...God...Gaston, are you kidding me?" Arielle yelled, voice quivering, hands clenched to fists.

"I don't understand," he stammered in shock.

"Annabel...Annabel..." she exclaimed, frustrated. "She wants to kill me. She's tried five times, Gaston, and she's come pretty close. I'm sure one of these days she'll succeed. I'm really tired. I'm not sure how long I can go on like this." She pressed her lips together and tears welled, blinding her.

"Annabel has tried to kill you five times?" he said, eyes wide in shock. "She never told me that," he added.

"Well it's true," she said furiously.

Gaston watched her intently, shock spread across his face.

"She said she was after Sebastian, she never said anything about you."

"Oh—My—God!" Arielle exhaled deeply. "She's made my life a living hell. Maybe if she does kill me it'll stop, all this hatred between you, Annabel, and Sebastian." She was now in tears and sobbing hard. His face softened and she saw apprehension taking over him.

"Arielle, I don't want to hurt you! I don't want to kill you! I love you. I want to be with you. I would never hurt you, Please don't sob," he said, overwhelmed with anxiety.

"Gaston, you're going to hurt me if you prevent me from being with Sebastian. Might as well kill me, because I can't live without him. I fell in love with him way before I ever met you," she said in sheer desperation.

"I love you, Arielle," he said passionately.

"Gaston, if you really search deep in your soul, you'll find that I'm just a challenge for you. I'm someone Sebastian has, and you now want. It's really the old game for you. Please... if your feelings are real then you must understand I can't change the way I feel toward Sebastian. How could you destroy years of precious friendship over me, over a girl? That's something I'll never understand. There's not a guy on this planet who would make me sever my friendship with Eva and Gabrielle. I just can't fathom what you've done."

Gaston stood completely still, lost somewhere in a tidal wave of thoughts.

Suddenly Arielle's mobile went off. She pulled it out of her purse with a quick movement and answered.

"Hello."

"Arielle, where in bloody hell are you?" Gabrielle's voice came out loud through the mobile and full of concern.

"I'm on my way, Gabby," she said, looking at Gaston's face. She shut the mobile off.

"If we'd met another time and another place, things might've been different, but not now. Please try and understand, Gaston. I'm in love with Sebastian. I'll never go with you."

Gaston looked lost in his thoughts, unable to say a word. It seemed that this time travel issue had him totally confused. Arielle used that moment, and without getting any resistance from Gaston she pulled away and started to walk toward the stores. Her head was spinning and she couldn't believe she got out of the situation that easy. She looked back and he was still standing there watching her with that stunned look. She turned and, looking away, accelerated her pace to a sprint and reached the first shops of the mall. She exhaled deeply and suddenly his voice filled her ears as if he was standing right next to her.

"This conversation isn't over Arielle, not by a long shot!" She looked back and gasped. He'd disappeared into thin air. She gulped a huge amount of air to fill her suffocating lungs and it wasn't long before she saw Gabby and Loren come into sight. She breathed in relief and practically ran toward them.

"Where've you been?" Gabby asked. "We've been waiting here for over an hour. Why didn't you call?" Arielle stopped running when she got closer. She took several deep breaths and stood still trying to calm herself down.

"What's wrong?" Both Loren and Gabrielle asked moving closer.

"You'll never believe it, in a million years," she gasped.

"Come out with it," Gabby said shaking Arielle eagerly. "We're dying here," she added. "Just a metaphor," Gabby chuckled, looking at Loren.

Arielle hauled a deep breath and spilled the details about her encounter with Gaston. Loren looked alarmed and Gabrielle gasped as a worried look spread across her face.

"Where is he?" Loren asked.

"I don't know; he was there a moment ago," she said and pointed toward the end of the parking lot, "And now he's gone."

"Are you all right?" Loren asked with extreme concern.

"Yes, I'm fine, just a bit shaken up." She took a deep breath and tried to relax. She paused for a moment, pondering a thought that made her shiver, and winced.

"What is it?" Loren asked.

"Loren, I'm at a bit of a loss and worried," she murmured.

"What about?" Gabrielle chimed in.

"I'm very worried because my necklace didn't prevent Gaston from coming near me," she said.

"Arielle, the necklace didn't work because Gaston didn't try to hurt you. He told you he loved you, right?" Arielle nodded in agreement. "The necklace has incredible powers that sense the deep emotions of people around you and it responds severely only to those who are looking to harm you."

Arielle met Loren's gaze, eyes narrowed, lips tightly pressed. Silence stretched between them as their thoughts plunged into deeper alertness.

"I'm worried about you and my brother," Loren said suddenly.

"I don't want to say anything to Sebastian," Arielle said stubbornly. "I think I can handle Gaston. I'm sure he'll never hurt me, maybe I can talk some sense into him."

"You're planning on seeing him again!" Loren cried out.

"No…no…I'm not planning anything like that, but I've a feeling that Gaston may have other plans. For once I want to deal with this my own way. Remember that you even told me, I have your mother's necklace on, so I'm protected." Arielle didn't believe that, not for a moment. She knew that Gaston's compelling made her want him even if it was for a short moment. She fell in his arms as if it was the most natural thing she'd ever done. She wanted Gaston to hold her, she desired his hot kiss and she wanted to stay there for the rest of her life until the fog cleared out of her head. That was something she didn't tell Loren or Gabrielle. She didn't want to make this a huge issue. She tried to suppress tears from welling up. "How do I explain that to Sebastian?" she asked.

"You must tell Sebastian," she heard Loren's firm voice. "He has the right to know."

Arielle nodded, trying to calm Loren.

"Okay, I will," she said. Twenty minutes later the three of them were lost in the world of shopping, moving from one store to another and having a great time. Arielle had almost forgotten about Gaston until they sat down to have lunch. Gabrielle and Arielle were starving, so they ordered sandwiches and cokes while Loren ordered water. The girls teased Loren about her order, but she just smiled, pleased to be out shopping with them. When their order arrived, they sank their teeth into the bread and moaned simultaneously with pleasure, making Loren burst into laughter.

"Hungry are you?" Loren chuckled.

"Uh huh," Gabrielle muttered with a mouth full of food. Arielle laughed with Gabrielle's expression and so did Loren.

"But all fun aside," Loren said again. "You must tell Sebastian."

"Oh, Loren, please don't make this such a big deal."

"Arielle, I think you don't quite understand the depth of the immortal mind. Gaston will attempt whatever he can to persuade you and that includes either breaking the immortal code or set up a trap to have Sebastian killed," the tone of her voice was elevated. A lengthy silence lingered between the three of them. Arielle glanced between her two friends and saw the determination in their eyes.

"All right...all right...I'll tell him all about it," she promised.

"Great!" Loren exclaimed. "I have an appointment in 30 minutes," she added. "I'd like to see you safe in the car if you don't mind." Her expression was determined as she pushed her chair away from the table and stood. "I'll feel a lot better about that, if you don't mind."

"No, I don't mind," she said and smiled at Loren lovingly. "We're done shopping anyway and I'd like to get home."

Gabrielle agreed. They paid their bill and, picking up their bags, stood to join Loren. They walked to the parking lot and Arielle took a deep breath, trying to remain calm. If he was watching her she couldn't tell and didn't want to know. They stopped at Gabrielle's car first. She hugged Loren and Arielle warmly.

"I had a great time. Let's do this again soon." She slipped into her car and took off smiling and waving. Loren and Arielle turned and took the long walk to the end of the parking lot where Arielle's car was parked.

"Why in the world did you park way out here?" Loren asked. Arielle looked around and there were hardly any cars left in the lot. She laughed and shook her head.

"When I arrived there wasn't a single parking spot left. I think I got the last spot at the time." They were now standing in front of the car. They hugged and promised to call each other soon.

"Thank you, Loren, I love you," Arielle said.

"I love you too, don't forget to tell Sebastian," she said, and gave her a meaningful look.

Arielle nodded and smiled. She pressed the unlock button on her key fob and pulled the door open. She threw the packages in the back and slipped in the driver's seat.

"Lock you doors," Loren called out just before Arielle shut the door. She looked at Loren again, smiled and pressed the lock button down. She chuckled at Loren's intense concern about her safety. She backed up from her parking space and drove off waving at Loren one last time. She looked back at her rear view mirror and Loren had disappeared. Arielle laughed aloud; she'd never get used to the immortal speed. While driving out of the parking lot she took another careful look around but there was no sign of Gaston. She felt pressure behind her eyes and knew it was anxiety.

At the first red light she let go of the wheel and pressed her eyes with the back of her hands. She took a moment to recall all that took place and exhaled deeply. The anger and fear were all mixed up and burst out in the form of tears. She wiped her eyes and pressed her lips together in frustration. Someone blew a horn and, looking up at the light, she realized that it'd turned green and she was blocking traffic. She waved to the car behind her politely and drove off, her thoughts turning to Gaston once again.

She wondered if he really understood how she felt and if maybe he'd go away without incident. That was a lot to hope for, but she didn't know what else to do. She pressed on the gas and turned the radio on. Music always soothed her nerves. When she reached the house she was glad to see Sebastian's car in the garage. Against Loren's advice and Gabrielle's insistence she decided to keep the incident with Gaston to herself for the night and maybe until after Gabrielle's wedding. She grimaced at the thought, but wanted to believe that Gaston would leave her alone. She thought she saw a bothersome look in his eyes, when she told him that she'd extremely unhappy if he hurt Sebastian. She believed that he loved her because he could've done something worst but he didn't. So she resigned herself to trusting her intuition this one time.

She pulled in the garage and before she even opened the door Sebastian was standing next to her car waiting for her. He reached down, pulled her into his arms and bending down, took her mouth in his, and she was lost in his intoxicating immortal scent.

"Hey, baby," he murmured against her lips. "Did you have a good time with Loren and Gabrielle?"

"Yes," she whispered, nestling closer to his muscular body. They walked into the house wrapped in each other's arms.

"Did you miss me at all?" He nuzzled her hair with a soft chuckle. She exhaled quietly.

"I spent my entire day wondering where you were and what you were doing," she said mockingly, soft laughter escaping her.

Her remark made him wince and look down at her regretfully. He remained silent for a moment. He paused inside the bedroom and turned her to face him.

"Did you think that my question was ridiculous?" he asked, sulkily. Arielle moved closer, cupped his beautiful face between her hands, and covered his lips with hers.

"Sebastian, you never have to ask if I miss you. For your information, you're a permanent fixture in my head. There's not a single second in my life that I don't think about you. Ever since the moment I set eyes on you, you have occupied every one of my thoughts, dreams, desires, and needs. So you see, I find it funny that you ask me such a question." She was filled with love and lust for the amazing man standing in front of her.

"Thank you, baby," he murmured.

His arms trapped her in a tight embrace and crushed her lips beneath his. He felt her body trembling as she moved into him and every muscle in his body locked. Anticipation ripped right through his veins and he groaned in desperation. He heard her soft chuckle and that infused his passion. He was aroused and she knew it. She took his shirt off with one quick movement and a wide smile spread across his face. He then pulled her top off. Then it was his pants then her pants until every stitch of clothing was piled on the floor by the side of the bed. They stood completely naked, fused together, unable to feel the cold temperature.

He lifted her and set her on the bed without breaking the kiss. She wrapped her arms around his neck and pulled him down on top of her. Wrapped in his steel embrace, she moaned in exhilaration. His weight pressed her firmly against the mattress and she stopped breathing. The kiss deepened and they merged into a sweltering blaze that took their minds and senses to another dimension, until they both surrendered to the release that shattered them and drove them to the peak of ecstasy.

Arielle couldn't imagine how the honeymoon could offer anything more powerful, more mind-blowing, more potent than what she was experiencing right now. However, Sebastian, the man of her dreams, the man who would be her husband, assured her that there would more...that was something she couldn't grasp, and she wasn't going to try. She would just wait...

Sebastian pulled back and grinned down at her. She put her hand behind his nape and pulled him back down, her tongue circling his lip line. Sebastian inhaled a deep breath and crushed her lips beneath his again. He finally pulled back and rolled off of Arielle, chuckling and laid on his back. He slipped his arm underneath her and pulled her close to his side. She laid her head on his shoulder; one arm resting on his muscled chest, one leg wrapped around him. Sebastian groaned at the feel of the soft warm skin of her leg around his thigh. She closed her eyes and exhaled utterly gratified. Sebastian lifted slightly and pulled the covers over them. He closed his eyes and remained motionless, still wrapped in the aftermath of their scorching encounter. He was at the crest of sleep when he sensed the steady thudding of Arielle's heart against his side, and oh... so close to his own dead heart. He inhaled deeply and smiled blissfully. She was his private treasure, his salvation from a lonely immortal journey for centuries to come. That was the last thought he had before sleep claimed both of them.

Chapter 10

ARIELLE DECIDED to spend a couple of nights with her parents while Sebastian and his immortal friends celebrated the last week of Troy's bachelorhood. She loved spending time with her parents and taking the so-familiar morning walks with her father in the garden. She noticed that her father was walking much slower during their walks, and stopped a few times to take a rest before he could go on. She felt a pang in her heart and tried to hide welling tears. She smiled, knowing that his heart medication had a lot to do with being so tired, but she encouraged him to continue the walks and he did without complaining.

Arielle was avoiding discussing the Gaston incident with Sebastian. She didn't want to ruin the bachelor celebrations and didn't want to create any unexpected problems so close to Gabrielle's most important day. She was on one of those morning walks with her father when her mobile rang.

"Hello!" she said softly.

"Arielle, it's Loren, how are you?"

"Oh, fine, and you?"

"Fine…fine…" her voice trailed.

"Is there something wrong?" Arielle asked.

"Oh! No, not really, I just wanted to talk if you have a moment."

"Can it wait?" Arielle asked kindly. She loved talking to Loren, but not now. She should've never answered that call. Her time with her father was very special. She didn't want anything or anyone to interfere.

"I'm sorry, I didn't mean to bother you," Loren said.

"You're not bothering me, I'm spending a little time with my father and we're the midst of a conversation. If this can wait I'll be happy to call you a little later. Will that be okay?"

"Oh, sure, call me when you can."

"Thanks, we'll talk soon," Arielle promised.

"I love you, Arielle," Loren said pleasantly.

"Me, too," Arielle chuckled and snapping the phone shut dropped it in her jean pocket.

"Who was that, Pumpkin?" her father asked.

"Sebastian's sister, Loren."

"She's a very nice and beautiful girl," her father said.

"Yes, she's wonderful,"

"Is there something wrong?"

"She didn't say, daddy, but it didn't sound like anything was wrong,"

"Why didn't you talk to her?" her father said.

"I'd rather talk with you," Arielle said and planted a soft kiss to his cheek.

"Thank you, darling, I love our talks and especially the morning walks. I've missed them so much. I knew when you left for college that things were changing. I just didn't know how much," he chuckled gloomily.

"I'm sorry, daddy, I miss our walks and talks just as much," she said and looked down at her hands despondently. Her father stopped walking and turned to face her. He put his finger under her chin and lifted her face to look at him.

"I'm very proud of you, and all that you've accomplished. Your mother and I couldn't have asked for a better daughter," he said, teary.

"Thanks daddy, I love you both so very much and I want you to know that I couldn't have asked for better parents," she said and embraced him warmly. She pulled back and gazed deep into his eyes. "You'll always be my number one man."

"And you, my number one girl," he said and stroked her cheek lovingly. "I think you made an excellent choice with Sebastian. He's a wonderful young man with an amazing future and he seems to love you so very much."

"I know, daddy, and I love him just as much. He's so good to me. I guess I'm a very lucky girl," she laughed happily and he laughed with her. Her mother called them for lunch. She put her hand through his arm and they walked back to the house.

*   *   *

It was the day before Gabrielle's wedding and Arielle watched her emotional friend, who was full of excitement, animated and trying not to fall apart from happiness. Arielle was caught up in that excitement, as she knew how close her own wedding day drew.

Gabby's wedding gown was one of the two Arielle fell in love with and she absolutely adored it. It was an ivory strapless gown of silk and satin, adorned with Venice lace. The bodice was fitted, embroidered with jewels and flowers, while a silk sash wrapped exquisitely around the waist. The skirt flared beautifully outward, giving it a dramatic look. She also chose a long train with a wonderful veil, capturing a 16th century look.

Arielle, Eva, and Loren's dresses were strapless, light taupe, brocaded with silver trim. The soft silk fabric had a raised design and the silver trim looked like metallic threads. They looked like they were from another era and that's exactly the theme Gabby chose to honor Troy, the man who changed her life for centuries to come. What Arielle loved about these dresses was the 16th century style that was appealing to the immortal boys.

It was now the morning of, and everyone was filled with excitement.

The wedding was very similar to Eva's, with a few small differences. The people standing in front of the vicar at the altar were Gabrielle and Troy but the rest of the players were pretty much the same.

She remembered vividly Sebastian revealing to her how he felt when he saw her coming down the aisle in Eva's wedding. She couldn't help gazing into his gorgeous eyes while walking down the aisle this time around. He was watching her intently with a brilliant smile on his beautiful face and knowing what he was thinking made her shiver with excitement. She smiled wide and he moved his lips letting her know that he loved her. Gabrielle and Troy's vows were so beautiful they made Arielle well up with tears, and Eva, unable to cry any longer, smiled, filled with joy.

The reception was incredible and the music fantastic. They all danced throughout the night and had a wonderful time. It was around two in the morning when they left the county club and Arielle couldn't help taking a careful look around while keeping close to Sebastian. He understood her anxiety and held her tight against his body, providing the security she needed, but there was no sign of Annabel or Gaston this time.

Gabrielle and Troy were leaving for Italy the very next morning. They would make a short stop at Troy's estate and from there fly to Sydney. Their final destination was the exotic Islands in the south Pacific. *Gosh that'd be just amazing,* Arielle thought as Sebastian held the door of the car open for her and she slipped in the passenger seat. Her thoughts were full of Sebastian and eager to get home and be in his arms with no worries at all. He pulled in the garage and using his incredible speed he was already standing outside her door holding it open for her. The next few moments were a complete fog. All she remembered was stepping out of the car and the next thing she was in their bed totally undressed, enfolded in his arms.

"What a feeling!" She heard him moan in excitement as his hands traveled eagerly all over her body touching every inch, every grain of her until he stopped and pressed at her most sensitive spot making her grown with hunger for him.

How did I stay away from this for more than three weeks, I'll never understand, Sebastian thought and pressed his lips together in wonder.

"I'm sure you knew what was coming, didn't you?" he whispered, totally out of breath while gazing into her beautiful sapphire eyes.

"I'm not sure that I know what you're referring to," she replied with amusement, while gasping for air. Her body burned, her skin shivered, her muscles tightened and she wanted more and more. His tongue pushed tenderly her lips apart, landing in her mouth and she tasted that amazing immortal scent. The kiss started soft and tender and deepened to a passionate, eager, hungry kiss that took her breath away. His arms locked around her hips and he pulled her underneath him, as he shifted eagerly pushing her thighs apart, making her writhe in his arms unable to wait any longer. She bowed her hips upward, wanting to take him in but he wasn't ready; he pulled back, making her wait, driving her crazy. After his three weeks of rejections she'd become obsessive with her unlimited wants of this beautiful man. She just couldn't get enough of him.

"What are you doing?" she asked breathlessly, and all she could hear was his soft chuckle.

"Is there something you want?" he murmured, voice totally amused.

"Mmmm...please Sebastian, why are you doing this?"

"Because, I want you begging for me. I don't want to be the one acting so eagerly each and every time we make love," he murmured, and laughed, as he lowered himself slowly on her eager, soft, beautiful body. He hauled in a deep breath, and pressing fervently entered her with a hard push and she cried out in sheer ecstasy. His movements sent hot waves through her veins and she was unable to consider any other thoughts, except for the fact that she wanted more. Her legs wrapped around his hips, pulling him further in, and he growled in bliss as the rhythm picked up bringing tears to her eyes. She felt encircled in a warm blanket of ecstasy that took her mind in higher levels of pleasure.

"One more month," he murmured gasping as he pulled back out making her gasp in shock.

"Where are you going?" she cried out desperately, as she wrapped her arms around his neck in an attempt to pull him back in, but before she could finish the though he plunged right back in with a loud growl bringing both of them to an exquisite climax, as tears of pleasure rolled down her face.

"Is this going to be an eternity for us?" she asked.

"Yep, this is exactly what our life is going to be for eternity..." he licked the tears off her face with a smile.

"I love the salty taste of your tears," he murmured and ran his tongue over his lips wanting to take every bit of that taste in his mouth.

Arielle's mind was in a fog as she was still folded in the aftermath of their amazing encounter. Her thoughts ran wild and a smile lifted her lips.

Why am I the lucky person he chose to love? I just can't make any sense of it. He's the most amazing, the most beautiful, the most incredible man on this earth. I know I'm not special and I'm not as stunning as the immortal girls who would die to have him by their side, so why me? Nothing makes sense to me, but I'm willing to ride this train as far as it will take me since I'm irrevocably in love with him.

He watched her in wonder and before she had a chance to move he'd unclipped her necklace and gazed into her eyes, reading her very soul.

"I just couldn't stand not knowing what you were thinking." His lips curved up into that beautiful smile and a blinding brilliance crossed his eyes.

"Arielle…how many times do I have to tell you there's no other person out there who would ever make me feel the way you do? It's like our souls were looking for each other, and they finally met, and nothing is going to keep them apart. I love you, baby, I need your eyes to get my energy, I need your touch to feel whole and I need you to make my body feel like a real man should feel." He clipped the necklace back on, and gathered her in his arms, as they laid next to each other in utter bliss. "Thank you for loving me," he whispered softly in her ear, as they drifted off to sleep.

*   *   *

It seemed awfully quiet without Gabrielle home, but Loren, Eva, and Arielle spent a lot of time shopping and getting ready for Arielle's wedding day. The weather was warm but they still seemed to get the usual amount of rainy days that brought a little melancholy in everyone's day.

In Arielle's case, Sebastian kept her happy at all times with his wonderful attitude. They kept up with their evening walks on the beach even after a rainy day. They were now only three weeks away from their wedding day and they both were on edge. The funny part was listening to Sebastian going on and on about having to be away from her for a whole week. He did actually sound exactly like Troy and Ian, just like a little boy with a temper issue. It was one of those evenings when they were taking a walk on the beach that he stopped and, gazing in her eyes, smiled softly.

"I think the idea of brides and grooms being apart the week before the wedding is utterly silly," he said, for the millionth time, and she laughed, reaching up to meet his lips in a blissful kiss.

"Well, you'll have to live with that, as you have no choice at all," she said, with an indulging smile. He pulled her tighter against him while his eyes stared deep into her soul.

"I guess you forgot with whom you're dealing," he whispered through the kiss. A wide smile spread across his face. "I can take you away, somewhere on the other side of the world and marry you. You wouldn't be able to prevent me from doing that no matter how hard you tried. What do you think about that?"

His eyes searched hers for an answer and she broke into a hearty laugh, knowing he was right. She threw her arms around his neck and their lips met passionately, reassuring him that she was ready to follow him to end of the earth.

They walked for a couple of hours holding hands, fingers intertwined, hearts filled with delight in silence. It was in that silence that she recalled the Lanes parking lot incident and repressed a reaction to the cold chill that ran down her spine. It'd been well over three weeks since Gaston popped unexpectedly into her life. She'd successfully blocked every thought about the incident by staying extremely busy. She helped Gabrielle with the last details of her wedding and she was pleased to see that Gabby's wedding day was absolutely faultless. Once Gabby left for her honeymoon, Arielle concentrated on the last minute items for her own wedding that was less than a month away.

Tonight the long, quiet, blissful walk with Sebastian unexpectedly brought back every unpleasant moment of that day. A rush of thoughts came blasting in like a roaring river in a rainstorm. Instinctively her hands moved up and covered her ears. She pressed hard, trying to prevent the noise from painfully pounding her temples. Loren's words kept hammering her thoughts now. "You must tell Sebastian! You must tell Sebastian! He has the right to know!" Gaston's compelling was something she'd prefer to conceal from Sebastian because she didn't know how to explain that part. This would make him angry. She was afraid of his reaction and what he might decide to do about Gaston.

She hadn't finished her last thought and was startled by Sebastian's hands reaching around her neck. She heard the snap of the clasp and saw the necklace fall into Sebastian's hands.

"You've been distracted for over a half an hour. Is there something bothering you, baby?" he asked, his voice soft.

She felt the weight of his gaze and stopped walking. He turned her to face him, gathered her in his arms and bending his head, kissed her gently at first and then the kiss deepened to a more passionate, more scorching kiss that spread wild desire though every nerve and muscle in their bodies. The want was so palatable that she gasped and he moaned still tangled in that embrace and kiss.

He finally pulled back and, inhaling deeply, cupped her face with his hands and bored through her eyes. Arielle gasped aloud and her brain went into panic mode. She was totally unprepared to discuss the details. All she could think about was Gaston's compelling actions that made her succumb to his embrace and the passionate kiss that was now creating this alarming anxiety.

Sebastian's gaze grew intense and a shocking expression spread across his face. His jaw tightened, eyes narrowing to slits, hands clenching to fists, and a loud growl of rage escaping his tight lips.

"When were you planning on telling me about this?" he roared wrathfully.

The tone of his voice set Arielle a few steps back, while their gazes remained locked. His lips were pulled back in rage, he broke the embrace and drop his hands to his side. He moved back, creating a bigger distance between them. His expression was that of pain, mistrust. and agony.

"You made out with him?" he asked, screaming in utter disbelief. Arielle froze in place. Her body started to quiver. She sent a quick glance his direction and quickly averted her gaze down to her feet. She tried to speak but nothing came out of her mouth. She heard him haul a deep breath and his cold voice sheared through her skin, bringing prickling tears to her eyes.

"So?" he screamed again. "What have you to say for yourself?"

Arielle remained silent through his ranting and yelling, stunned by his reaction. She finally hauled all the strength she could unearth and resisting the urge to just stomp away, she moved forward and halted a hair's-breath from him. She lifted her face and her eyes scanned his face. Defiance locked her jaw, as she felt anger surging through her body.

"You always ask me to trust you," she said bitterly. Her face was flushed and hot tears of anger streamed down her cheeks. "Where's your trust in me?" she said through clenched teeth. "Or have you set rules that apply to you and are different for me?" Her gaze held his and his look was that of shock.

"What are you saying?" he asked, confused. "Arielle! I saw clearly what happened in your eyes. You can't deny any of it."

Arielle met his gaze again and pressed her lips together in exasperation. She looked out toward the ocean and hauled in a deep breath. Silence stretched and she finally turned to face him, face full of defiance. "I'm not trying to deny anything," she spit out the words. "And no...no...no..." she screamed in fury. "You didn't see what happened. All you did see was what you chose to see and then you exploded in anger like a child," she accused.

Sebastian pulled back in stunned shock and flinched at her anger.

"Arielle, I saw you in his embrace, and you didn't look like you were fighting your way out of it or the kiss, you were fully engaged, face filled with anticipation," he growled. His face was stretched with anxiety, teeth clenched. He put his hands against his eyes and pressed hard, trying to erase the vision of Arielle and Gaston intertwined in a loving embrace. A barely audible curse escaped his lips and she winced. She waited until he was quiet then reached for him overwhelmed with unclear emotions about his reaction. Her gaze was fixed on his face, as he abruptly pulled back. He looked down still clenching her necklace tightly in his hand. He was lost in thought as he bounced the necklace back and forth from one hand to the other. Time stretched, as she waited patiently for his next move, he finally drew a deep breath, resolve in his emerald eyes.

Moving fast, he gripped Arielle's hand, pulled it close and holding it open, dropped the necklace in it and pressed her fingers softly to close around it. Then he flashed a quick glance at her one last time, and turning around, stomped away like a spoiled child.

Arielle threw her hands up in the air and let out an exasperated breath. She was feeling a surge of fury spreading across her nerves;

she looked around at the empty beach and slumped down onto the sand. She pulled her knees tightly up to her chest, hands braced around them. She sighed and dropped her head down. Her thoughts reeled and fear hung over her. He was leaving her and she was sure this time it would be for good. He told her once that if he thought that she didn't love him any longer he would disappear. Tears blinded her and frustration surfaced.

"I thought you trusted me, but you're a liar."She whimpered aloud without realizing it and groaned bitterly. She didn't fathom that Sebastian heard every word she said even though he was almost home. He stopped in his tracks just before he crossed the threshold and heard her quiet whisper once again.

"You only saw a small part, your anger about Gaston blinded your vision. I guess you don't love me enough..." she said talking to herself aloud. His muscles tightened at those words and his chest clenched. "Sebastian!" she cried. His breath caught at the sadness in her voice. "I was right after all," she said again. "You were just a dream! Gaston succeeded without having to lift a finger," she sighed bitterly and sobbed.

She sat there for what it seemed to be centuries. She finally stood, wiped her eyes, and decided to go home. It was now twilight and the water looked dark and uninviting. She turned with a heavy heart and gasped as she fell right into his arms.

"Sebastian!" she exclaimed. "Sebastian! I thought you were gone."

"I was, but I heard what you said," he murmured. "I'm not a liar Arielle, and if I didn't see what really happened, I'd like to see it now." His eyes narrowed, voice compelling. She gazed up and their eyes locked.

 *Chapter 11*

"OKAY THEN, I WANT you to see everything that took place, not just the embrace or the kiss," she whispered.

She remained silent while he bored into her eyes and she recalled every detail about her meeting with Gaston. It had been a while and they were still standing, their bodies a hair's-breath apart in a stunned silence. She watched intently as his expression changed slowly from anger and fury to remorse, to apology, to the "forgive me" look.

She was filled with warmth and love for this man, the only man in her life. The man she wanted like no other, the man who took her to incredible heights in bed, reaching emotions of ultimate ecstasy. She was sure she couldn't live without him. His arms tighten around her and he crushed her against his hard, muscular body. His mouth found hers in a hungry, obsessive kiss and she moved into him, surrendering mind and soul. They clung to each other like magnets, heat and fire pulsing between their bodies like opposite conductors.

"Why didn't you tell me, baby?"

"I was afraid of what you might do. It's so close to our wedding day and I didn't want any problems. After all, he really didn't hurt me."

"Didn't hurt you? What are you saying? He compelled you to want him," he said softly. "What if he took you somewhere, what if he went a lot further than just a kiss and an embrace?" his lips were stretched in sheer anxiety. "I can see that he's obsessed with you and he might even break the immortal code."

She watched him carefully. "Can he make me love him and forget you?" she enunciated each word.

"Yes, he can," he said thoughtfully.

She moved closer to him and wrapped her arms around his waist.

"I love you so much!" she whispered, lifting herself on tiptoes to touch his lips. He bent down and kissed her hard, possessively, selfishly.

"I have to do something," he murmured looking ahead. "I can't let him do this. Gaston harbors a lot of anger against me and he'll do everything he can to persuade you."

She watched his expression change to distress. She tugged his shirt, making him look down at her. "Sebastian, there's not a person in this world who could make me stop loving you. I can't live without you. I can't breathe without you. I need you with me to feel whole."

Sebastian squeezed her tightly as they walked in the house. "I feel the same way baby, that's why I have to do something. Loosing you would be the end of me."

His mouth found hers again and the kiss became deeper, limitless.

They readied for bed without any more discussion about Gaston. Once in bed, Arielle pull the covers back and stretched leisurely. suppressing a yawn. Sebastian was watching her intently, wide smile spread across his face. His arms slipped around her and he pulled her hard against him. "I'll kill anyone who touches you," he murmured lips against hers.

Arielle move into him seductively and he loved every minute of it.

"Can he compel me to do things I don't want to do forever? Or just for a small period of time?" she asked full of curiosity. Their gazes were locked.

He winced and groaned but replied, "Yes he can, but..." he paused.

"But...but...what?" she asked eagerly.

"Immortals regard the breaking of the sacred code a very serious matter. It's an oath that should remain unbreakable as long as the immortal roams this earth. When an immortal compels a human to love them, he has to use a lot of his body energy. He will need an enormous amount of Salve to prevent his energy from draining his body quickly. The intake of vast amounts of Salve in the long run will create problems for his self-preservation and the body will slowly perish."

"Gosh!" she murmured. She was quiet for a moment. "Well, I suppose that's a good thing, right?"

"No, not really. He can compel you for as long as he wants to satisfy his desires and then let you go." He looked anxious as he continued. "I'm sure that he knows how long he can sustain the compelling without trying to kill himself. Gaston was extremely resourceful when we were growing up. I've no idea when he was turned or who turned him but I'm sure his immortal capabilities are now very dangerous."

Arielle shivered at those words and snuggled closer to him, into her own private sanctuary, Sebastian's warm embrace.

"How can I fight against something like that?" she asked, distressed.

His arms closed tightly around her. He pulled her closer and gasped as he felt her breasts press against his muscled chest. His mouth found hers and the kiss deepened to that of absolute consciousness, wild desire and hot sensation that traveled through every fiber of their bodies and shattered both, leaving them breathless.

He pulled back, gasping. How can he get so worked up each and every time he felt her touch? He groaned as he heard the blood pounding his ears and his pulse thudding his temples painfully. He hauled in a deep breath trying to control his desire. He heard a soft chuckle and felt her turning to her side without leaving his embrace. She shifted and he pulled her closer, spooning his naked body around hers. He heard her breath easing and her body relaxing in his arms. He smiled warmly. He shifted again. Her skin was soft, exciting, and he trembled at the feel of their naked bodies flush against each other. He nuzzled her hair, and gave her a soft squeeze.

"I love you, baby," he murmured softly brushing his lips against her ear.

"I adore you," she whispered in a barely audible voice.

Arielle felt his warmth and knew that this was where she wanted to be for the rest of her life. Eyes closed and on the brink of sleep, she tilted her head up searching for his lips, and he locked them eagerly to a deep passionate kiss. His muscles tensed with excitement and he stopped breathing. Suddenly he froze, as a quick vision of Gaston and Arielle in that tight embrace, and their lips locked in that kiss shuddered his awareness and his pulse leaped to high intensity. Arielle was at the very edge of unconsciousness but she felt his pulse pounding against her body and her eyes snapped open.

"What's wrong?" she asked.

"Nothing, my love…" he muttered. "Go to sleep." He pressed his lips against her temple until he felt her relax again, utterly motionless. He snuggled closer and groaned quietly, suppressing the overwhelming emotion of needing more each and every time the heat of her body touched his. He listened blissfully at her soft breathing, and felt the pleasing rhythm of her heartbeat, filling him with shattering emotions. His heartbeat had been stilled for over 500 years and the forfeiture was that of an endless horrible emotion. Immortality was what he had to accept in order to survive on this earth for centuries to come.

Somewhere in the midst of that thought he dozed off, only to wake a few minutes later, shaken by another thought that settled in the center of his very core. He gazed down on Arielle's peaceful sleeping face and realized that it was just a vision. She was still in his arms safe and sound. He bent down and pressed his lips softly on her bare shoulder, shivering at the touch of her soft satin skin.

His thoughts turned to the moment at the beach, when he looked into Arielle's eyes, and saw that Gaston was conspiring with Annabel to unearth ways to destroy his life. He couldn't fathom how an argument over a beautiful girl who attended his 20th birthday would unravel in such a wild way 500 plus years later. Gaston and Sebastian's parents were friends. The boys played and spent time together ever since they were 3 years old. He never knew anything about Gaston's immortality during their 17 years of friendship. They loved each other, and their friendship was strong and deep, more like brothers. Why didn't he ever talk about his immortality? Sebastian would've never had divulged Gaston's secret to anyone. He'd loved Gaston and trusted him with his life. He felt a pang knowing that Gaston never trusted him. He groaned softly. "How did it ever come to this?"

His mind journeyed back to that hurtful night when their friendship was severed. He didn't see Gaston for two years after that, not until his wedding day to Annabel. He hadn't invited him, so he was sure that Gaston was Annabel's guest. He'd never known how he met Annabel, but now he understood. They frequented the same immortal circles. He saw Gaston a few more times and their meetings were always cordial but never friendly. After he left Annabel he never saw Gaston again.

Gaston's name surfaced approximately three times in this century but to this day Sebastian hadn't laid eyes on him. He wasn't going to allow him and or Annabel to destroy his life. A life filled with the existence of this incredible girl who was nestled safely in his arms. Arielle made his world orbit around her. Time stood still each time they were together. He thought back at their encounters and heat spread, claiming every nerve and muscle, making him ache for her in an indescribable way. He muted a groan and tried not to wake her.

During his very long immortal existence he'd had frivolous affairs with many females, but he'd never met anyone like Arielle. Their encounters were like massive tidal waves and monsoons all wrapped in one. Every time their bodies merged, his emotions were draped simultaneously in heat, intoxication, passion, and exquisite blissfulness. He was overwhelmed with the desire to explore and possess every little grain of her beautiful body, to watch her surrender unconditionally to his every desire and wish. What he found inconceivable was the fact that each encounter left him with a different emotion; one that was greater and more palpable than the one before and he just wanted more.

Sebastian stayed awake a large part of the night. After a lengthy consideration of every possible angle to his problem with Gaston, he came to a firm conclusion. Christian and Isabella were going to become Arielle's invisible bodyguards. This seemed to be the perfect solution. He trusted both of them and knew they would provide the safety blanket Arielle needed every moment she was away from Sebastian. Annabel didn't know Christian or Isabella and she wasn't going to link them to Arielle and Sebastian's group of friends. Gaston was sure to show up again and Sebastian wasn't willing to expose Arielle to his sick methods. He could see in Arielle's thoughts that Gaston was obsessed with her and determined to persuade her. Sebastian's lips twisted at the thought. He glanced down at Arielle's peaceful face, pressed his lips softly against her temple and closed his eyes, hoping it would all work out.

* * *

He woke early in the morning and Arielle was still sleeping in his arms, her bare soft body pressed firmly against his. He smiled blissfully and couldn't resist the impulse. He bent and took her mouth with his. She shifted and stretching groggily open her eyes to meet that deep green gaze that turned her world upside down and she kissed him back fervently.

"Good morning," he murmured his lips still on hers. "Did you sleep well?"

"Mmm..." she mumbled, blissfully. "Every time I'm in your arms I sleep perfectly." She turned to face him without leaving his embrace.

"You're so warm," she whispered and shifted even closer. He chuckled and held her tightly.

"What are your plans for the day?" he asked tenderly.

"I can't think right now," she said gasping, feeling him aroused under the covers. Sebastian smiled, drew a vast breath and, shifting his hips even closer, he felt her quiver.

"Whatever do you mean by that?" he asked pretending nonchalance.

"You...you..." she mumbled and gazed into his eyes.

All Sebastian could see was a dark blue ocean filled with thunderous desire. His body struggled for control and failed miserably. His gaze moved from her eyes to her mouth to her beautiful long alabaster throat, rested on the stunning mounds on her chest and he gasped. His hand moved slowly, encircled one of those mounds and pressed softly massaging and stroking, sending a sweltering wave of heat throughout her body. He then bent down, set his mouth on the other, and lapped eagerly, hungrily, ravenously. She cried out, struggling to breathe. She was lost in a sea of wonder and awe. Sebastian was having a hard time trying to hold back, to enjoy this amazing creature in his arms for a long while, but he failed. He pulled her underneath him; conquered her, and she surrendered. Burning lava enfolded them, muscles tightened and senses soared to incredible heights. They shattered and crashed, fulfilled and spent. They remained in a tight embrace, unwilling to let go.

"You'll be the death of me," he murmured. She chuckled blissfully at one of his favorite phrases. His mouth found hers and he crashed her lips beneath his with scorching desire. His thoughts whirled in unimaginable places. He held her gaze for a long time and a wide smile lifted his lips.

"What is it?" she asked inquisitively.

"Nothing…" his voice trailed off and he chuckled. He shook his head, wondering if he'd lost his mind or maybe he was at the verge of going crazy. How could he explain that his endless desire for her was something that pushed his thoughts to a far-reaching level? How could he tell her that all he wanted was to essentially devour her whole, make their bodies fuse so they'd never have to be apart? He certainly couldn't say all that. That wasn't the thinking of a rational man. He chuckled again trying to wipe away all these crazy thoughts. She was watching him intently waiting for him to say something.

"What's on your mind, love?" she asked curiously.

"Nothing…nothing at all," he said again and laughed quietly.

"It doesn't seem like nothing to me," she said probingly.

"I was just thinking about how I love just being here with you," he said softly and pressed a soft kiss on her lips.

"I feel the same way," she was quick to reply. "I want to just spend a whole weekend doing nothing but lying in bed with you," she said thoughtfully. "But somehow it's never worked out that way. Something always comes up. We either have to meet someone, or someone is coming over, or you have some emergency at the office, or a crazy phone call, something… something…something…ugh!" she cried out in exasperation, pushing the covers off and throwing her hands up in the air.

Sebastian burst out into laughter, while gathering her even closer in his arms. "We're here now, baby," he said tenderly and his mouth closed over hers. She gave into the kiss with so much passion that he drew back gasping, brows lifted, wide grin spreading across his face.

"Well…whatever this is about please keep it up," he hauled in a deep breath, eyes filled with wonder. She swallowed hard and finally broke out into a hearty laugh.

"Well…speaking about always something coming up…" her voice trailed off.

He lifted on one elbow and gazed down at her, watching her with a soft smile. "Yes, I'm listening," he said, amused.

"Loren and Eva are coming over. We made an appointment to spend a few hours at a spa."

"A spa!" he exclaimed, chuckling. "So...my massages don't meet your standards?"

Arielle gazed up at him with an appealing look in her eyes. "When you start what you call a massage, it escalates to something much different," she said, blushing.

Sebastian ran his fingers gently over her cheeks. "Blushing, my love?" He chuckled. She smiled.

"What time are they coming?"

"At 1:00 o'clock, the appointment is at 2:00."

"Well...it's now 9:30," he whispered softly. "What are you planning on doing between now and then?"

"Um..." she chuckled. "I have a suggestion for you," she mumbled, arms wrapped around his neck tightly. His eyes filled with delight, focused on her lovely face.

"I'm listening!" he murmured, brows arched in question.

"I'll let you massage me. How does that sound?" She giggled blissfully.

"Oh...do you think I can meet your standards this time?" he murmured as he brushed his lips against her ear.

"I'm hoping you can. This will be your last chance," she said, trying to suppress a laugh, holding his gaze. Her hands moved down, caressing the hard planes of his back and he moaned bursting with anticipation. She chuckled softly and her lips were on his, probing inside his mouth to taste his immortal scent. She suddenly pulled back from the kiss.

"I'm going to get a glass of water, do you want me to bring a glass of Salve for you?" she asked. His eyes snapped wide open.

"Right now?"

"Yes, right now," she chuckled and jumped out of bed. "Stay as you are, I'll be right back," she said, looking down at him with lust and desire. She ran her tongue over her lips slowly, trying to savor every bit of his immortal scent left from the last kiss. He could feel the heat of her gaze and saw the glow of her wet lips and he nearly fractured.

"No, I...I don't need anything," he finally said. The words struggled to leave his lips as he fought the desire to jump out of bed and pull her back in his arms. He watched her walk seductively out of the room, looking back at him with a soft smile. He moaned aloud at the sight. When she disappeared down the hallway he pushed the covers away and stretched leisurely. He put his hands behind his head propped up on the pillows and closing his eyes, waited impatiently. He chuckled at the blistering desire and sizzling thoughts that occupied his mind each and every time they were together. A loud crash of a glass hitting and shattering on the marble floor locked his muscles to an alarming position. His immortal hearing caught each and every one of the shards as they hit and shattered across the kitchen floor. His eyes narrowed to slits fixing his gaze toward the bedroom door. There was a moment of stony, creepy silence. He heard his blood pounding his veins and a cold chill ran through his body.

"Arielle!" he called out, as he sprang out of bed. He listened for a reply from the other room but nothing, except cold silence. "Are you all right?" he called out again as he ran toward the kitchen. The eeriness of the quiet turned his muscles to unbending steel. He stepped into the kitchen ready to face anything that came along, but the room was empty. His eyes scanned the area wildly. He ran over the sharp pieces of glass that were spread across the kitchen floor and using his immortal speed searched every room in the house, including the garage, and backyard, but no sight of Arielle. His breathing was elevated, as rage started to boil in the pit of his stomach. He stood lost in the middle of the backyard, unable to ponder a single thought, unable to move.

"Oh…God…please—no—not again!" he gasped aloud, conscious of the significance of the moment. "Arielle!" he cried out, pain searing every muscle, every vein.

 *Chapter 12*

SEBASTIAN WAS FROZEN in shock and nervous silence. Where was she? What happened? Who was in the house? How long had they been in the house hidden and waiting? His mind was whirling wildly, but he couldn't answer any of these questions. This was surreal...what were the odds of this befalling them all over again? He growled furiously as wild thoughts began to churn in his bewildered mind. His eyes narrowed, and he cursed aloud, as he contemplated several possibilities. It was totally unreasonable to suspect a Russian mafia conspiracy, because that chapter had been firmly closed by the immortal group a while back. This was different; he could feel it in his bones. He winced at the name that flashed into his brain like a brilliant neon sign. "Annabel!" The icy eerie possibility of Annabel abducting Arielle was choking him to the point that he couldn't breathe. Anger, resentment, fury, desperation, and guilt filled him. He sank to his knees in the middle of the backyard and, wrapping his hands around his body, growled in anguish.

Arielle's face emerged before his eyes, and the pain was like none he'd ever experienced before. He crashed to the ground panting hard. *"Oh...God...please don't let Annabel hurt her!"* he prayed pressing his eyes shut. He curled into a fetal position gasping for air. The loss that engulfed him reduced the strong immortal to a bundle of pain-filled flesh. He remained unmoving for the longest time. He finally got to his feet and forced himself to walk inside the house. Entering the kitchen area again was excruciating, every step sheer torture. He looked down at himself in astonishment, realizing that he was completely naked. He dragged himself into the bedroom drained of any motivation or ambition, and threw on a pair of jeans.

A raw scream escaped his lips, snapping his muddled mind back to reality. Annabel had done the unthinkable, and he wasn't able to prevent it. He hadn't been able to protect Arielle inside their own private home. *How ironic is that?* he thought, and let out a harsh laugh. His emotions mixed with the anguish reeling in his head. The struggle to accept Arielle's kidnapping became even harder. The pressure in his head throbbed like a roaring river. He was standing in the middle of the kitchen again when he felt this excruciating pain, and pressing his hands hard against his temples, succumbed to unconsciousness. When he came to, he opened his eyes, and glanced around, thoughts unclear. He tried to grasp the situation; he couldn't remember why he was lying on the floor half naked. He looked down on himself and saw blood dripping from different spots on his torso and upper arms. He looked closer and noticed that several of the shards scattered all over the floor had pierced his exposed flesh when his body collapsed. Anxiety, helplessness, and insecurity enfolded him once again. He remained sitting on the floor trying to regain his clear thoughts and immortal control.

A woman's face emerged before his eyes and his jaw muscles locked as a loud curse escaped his lips. "Annabel, you bloody bitch!" he screamed. "You ghastly bitch! You're going to pay! I'll follow you to the end of the earth and shred your body to little pieces."

Sebastian kept shouting with clenched teeth. The thought of Annabel harming even a single hair on Arielle's head drove him to the edge of insanity. He stood and marched from room to room screaming and cursing. He knew that he needed immediate help. He wanted to make sure Annabel didn't have the chance to make Arielle's capture any more complicated.

His first thought was Eva. He knew the spiritual relationship between Eva and Arielle was a special one, and they had gifts and abilities to connect with each other in mind and consciousness. He felt anxiety knowing that Troy and Gabrielle were away on their honeymoon. He was sure that Eva was the one he needed right now. He slumped in his chair, picked up his mobile and speed dialed Eva. She picked up on the first ring. Sebastian hauled in a deep breath.

"Eva!" he cried despondently.

"Sebastian! What's wrong?" Eva asked, alarmed. She could feel his anguish through her special gift. Something was terribly wrong.

"Eva, Arielle's gone," he said despairingly.

"What do you mean gone? Did you have an argument?"

"No…no… nothing like that. I think Annabel took her."

There was a stunned silence, and then Eva's voice came out utterly dumbfounded. "What!"

"I think Annabel kidnapped her," he said, again in a voice barely audible.

"When? How?" Eva grumbled.

"Eva, I need you, please come over," he said, and the phone went dead.

Eva stood there, looking at the phone thunderstruck.

"What's going on?" Ian asked, noting Eva's stressful expression.

"Arielle's been kidnapped, and Sebastian thinks it's Annabel."

"Oh no…"Ian's voice trailed thoughtfully, and gave Eva a concerned look. "He must be devastated."

"He sounds shattered, we must go," Eva said. They jumped out of bed and using their immortal speed they were dressed and out the door in no time.

"He needs us," Eva said, reaching for Ian's hand, as the car sped away from the house.

"We'll find her, Eva," Ian muttered as he patted her hand affectionately. He knew they were rushing into a dreadful situation. He also knew that Arielle and Eva weren't just friends, they were more like sisters.

"Ian, I hate that bloody bitch," Eva said. "She and I have unfinished business and I'm willing to go the extra mile to make her pay." She moaned, thinking of her best friend, pressing her lips together in frustration. "If she hurts Arielle, I'll make her feel pain like she never has before. She'll die slowly, painfully in sheer agony." Her hands were now balled into tight fists. They remained quiet the rest of the way.

* * *

Sebastian sat, unmoving, lost in thought. His arms ached for the love of his life; his soul yearned for her touch. He couldn't think straight.

He didn't know where to start to look for her. It'd been over 2 hours since Arielle disappeared and he knew that Annabel could've moved her to the other side of the world. He tried to think reasonably, trying to get inside Annabel's sick mind. Annabel knew that they were getting married in three weeks. This thought provided slight comfort to Sebastian. Annabel was resentful, insufferable, and repulsive, but she thrived on other people's misery; especially Arielle's.

He was sure Annabel would keep Arielle her prisoner and very much alive at least until the wedding day. She'd want to watch Arielle suffer and indulge her sick self in Arielle's excruciating pain. Watching Arielle's agony would make Annabel happy, and she would exult over her huge win that destroyed both Sebastian and Arielle. His next thought made him recoil. The problem was that after she'd accomplished that first part of her plan she would kill Arielle. Sebastian cringed at the thought, clenching his teeth tightly. He shut his eyes and pounded his fists on the armchair, growling in desperation.

Suddenly a frightening thought made him jump out of his chair and run into the bedroom. He looked around frantically, but couldn't locate what he was looking for. He drew a deep breath and exhaled optimistically as a smile painted his lips. That smile was short-lived, when another thought made him turn and walk into the bathroom. He groaned in despair as his eyes fell on the small shelf by the mirror. His jaw clenched and another loud curse escaped him. Arielle's necklace was lying on that shelf. He roared in misery and his muscles tightened. *Oh, my God! What else is going to go wrong?* he thought. His mind drifted to unreasonable places and he was unable to make sense of a single thought. He picked up his phone again and called Loren. He needed his sister's moral support.

"Loren, something's happened," he said.

"What is it?"

"I'll explain when you get here."

"Sebastian! You sound terrible. Is this something that I can share with mother?"

"No...no, don't get mother involved. Just come over please, as soon as you can."

"I'll be right over," Loren said, filled with concern. Her brother didn't sound like himself. She was sure something was terribly wrong and she would part the ocean for Sebastian if that's what needed to be done. She was out the door in a matter of seconds.

Next call went to Christian and Isabella. Isabella answered the phone.

"Isabella, it's Sebastian," he said gasping nervously.

"What's wrong Sebastian?"

"I need you both to come over. I have a major issue and I'm sure I'll need all the immortal help I can get. I'll explain when you get here."

"All right, we'll be right over." When she put down the phone, Christian was coming out of the shower.

"Who was on the phone, baby?" he asked.

"Sebastian's in some kind of trouble. He sounds absolutely horrible. He said he needs our help and he'll explain when we get to his house."

Christian gave her a thoughtful smile, but didn't ask for further details. He dressed quickly and they left the house without another word. Christian drove steadfast, wordlessly, filled with anticipation as to what type of major issue could this be. Sebastian was one of the most amazing people he'd ever met. He'd met him through his brother Pierre, who was Sebastian's best friend, and he simply worshiped the ground he walked on. He admired his success, his motivation, his innovation and his sound decisions. He was forever thankful for the way he'd taken care of Pierre's family. He'd treated them all just like his own family. Christian had been more than happy to move to Brighton with his wife Isabella to try and make Sebastian's life a little easier by watching over Arielle at school.

"I wonder what's so major," he mumbled.

"I don't know," Isabella replied, "but Sebastian sounded terrible."

"You don't suppose that Annabel's the issue, do you?" he asked, looking over at Isabella skeptically.

"It just might be. Sebastian was rattled." They remained silent for the rest of the way.

Sebastian was still lost in thought when the doorbell brought him back to the task at hand, and he ran to open the door. When Ian and Eva stepped inside the threshold, Eva fell in his arms, and they held each other. Eva wanted to cry so badly, but as an immortal, she couldn't do that any longer. The pain was shearing her skin to an excruciating level. It wasn't long before Loren and Nathan walked in, followed by Christian and Isabella. They all gathered in the library.

"What exactly happened?" Eva asked impatiently. Sebastian looked around and saw all the concerned faces that he loved and trusted with his own life.

"I think Annabel broke into the house while we were in bed. Arielle went to get a glass of water and she was gone before I knew what occurred." Sebastian groaned. They remained silent, waiting for his directive.

"Eva," Sebastian said glancing at her. "You have the gifts I need to find Arielle. Once we know the location it'll be simpler. I'll call the rest of our friends for help, and we'll deal with Annabel and her buddies, like we did in St. Jean De Luz."

"I'll do everything I can," Eva murmured.

"What about her necklace?" Ian asked. "How did she ever touch her without repercussions?"

"Ugh!" Sebastian cringed. "Arielle took it off last night when she took a shower and I found it this morning lying on the shelf in the bathroom."

"Oh, no..." Eva's voice trailed off. Loren was standing by the large window, scrutinizing Sebastian's face.

"Sebastian," Loren said, trying to get his attention. "I remember Arielle attending several of the secret society meetings with mother and Professor Allworth earlier this year," she chimed in softly. She walked up to Sebastian and, taking his hands lovingly in hers, continued. "I'm sure she learned a lot about using the mystic in that little black book."

"Yes, that's right," Eva, said, nodding in agreement. "Arielle and I spent a lot of time with that little black book after each one of those meetings. She and I did a little bit of that mind linking, trying to find out if it actually worked. We found out that every little thing in that book is reliable."

Sebastian's gaze was fixed on Eva's face. He was hanging off of every word that left her mouth. Eva noticed a flash of hope crossing Sebastian's eyes.

"What type of connection was that?" Sebastian asked, extremely interested in Eva's remarks. His thoughts were churning in a painful conflicting sort of way trying to balance the loathing he felt for Annabel and the mandate that was on hand for control in this situation. Eva sighed.

"Arielle and I discovered the secret of mind contact in the pages of the book. We were able to establish wordless communication with each other, just in case one of us was in a dangerous and defenseless situation. It creates a sort of map in our heads that outlines a path that leads to each other."

"How?" he asked eagerly.

"In the book, it's called clairvoyance," Eva said.

"How does it work?"

"Information is transferred from one mind to the other by simply using one's sixth sense. Arielle and I can access each other's thoughts and pass information to help each other."

"Eva!" Sebastian was flabbergasted. He moved across the room and halted in front of her. He stared at her steadily for a long moment and suddenly a wide smile painted his face. He lifted her and twirled her around in exhilaration. "That's exactly what we need," he said, eagerly. "Oh Eva, you've always been a special friend to both Arielle and myself."

"Sebastian, I know that Arielle will look for the right moment to connect with me and I'll be ready for her."

"How does that work?" he asked, filled with anticipation.

"It's on page 136 of the little black book," she said, voice low and mysterious. A wide smile spread across her face.

"Eva, you have to do this. If I can't get her back I'll surely die," Sebastian said, and grabbed her hands in desperation. "There's nothing in this world if she's not here with me. I'm sure you know that." His voice was so despondent, and his pain so palpable it made his friends shudder.

"Oh, God! Gabrielle would die, if she knew," Eva said, and ran her hand through her hair anxiously.

Sebastian was quiet for the longest time. "The house is empty," he murmured. "It feels cold and strange without Arielle in it." He pressed his lips together and his hands against his eyes. "Right now it seems that death would be sweeter than the way I feel without her." A painful tug clenched his chest.

"Sebastian," Ian said, putting his hand on his shoulder. "You have to get a hold of yourself, old chap. Your mind has to be clear in order to make the right decisions. We're all here to support you and we won't leave until Arielle is home safe."

"Thanks, Ian, it's hard to keep my mind straight. It's only three weeks left until our wedding day. I'm so hurt that I'm afraid I'd fall completely apart," he said, looking around the room frantically.

"Don't worry buddy we're all here," Ian said, again reassuringly.

Sebastian nodded thankfully. "Eva, do I need to get the book?" he asked, turning to look at Eva again.

"I think that would be most advisable," she replied.

Sebastian got out of his chair and walked into the bedroom. coming back in a few minutes, clenching tightly in his hand a small leather black book.

"Well...here it is," he said handing it to Eva. "I need to understand how the connection works," he added. Somehow Sebastian was feeling the eccentricity of the magical touch between two minds and it was overwhelming him.

"Great!" Eva murmured. She took the book from Sebastian and slowly flipped through the fragile pages. She stopped on pages 136 and 137. Her finger moved slowly over each word and each symbol between the two pages and she stopped when it reached a precise spot.

"What's that?" Sebastian asked inquisitively.

"That represents the connection thread between Arielle and me," Eva said, pointing at a particular spot on the page.

"Are you saying that you can find Arielle by following the words on that page?" Loren mumbled, thinking that the whole thing was a bit maddening.

"If we can manage to enter each other's thoughts at the right time, then yes, she will let me know where she is."

Loren had a lot more questions but she remained quiet after a moment's thought. However Christian's curiosity had piqued to wonder.

"Eva, I don't want to bother you, but can you elaborate on that theory? I'm personally involved in that type of interaction," he quantified.

"How so?" Eva prompted.

"I belong to a group that specializes in Mentalism."

"Oh, excellent!" Eva cheered.

"Do you want to discuss specifics about what's on that page?" Christian pushed on.

Eva's eyes were fixed on the open book and she didn't bother to answer Christian's question. She looked away and focused somewhere in the distance, but nowhere specific. They all approached Eva and stood behind her trying to catch a glimpse of the page. The left side was full of hieroglyphics and small symbols. However, the right page was mostly empty but for two heads showed on opposite sides of the page, facing each other. There was a gold line connecting the heads just behind the temples.

"Eva, what do you see on that page?" Christian asked putting his finger on the gold line and moving it from one end to the other.

"The ends of the line touch the spot where the brain is located in each head," Eva said, pointing with her finger at the exact place where the line was ending on each cranium figure.

Eva stood and walked into the kitchen, ignoring the broken shards on the floor. She set the little book on top of the counter thoughtfully. Her fingers drummed the counter as she focused on the written script on the left page.

"Tell me you can find where she is," Sebastian interrupted Eva's thoughts. He leaned against the doorframe between the study and the kitchen, arms crossed over his chest. He was consumed by stress and wanted to do something. Eva turned to look at him. Sebastian didn't understand how it all worked together, but he trusted Eva. He vividly remembered the weird sensation he had last year at St. Jean De Luz when Eva summoned him to save her and Arielle when they almost died. The pull was of enormous power and it brought him all the way to the place he needed to be. Now he was trusting Eva to guide him to where Arielle was taken. Sebastian pushed away from the doorframe and came to stand right over Eva's shoulder. He peered down on the open page.

"Somehow I don't see much in those symbols," he said.

"Ahh...Sebastian there's a huge secret world behind each letter in this little book," Eva replied. Loren and Isabella came closer as they seemed to be mesmerized with Eva's knowledge. Eva's face unwavering while her finger moved slowly across the page and her eyes scanned each letter and each symbol carefully.

"All right, I think I want to try and see if I can make contact with her," she whispered to Sebastian. "How long has she been gone?"

"3 hours and 15 minutes now," he replied without hesitation.

Everyone moved into the study and sat down waiting for Eva to give them some kind of information so they could help. Eva remained in the kitchen by herself for a while. She finally walked into the room and sat next to Ian.

"What happened?" Sebastian asked anxiously.

"From what I can gather she's either sleeping or unconscious because there's no activity with her brain. I can't meet her thoughts. Maybe Annabel drugged her until she gets to her desired destination. Don't worry Sebastian, I'll communicate with Arielle. We just have to be patient." She looked around and finally she said. "If any of you have something else to do you can go on, Sebastian will call you when we have something."

"We are not going anywhere," Isabella said and Christian agreed. Sebastian acknowledged them thankfully.

Loren walked up to Sebastian and put her arms around him and he held her tightly. She pressed a soft kiss on his cheek and whispered, "I love you Sebastian. Please don't worry; we'll get Arielle back." He nodded and sat in the big chair waiting.

"Eva, can you tell me now a little about this ability you and Arielle have to link your thoughts?" Christian asked, again. "Like I said before, I'm very interested in Mentalism."

"Indeed," Eva said. She seemed to have forgotten his previous statement.

"Yes, I studied about it at the university with a special group of students who were interested in the incredible indicators that the brain can provide, channeling from one mind to the other." Everyone but Eva looked at Christian in fascination.

"Very well," said Eva, and started to explain. "Each of the two people who want to link their thoughts concentrate their energy within their mind and soul almost like accelerating their sixth sense. The sixth sense is the secret and unique ability to read someone else's thoughts. You literally channel into the other person's mind and you can vividly see places the person you're channeling with is passing, such as names, streets, and places that will lead you to them. Sometimes the signs aren't very clear and then others are so clear they can rattle the mind to high anxiety." Eva took a deep breath, ran her tongue over her dry lips, sighed and added, "I've had the ability to reach into the subconscious of people I was looking for and find them. Arielle and I were in different places when we tried this. We had the ability to channel unspoken thoughts and feelings and communicate through space. Something called Telepathy; what you called Mentalism. I knew exactly where to go to find Arielle. We then knew that what this little book told was the absolute truth."

"So, you can work your way into someone's mind, and uncover the key to their thoughts and probe to locate your target, right?" Christian quantified.

"Exactly," Eva said, smiling. They all seemed to be obsessed with the idea of Eva connecting with Arielle. Christian and Isabella stood up and smiled sympathetically at Sebastian.

"Sebastian," Christian said. "I'm a bit familiar with this subject and the fact that Eva and Arielle possess that amazing ability makes me feel very sure it'll all work out. Maybe it would be best if Isabella and I went home. We don't know how long it'll take for Eva and Arielle to communicate. Call me when you know where you want us to be. We'll be available to you at any time."

Sebastian nodded in agreement. He turned to Eva and smiled.

"Eva, that's absolutely amazing!" Christian said.

Eva tried to enter Arielle's thoughts but she'd been getting utter silence.

"It's—" Eva started to say but stopped mid-sentence and shifted uncomfortably. A shocked look in her eyes didn't escape Sebastian who moved quickly closer and stared intently at Eva. She lifted her hand to her mouth and ran her finger lightly across her lips. She hauled in a deep breath and disbelief spread across her face. Her hand movement over her lips became forceful, while disgust spread across her face. The feeling of lips pressing hard against Eva's was so palpable that she gasped aloud.

She looked as if she was suddenly aware of someone's presence. Eva was absolutely certain that she'd entered Arielle's consciousness. Someone was with her and that someone wasn't Annabel. It wasn't but a second later and she felt a jolt that nearly threw her out of her chair. Arielle's thoughts and emotions were pouring into her head. *"No...no...let me go!"* Eva mouthed, as she lifted her hands and thrashed out into the thin air, as if she was pushing against something or someone. Eva recoiled as Arielle's emotions kept coming filled with anguish and disgust. *"What have you done?"* Arielle's voice was elevated. *"You're crazy! Where are you taking me?"* Eva felt each and every emotion piercing her very soul.

Eva's body reacted to Arielle's anxiety; as she jumped out of her chair, waving her hands wildly, pushing hard against the thin air. Stony silence fell in the room, while everyone stood motionless, watching Eva.

Christian and Isabella had reached the front door, but stopped. Ian and Loren stared in shock while Ian dropped to his knees in front of Eva and, taking her hands in his, tried to stop her from thrashing against the empty space in front of her. Sebastian watched her face intently. Eva's eyes were wide open and abruptly she pulled her hands away from Ian. He blinked in shock but remained quiet. They knew Eva had connected with Arielle's inner thoughts. Eva finally dropped her face into her hands and, hauling in a deep breath, exhaled forcefully.

"What happened, Eva?" Sebastian asked in desperation.

Eva looked up slowly, confused. "She's fighting to keep someone from touching her."

"Who? Who is trying to touch her?" Sebastian asked again, faced filled with tension.

"I don't know...I don't know..." she repeated, voice fragmenting. She'd tried to pierce through Arielle's very soul. Her eyes scanned the room and suddenly she smiled. "She knows...she knows I'm trying to communicate with her," she said softly. Sebastian exhaled deeply. "She's letting me see that she's in some type of vessel," Eva murmured. "I can see water through large portholes. It looks like she's held in a cabin."

Everyone in the room was frozen in place. The silence stretched but nobody moved. Eva looked like she was on a rollercoaster.

Abruptly, her eyes widened, her jaw tightened and she started to hyperventilate. She grabbed her chest, gasping out loud, trying to breathe, hissing, as if she was suffocating. Her eyes shone with fear and stunned shock. Ian jumped out of his seat and together with Sebastian pulled her up from her seat. She was dead weight.

"What's wrong baby?" Ian asked fearfully.

"I can't breathe…I can't breathe," she gasped and shortly after that she collapsed. Loren ran into the kitchen and grabbed a towel. She soaked it in cold water and running back placed it on Eva's forehead. A little while later Eva opened her eyes and looked around feeling weak. She brushed her hair away from her face let out a huge lungful of air.

"Are you all right?" Ian asked hovering over her excitedly. He pressed his lips softly on her forehead and waited for a reply. Eva blinked, as discontent pounded her thoughts.

"I'm fine," she said, tilting her head back. "I'm a little disappointed that I didn't see the person who's holding Arielle."

"What happened? You had a hard time breathing and you passed out," Sebastian said.

"I'm sure that whoever is on that boat sedated her to keep her from fighting. I felt every bit of it."

"Why would anybody want to do that?"

"I don't know, Sebastian, I don't know. We have to wait for her to wake up."

Sebastian exhaled, consumed by anxiety. He walked over to the big chair and slumped down, dropped his face in his hands and let out a deep sigh.

Chapter 13

"THIS IS SURREAL," Christian whispered to Isabella. They decided against leaving the house for the time being. The raw experience of the channeling between Arielle and Eva mesmerized them, and they wanted to see it through.

Eva shifted uncomfortably. She clasped her hands firmly and gave Ian a pleading look. Ian seemed to understand her sign and moving closer. He put his arm around her and held her tightly. Eva's look didn't escape any of her friends. Sebastian was going out of his mind; he needed something to distract him, so he picked up the remote and turned the telly on. He was sure that they were all tense, waiting for something to happen.

"There's plenty of Salve in the fridge," Sebastian said softly. The news on the tube seemed to absorb their attention for a short time, easing the tension in the room. He drank a glass of Salve and paced a few times, before finally sitting back down, lost in thought.

Eva felt Sebastian's distress and wanted so badly to be able to do something. It had been about an hour since the last channeling with Arielle. Eva was in deep conversation now with everyone about school coming up in the fall. She was in the middle of discussing the classes she was going to take when she seemed to be drifting away and she flinched.

Loren was watching Eva carefully, her gaze moved from Eva to Sebastian, who was still lost in thought, and then back to Eva. Eva's face was flashed as she moved her hand up and with her finger rubbed her lips back and forth, as if she was trying to wipe something away.

"Why do you keep doing that?" Ian whispered in her ear, leaning much closer. Eva set her lips against his ear. making sure that what she said to Ian didn't reach Sebastian's ears.

"Someone's touching Arielle," she murmured. "I can feel their lips pressing against hers and their hands touching her body."

Ian recoiled. He stared in Sebastian's direction, wanting to make sure he didn't hear any of it. He was still sitting silent, overwhelmed with devastating emotions, face hard, jaw clenched.

Sebastian heard the quiet and noticed that the vigorous conversation between his friends about school had suddenly stopped. He jerked his head up and he noticed that they were all watching Eva. He turned and gazed at her for what it seemed to be eternity. His eyebrows lifted in amazement as he watch her wiping her lips over and over again. Something she did a while ago before she channeled with Arielle. He jumped up and, walking to the other side of the room, stood in front of Eva once again.

"Eva," he said, but she seemed to be lost in her thoughts. "Eva," he called out anxiously. Eva lifted her gaze and the expression in her eyes sent chills down his spine. Eyes widen further, breathing elevated. He could almost read her thoughts.

"It's not Annabel…right?" he asked, anxiety choking his words.

"No," Eva gasped.

"Who is it Eva?" body muscles clenched, voice icy cold.

"Gaston," Eva mumbled. "It's Gaston."

The loud growl that escaped Sebastian hit the walls like lightning and bounced back several times making everyone in the room recoil. He fell to his knees, pressing his hands hard against his temples. Rage painted his face and the sickening sensation in the pit of his stomach rose quickly stopping at the bottom of his throat, shearing every fiber in his body, burning every nerve like a blazing fire.

Eva tried to focus on the thread that connected her thoughts with Arielle. The connection broke, leaving her with a sickening sensation. She looked up to meet Sebastian's gaze.

"Don't worry, Sebastian, give it a little time. We'll find her. Arielle's very smart. She knows how to keep away from his gaze."

"God…Where's he taking her?"

"She doesn't know. All she's sending to me is water. They're still on the boat. She and I will reestablish this connection once she knows where he's taking her."

"Gaston holds a strong resentment against me," Sebastian mumbled bitterly.

"I knew that son of a bitch was going to do something," Loren cried out. "I told Arielle to tell you about him three weeks ago, when he showed up at the Lanes parking lot."

"Oh, Loren, how I wish you'd told me," he said sadly. "I didn't find out about Gaston until last night and it was too late to form any type of plan. I just didn't think he would be so bold as to come into the house when I was here." He looked lost in thought again, as he drew a huge breath and his voice came out in a throaty sound. "I know that he's madly in love with her so, I'm fairly sure that he isn't going to hurt her." He winced.

"I wouldn't trust him, Sebastian," Ian said.

"I don't trust him, Ian, not for a moment, but I have to think this way to keep my sanity," he replied. "I'm very sure he'll try to compel her, but Arielle's smart. We talked about that in detail last night, and I hope that she remembers all I told her. She knows how to keep her eyes away from his gaze. However, that can't go on for too long. He'll get to the point that he just might hurt her." He grimaced. "That's why we need to do something. I need to find her, God! I need to find her soon," he mumbled.

"What if he keeps her drugged?" Isabella asked quietly. Everyone looked at her in surprise.

New fear took over Sebastian's expression and he growled. "I didn't think about that, Oh...God!" he said again.

His friends heard the pain in his voice and watched him with extreme concern. Silence stretched between them. Sebastian looked tired and completely drained.

"Sebastian, I'm fairly sure he wouldn't try anything without her consent. You know the immortals oath is sacred, and he's not going to break it unless he doesn't care about his own life and I find that hard to believe. But even if he decided to do that eventually, that will give us time to find her." Eva said.

Sebastian stared at her thoughtful but at the end he had to agree.

"Who is Gaston?" Christian asked inquisitively.

"Gaston was my best childhood friend," Sebastian replied. "This resentment started way back in the 1500s in Calais. That's when he fell madly in love with Arielle."

Christian and Isabella gasped in astonishment. Christian hauled in a deep breath.

"How in bloody hell did he ever meet Arielle in Calais?" Christian asked, astounded. "Sebastian, you must understand that you sound a bit crazy to Isabella and me, making a statement like that," he furthered.

"A statement like what?" Sebastian asked, watching Christian, as if he should know what he was talking about.

"Are you serious?" Christian exclaimed. "How could Gaston have met Arielle 500 plus years ago? She's human!"

Eva knew now that there was no way she could get out of providing details on the time travel adventure in Calais.

"It was Arielle's birthday present from me," she chimed in. "I wanted her to meet Sebastian when he was a mortal man. So we decided to go and attend his parent's annual gala. Sebastian was 20 years of age at the time."

Christian, Isabella, and even Loren were hanging on every word, utterly shocked.

"You can time-travel!" Isabella cried out, watching Eva intently.

"Yes," Eva said. She looked around and smiled at their shocked astonishment.

"Well..." Loren's voice trailed off. "Now I've heard everything."

Sebastian looked around unable to hold back his sadness. However, the ability of Eva to communicate with Arielle gave him the reassurance he needed so desperately right now. He looked up at Eva, a smile barely touching his lips.

"Sebastian, why don't we all go home so you can rest a bit? I'll keep you informed as soon as I'm able to link with Arielle. You're just a text away, and we can be here in a matter of seconds, you do need to rest!" She emphasized. "We've been going at this since this morning. It may take a while for Gaston to get to their destination. That's when Arielle will be able to find out a name, a landmark, or a place that'll give us an idea of where to start."

Sebastian knew Eva was right. Patience would have to be the most important thing right now. He nodded in agreement.

"I'll stay here with you," Loren said. Sebastian smiled softly at his sister. He was happy that she decided to stay. He didn't want to be alone.

"Thanks, Loren," he said and put his arm around her. He thanked his friends for coming and spending the day with him. He needed their support and advice.

Eva hugged him tightly. "I love you Sebastian. We'll have Arielle home soon. I promise you that," she said encouragingly.

"I love you Eva, thank you," he whispered in her ear. Eva smiled as they walked out.

Sebastian hugged Isabella and shook hands with Christian and Ian, then stood at the closed door unmoved for several minutes. He finally looked up and met Loren's gaze.

"Come and sit here with me," she said softly and motioned for him to join her at the sofa. "It's going to be all right. Eva seems to be able to communicate with Arielle. When we find out where he's taking her, then we'll tear the place apart and bring her home."

"Thanks, Loren. Right now, I need all the encouragement I can get," he said, and set his hand on hers. "I feel so alone, and so hurt, I can't live without her." He gritted his teeth, as an icy cold sensation coursed down his spine. "God...it hurts so bad!" he groaned. "Loren, I can't be in this house without her, I can't sleep or even imagine waking up without her in my arms." He sighed deeply, as waking doom surged through his mind. He remained silent, buried in his thoughts and Loren closed her hands around his in a sisterly attempt to ease his pain.

Sebastian's wretchedness ran intensely within his very soul. As an immortal he had never before experienced this mind-blowing, sheering pain. Eva had promised to call him as soon as she was able to resume contact with Arielle. He drew in a deep breath and dragged himself out of that sofa. He needed some air; he was suffocating in his horrifying thoughts.

Loren sprang out of her seat to follow Sebastian. When she stepped into the kitchen her jaw dropped and her body stiffened. "What in bloody hell happened here?" she cried out, glaring at the countless pieces of bloody sharp glass that were spread across the floor.

Sebastian gazed back at Loren for a short moment; eyes filled with despair, hands clenched into tight fists, but remained silent. He finally muttered something inaudible and, turning around, he disappeared through the door leading into the garden.

He walked through the trees and with a few long strides, reached the edge of the property and stood under a large Hawthorn tree. He leaned against its trunk, focusing his gaze toward the fine line where the sky met the ocean. He wanted to be alone; he wanted to reflect and get his thoughts in order. The revelation that Gaston was the person who'd placed Sebastian's life into a crushing cyclone wasn't a big surprise. What was astounding was Gaston's boldness to strike inside their home. His lips twisted and his stomach clenched, as every muscle in his body turned hard as steel. The fury was so intense that he could've crashed a bolder into fine dust.

He was pondering scenarios of confrontation when suddenly Arielle's shockingly blue, blue sapphires emerged in front of him and his breath held in his throat. He growled angrily at the thought of Gaston being in close proximity of Arielle's soft satin skin, elegant curves, flawless face, and sensuous lips. His arms ached for her, his senses painfully consumed by the mere thought of her. At this point there was nothing he wanted more than to have her home safe. He was sure that Gaston was unaware of Arielle's gifts and her ability to mentally communicate with Eva. He had no idea about all the spells Arielle had learned attending the secret society with his mother and how to use those spells to help her in difficult circumstances. Those abilities were a plus for Arielle and a disaster for Gaston.

All that Sebastian needed was Eva's word as to where Gaston took Arielle. Armed with that information, he would contact all their friends, and have them assist in getting her home. He decided to text the guys just to give them advance warning about the situation. He pulled his mobile out of his jean pocket and text a few words to Pierre, his oldest and dearest friend.

"Pierre, I need your help."

It took but a couple of minutes before he received a reply.

"What's wrong?"

"An old friend from my mortal years has kidnapped Arielle. He's utterly obsessed with her."

"Do you know where she is?"

"No, not yet, but I'm in the process of finding out."

He was startled when his phone rang.

"Hello!" he answered anxiously. Pierre's voice was on the other end.

"How about if I contact the others and we come to Brighton to be with you? I think more brains will bring better results. After all, I need the break."

"I welcome your offer, old friend," Sebastian replied. "I need a few more ideas. If you want to come, I'll be grateful."

"All right Sebastian, don't worry, man, we'll find her."

"Thanks," he said, closed the phone. and slipped it into his pocket. A little while later he heard back from Jacques, Antonius, Giani, Gerard, and Jon. They were all on the way. Hope filled Sebastian's lungs and hauled in a deep breath.

Loren looked out the window and saw him leaning against the tree and felt a painful twitch in her gut. She studied his expression and was sure that she understood the anxiety sheering his very existence. She chose to leave him alone and decided to clean the mess off the kitchen floor. She needed to give him time to cool down and come back inside. By the time she put the broom away Sebastian walked in and she ran to him. She put her arms around him and held him close.

"We'll find her Sebastian, please don't worry," she said. He held her and they stood in a warm embrace trying to find comfort in each other.

"Please don't say anything to mother," he said quietly. "I don't want her to worry."

"I won't, but what about Arielle's parents? What if they call?"

"They're away for 10 days with Gabrielle's parents and Eva's mother. They usually don't call when they're away."

"Oh, that's good!"

"Yes, it actually is. It's one less thing to worry about right now," he said, letting go off Loren and walking to the fridge to get another glass of Salve.

"God...I wish Eva would call," he groaned. He twirl the glass in his hand and for a long moment watched the red liquid swirl.

"She will, Sebastian, I'm sure she will," Loren said, pursing her lips, gut filled with anxiety.

Oh, please, God, Loren, thought. *I can't stand watching Sebastian. He's in so much pain.*

The clock ticked away as Sebastian settled into his large chair to wait for Eva's call. Thoughts of Arielle surged into his head and his lips slowly curved. She'd dropped into his life full of vigor and determination for the future—their future— together. She filled his bewildered existence with passion for life, tenderness, and heart-pounding exhilaration. Her striking splendor focused his life toward a path of pure ecstasy. He just couldn't believe that an intangible eye-connection on that beautiful August day at the beach of St Jean De Luz turned to an astounding heart-pounding affirmation that he'd found the *one.* He wanted to anchor the rest of his existence right next to the girl who enveloped him with a palpable thirst for life. What a significant moment that was! His breath caught at the thought.

*   *   *

It was 1:30 in the afternoon when Eva and Ian drove home lost in weighty thoughts. Ian wondered how far Gaston was going to take this game with Arielle and Eva was overwhelmed with wretchedness. She was eager to reach out to Arielle, as soon as she regained consciousness. She was sure that Gaston was keeping her sedated in order to make it easier for him to move her as far away from Sebastian as possible. She was convinced he would try to seduce her, hoping that in the long run, he'd win her over. He wanted Arielle in the worst way. Eva felt his fervent kiss on her lips, through Arielle's mind. She felt his passionate touch on Arielle's body that alerted her very essence. Gaston was up to no good. She frowned and the atmosphere in the little car deepened considerably.

Ian helped Eva out of the car and pulled her into his arms tenderly. He bent down and brushed his lips seductively against hers and Eva blinked, a hot sensation rippling across her muscles. She reacted instantaneously by wrapping her arms around his neck and deepening the kiss to sweltering. Ian's arms closed around her and pulled her even closer.

"I love you, Eva," he murmured through the kiss.

"Mmm," was her reply, eyes closed, searing heat coursing through every nerve, every muscle. She reluctantly pulled from the kiss and gazed into his loving eyes. "I need to connect with Arielle, baby," she said, pressing her lips anxiously.

"Okay."

In the house, Eva laid on the sofa closing her eyes, waiting impatiently for Arielle to give her a small sign that she was alert again. Ian settled in the large recliner with a book, trying hard to keep Eva out of his thoughts. He thumbed boringly through several pages totally uninterested in reading. His eyes moved slowly and focused on Eva as she shifted and changed positions trying to get comfortable on the sofa. He dragged in a deep breath, and yanked his gaze away fighting hard the urge to lie next to her and take her in his arms. He failed miserably as he gaze moved back on her and his eyes traced lustfully every little curve of her body that moved, tensed and relaxed over and over again.

His muscles tensed and he bit his lower lip fighting to keep calm. Unknowingly Eva was sending waves of intoxicating desire his way and heat coursed quickly through every muscle in his body. Eva kept her eyes shut but she felt the heavy weight of his gaze and turning around she met his blistering gaze. Passion surged through her and Ian lost it. He leapt out of his chair using his immortal speed and, picking up Eva, he carried her to bed. His mouth covered hers fervently and ripples of exhilaration coursed through their bodies. The passion that enveloped them was beyond human grasp. They lay motionless for a long time, smoldering in the aftermath of their amazing encounter. They laid quietly for what it seemed to be a century. The sound of the clock in the foyer stroke 3 times and Ian turned to his side. Eva opened her eyes and looked over at Ian sending him a warm smile. Ian gathered Eva in his arms and she pulled herself even closer serenely.

"Eva," Ian whispered trapping her gaze. "I'm hurting for Sebastian," he murmured. "I can't even fathom being without you, not even for a moment. I'd have to kill someone," he said seriously. He held Eva tighter, voice filled with emotion.

"I know…" her voice trailed off. "I wish there was something we could do, but until Arielle decides to connect with me, we are at a loss," she said. Slowly Eva eased herself away from Ian's embrace and sat up, taking a deep breath.

"Where are you going baby?" Ian asked.

"I'd like a glass of Salve, would you like me to bring you some?"

"No, I'm good," he said, with a deep sigh, sending Eva a warm smile. Eva swung her legs over the side of the bed and set her feet on the floor. Ian watched her with a wide smile on his face, but Eva didn't stand up, she sat there totally unmoved. She looked frozen in place. He frowned, as he waited for a short moment and when Eva didn't give a sign of movement, he sat up, and moved across the bed quietly. He sat next to her placing his arm about her.

"What is it, Eva?" he murmured, softly. Eva's gaze was surging into a distant unsettling place. "Is it Arielle?" he asked, voice barely audible. Eva nodded without replying.

"Come on, Arielle!" she urged, pushing her hair away from her face and stifling a growl. "Give me something," she pleaded, and letting out a deep sigh, she halted at the end of the bed totally unmoved.

"What's going on?" Ian asked eagerly.

"We're connected. She's aware of me and she's letting me enter her thoughts to see what is going on. They're getting out of the boat," she murmured. "She's trying to get her bearings, looking for something to help us find her." Eva was piercing through the empty space, her eyes moving wildly from one side to the other, searching the empty space in their room. She reached over and clasped Ian hand. "She's asking Gaston where they are," Eva said.

"What's he saying?" Ian asked.

"He says it's a surprise," Eva whispered, pressing her lips together. "Oh, Ian, she's very frightened," Eva dragged in a deep breath. "They're walking up a poorly-lit pier…" Eva furthered. "Gaston and another man are right behind her. She doesn't know the other man; she has never seen him before."

"Where in bloody hell are they?" Ian asked anxiously.

"She isn't sure," Eva replied. "It's very dark and hard to see."

"It's dark? But it's only 3 o'clock in the afternoon," Ian said, astoundingly.

"It's dark at the place they've arrived," Eva said. Ian closed his eyes, trying to consider all the places that would be several hours later than Brighton. Unfortunately he was fooling himself, as he knew that they could be just about anywhere in the world where it was nighttime. He let out an exasperated breath, as his mind whirled wildly, accepting the fact that without Arielle's help, it'll be near impossible to locate her.

"Wait! Wait! I think I see something coming up in the distance," Eva exclaimed pressing Ian's hand harder. "A light of some sort." Eva's eyes were searching the empty space again wildly. "Oh, no..." she added, disappointingly. "They're headlights, a car is waiting for them," she murmured. "Arielle's trying desperately to see a sign, something she can give me." A long silence fell in the bedroom. Ian got out of bed to retrieve his book from the recliner, and coming back, he laid down in bed next to Eva, waiting for something they could take to Sebastian.

"Arielle's letting me know that she can't see a thing outside the car. Gaston is sitting next to her, his arm about her, whispering to her that he's not going to hurt her." Eva's breathing picked up speed as she could feel Gaston's arm tightening around Arielle. Ian noticed and, putting the book down, he moved even closer.

"What is it, baby?"

"It's Gaston, he's holding her and Arielle hates it."

"Still in the car?"

"Yes, but it's very strange. Through her mind, I can see that there is an eerie darkness outside the car. No lights, no street signs, no traffic. Where in bloody hell is he taking her?" Eva stood up and started to pace. "She's having a hard time concentrating until she gets away from Gaston," Eva grimaced, looking into the empty space in front of her. Suddenly she stopped, her cold gaze fixed on something in the distance.

"What? What?" Ian asked noticing the icy look on Eva's face.

"The car has stopped. He's helping her out and they're walking up a large staircase. I can see a large double door held wide open by a tall young woman. She's smiling at them and greeting Gaston warmly." Eva was immovable staring through Arielle's eyes, trying to inspect the inside of the house. "I can see a lot of wall paintings, portraying ocean sceneries. There are rich decorations, elegant details, and large windows, reflecting total darkness outside. Oh…Ian…there are no signs anywhere to show where she is. I feel her anxiety. Gaston is telling the woman to show Arielle to her room. I can see her going up a long staircase and walking down a long corridor with many doors on either side. They're now standing at the very end of that corridor. The woman opens the door and, stepping aside, she is letting Arielle inside. She's now gone and Arielle is left alone. She's crying!" Eva says through clenched teeth. "She's plummeted on the bed sobbing uncontrollably."

"Talk to her, Eva," Ian pushed anxiously. Eva blinked and drew a deep breath.

"*Arielle, Arielle,*"

"*Yes,*" Arielle thought anxiously.

"*We're all here, ready to come and help you. Don't be frighten, he's not going to hurt you. Don't look directly in his eyes, try to buy time.*"

"*How is Sebastian?*" Arielle's emotions were shattered.

"*He's devastated,*" Eva passed the thought to her and bit her lower lip. "*Try to look around and find something, even a little piece of paper, or a book, or a sign, something that might give you the name of the place.*"

"*I'll try.*"

"*I'll be here waiting for anything you can give me to help us find you.*"

"*Tell Sebastian I love him and I'm sorry for missing our wedding day.*" Arielle whimpered.

"*You're not going to miss your wedding day. We're going to find you way before then.*"

"*I love you, Eva,*" Arielle said.

"*I love you, too,*" Eva replied, feeling a heavy rock sitting in the pit of her stomach. "*Go take a shower and rest. That'll keep Gaston away from you for a while if he tries to come in your room.*"

"*But where do I look for signs?*" she asked Eva.

"*Check any place in the room, every corner, every closet, and finally the surroundings when you get to go outside. There has to be something like a name or landmark that'll help us find you sooner. Gaston isn't aware of our ability to communicate, so he has no reason to hide anything from you now.*"

"I hate him, Eva," Arielle's thought came across forcefully. "And Eva, one more thing. Tell Sebastian that everyone here is an immortal. I haven't seen a single human."

"Arielle, don't worry about that, go and take a shower and then get in bed, you do need to rest. I'll update Sebastian, let him know that you are all right, and I'll wait to hear from you. Again, look through everything in your room. Check the corners of the closet, the drawers, you might notice something that will give us an idea, a start."

"All right, Eva, I will," Arielle conveyed to Eva, trying to keep her thoughts steady even though she was shattered inside. Eva however smiled, sure that they'd find something. Her connection with Arielle was clear and their communication a relief to both of them. Once she knew their connection was broken for the time being, she picked up the phone and called Sebastian. He picked up on the first ring.

"Eva, anything?"

"Yes, I communicated with Arielle. She's fine, just a little frighten. She told me to tell you that she loves you." A loud groan followed on the other side of the phone and Sebastian let out a low curse. "Sebastian, it'll be okay. She's going to try and get something, a name, a tag, anything that will tell us where she is. When they arrived, wherever that place is, it was dark and couldn't see any signs, traffic, car tags or anything like that. She was picked up and taken to a very large home. Gaston had an immortal woman show her to her room. He didn't tell her where they were, even though she did ask him several times."

"Son of a bitch," Sebastian cursed again. His voice was filled with pain and anticipation. "Eva, this is way worse that when the Russians took her for those horrifying two days. This is a different scenario. These are immortals and capable of disappearing at a moment's notice to any corner of the earth."

"Sebastian, I know, that's why you need to get ahold of yourself and try to move slowly and carefully. Arielle's smart and she's going to find that particular something that'll help us locate her." Eva's voice was tender and reassuring.

"Call me as soon as you have something," Sebastian said.

Eva woke in the middle of the night, muddled by sleep, eyes shut, mind confused, and a strong sensation of unease spread across her body. She struggled to understand. Her head was pounding and, lifting her hands, she pressed them tightly against her temples. Slowly she tried to think and was abruptly jolted to consciousness. She sat up on the bed and pushed the covers away. She realized that Arielle was trying to connect with her mind. She swallowed hard shaking her head, trying to get her bearings.

"*Eva, wake up!*" Arielle's desperate voice bored through her mind.

"*I'm here, Arielle.*"

"*Eva, they have me locked in this room. I feel like a caged animal,*" she whimpered. "*I have no one to talk with, nothing to do and the telly isn't working, so I'm totally cut off from the world except from you,*" she murmured anxiously.

"*Arielle, listen to me carefully. Don't be scared of Gaston, he's not going to hurt you. You need to buy time while looking for that something that will be the key to help us find you. Can you do that?*"

"*Yes,*" she replied, voice still shaken. The connection was broken once again and Eva cursed. She lay back down, exhaling deeply.

"What is it, baby?" Ian asked, and pulled her in a tight embrace.

"We don't have anything that will help us," she said regretfully. "She's going to search and when she has something she will contact me." The night came and went and she didn't hear anything from Arielle. Sebastian called first thing in the morning but to his disappointment Eva had nothing new. It'd now been two days and there had been no news. Eva and Arielle remained aware of each other's existence and thoughts, but they tried to preserve their energy for when Arielle actually found a real clue. Arielle had nothing at this point. She didn't find anything in her room that would give her a hint of her whereabouts, and she hadn't been allowed outside the room. She lay down and closed her eyes, gripped by fretfulness. "*God please help me! I want to go home,*" she prayed, sincerely. Tears trickled slowly down her cheeks, dampening her hair.

 *Chapter 14*

ARIELLE PULLED GENTLY away from Sebastian's kiss and he let her go reluctantly. She sat up and, turning, she set her feet on the floor. She felt Sebastian's strong hand pulling her back. Arielle turned and let her gaze glide over his faultless body. Her lips curved, she bent down and set her mouth on his passionately in a sweltering kiss. His lips moved underneath hers with ravenousness and his arms wrapped tightly around her pulling her slowly back on the bed.

"Where are you going baby?" he whispered on her lips.

"I'm just going to get a glass of water. Don't move, I'll be right back," she murmured and chuckled blissfully. He released her lips unwillingly, and she jumped out of bed, a wide smile spread across her face. Every time they kissed he left her breathless. She was thirsty, so she made a beeline toward the kitchen. She stood naked in the middle of the room trying to decide if she needed to turn the light on or leave it off. It was a beautiful summer night, exhibiting a spectacular full moon that was nestled in the middle of a steely sky. Its brilliant light slipped through the large window and lit up the room. She smiled, eager to get a glass of water and hurry back into Sebastian's warm embrace. She grabbed a glass from the cabinet and reached in the fridge for the water pitcher. Suddenly an arm of steel held her immobile in a tight embrace and a hand holding a cloth pressed against her face. She felt fear spreading across her body, fighting to breath, feeling suffocated. The glass slipped from her hand and shattered on the floor with a loud crash. That was the last thing she remembered before she lost consciousness.

Arielle opened her eyes thoroughly confused. She felt drowsy and her throat was dry and raw. She glanced around awkwardly but nothing looked familiar. She was completely alone in a dim lit room. She pressed her eyes shut and shook her head. *Where am I?* she thought. *Am I dreaming?* She opened her eyes slowly, thinking she was going out of her mind. She tried to clear the fog from her brain and the haze from her eyes, but the surrounding didn't change. She was lying in a bed but not her bed. She carefully studied every item around the room, but nothing was forthcoming to her. She shut her eyes tightly in sheer desperation. *Where am I? How did I get here?* she thought, still a bit lightheaded.

She lay still for a short moment, reaching deep into her thoughts and suddenly her eyes snapped open, as reality came slamming back into her brain. She sat upright and stared in disbelief. She was sure that she was in what it looked like a large cabin used as a bedroom. She remembered being naked in her kitchen. She looked down at herself and she was in a pair of jeans and a top totally unfamiliar to her. Her lips twisted and she could feel her heart hammering her chest painfully. She took another look around; there were 2 portholes on the panel wall behind the bed and a door directly across. She was sure that she was in a vessel and that door most likely lead to the upper deck. She couldn't hear any noises, but she could unquestionably tell that the vessel was moving across water. Her eyes narrowed as the last moments of her getting a glass of water in the kitchen flashed clearly into her mind. *What in bloody hell happened?*

A vivid memory of a steel-like embrace and a cloth pressed against her face made her shiver. A lump started to form in the pit of her stomach and it was climbing fast up to her throat, as panic coursed across every muscle.

A face flashed before her eyes and her heart stopped. Fear was swirling like a gale force shearing every inch of her flesh. *Oh—my—God—Annabel!—She's finally done it!* She gasped, shocked into stillness. Instantly she reached for her necklace and froze. Her neck was bare. The blood drained from her face and she felt faint. She was her prisoner and totally unprotected. She was now sure that Annabel sedated her and took her from her own home. She'd made a promise to never allow any woman to marry Sebastian and it looked like she'd kept her promise. Swallowing her panic, she tried to gain some control of her senses. *Eva,* she thought in shear fright. *I need to talk to Eva, I need to try and enter Eva's thoughts,* she mumbled to herself. She felt blistering tears burning the inside of her eyelids, as anxiety heaved through her brain. *I'll let Eva know where I am so she can help me, but where am I?* Her thoughts were whirling wildly making her sick. *Oh—God—! What do I do? Please help me.*

The sound of footsteps descending to the lower level made her stiffen. She forgot to breathe as fear cursed through her body. She glared at the closed door, holding her breath. Her horror was gripping every muscle and anxiety was smashing against her brain cells like thunderbolts. The footsteps were closing in and each step was pulverizing her very essence. She shackled her fear, lowered her head, shut her eyes, and waited with tormented breath.

"You're up!" A man's velvety voice reached her ears. Her head snapped in utter shock. She stared, eyes wide open, a scream stuck on her throat.

"Ga...st...on..." she finally cried incoherently.

"At your service, my princess,"the said with a smile.

"Where are we?"

"Oh...my sweet, that's my surprise," he said.

She looked thoroughly confused. He took that chance and continued. "You slept most of the way."

"Most of the way to where?" she shrieked, "Most of the way to where?" she stumbled this time, the words barely audible.

"Don't worry about the details right now, we'll talk later," he said; his gaze trapped hers. He moved closer and leaning over her he put his arms around her.

"No...no...let me go!" she screamed thrashing her hands against his chest.

"Calm down Arielle," he said, his voice soft and completely unruffled.

"What have you done?" she yelled, looking at him with horror in her eyes. "You're crazy! Where are you taking me?" she cried out again. "I'm getting married in three weeks, you can't do this." Her voice was elevated. He put his finger on her lips and she stopped talking. His eyes were now filled with fury.

"Arielle, you better listen to me and listen well." He bent down and lifted her out of the bed, as if she was weightless. He set her on her feet right in front of him and bored through her eyes. "You're never going to marry Sebastian. That part of your life is over," he said, through clenched teeth. "Do I make myself clear?" His eyes hardened.

"Gaston, what are you saying?" she asked, eyes filled with anxiety. She was stunned to find herself in his steel embrace, trapped unable to move. She was sure she could escape much easier through a concrete barrier than his embrace. He lowered his head and set his lips on hers and pressed hard seductively, demanding, but she didn't reply. His lips firmed and his demand became haughty, dominant. She could fell his lips hungry, aching, possessive and she felt frantic. She finally pulled back and screamed.

"Go away, Gaston, I don't want you now, and I never will," she was now sobbing hard, eyes pleading with him. "Please, let me go—, please, let me go…" she pleaded again and again gulping back tears. His eyes went cold. The bright blue turned dark and his voice bellowed.

"You're going to have a life with me and me only. I'll have you weather you like it or not, so I'd suggest that you get used to the idea." His voice was hard and his glare unforgiving. She was still trapped in his embrace, unable to move away.

Arielle had never felt this angry before. Inside rage fueled and spread across every fiber of her body, drawing a deep breath she shrieked. "I'll never have a life with you, I'd rather die." She cursed inward and his answer was another hard embrace and another scorching kiss. As soon as he let go she started to scream again. He moved in that immortal speed and before she knew it she was unconscious again. He laid her slowly back on the bed and, taking her mouth, he ravished himself with another kiss.

His arrangement was ordinary nothing complicated, but it would be a lengthy one, until he'd convinced Arielle that this was now her new life. She would forget all about her love for Sebastian and the life she had with him. He felt a pang thinking of her rejection, but he knew it would take time to change her mind. Swooping down one more time he pressed his lips on hers passionately. She would remain unconscious until they reached their destination. *There is no way that anyone would be able to find us,* he murmured. *I'll keep you with me forever.* He chuckled blissfully and walked out of the cabin closing the door behind him. He crossed the corridor in a few short strides and climbed the steps smiling.

When he stepped onto the deck, he saw Oliver Stabelton, his best friend, waiting patiently, sprawled on a lounge chair, dark sunglasses on, and a drink in his hand. He had agreed to help Gaston in this venture.

Gaston had moved Arielle quickly, using his immortal speed, and met Oliver in his hometown Sidney. From there, Oliver and his crew had agreed to take Gaston and Arielle to their final destination. Oliver didn't get a good look at Arielle when they boarded, but he knew that Gaston's obsession for this girl was beyond any limitations, beyond any rational thoughts. He'd known Gaston for over 500 years and he'd never seen him more determined to capture a person's attention. He was head over heels in love, and that alone convinced Oliver to offer his help and his crew to kidnap Arielle, and take her to his private home in Fiji. Gaston would keep her there until her heart body and soul had surrendered to Gaston.

"How did it go, mate?" Oliver asked, amused. Gaston shrugged, as reality slammed hard into his brain. Arielle's rejection enveloped him and he tried hard to mask his agonizing emotion. He realized that it would take a long time to make her forget Sebastian. He swallowed his anger and a low curse escaped this mouth. Oliver's creepy gaze didn't falter. "What's wrong old friend?" he said again, trying to hold back laughter. "I thought after 500 years, you'd have a supreme understanding of how women think. They've always been a huge puzzle for us men."

Gaston snorted at Oliver's words. What defined Gaston was his relentless and tireless pursue to capture everything he went after. And now he was on the hunt for Arielle's body and soul.

"I was sure I understood everything when it came to women, but Arielle's different. She's not like any other woman," he said, and groaned anxiously but filled with hope.

"Is she awake?" Oliver asked.

"She was, but she got hysterical, so I decided to sedate her once again. I want her to remain quiet and stress-free until we arrive in Vatulete." His lips twisted.

"Gaston, relax—mate—I've never seen you this upset. It's going to be all right. She's now here with you and you can take all the time in the world to convince her that she should be with you," Oliver added and chuckled mischievously.

"What if she never accepts me?" Gaston paled at the thought.

"It's going to take a lot of effort and time to convince her that she has no other options," Oliver said. Gaston was sure that this was going to be an uphill battle. "We have one more hour before we reach the shore. Sit down and have drink with me," Oliver furthered. "I know you enjoy having a sip of brandy here and there instead of Salve, don't you?"

"Yes, I think I do need a drink."

"I must say that your story is an extraordinary one," Oliver said. "What are the odds of something like this happening to one of us?"

"What do you mean?" Gaston asked curiously.

"I mean, when have you ever heard anything quite like this? Arielle's time-travels weaved such a tight web around your immortal life, that you can't breathe, you can't think, you're trapped."

Gaston's face-hardened. "It's complicated, but there's nothing I can do now, I'm doomed."

"I hope you've thought of the consequences and the detestation that you'll have to overcome," Oliver continued. His gaze fell on Gaston's face. He looked as if he was evaluating Oliver's words.

"What exactly are you referring to?"

"Gaston, you're not only taking her away from Sebastian. You're depriving her of her family and close friends. She'll loath you for days and years to come."

"I'll take care of that," he said smirking.

"Don't even think about breaking the immortal code, because the consequences of that are severe. You know if you do that, you'll perish in a matter of time."

"Yes, I know, and I'll try everything possible before I get to that point. I want her and I'll have her no matter what I have to do. I'm determined to risk it all." His expression was blank. Oliver shrugged and stared down into his glass. Gaston swirled his drink inside the glass in complete silence and sipped slowly without saying another word. The discussion veered to other subjects, but Oliver could tell that Gaston was mentally disengaged, and he shook his head in wonder.

"I think, I'll go check on Arielle," Gaston said, and stood, leaving his glass on the small table next to his chair.

"I'll go with you if you don't mind," Oliver said. Gaston didn't reply, he just moved eagerly toward the stairs that led to the lower level. He crossed the corridor with short strides, Oliver on his heels. He stopped in front of the narrow door and turned the nob quietly. He swung the door wide open and crossing the threshold he reaching to his left and turned the light on.

Oliver walked closer to take a closer look at the girl who'd stolen his best friend's soul and mind. He stopped next to the bed and looked down on her, his gaze sweeping over the soft motionless body that was lying unconscious. A wide smile spread across Oliver's face as his eyes traced the gorgeous curves, the bare shoulders, the swells under the t-shirt. His gaze lingered for a long time over that beautiful sight. He forced himself to move his gaze slowly to her face. Her complexion was creamy white, like alabaster. Her hair a radiant wave of sunburn spread across the pillow. Her features were refined; her lips were full and luscious slightly parted, reflecting a shade of pink. Her nose was petite and quite sexy. Her eyes were closed but her lushes were long and he was sure they would complement the gorgeous blue eyes Gaston spoke of so often. A faint aroma of freesia reached his nostrils and he shivered. Silent waves of excitement coursed through his body, and quickly he stepped away from the bed, letting out a muted curse. She was anangel! She was that, and much more, he was sure. After this, he wholeheartedly understood Gaston's obsession.

"We should be arriving in 30 minutes," Oliver said, his gazed roaming over Arielle's body one more time and, swallowing another curse, he turned away. "I'm going upstairs," he said, his jaw clenched. He walked outside and climbed the steps quickly. Oliver was shocked by the powerful urge that swept over him when his eyes fell on Arielle. He shook his head one more time and groaned in disbelief. This was his best friend's obsession, not his.

Gaston remained behind for a few more minutes. He kept his gaze on Arielle's face. He was dead set to sway her his way. He was ready to offer his body and soul and he wanted to convince her to give him the same in return. This was something he had to have, as he just couldn't live without her. That was one fact he couldn't escape any longer. He spent years after she left Calais to try to get over her, but he never did. Deep inside she had remained his one and only desire.

He swooped down and pressed his thirsty lips on hers. He ran his hand softly over the swells under her shirt and hauling in a frustrated breath he swung back and left the room closing the door behind him. He climbed the steps and crossed the deck with a few strides, cursing out loud. He reached the small table that held his brandy and with a deep groan he picked up the glass and drained it.

* * *

Arielle open her eyes slowly. Her mind was in a thick fog; thinking, feeling or understanding seemed to be nonexistent emotions. She tried to lift her arms, but she couldn't. It felt as if she was trying to lift solid blocks of concrete. Her eyes were burning, her temples were throbbing and her throat was dry. She pressed her eyelids shut hoping that she would snap out of this dreadful dream. She ran her tongue over her dry lips and tried to blink several times to clear the thin film that was obstructing her vision. *This has to be one hell of a bloody dream,* She thought, and chuckled. *I'm trapped in this horrific nightmare and I can't wake up.* Her intuitive intensified, as images started to trickle into her mind slowly at first and then they reeled wildly until they skidded to a halt. She gasped as the recent memories poured in. She was still lying in the same bed but the room was now dark. *How long have I been lying here?*

Her eyes inched over each item in the room all over again. There was a small dresser against the opposite wall, a nightstand next to the bed, and two chairs. Suddenly, through the shadows, her gaze stopped on the portholes above her head and she froze as Gaston's face emerged in her mind and she cursed inwardly. She sat up in the dark and lifted her hands to wipe moisture that was trickling down her face.

Her fear was now so dense; it blocked her thoughts one more time. Her hands balled into tight fists and her nails cut through the skin of her palms, spreading pain across her muscles. She welcomed the darkness inside the cabin; it helped conceal her emotional stress. She was at a total disadvantage with Gaston, without her necklace, however she still had Eva. *I have to remain calm,* she thought to herself. *I need to find out where he's taking me. I need to get something that will help Sebastian and my friends find me.* She struggled to focus her thoughts on Eva, but Sebastian's face kept filling her mind. *Sebastian!* She whimpered his name, and felt his image envelope every fiber in her body. Her lips move again, repeating his name over and over again and she started to sob quietly. *God, what am I going to do? Will they ever find me?* Panic coursed through her nerves and fear traveled like lightning, searing every pore in her body.

She had a wild thought of trying to escape, but how could she even opt on an escape plan if she didn't know where she was? According to Gaston she'd slept most of the way to this boat and for how long she had no idea; she'd lost complete track of time.

Footstep in the corridor made her skin crawl. She kept her eyes shut, hoping that Gaston would leave her alone. She heard the doorknob turn and the door creaked as it opened. She heard him approach and he stopped next to the bed. He had to be very close because she could smell that intoxicating immortal scent. Only in this case it was turning her stomach inside out.

"We're here, princess," he whispered in her ear and brushed his lips against her earlobe. Arielle stifled a scream and opened her eyes slowly. "Please don't be scared of me and don't scream. I'm not going to hurt you, I've told you that over and over again. I'm in love with you, I wouldn't hurt a single hair in your head," he said, and his eyes locked with hers. Arielle recoiled, and yanked her eyes away, avoiding his immortal power to compel her. He gave her his hand to help her out of bed but she pushed him away.

"Where are we?" she mumbled without moving.

"I'll tell you later. Right now we need to get out of the boat," he said, voice firm. He took a step back and kept his eyes on her. Arielle sat up and swung her legs over the bed. She groaned and came to her feet, not realizing she was still in a deep haze from being sedated. She wobbled and lost her balance. Gaston reflexively closed his arms around her and pulled her against his hard body to steady her. He cursed inwardly, as severe desire spread through every muscle in his body.

Mortified anger flooded her mind and she tried to pull away. His arms locked around her unyielding like a steel cage, his male hardness pressed against her body. His mouth found hers and his kiss was hard, passionate, and fervent. He moaned and Arielle understood that he was kissing her into forfeit and she wasn't going to let him succeed, so she locked her lips against his. Her disbelief was intermingled with something much bigger, a suffocating revulsion. Gaston noticed tears running down her face and immediately he let her go. He pulled back, as resentment against Sebastian grew even larger. He bit his lower lip, and turning around, he walked toward the door.

"Come on Arielle, we need to leave this boat," he said, without looking back.

"Gaston," she screamed, and he froze. His jaw clenched, his muscles clenched but he didn't turn back to look at her.

"What is it, Arielle," he asked, voice low and calm.

"Where in bloody hell are you taking me?" she cried out. "You can't do this, I'm not going along with your sick plan," she said, and started to sob. Gaston turned around slowly and glare at her, frustration spread across his face. Arielle gasped as he moved using his immortal speed and he was now standing right in front of her. He met her gaze and trapped her in his arms one more time.

"I hate to disagree with your statement, my beautiful princess, but you are going to be with me for a very long time. Therefore you might as well get over yourself and relax. You have nothing to say about this."

Arielle gritted her teeth and *humphed*. "That's ridiculous!" she shrieked. "I'm not going to be with you. I'm in love with Sebastian."

Jealousy coursed through Gaston's body and hit him like a ton of bricks.

"We'll see about that," he said through clenched teeth. He took her arm and pulled her toward the exit. He helped her up the stairs and they were now standing on the top of the deck. She looked around and saw several men moving about the boat but she couldn't see their faces. The night was warm and clear. The moon looked like a huge preciouses stone, nestled in the middle of an enormous silver platter. The sky was crammed with millions of brilliant starts. Under different circumstances, she would smile at the splendor of the night but not tonight. The huge boat had docked against a long poorly lit pier, that lead to somewhere in the distance. Gaston grabbed her wrist and lead her to the side of the boat, and helped her step over onto the pier. There was no need to try and jerk her hand back; his grip was hard as steel and she twitched from pain.

"You're hurting me," she whimpered.

"Then stop fighting me," he said quietly.

How is Sebastian ever going to find me? She reached for Eva's thoughts and mentally invited her in her head to see, what Arielle was experiencing. She continued to walk next to Gaston with Oliver close behind them. As they reached the end of the pier, she could smell the ocean and the strong scent of moist soil filled her nostrils making her flinch.

She tried to survey the area, but it was dark and even in the moonlight she couldn't see anything. Turning to her left, she noticed a set of headlights that were heading their way. A large limo pulled up and the driver jumped out to greet Gaston and Oliver with their first names. He moved around and held the doors open for them.

"Get in," Gaston said softly, but his voice was hard, so she climbed in without any arguments.

She cleared her throat and asked quietly. "So, where are we going?" she waited for an answer, but he didn't reply. She turned to face him in the dim overhead light and all she could see was lust in his eyes and she recoiled. The hurling started all over again in the pit of her stomach as the car rolled into the dark street of this unknown place. She was sure Gaston had used something like chloroform to put her to sleep. Just before she lost consciousness, she remembered the sweet smell when he pressed a piece of cloth over her face. She was still feeling the aftermath of that; her vision was fading in and out. She stared out the window, trying to see something that would give her a small clue of their location, but even with the moonlight there was nothing to see, nothing but trees, water, trees, and more water. Her awareness was telling her that she was here with Gaston, but her body was refusing to believe it. Her jaw muscles tightened and she was sure that if her friends couldn't find her, the result would be dreadful. She closed her eyes and mentally tried to connect with Eva.

"Eva, are you there?"

"Yes, Arielle, I'm here, we're all here," she replied. *"Are you with Annabel?"*

"No, it's not Annabel, It's Gaston."

"Gaston!"

"Yes, Gaston. Oh, God, Eva help me."

"I need you to see something that'll help us find you."

"I'll try my best to find something. Don't leave me."

"I won't, Arielle. Don't worry, we'll find you."

"Tell Sebastian I love him."

"He says the same back."

At Eva's reply, Arielle felt a twinge in her chest, and pressing her lips together, she let out a sigh.

Gaston and Oliver turned and looked at her intently. Their immortal ability made them aware of her anxiety. Oliver stared at her thinking how beautiful Arielle was and smiled delightfully. Gaston reached over, and putting his hand over Arielle's shoulders, he leaned closer and whispered in her ear.

"There's nothing to be afraid off, I'll never let anything happen to you. I love you..." and brushed his lips softly against her ear. Arielle recoiled. "We're almost there," he added, a bit louder.

"Where is there?" she stammered.

"Fortitude is a virtue, my princess," he chuckled.

"Stop calling me that," she said fiercely, and glared back at him. Gaston gazed across at Oliver and smiled.

"I can see this is going to be a challenge for you mate," said Oliver with a throaty laugh, "but I'm sure you're prepared to fully enjoy the ride," he furthered, and they both laughed.

 *Chapter 15*

ARIELLE HAD NO IDEA what all that was about. She dragged in a deep breath, and turning her eyes to the window, she stared out into the darkness. She got lost in her thoughts, as Sebastian's flawless face emerged before her eyes and she sensed his deep green emeralds enveloping her. She shivered with excitement as she recalled their last encounter. Her love for him was so powerful; she could feel it in her bones, in her soul, in her very existence. She couldn't live without him. She was trying to convince herself that she was entangled in a dreadful nightmare and soon she would wake up. She eased back on the seat and closed her eyes, hoping the nightmare would go away, but sadly, when she opened them again, she was still seated in the car next to Gaston. Restless thoughts whirled wildly again, as she had no idea what the next step was going to be.

The car stopped and her wits came back, slamming her brain into complete awareness.

"Eva, the car's stopped," she sent a mental update.

"Play along, Arielle, until we find out where you are."

"Come on, princess," she heard Gaston's strong voice, as his hand grabbed her arm and pulled her out of the car. Arielle pressed her lips together in sheer distaste of the word *"princess"*; she hated the sound of it. Her muscles locked as she felt Oliver's hand pressing against the lower of her back. She looked back at him in utter shock and noticed a creepy smile on his face. She didn't like the look in his eyes, but Gaston didn't seem to pay any attention to any of that. She was now out of the car, as an awakening sensation soared across her body and mind.

She was standing on a round cobblestone driveway in front of an enormous house that at first sight seemed to be nestled in the middle of a thick forest. Besides the huge structure that was brilliantly lit, all she could see were trees and more trees that surrounded every inch of the property. A large marble staircase led up to a tall double door with bright light fixtures on either side of the wall. They walked up the steps and stopped in front of the doors just as they opened, framing a large man. His eyes swept over them and a smile painted his face.

"Mr. Stapleton, Mr. Bertaud, I've been waiting for you. I've everything set up, per your request," he said respectfully. His eyes swept over Arielle and, stepping to the side, he motioned with his hand. "Please come in."

"Thank you, Edward," Oliver said, and patted him on the back.

"Another immortal," Arielle mumbled, groaning. She'd forgotten the impeccable hearing immortals possessed. Edward flushed at the comment and looked up at Oliver. He made some kind of motion so Edward remained silent, sending an acid look her way.

"Is this your house?" she asked looking up at Gaston. He turned to look at her and shook his head.

"No, it belongs to Oliver and we're his guest," he said, and looked away.

"Oh," she said, and *humphed*.

"Arielle, please make yourself comfortable and anything you need, please let Cecil know," Oliver said, pointing somewhere to the left, but Arielle dismissed his comment, keeping her head stubbornly straight ahead.

"I don't need anything from you," she said sharply.

Oliver's voice came out calm and unruffled. "Just in case you do need something, Cecil will be at your disposal." He chuckled at Arielle's repudiation. Arielle kept her gaze straight ahead, trying to ignore their existence, and *humphed* disgustingly. Everything inside the house looked lavish, elegant, typical of immortals, but Arielle wasn't impressed. She felt Gaston's arm on her lower back pushing her softly toward the staircase that lead to the upper level. She could hear the low chuckles from the guys behind her and her anger flared.

A beautiful girl was waiting at the bottom of the stairs. She was sure that she was another immortal. "Cecil, this is Arielle," Gaston said, as they approached her, "Arielle this is Cecil, she'll be at your beck and call." Cecil gazed at Arielle without saying a word, her face unreadable. Gaston's hand burned her skin as he pressed softly against her back, encouraging her to follow Cecil. Her eyes glanced up, and she started to ascent the stairs and fell in behind the girl. She was sure that she was following her to what would be her prison.

"I'll see you in the morning," Gaston called from the bottom of the stairs. Arielle didn't turn to look at him, didn't acknowledged his statement. When they reached the top of the landing, Cecil turned to the left and walked down a long corridor. Arielle peered into all the rooms they passed and she noticed a couple of women moving about. They stopped as she passed and she felt their stares piercing through her. Just from the quick look she gave them, she knew that they were immortals. She inwardly cursed. *This house is crawling with immortals.*

"*Eva, are you getting all this?*"

"*Yes, I'm still here. Try to find something that'll give us a start. We're all here waiting with bated breath.*"

"*I need you, Eva; I need you now more than ever.*"

"*Remain calm, I'm here, I'll not leave you.*"

"*What do I do with Gaston? He seems to want to touch me all the time. I hate him, Eva, he makes me sick.*"

"*Try to endure. A kiss and embrace won't harm you. He'll not try anything more than that. Remember, he's an immortal. They prefer the girl's consent when they're in love, and he's in love with you. He'll give you the time you need. Immortals need total submission before they move to a final encounter. That'll give us time to find you.*"

"Here you are," Cecil's velvety voice broke her mental connection with Eva. Arielle gave her a quick unhappy look that she seemed to totally dismiss. Her face was expressionless as she walked into the room and turned the light on. Arielle blinked, trying to adjust her eyes to the bright light, and walked inside grudgingly. She stopped in the middle of the room and looked around giving it a careful stare. It was quite large for a bedroom. Rich blue, elegant draperies covered three large windows. A stunning dresser rested against the wall with large ornamental chairs on either side. A bed occupied a large amount of space with nightstands on either side. A full-length mirror covered one of 4 ornate panels that seemed to be part of a wall closet. Across from the bed, a large plasma telly hang from the wall, and a few paintings decorated the empty wall spaces. Fresh flower arrangements rested on three different small tables.

Arielle turned and faced Cecil, who was standing at the door waiting for Arielle to dismiss her. Arielle ignored her and, turning back, she walked over to a chair and sat down without saying a word. Cecil took that as a dismissal and walked out, closing the door behind her. Arielle's head snapped upward and stared at the door in utter shock. She clearly heard the lock fall in place. *Good god! I'm a prisoner!* The thought crashed against the walls of her mind and reality sunk to the bit of her stomach like an oversized bolder. Profound wretchedness settled deep into her bones. She fell on the bed and started to sob uncontrollably.

When she next opened her eyes, the clock by the nightstand displayed 3:30 in the morning. It was still dark outside. She got out of bed and shuffled into the bathroom. She needed to take a shower and try to find something that would help Sebastian to locate her. She let the hot water run on her aching body for what it seemed to be eternity, as her thoughts journeyed to a happier place, *Brighton*.

Tears rolled down her face as she finally turned the water off. She was ready to start searching for clues. She wrapped herself in a bath towel and walked back into the bedroom. She strolled around the room slowly. She looked out the window but it was still dark. In the distance she could see the ocean, the moon a huge reflecting, gleaming sphere that splattered silver spurts all across the waves. Everything else looked dark. There were no lights in the distance, nothing that would convey the existence of other life anywhere near this place. She pulled the curtains closed; disappointed, she turned around and went back to the bathroom to pick up her clothes.

She was shocked to find them gone. She tried to recall what she'd done with them, but was sure they were on the bathroom floor just before she walked into the shower. Cecil must've slipped inside the bathroom while she was in the shower and taken them away. What if it was Gaston? She felt an eerie sensation that made her skin crawl. She walked back in the bedroom and sat on the bed, trying to reflect.

She slipped under the covers still wrapped in the bath towel and soon drifted off.

Next time she opened her eyes, it was daylight. She could see a slither of light coming from the closed curtains. She sat up and realized she was still wrapped in the bath towel. She slit off the bed and noticed a tray with a glass of milk and what it looked like toast and a ball of fruit. She ran her fingers through her hair, pondering all the questions that were flooding her mind. *Who came in while I was asleep? Was it Gaston or Cecil? When?* She finally realized that she needed something to wear. She couldn't keep that bath towel wrapped around her for however long she was going to be kept in this room. Reluctantly, she walked over to the dresser.

She pulled the top drawer open and her jaw dropped. Several pairs of expensive underwear and bras were carefully folded and put in place. She pulled the second and third draws open in utter shock. Lingerie upon lingerie, sleepwear, nightshirts, and anything a girl might want. Each item neatly folded and carefully stored. Astounded she looked through them only to find them all in her size. Stunned she walked over to the closet pulling the doors open, and she gasped out loud. The closet was filled with clothes, her size. Dresses, Jeans, T-shirts, sweaters, and much more. A large section held very elegant shoes and sandals her size. She staggered backward totally thunderstruck.

"Oh...my...god...Eva! Eva! *You'll not believe this. Are you there?"*

"*I'm here Arielle, did you find something?"*

"*Eva, I'm shocked beyond belief. The dresser drawers are full of expensive lingerie; sleep wear, bras, and underwear, all in my size. The closet is full of new clothes and shoes in my size!"*

"*It sounds like he had it all planed out, Arielle."*

"*I'm suffocating in here, Eva."*

"*Try to find something. Maybe a tag on the clothes that would show the shop they were purchased from."*

"*What if he manifested everything?"* Arielle thought.

"*Well that might be true, but it doesn't hurt to try. I know you'll find something. Be patient and try to check everything in detail."*

"*All right, I will."*

Arielle broke the connection with Eva and sat back on the bed. She wasn't going to use any of the lingerie Gaston bought for her. Cheating was the word that slammed into her mind. She thought she would be cheating on Sebastian by putting on gifts Gaston purchased for her. She sat there for a long time pondering the thought and finally realized she couldn't walk around with that bath towel. Her clothes were gone so she had absolutely no choice but to wear something.

She chose a pair of underwear and a bra. Next she walked to the closet and picked a pair of jeans and a T-shirt, noting the time on the clock with the corner of her eye. It was 10:30 and she was completely alone. Her stomach growled, but she wasn't going to touch the food. She needed time to search for clues. She walked over to the door and turned the knob. It was locked. Inwardly she cursed and turning around she walked over to the window and pulled the curtains open. She blinked as the sun flooded the room. The view took her breath away.

The garden was a lush green with a large variety of flowers and rich breathtaking colors. At the end of the property stood a thick layer of huge trees and over the treetops in the distance she could see the ocean meeting the clear blue sky at the end of the horizon. The white sandy beach welcomed the waves that rolled in and kissed the sand. It was hard to pull her eyes away from that magnificent sight, but she needed to study her surroundings. She walked to the other side, pulled the curtains open and gasped. She was looking at a tall mountain in the far distance and a dense forest of tall trees between the end of the property and the mountain. Again she couldn't see any sign of life. She tried to open the windows but they seemed to have a special lock that wouldn't budge. She mouthed an oath that startled her. She was utterly upset and overwhelmed with the unknown.

She was ready to face Gaston and give him a piece of her mind, but the morning came and went and Gaston didn't show up. She saw Cecil come in but not a word was spoken. She felt like a wild animal trapped in a zoo. The night they arrived in this house was the last time she saw Gaston. He'd asked Cecil to show her to that dreadful room where she'd been a prisoner for two days now. She spent her time thumbing through a few books that were left on the table, but mostly laying on the bed staring at the ceiling, pondering her options. The telly was there for mere display, because it didn't work.

Arielle was completely shielded from the outside world. She was going stir-crazy in that room, and if not for Eva and their ability to communicate, she would've been completely shattered. Maybe that was what Gaston was trying to achieve. He was trying to break her spirit and gain control over her body and mind. She was getting angry, mostly because he didn't have the guts to face her. She thought it quite strange for a man who vowed his undying love for her to leave her in a locked room without so much as visit.

Cecil came to her room twice in the morning, twice at noon, and twice in the evening bringing a food tray and placing it on the small table by the dresser. Then she would come back and take it away. The food was always untouched. She never looked at Arielle and never uttered a single word. Arielle thought she looked uncomfortable having to be the one to perform that duty. A couple of times when she picked up the full tray, Arielle thought she had an astonished expression on her face, but she remained quiet.

Every time she left the room she locked the door behind her. Arielle clenched her fists. What were they doing? Why were they afraid to let her out of the room? Where was Gaston? Resentment built up and coursed through her like a tidal wave. She was determined to find something to help Sebastian find her. *God I miss him so much!*

She lay back on the bed lost in the passion that embraced her every time thoughts of Sebastian flooded her head. She honestly didn't know if she could live without him. She wanted to cry but knew she had to keep her mind clear. She would have to try and concentrate her efforts in convincing Gaston that after two days she was willing to surrender. That would be the best way for her to find out her location. It would have to be done carefully because Gaston wasn't a fool and certainly not stupid. She would be angry at first and then she would slowly compromise. She thought that was a good plan and she was pleased with her decision. She was starving but she wasn't going to touch the food until she thought it was the right time. She was quite stubborn and would endure.

On the third day Gaston came to see her. She was alarmed that she felt a bit happy to see him. She desperately needed to talk with another person. Cecil wasn't much of a talker. She was actually not a talker at all. In the last two days they hadn't exchanged a single word. Arielle was extremely angry with him for leaving her locked in this room for two days. She wanted to give him a piece of her mind but she held her tongue. He walked in smiling, but she didn't smile back.

"How do you like your room?" Gaston asked.

Anger blazed in Arielle's eyes. Infuriation washed over her like an explosion of an atomic bomb. "I think what you really want to know is how do I like my prison cell? Isn't that right?" she grumbled, her voice irritated. She didn't hear his reply and she didn't care at this point. She knew the answer. All she wanted now was to find something to help Sebastian find her.

She stood and walked around the room, feeling the walls closing on her. She tears of desperation welled up, burning the insides of her eyelids. She shut her eyes and remained unmoved with her back to Gaston. Her lips moved quietly, praying inwardly and she wrapped her arms around her body lost in her nightmare. Startled she snapped her eyes open; Gaston had moved with his immortal speed and stood in front of her. His eyes were on her face, his hands cradling her jaw, his thumbs softly wiping her tears away. She tried to look away, but his hand was a steel trap. Clear blue eyes bored through hers and she was lost. Her breath caught and her heart hammered her chest wildly.

"Why are you crying?" his voice was velvety soft.

"I want to go home," she whimpered.

Gaston felt a pang in his chest. He loved her so much; he hated to see her cry. "I love you, I don't like to see you cry, but I need to do this," he said.

"What is it you need to do?" she asked without looking at him.

"I need to convince you that I'm the right guy for you. Nobody else, and that includes Sebastian, will ever love you as much as I do. I know it's hard for you to believe, but it's true," he murmured, his lips brushing the side of her cheek. "You will be with me forever,"

"You forget that I haven't agreed to be with you," she said firmly.

"Oh, but you will," he said smirking.

"You seem to be sure of yourself."

"Indeed. I'm crazy about you."

"I don't believe you," she said, firmly.

"Why is that?"

"You've locked me in a room for two days, like an animal," she said. "I'm going out of my mind."

"I had another commitment that kept me away. It wasn't my intention to keep you locked in the room, but I didn't want you to wonder alone and maybe have something happening to you. Cecil is my private assistant and she had orders to make sure you're safe." His eyes were searching her face.

He didn't try to hold or kiss her, however he was standing very close. Close enough to make her uncomfortable. Close enough for her to breathe in his intoxicating immortal scent, which made her ache painfully for another man. He looked over her shoulder and his gaze fell on the food tray that was sitting totally untouched.

"Are you on a hunger strike? Or you just don't like the food?" he said, and chuckled. "Would you like for Cecil to bring you something else?"

"I'm not hungry," she said stubbornly.

"Do you go three days without eating when you're at home?"

"No."

"Then why here?"

"I hate being here. I miss my parents and my friends," she said.

"Arielle, I know your parents are away for a whole week and your friends have their own lives. What you're really saying is that you miss that son-of-a-bitch Sebastian. The man who betrayed his best friend by selfishly taking away the only girl that best friend loved." His face radiate a blazing fury. "He's never going to have you. You're mine and I will love you forever." A look of satisfaction filled his eyes.

Arielle was horror-struck but masked her feelings and remained quiet. She wasn't going to get him angry. She was going to follow her plan and endure. His hands cradled her face, making her look up at him. His gaze fell on her lips and, bending, he kissed her softly. Arielle tried to resist but remembering Eva's words she forced herself to relax. Gaston felt her yielding, wrapped his arms around her, and moaned with gratification.

His eyes bored directly into hers and his compelling caught her by surprise. She was now complete under his control. His arms pulled her against his hard muscles and, bending down again, he kissed her sensual lips hungrily, possessively. Her body quivered and she sank into the kiss utterly captivated. Gaston groaned delighted with the results. The kiss was soft at first and then deepened to blistering. He moaned fervently as their lips melted into a more seductive enthrallment. Her lips parted inviting him inside and his passion was palpable. Her perfume filled his nostrils with the intoxicating aroma of freesia and he groaned. His eyes closed in utter bliss and his muscles locked as she shifted pressing herself deeper into his embrace. Her warmth coursed across every muscle, every nerve, and every morsel of his existence. His male rigidity ached as he plundered into the kiss. *God!* he thought. *If this is heaven, I'm never going to let her go. I'll sell my soul to the devil to keep her in my arms for eternity.*

A few minutes passed and he was still lost in the bliss of Arielle. He'd forgot that his compelling would fade. He was startled when she pushed against him and he snapped his eyes open. Inwardly he cursed knowing that'd he messed up his chance by losing himself in his wild passion. Arielle blinked and her face-hardened.

"What...are...you...doing?" she demanded, trying to keep her voice down.

His voice was velvety soft, full of passion, desire, and frustration.

"I'm in love with you," he groaned, pulled her hard against him, trapped her arms and kissed her hard, demanding. He pulled back and watched her waiting for her to scream again, but she didn't.

Arielle knew it was her fault for letting him compel her. She would make sure it didn't happen again.

"What? No screaming, no cursing?" His eyes never left her face.

"I want to be alone," she murmured and turned away. "I'm tired."

Gaston was dumfounded. Her reaction wasn't what he'd expected. He pursed his lips, turned, and walked to the door. He was pleased with the results. She didn't scream, didn't hit him, and didn't push him away. For Gaston that was progress. He smiled wide.

"If you need anything, push this button." He pointed to a white small button next to the light switch. "There are people here to fulfill your every wish." His eyes were still searching her face.

"I wish to go home," she said.

To that he didn't reply. He opened the door and stepped in the hallway. "I'll be back to see you a little later," he said softly. The door closed behind him. Eva was right; her plan was working. He didn't lock the door.

Eva, Gaston compelled me. He caught me by surprise and I didn't have time to look away.

Yes, I felt the kiss, I want to throw up.

Same here. I'll be more careful next time. Don't tell Sebastian, I don't want him to worry," she sniffled.

I won't. He's in a pretty bad mood.

I'm not sure I can keep up the charade; I don't have any warm emotions about Gaston. All I have is loathing.

Arielle, you must stay calm, we're going to find you, trust me. I've never failed you and I'm not going to start now. Do you trust me?

Yes, I do.

Please try to look for clues. Look at things a lot closer. Find details, anything that might be of interest. I'm connected with your thoughts so let me know when you find something.

Eva pursed her lips in frustration. It had been two and a half days and they had absolutely nothing. They didn't know where to go, where to look.

 *Chapter 16*

UTTERLY FRUSTRATED, ARIELLE walked to the window and looked outside, trying to collect her thoughts. She gazed at the ocean, filled with exasperation, and groaned. Slowly she turned and her eyes fell on the beautiful painting next to the window. It portrayed a picturesque sandy beach and crystal blue waters. She closed her eyes and could almost feel the warm breeze brushing against her skin, almost hear the waves lapping against the shore, and smell the lushness of the sea mist. Loneliness enveloped her remembering another painting, a birthday gift from Sebastian. She sighed profoundly as her eyes roamed the painting, trying to absorb every little detail. Suddenly her eyes stopped at the bottom right corner of the canvas. It wasn't the signature of the artist she was focused on, but the small letters below the signature. She peered much closer and her breath held. V Fiji, were the small letters below the signature. *V Fiji,* she repeated inwardly. Her alertness piqued, she moved to the next painting, and the next. She verified that all four paintings had the same letters. Her heart began to race and she felt like screaming aloud in sheer bliss. She immediately mentally spoke to Eva.

Eva! she exclaimed.

I'm here, Arielle, did you find something?

I think so.

What is it?

There are four paintings in this room and at the bottom of each is the painter's signature along with two more words. V Fiji. Eva, I think I'm in

Fiji, possibly at one of the islands that begins with the letter 'V.' I'll check further; maybe I can find something more.

Arielle, that's great! That will give us a place to start. I'll contact Sebastian right now.

I love you, Eva, she sobbed.

I love you, too, Eva replied.

*   *   *

Arielle closed her eyes. She was now filled with hope and anticipation. She strolled back to the window and gazed at the thick forest. The leaves swaying in the breeze made her smile. The smile froze when she spotted a black car pulling away from the house slowly. She focused on the tag FIJI LD-432 and her heart thudded.

Eva! Eva! I'm in Fiji. I am looking at a car that's leaving the house and the tag shows Fiji. And there's one more thing.

What is it, Arielle?

There's a very tall mountain behind the house.

Arielle, that's great! That's a huge clue. There are very few islands in Fiji with mountains or high elevations.

Fiji! Eva thought. She resisted the need to scream. Her inward shock was overwhelming, but she kept the need in check. She didn't want to frighten Arielle any further than she already was. She knew there were over 300 islands in Fiji, which made their search a bit more complicated.

Fantastic! I'll contact Sebastian; let me know if you see anything that might make the search easier. We'll ready to leave for Fiji at once. Everyone's here. Be brave; try to keep Gaston clueless.

Excitement flooded Arielle's mind and she felt overwhelmed. She tried again to open the window. She was so obsessed with getting some fresh air that suddenly she felt smothered. She was trapped and needed to be outside. She started to hyperventilate and staggered to the bed. She inhaled huge amounts of air, and exhaled deeply. She did that several times, but it didn't seem to help and she fainted. She opened her eyes slowly and blinked several times. She lay in bed, trying to recall the last thing she remembered. Footsteps alerted her and she sat up facing the door. The knob turned slowly. Gaston pushed the door wide-open, expression filled with joy.

"How are you feeling?" he said softly.

"As well as can be expected considering I can't even open the window to get some fresh air," she replied with a frown.

Gaston approached. "Would you like to take a walk?"

"Outside?" she cried out.

"Of course. Where else?" he said, chuckling. He looked at the table and saw the tray of food completely untouched.

"Not hungry, love?" he added, as if it was natural. He stood by the bed looking down at her. "Arielle, you have to try and adjust to your new life. I wish I could make you understand how happy I can make you. I can give you the world and more," he said, and sat next to her.

"I want to go home. I miss my parents and friends," she whimpered not looking at him.

"You can have all that back, with one request," he said, the smile never leaving his face.

"What is that?"

"You'll have to give up Sebastian. You're never going to marry him and he's never going to be in your life." Arielle winced, but she didn't say anything. "I'm in your life now. You...are...mine..." he said, his voice was soft but firm.

I'll never be yours, she thought. She remained quiet, following Eva's advice to keep him clueless. He was suddenly on his feet and pulled her up, trapping her in his embrace.

"What's wrong with me?" he asked. "Why don't you want me?"

"Gaston, I'm not ready to give you an answer right now. I need time," she said and pressed her lips together.

"I need to know your thoughts right now," he pressed.

She kept her face blank and her voice came out calm and steady. "Gaston, you're beautiful, you're astonishing, any girl would die to be with you, but not *me*. At least not right now. I'm in love with Sebastian. I've already given myself to him, body and soul. I can't just change the way I feel just because you asked me," she stated.

"I do understand that you need time," he murmured. "But I want you to know that I don't want any other girl. I've only ever wanted you and you alone," he said, trying to reason with her. "I'll give you all the time that you need, and oh! How I wish you'd change your mind. It'll be much more gratifying that way," he said.

"What do you mean?" Arielle recoiled. She knew exactly what he was talking about.

"Arielle, I'm not going to hurt you, I love you and I'm not going to force you into anything. However, I'm here to stay, so it's your decision on how you want to go about this, I mean about us. I'll wait for you, for as long as you want me to wait," His voice dropped to a mere whisper.

"You might have to wait for a long time," she warned.

His eyes narrowed to slits and then he smiled wide. "I'll wait..." his voice trailed. "Remember that I've all the time in the world," he said and chuckled.

Eva's advice was working wonderfully. Arielle needed to remain calm and let Gaston believe that she needed time to adjust. She needed that time to find some more clues for Eva. So when his hand cradled her jaw and pulled her face up to meet his, she didn't resist. His lips pressed against hers softly and then he let her go.

"That's better," he said. "There's no need to fight me, I'll never hurt you," he said, again softly.

She nodded and he kissed her again.

"Are you hungry?" he asked. Arielle couldn't see any reason to resist food any longer. She was starving.

"Yes," she replied.

Gaston smiled, pleased, and, taking her hand, pulled her toward the small table with the food tray.

"Is this okay or would you like something else?"

"No, that's fine," she replied. She sat in the chair and Gaston took a seat across from her.

"Gaston, can I ask you a question?" Arielle said.

"Anything at all," he replied, eagerly, happy that she was finally talking.

"Why did you lock me in the room for two days?"

"Oh, that," he said and waved his hand dismissively. "I didn't want you to wander in the dark before you got familiar with the house and the surroundings," he said softly.

"Oh," was all she said. She sank her teeth into the sandwich and he watched her blissfully. She drained the milk and ate half the fruit in the bowl.

"I love you," he murmured. "I'll never get tired of telling you that."

She forced a half smile and that seemed to be enough to send Gaston to silly blissfulness. When she was finished eating, she stood and went to wash her hands.

"Would you like to take that walk now? I'll show you the house and the property," he offered.

"Yes, I'd love that," she said eagerly. "I need some fresh air." She was going to look for obvious clues. She wiped her mouth and stepped out of the bathroom. Gaston took her hand, a smile on his face and led her out the door.

He showed her the house and introduced her to the help. She noticed that there were 4 women and 3 men who took care of the house. They were very nice, very friendly and all of them immortal. So in total there were 11 immortals in the house, including Cecil, Edward, Oliver and Gaston. She was gathering all that information and passing it telepathically to Eva.

They finally stepped outside into the glorious day. Arielle inhaled a large amount of fresh air and it seemed to give her amazing strength, renewing her mind and body. They walked slowly toward the end of the property and she was astounded. The density of the forest was totally breathtaking. She could smell the ocean and it made her smile.

"Why are you smiling?" Gaston asked. He'd been watching her face and her changing expressions.

"Oh, several reasons," she said.

"Can you share any of those reasons?" he asked, imploringly. She remained quiet for a short time. When she spoke her voice was soft like a whisper.

"I can hear the waves lapping against the sand, smell the salt of the ocean and feel the breeze from the trees brush against my skin," she said.

Gaston squeezed her hand and she looked up at him. His face was blissful and jubilant. "All I can see is you," he murmured, and she laughed. Her laugh stroked his very soul. He couldn't remember another moment in his long life that he felt as happy as he did right then and there.

However Arielle's thoughts were far from Gaston; they were resting on another flawless face and she sighed inwardly. She looked back and saw Oliver watching her intently from a window on the second floor. An uneasy shiver coursed through her body and fear spread.

"What's wrong with your friend?" she asked, looking up at Gaston.

"Who do you mean?"

"Oliver, of course," she said, pressing her lips together.

"Why? Did he say something to you when I was gone?"

"No, I never saw him, but when I do see him, he has a creepy look on his face," she said.

"Don't worry about Oliver. He's happily married. He just admires a beautiful girl when he sees one." He chuckled.

"Where are we?" she murmured. She tried to make her voice totally indifferent.

"We're on a beautiful island. Away from any person who would interfere with you and me getting to know each other," Gaston said softly.

"What island?" she asked. "Gaston, I can't leave and I can't tell anyone else, so why can't you tell me?" Arielle's voice was a little shaken but filled with anticipation that she might be able to tell Eva her location tonight. "Are you going to keep me in the dark for as long as we're together?" she asked casually.

He seemed to bonder the thought. "I'll tell you tomorrow."

"All right," she agreed, not wanting to alarm him.

They spent a considerable amount of time walking through the beautiful manicured gardens, the twisting paths that stretched among the flowerbeds, and the perfectly trimmed hedges. Three large fountains made the view even prettier. When they reached the edge of the property her breath caught from the stunning beauty of the forest that stretched ahead. Arielle's eyes traveled across the large trees plush with dense foliage, countless trunks and branches covered with moss.

Gaston took her hand and pulled her down a small trail filled with green sprouts, swaths of beautiful ferns and amazing vegetation growing in frenzied abundance. She heard the sound of running water and soon they came upon a wide creek with crystal clear water rushing down from the mountain toward the ocean. The beauty of the place was something she couldn't get over. They were deep into the woods when she noticed a gray building nestled in the middle of the forest. It looked like a church with a narrow structure attached to the right of it. The narrow structure was taller than rest of the building but the thick trees prevented her from being able to see the top.

"What's this building?" she asked Gaston, pointing at the structure.

"That's a very old church, with a tall bell tower. It's not in use any longer. Just a beautiful structure that remains as an old landmark," he said quietly.

"Does it have a bell on the top?"

"Yes, the belfry reaches way above the trees. The density of the forest doesn't give you a clear view from the ground.

"Can we go there?" she asked.

"How about doing that tomorrow," he suggested. "It's getting late and I have another commitment in about an hour."

She nodded agreeably and he seemed very pleased. Anxiety crept over Arielle. She wasn't sure how long she could keep up the charade.

"Are you tired?" he asked.

"I'm not," she said softly. There was a long pause and then he took her hand again and turned toward the house. When he left her at her door, he drew her closer, leaning in, he pressed a passionate kiss on her lips. Arielle tensed then raised her head and kissed him back. Utter shock coursed through Gaston's body and his breath shivered.

"Thank you," he murmured. "I'll come back later. We'll have dinner downstairs in the dining room. Will that be all right with you?" he asked softly. She nodded in agreement and he walked away in sheer shock.

Gaston couldn't contain himself. He couldn't believe the change in Arielle.

When the door closed, Arielle let out a low growl. She fell on the bed and closed her eyes hauling in a deep breath. Her resentment toward Gaston grew by the minute. The frustration over having her life interrupted in such a horrible manner was mammoth. She wanted to believe she was living a nightmare, and any second now she'd wake to discover that the recent events were just a dreadful hallucination. She wanted to be back in Sebastian's arms. She wanted to get lost once again in that deep green ocean that made life worth living. She wanted to be there for her wedding day. Scorching tears welled, burning the inside of her eyelids and searing soft skin as they trickled down her face. She got out of bed and walked over to the window.

Gaston, on the other hand was delighted with the outcome. He had absolutely no reason to suspect anything unusual. They were in a remote island, thousands of miles away from Brighton, and Arielle had absolutely no way of communicating with a single soul. He smiled, trying to convince himself that maybe Arielle realized there was no way out of this situation. This was now her new life. So he thought...

 *Chapter 17*

GRITTING HER TEETH, Eva speed-dialed Sebastian. "She's in Fiji," she said breathlessly.

"Fiji!" His voice hitched, and his body stiffened.

"Yes," Eva said. "She's not sure where in Fiji, but she thinks the island's name may begin with the letter V."

"Why in bloody hell Fiji?" he cried aloud. The surprising awareness that they actually had a firm location overwhelmed him. Swallowing a curse, Sebastian drew a deep breath. "Is she all right?"

Eva understood his state of mind. "She's fine Sebastian. She also said that there's a tall mountain behind the house. As you very well know there aren't very many mountainous islands in Fiji. That's a great clue and we should be able to minimize the number of Islands we need to search," she said.

"I agree. I'll do a little research and have the details when you get here," he said.

"Ian and I will be right over," she said softly. They were dressed and out of the house within a few minutes.

They were stunned to find all of Sebastian's immortal friends there, ready to offer him their complete support once again. Eva looked around and smiled wide. Thirteen amazing, robust, vigorous immortals were more than ready to rescue Arielle. Jon, Pierre, Jacques, Antonius, Girard, and Giani warmly greeted Ian and Eva. They'd all rushed to Sebastian's side. Christian and Isabella were there. Loren had never left, and even Nathan Shilton came to help his friend in his time of need.

They all gathered in the library to put down a well-thought-out plan. Sebastian sensed his world was coming apart, and he was struggling desperately to grasp his levelheadedness. His heart thudded with eagerness as something very powerful surged through his thoughts. His arms ached, his lips twisted, he couldn't imagine his life without Arielle. He loved her deeply, powerfully, and passionately. He needed her more than he needed air. She needed to be back where she belonged—in his warm embrace. He turned to face his friends with a thankful smile. "I just can't tell you what this means to me. I'm confident that together we can bring Arielle home safely, because without her I'm completely lost." Sebastian wasn't sure whom he was trying to convince about her safe return; his friends or himself. He drew a deep breath and tried to still his mind feeling his pulse pounding his temples wildly. He started to pace again.

He stopped pacing and scanned over the eager immortal faces. "It's déjà vu all over again," he said bitterly. "We have to put in place a foolproof plan that will guarantee her freedom without creating problems for any of us." He stopped pacing, sat and began to elaborate on the bit of information Eva had provided thus far. "Eva connected with Arielle," he said. "She's in Fiji!" He saw everyone's face reflect shock and continued. "The name Fiji is displayed on a few paintings in her room, right below the artist's signature. She also saw a Fiji tag on a car leaving the house. So we're sure she's in Fiji, but exactly were, we're not sure."

"Is Gaston the same guy who was at Eva's wedding reception with Annabel?" Giani asked.

"Yes, he's the same rogue," Sebastian said. A curse escaped him and he pursed his lips irately. "Something that maybe helpful is that Arielle noticed the letter V preceding the word Fiji on those paintings. She also told Eva there's a tall mountain behind the house. She'll continue looking for landmarks and other things to help make our search easier." He breathed deep and continued. "The presence of the letter V led Eva believe that the name of the island may begin with the letter V. This won't be an easy undertaking, but given our speed and ability we should be able to find her," he said anxiously and looked around the room to get his friends' approval.

They all nodded in agreement. Sebastian rose and started to pace again, hands clasped behind his back. "The fact is that out of 322 islands in Fiji, only 106 are inhabited," he continued. "I'm afraid my assumption might not be accurate, but after doing some quick research, the number of islands that begin with the letter V are exactly 7. Taking into consideration the existence of a mountain, the number of islands we should be interested in narrows to exactly 5. I think we should first check those islands and if we can't find her there, then we'll spread across Fiji and check every inch of the remaining islands." He winced at the thought of not being able to find her quickly. He was, however, determined, as was everyone else in the room.

"Do we have anything else that might help to locate Arielle quickly?" Jon asked, gazing at Sebastian thoughtfully.

Sebastian's lips twitched in anxiety. "Arielle told Eva that the house has three levels, with countless rooms and long corridors. That makes me believe the house is massive. She also said it's hidden in a dense forest between the ocean and a very tall mountain."

Jacques turned to face Eva. "Eva, let us know as soon as you have something more from Arielle."

"Our minds are open to each other. I will text when I have something new," Eva promised.

Sebastian looked around to be sure there were no other questions before he continued. "There are 5 islands that begin with the letter V and are mountainous and there are thirteen of us. Do you want to make your own choices or do you want me to do it for you?" Sebastian asked, glancing around the room.

"Go ahead, Sebastian," Antonius said, eager to get started.

Sebastian quickly wrote down the names of the 5 islands, then made the assignments. "Viti Levu is the largest of those islands, so I think Christian, Isabella, Loren. and myself will search that area together," he said. "Vanau Levu will need a few people as well, as it's the next largest in the bunch, so Nathan, Ian. and Eva will go to that one." He assigned Vanua Balavu to Jon and Piere, Vatu Vara to Antonius and Giani, and finally, Vunisea to Jacques and Girard.

"Hopefully," he said, "she'll be on one of those islands. If we don't find her in any of those islands we'll regroup and scan every inch of the other islands as well." His expression was wrathful, muscles clenched, lips stretched to a thin line. "The fact is that she's in Fiji," he continued. "Anything you find, make sure we know. Now's a good time to exchange telephone numbers if they've changed from the last time we did this," he said. chuckling bitterly. He hauled in a deep breath, made 10 copies of the list and handed them to each one.

A couple of hours had passed since they'd gathered in the study, and they were all eager to find Arielle. As they started to disperse Eva's voice drew them all to a halt.

*   *   *

Arielle got out of bed and wiped her tears away. She walked to the window overlooking the dense forest that extended all the way to the foothills of the mountain. She squinted at the bright sunlight and focused toward the place where she remembered seeing the gray bell tower. She smiled wide when she saw out in the distance the top of the gray structure peering through tree canopies in brilliant gold and a bell that was now sparkling in the sunlight like a jewel of freedom. *Her freedom.*

*   *   *

Arielle's thoughts surrounded Eva, and Eva's expression became intense.

Hmm, Sebastian thought, brows lifting inquisitively. He moved close to Eva and waited agonizingly. Eva listened fixedly, making notes, using a vastly superior note-taking method, her mind-map. She founded that easier to use to recall details and scan through them quickly with accuracy anywhere, anytime. Arielle's voice came through fervently.

Eva, are you there?
Yes, Arielle, we're all here,
Is Sebastian there?
Yes, he's right here.

Eva pursed her lips feeling Arielle's sadness. Her eyes flickered to Sebastian and she could clearly see his excruciating expression.

"What's she saying?" Sebastian asked eagerly.

"She's asking about you," Eva said and he groaned painfully.

Eva, Arielle's thoughts came pouring into Eva's mind. *Gaston just left the room. I took your advice and made him feel at ease. He thinks I might be considering his offer. I took a walk with him and found that a very thick forest surrounds this house. I can see the ocean on one side and the mountain on the other. There's nothing in sight but trees, water and more water. I did notice an old church in the forest adjacent to the property. A gray narrow medieval-type of bell tower is attached to the right side of the building. The church itself is located on the west side of the property facing the foothills of the mountain. I couldn't see the top of it from where we stood.*

The density of the forest didn't give me a view of the top and Gaston wasn't going to take me up close. However, windows surround my room. I looked outside as soon as I got back and located the bell tower in the distance; I'm looking at it right now. It peeks over the thick canopies; the top of the belfry is gold and the bell sparkles in the afternoon sunlight. A wall approximately 10 feet high surrounds the property. There's a main gate and 3 smaller gates that exit to the rainforest. There are surveillance cameras inside the house. Finally she stopped pouring thoughts into Eva's head, waiting for Eva's response.

Arielle! That's great news. We now have a couple of landmarks: the mountain and the bell tower. You know that's more than enough to find you. I'll be open to your thoughts and anything else you give me I'll pass it on to the others," Eva thought joyfully. Her spirit was now calmer, which inadvertently eased Arielle.

"What is it?" almost everyone in the room asked in unison. They'd turned to face Eva.

She folded her arms and pursed her lips. "Arielle found another important landmark." She told them all about the bell tower. "She also said there's a wall with security gates around the property and she's pleading for us to find her soon."

Sebastian clenched his fists and his growl was loud and heartfelt by his friends.

"Sebastian, are you going to be all right, man?" Nathan said understandingly.

"Yes...yes..." he mumbled, and his voice drifted. Frowning he looked at his friends. "Keep in touch at all times."

That was his last request. Soon they were all gone...

* * *

Jon and Pierre arrived at Vanua Balavu eager to find Arielle. It didn't take long to cover the small island and find out that there were absolutely no large estates or tall mountains. The few people inhibiting the area spread between small villages nestled along the coastline. They did observe the amazing scenery and the breathtaking blue waters. It was a tropical paradise but not where they'd find Arielle. They texted Sebastian and advised him of their findings. They agreed to join Ian, Eva and Nathan in Vanua Levu.

As soon as Antonius and Giani arrived at Vatu Vara they became aware that this island was also sparsely populated. It was covered with dense tropical jungles and limestone cliffs. Lagoons enveloped the island in a teal embrace. The beaches and broad-fringing reefs surrounding the island were amazing and draped with pure white sand. But there were no signs of large mountains or large estates. This island was definitely not the place where Arielle was held. Jacques and Girard reported the exact same findings from Vunisea. They all texted Sebastian and he asked the four of them to join him at Viti Levu. This island was the largest in Fiji so he could use more people to cover every inch.

"Have you heard from Eva?" Antonius texted.

"No, not just yet, but Jon and Pierre are going to join Eva in Vanua Levu," he replied.

When Eva, Ian and Nathan reached Vanau Levu, they were amazed by the rugged mountain range. "This may be the place," Eva said, glancing between Ian and Nathan. "We have the mountains and the ocean. We now need to look for a bell tower and a large estate somewhere in the middle of one of these rainforests," she furthered. Using their immortal speed, they decided to start at the south side of the island, move carefully and search the island in great detail. This was the second largest island in Fiji and it looked as if there was a possibility of finding Arielle hidden somewhere here. They would look for the three landmarks she'd provided. They passed gorgeous landscapes brimming with rainforests, coconut plantations and fantastic views of the ocean. As they moved slowly and vigilantly they noticed huge green fields of sugar cane on the west coast. The island seemed to be surrounded by magnificent coral reefs. Expensive plantations and private estates were appeared here and there but none of them nestled in the middle of any of the rainforests and or surrounded by a tall stonewall. However the view gave it a surreal kind of quality. Eva's mobile rang. She pulled it out of her jean pocket and answered.

"Eva, Pierre and I are going to join you. There's nothing in Vanua Balavu," Jon said on the other end. "I texted Sebastian and he agreed we should join you."

"Sure, come on. The more the merrier," she chuckled.

"Where are you?" Jon asked. Eva gave him their location and it wasn't long before he and Pierre joined them. They were getting deeper into the rainforests covered by thick canopies and she thought it would be a good idea to ring Sebastian.

"Sebastian, I think Vanau Levu might be the right place. We're going to look for the landmarks Arielle provided," Eva said.

Sebastian sighed, and anticipation flashed powerfully in his brain. He looked across the expanse of land, forest lines and ragged mountain peaks and shook his head thoughtfully. "Eva," he said faintly. "Viti Levu has high elevations and thick rainforests. There are high possibilities that we may find those landmarks here. Let me know what you find and I'll do the same," Sebastian said and ended the call.

* * *

Eva put the phone back in her pocket and *humphed*. She stood still for a moment and then followed the men as they resumed their search. They'd gone through every rainforest on the island, crossed every river, searched between the mountain, hills, and coastlines but they never found an estate surrounded by a tall stone wall to match Arielle's description or an old church with a tall bell tower. Her heart sunk and she felt deep disappointment.

Ian reached for her hand and she slipped it into his, pressing her lips together. "Sorry baby," he murmured. "We'll find her. She must be in Viti Levu if she's not here. Let's call Sebastian," he suggested and gave her a peck on the cheek.

"You're right, we've exhausted every inch of this island, every possible corner." She took her mobile out again and speed dialed. "Sebastian, she's definitely not here," Eva said disappointedly.

"Well, I've a strong feeling that she's here. Don't ask me how, I just do," he said anxiously. "Let's meet and we can continue the search together. The sun's going down but there's still a lot of daylight left. We're just now reaching the middle part of the island. We can see in the far distance the ragged peaks of a tall mountain and we're all sure that this is the right place."

"How do we find you?" Eva asked.

"Let's meet at the city of Nadi. It's a small quiet town. We'll wait for you at the entrance of the Nadi Garden of the Sleeping Giant. It's a main tourist spot and it'll be easy to find."

"All right, we'll be there shortly," Eva said.

*　　*　　*

It was a bit late in the afternoon but still a lot of tourists were walking through the gardens admiring the collection of tropical orchids, and all the other strange plants from Fiji. Loren walked up to the sign in the front and read out loud. "Two thousand varieties of orchids." She stood staring at the words as she read over them a couple of time and *humphed* in wonder. The others looked around; they already knew what they had to do and there was very little talk. It'd been less than an hour and they were pleased to see their friends approaching, eager to get on with the search. A few hugs and handshakes and they were on their way.

"Have you connected with Arielle?" Sebastian asked Eva.

"I have, and I've let her know we're close," she replied patting his hand.

Sebastian looked at her gratefully and gave her a warm smile. The thought of Arielle made his skin tingle, his arms ache and his heart pound. He felt his world falling apart without her in it and the sensation deepened. "This island seems to be heavily populated,"

Sebastian said. "But the east side is less populated and less visited. I'm of the mind that's the perfect place for the house and location Arielle described." He looked around and saw everyone nodding in agreement. They spread out and made sure to comb the grounds carefully without leaving a piece of earth unexplored or a single stone unturned.

They passed many historical sites, rain forests with waterfalls and remote villages. The steep mountains ahead of them had rugged peaks just as Arielle described. The cities and villages weren't very impressive but the beaches and rainforest were a different story. They were now reaching Viti Levu Bay at the northeast coast and all they could see were endless sugar cane fields, rolling grass hills and a mangrove-lined ocean seldom viewed by human eyes. Twilight was upon them but the immortal vision was just as perfect in the dusk as it was in bright sunlight. They'd arrived at the northern part of the island that looked the least developed and passed Navala, a very small village that seemed to be the last one with any type of civilization before they reached the thick line separating the sugar cane fields from the lush rainforest. On the left side mountain scenery appeared beyond the treetops and on the right side the coastline.

Sebastian's blood started to pound in his veins. "This has to be the island..." he murmured.

Viti Levu was quiet, drenched in the beauty of the twilight. A light breeze was blowing and the moon provided a clear view of the island but under the trees the shadows loomed like ghosts. They were now deep into the forest and it wasn't long before they stumbled at the steps of a Gothic architecture old church. To the right of the structure stood a huge gray stone bell-tower that seemed to rise and disappear above the tree canopies. Eva gasped and grabbed Ian's hand. They all knew they were at the right place. Immediately adrenalin kicked in and their minds became overwhelmed with inconceivable vigilance.

Blood pounded their ears while they tuned to every sound around them no matter how mild. Eagerness grasped their senses while watchfulness crept in. They talked to each other in that soundless immortal movement of their lips and stalked quietly like ghosts in the night. Sebastian's face radiated restlessness and his lips curved to a remarkable smile. Every grain in his body, every particle in his mind told him to run toward the house and not stop until Arielle was safe in his arms, but he resigned himself in pursuing Arielle's rescue according to plan.

When they reached the end of the forest line, a small gasp escaped Loren and she immediately capped her mouth with her hand. Eva put her index finger to her lips, making sure they kept quiet. They knew from Arielle that the house was full of immortals able to hear faint sounds clearly for miles away. The house stood before them like a silent giant in the night, dark and soundless, surrounded by a 10-foot stone wall.

Everyone was alert searching the shadows making sure there were no guards larking in the woods to prevent anyone from getting close to the wall. They couldn't dismiss the idea that Gaston would take extra measures to make sure nothing disturbed his plans. They moved through the woods like shadows in the night. They surrounded the house clearing every obstacle in their way, making sure to suppress any conflict that might alert the people inside the house. They found no one guarding the outside of the wall. They scaled the wall effortlessly and dropped on the other side soundlessly. They shrunk behind the large hedges growing against the wall and stood still trying to get their bearings. Inwardly sighing Sebastian kept his eyes wide open and his mind alert.

Antonius, Gerard, Giani, and Nathan were to clear the back of the house. Sebastian, Jon, Jacques, and Pierre were to clear the front, while Loren, Christian and Isabella moved to the left and Ian with Eva walked to the right.

It wasn't long before they observed men posted at four different locations close to the hedges in groups of two. Antonius saw a slight movement by a tall hedge a few feet from him to his left. He stopped breathing keeping in the shadows. He glanced to his right and saw Gerard, Giani, and Nathan. He pointed and they nodded letting him know that they'd seen the same movement. They searched the night and identified that in fact only those two men were guarding the back of the house.

The sound of a lighter clicking snapped their attention back to where the guards stood. The faces behind the lighter flame were that of two young males. They lit their cigarettes and the flame went out.

They exchange a few words and a couple soft laughs and turned to walk in opposite directions to safeguard the grounds in back of the house.

Antonius waved Gerard and Giani to cover the guy on the right while he and Nathan crept toward the guy on their left. Nathan picked up a large rock and threw it in the center of the backyard.

Both young men spun around on high alert to follow the sound. Before they realized what was going on, they were facing 4 very angry immortals. They had no time to alert anyone in the house or use their weapons. They were the first two victims of the night. The immortals noticed that both guards were human. Since they'd all agreed to keep their mobile phones on vibrate, Antonius texted the others to let them know that the two guards in the back of the house were eliminated, and that the guards were human, which made their job a lot easier.

Ian and Eva had no problem in eliminating their guards and neither did Loren, Christian and Isabella.

Sebastian, Jon, Jacques and Pierre scanned the front of the house, making sure they only had to eliminate two guards. They were aware that their friends had clear the back and sides of the house. However they'd have to be very careful, because Arielle told Eva that all the bedrooms faced the front gardens.

They saw their friends approaching from all sides keeping between the tall hedges and dense greenery surrounding the grounds. The stars were the only faint light and the night was dark and full of shadows. They weren't sure that they weren't going to face more guards than what they originally observed. They also had to disconnect the power to disable the cameras inside and disengage any alarms that might go off when they entered the house.

It wasn't long before they located and eliminated the rest of the guards. They moved quietly and searched the sides of the house to locate the power box. Sebastian gestured to a spot on the wall behind a tall bush and quickly opened it, slipped his fingers inside and pulled all the wires apart disabling all the power to the house. They remained quiet listening for any sounds or alerts but there was nothing.

They crept alongside the house and stopped at the front door. They paused and waited. Sebastian let Giani step in front of them, as he was the expert in breaking through any lock. He took a little tool out of his pocket and picked through the lock carefully; never more obvious that he was an expert. He then step aside and let Sebastian push the door wide open. They held their breaths worried about creaking sounds but there was absolute silence and they breathed in relief. They moved quickly inside and Ian closed the door behind them.

Based on the information they had from Arielle, most of the occupants were using bedrooms on the first and second floors. Only Oliver, Gaston, and Arielle used the third floor. Giani, Gerard, Ian, Loren, and Pierre took the first floor. Jon, Jacques, Christian, and Isabella crept up to the second floor while Nathan, Sebastian, Antonius, and Eva quickstepped up to the third floor. They were all to wait quietly until they saw Eva bring Arielle down the stairs and safely outside.

There was no further discussion but a clear understanding that they were to eliminate every single immortal in the house to avoid future revenge attacks and long battles from anyone who would remain alive.

On the top of the landing Sebastian glanced back and saw his friends prowling quietly toward the servant's quarters. His breath stilled as he felt Eva's hand slip into his. Holding tightly, she pulled him toward the left of the corridor. They reached the last door on the right and stopped to listen for any sounds but there was nothing but quiet.

 *Chapter 18*

ARIELLE LAY IN BED, hands behind her head, knowing that Sebastian was already on the island along with everyone else. Thanks to Eva and their wordless communication she knew her horrible ordeal was coming to an end. Soon she would be in Sebastian's arms. She closed her eyes and saw his beautiful face with those stunning flawless features. The muscular body with arms of steel, the amazing emerald ocean of his eyes, and the sensuous lips that made her lungs lock every time they kissed. Her emotions leaped, her breathing picked up, knowing that shortly they could go on with their lives as if nothing happened. Suddenly Eva's thoughts poured in her head and her heart skipped a beat.

Arielle, we're here. Stay alert but don't make any sound.

Oh, God, Arielle thought. Anxiety spread across her body not believing that Sebastian was but a few feet away. Her pulse raced and she sat up on the bed. She tip-toed close to the window and carefully lifted the corner of the curtain but couldn't see a thing. She stood silently waiting. She could hear the blood pounding her ears and rubbed her hands anxiously.

* * *

Nathan and Antonius stood with their backs to Eva and Sebastian keeping a watchful eye so nobody surprised them. Sebastian set his hand on the doorknob. The thought that Arielle was on the other side of this door made his pulse hammer his temples painfully. He turned the handle slowly, soundlessly and walked into the dark room with Eva on his heels. They saw clearly Arielle standing at the window with her back toward them, trying to pierce through the dark. Sebastian moved with his amazing speed and stood right behind her like a phantom, his pulse pounding wildly. He put one hand over Arielle's mouth and with the other pulled her tight against his body. *Oh! What a feeling!* he thought.

Arielle was so startled her legs nearly gave in. She started to struggle by pulling away from the hands she thought belonged to Gaston. She tried to yell but was unable to make a sound. The voice that caressed her ears calmed her senses and sent her heart leaping to new heights as tears started to fall uncontrollably down her face.

"Hey, baby, did you miss me?" he murmured, his lips brushing her ear making her legs limp. "Try not to talk; we need to move quickly and get you outside. Follow Eva, do you understand?"

She nodded and he took his hand away from her mouth. Arielle twisted in his arms and threw herself against him. Her arms wrapped around his neck tightly and her lips met his in a wild fevered kiss that sent pure fire between their bodies.

"Baby, we have to move fast," Sebastian whispered against her lips.

"I love you!" she murmured through the kiss.

"I love you, too, now go," he said firmly.

Arielle turned and fell in Eva's arms and they walked quietly down the corridor with Sebastian on their heels.

"Eva," Arielle whispered, but Eva squeezed her hand, and put her index finger against her lips signaling to keep quiet. At the top of the landing of the third floor they met Antonius and Nathan who were waiting for Sebastian. Both smiled wide when they saw Arielle and they exchange quick, silent hugs. Eva whisked Arielle quickly down the two sets of stairs and out the front door. Sebastian stop to talk with Antonius and Nathan in that inaudible immortal language and they readied to face Gaston and Oliver.

With Arielle safe out of the house they now could complete their plan. They checked all the rooms on the third floor but the whole left wing was completely empty. They focused their attention to the right wing. The first two rooms were empty. They opened the third door on the right and a loud snoring reached their ears. They approached the bed and looked down at the sleeping man, clueless of the danger lurking above his head. It wasn't Gaston so Sebastian waved his hand and walked out the door, leaving Antonius and Nathan to deal with Oliver.

He walked down the corridor and checked a few more rooms but they were unoccupied. He stood in front of the last door on the left, sure that Gaston was in that room. He turned the handle quietly and open the door just enough to slip in and scanned the room intently. He heard Gaston's low breathing as he entered the dark room. He approached the bed, light-footed on the floor. He looked down at Gaston and let his anger engulf him. He reached down, grabbed Gaston by his neck, and pulled him out of bed.

Gaston stood, watching Sebastian in utter shock. He'd never heard him approach the bed; so much for his immortal awareness.

"You know I'm here to kill you," Sebastian growled.

"Then why didn't you do it while I was asleep?" he asked, a hint of a smirk on his lips; but the truth was that reality had started to seep into his bones.

"Because I'm not a coward like *you* are," Sebastian enunciated. "I want you to be looking at me when I kill you," he furthered through clenched teeth.

"Where's Arielle?" Gaston screamed, eyes filled with loathing.

"She's out of this house in a safe place. She's where she belongs—with me..." he emphasized.

Gaston moved quickly to throw himself against Sebastian, but Sebastian saw him coming before he even moved and just before impact, landed him a hard blow in the middle of his chest. Gaston flew back and landed against the wall. He sprang back up on his feet and stormed at Sebastian with all the wrath of a hurricane. Sebastian's fist met him in mid-air, flipped him over his head sending him crashing against the dresser that splintered and threw shards of wood all over the room. Gaston's body stopped moving when he hit the wall with a thundering noise. He moaned audibly, but shaking his head, pushed himself away from the wall and stood, staring at Sebastian eyes on fire.

He seemed to assess his chances in this encounter, and with a sudden move, reached into one of the dresser drawers now exposed from the crash, and came back up holding a gun in his hand. He didn't hesitate. He fired and kept firing until he emptied the entire clip. Sebastian jumped to his left trying to avoid direct hits to his chest, but two of the bullets hit, spreading pain across his body. One went through his upper thigh and the other entered his left shoulder. Thankfully they didn't involve parts of the body that would immobilize him. What they did was make Sebastian angrier. Grinding his teeth he moved fast, grabbed Gaston's arm and broke it, sending the empty gun to the floor with a loud bang. He lifted his left arm and jammed an upright blow into Gaston's face breaking his jaw. Gaston growled and threw himself on Sebastian sending them both rolling on the floor. Gaston got some good hits on Sebastian's bloody shoulder and thigh trying to make him weaker but Sebastian was highly motivated by Arielle.

Gaston jumped up onto his feet, his back to the door, hoping to make a quick exit and leave Sebastian on the floor. He knew they would both heal soon so he backed off slowly and froze in place as his back came in contact with a hard unyielding body. Antonius raised his hands, placed them on either side of his head and gave a quick turn, ending Gaston's miserable life. He then let his lifeless body drop on the floor. Nathan walked in right behind him.

Sebastian smiled and walked slowly toward them. "Thanks," he said. "What happened with Oliver?"

"Oh, we went a few rounds. It wasn't easy; he was a large thug but all and all it ended well," he said glancing at Nathan. They laughed heartily.

"He shot you?" Antonius said surprisingly. "Was he sleeping with his gun on his pillow?"

"No, he got it from that drawer there," he said pointing to the shattered dresser. Nathan patted him on the back and they walked out of the room to join the rest of the group. When they reach the top of the landing they heard a lot of noise coming from the servants' quarters. They descended quickly and ran to assist their friends. They found that all of the servants on the second floor had been dispatched and they were all now on the first floor watching Giani go a few rounds with Edward. Oliver's bodyguard, was a large man with enormous fists and inflexible face. His enormous chest looked like a steel wall and his gaze filled with rage was penetrating through Giani's eyes.

He'd landed some good blows at Giani's midriff and he now stood across from him, hands on his hips enticing him to attack. Giani looked totally unruffled as he quickly glanced at Antonius and Gerard meaningfully; they smiled in clear understanding. Giani closed his eyes and inhaled deeply several times, stretching his arms away from his body as a faint smile touched his lips. Edward's brows rose inquisitively but he remained unmoved. Suddenly Gianni moved like a hurricane, flipping through the air like a boomerang, landing an uppercut and a hook to Edward's neck and face. Giani's body landed right behind him and as Edward spun around to face him, Giani took a swift turn and lashed a deadly thrust to Edward's throat. Edward lost his balance and backed into Sebastian who placed his hands on either side of his head and twisted hard, taking Edward's last breath away.

"And *he* makes 9 down!" Giani yelled excitedly, pointing at Edward's lifeless body.

"What happened?" Loren asked.

"We finished Gaston and Oliver. Arielle's outside with Eva waiting for us," Sebastian said anxiously.

"Well let's go then," said Ian smiling wide. The guys joked and patted each other on the back exchanging exciting moments of their fights with the immortals. Loren and Isabella talked about the large woman who'd bolted upright on her bed as soon as they entered her bedroom. She gave them a run for their money, but at the end she lost the fight. They walked through the foyer, out the front door, and scanned the area to locate Eva and Arielle.

Sebastian stepped down ahead of the group, unable to hold back his eagerness to take Arielle in his arms. His eyes pierced the darkness and spotted the women walking out from behind the hedges by the front gate. They both ran joyfully toward their friends.

The next few seconds were sheer pandemonium. Two shots resonated in the air, sucking the breath out of everyone's lungs. Their heads instantly turned to watch in utter shock, both Arielle and Eva swayed then stumbled as their legs scuffed the ground just before they plummeted face down. Stony silence covered the night like a cold blanket of death. Their faces were painted with a look of a shocked disbelief.

"Arielle!" A despondent scream escaped Sebastian's lips as icy cold fear slid deep into his bones. Strong footsteps running into the darkness away from the front gate broke the silence. Nathan whirled around and sprang in the direction the shots came from, sailing across the ground. It wasn't long before he was right behind the culprit. The man turned and gazed at Nathan's face that revealed an expression of blank calculation deadly to any human mind. His fear was so thick it clogged his mind. Nathan raised his hands, gave the guy's neck a quick twist and the man fell lifeless on the ground without a sound.

Back in the front garden the group was kneeling by the girls. Eva was coming around in Ian's arms but they all knew she would heal awfully fast. Arielle was moaning and shaking, tears rolled down her face as pain ripped through her body. Sebastian cursed through clenched teeth. Her shirt was covered in blood and Sebastian searched wildly to locate the injury. He finally realized she was bleeding from her shoulder. He ripped a long strip from his shirt and with Antonius' help wrapped her arm tightly to stop the bleeding. They both checked closer to make sure the bullet wasn't lodged inside her body. Sebastian wrapped his arms about her, lifted her effortlessly and held her tightly to him. Her body tensed and she shuddered, shaking like a leaf. His senses elevated, his lips tightened, and his brain went on overdrive worrying about her state of health.

"The bullet just grazed her shoulder, Sebastian, she's going to be all right," Antonius said, patting Sebastian on the back. Sebastian took a few minutes to process his friend's statement, the tension eased and his arms tightened around Arielle's quivering body. He looked down and met her gaze. He could feel her trembling and bent to cover her lips with his tenderly.

"You'll be all right, baby; it's just a scratch," he whispered. "I'll take you home."

Through her sobs she smiled, closed her eyes, and settled comfortably in his warm embrace. Sebastian tightened his hold on her and she buried her face in his chest, inhaling his immortal scent filling her soul with every inch of him.

Ignoring the pain, she wound one hand around his neck unwilling to let go. Sebastian looked down into her face and smiled, utterly content that she was safe and in his arms once again.

"I love you," she whimpered.

"I love you," he murmured back. Sebastian could clearly grasp the overwhelming emotion that was rooted deep down his very core. The love he held for Arielle was extraordinary. He couldn't breathe without her; she was the center of his universe, the essence of his very existence. Their gaze locked once again and he was lost in the deep blue ocean of her eyes. His smile deepened and he pressed his lips on hers one more time. He wanted to get her home, to enjoy her return, to make love to her, as he'd never loved her before. He felt the small hand resting on his nape, pulling him gently down to meet her lips for another kiss. His lips moved against hers softly then harder, increasing the pressure and intensity until both couldn't breathe.

"God, I missed you. I love you so very much!" he murmured.

"I love you more," she whispered breathlessly into the kiss. He laughed, but he was sure she couldn't possibly love him as much as he loved her. She absolutely wouldn't be able to grasp the strength of his passion for her. She would never understand that just by breathing she was providing the oxygen for his existence. That she was creating each and every bright sunrise in his life just by being next to him.

"Let's get her home," he said eagerly, and quickly they moved like shadows in the night. Arielle felt the immortal speed in her very core. It was almost the same type of breathtaking swirling she'd felt when Eva took her back in time on her birthday. She couldn't feel the pain in her shoulder and she couldn't breathe but knew she was safe and in the arms of the man who provided her own private utopia.

* * *

They reached Brighton at the end of twilight. Sunrise was on the way. The upper arc of the sun peeked above the horizon with a spectrum of colors ranging from lavender to sapphire, from orange to red. The evening dew was still clinging to the ground and cool mist was in the air. There were smiles on the beautiful immortal faces as they exchanged looks revealing a quiet loyalty that radiated among them. Arielle was home safe and they could all glow in the gratification of the outcome.

Arielle opened her eyes, shaking the swirling sensation away, still enveloped in Sebastian's steel embrace. She let out a low moan, suffering a thriving headache, and a sharp pain jabbing her left shoulder. Sebastian, sensing her emotion, looked down and their eyes locked.

"What is it, baby?" he asked anxiously. She hesitated for a brief instant as if she was considering whether she needed to tell him that she was in pain, but decided against it. His warm gaze touched her clear blue eyes and her lips curved in a dazzling smile. She got lost into that amazing emerald ocean of his eyes that reflected exaltation bold enough to make her forget all about the pain.

"Nothing," she murmured. "Are we home?"

"Yes, baby, we're a few minutes from home," he said gently.

Eva stepped closer holding a blissful smile. "How are you feeling, Arielle?" she asked.

"I'm fine," she said quietly. She glanced around and shaking her head asked in a soft voice. "Was I the only one hurt?"

"No," Sebastian answered. "Eva was shot as well, but she's already healed."

"Oh," Arielle whispered and *humphed*. "Way to go," she murmured. "I guess being an immortal is a big plus in a case like this, huh!" She rolled her eyes and pouted.

Eva chuckled and patted Arielle's cheek. "You're home safe and that's all that matters," she said.

Arielle grinning and pushed softly away from Sebastian's arms, flinching painfully. Looking up at him again she murmured.

"I'm okay now, you can put me down."

"Are you sure?" he asked warily. She nodded and loosening his hold on her he let her down hesitantly. Arielle smiled wide as she scanned the beautiful immortal faces surrounding her. She approached them and gave each one a heartfelt hug, and a huge kiss.

"I love you all," she said fondly. "Thank you for helping Sebastian." Then she walked back and stood next to Sebastian slipping her hand into his. He smiled blissfully as he tightened his grip on her hand and pulled her closer. He took his turn thanking his friends and they all patted him in the back warmheartedly.

"I'll call you all later," Sebastian promised as they waved and departed.

As they all disbanded, Loren glanced back and said, "I'll come over tomorrow to check on you."

Arielle waved with a smile. "I'll be there!" she replied.

Sebastian grinned, wrapped his arm around Arielle's waist and pulled her to him. "Let's go home baby," he whispered looking down at her exhausted face. He knew she was worn out, and most likely in a lot of pain.

"Did you miss me?" she asked softly as they walked hand-in-hand.

Sebastian dragged a deep breath, tightening his hold on her. "Oh God! Arielle, I thought I was going to lose my mind," he answered pulling her even closer. "I couldn't breathe," he whispered. "You don't understand, but I can't exist if you aren't here with me."

His face looked distraught as he recalled the last three days. She stopped to face him and reaching up on tip-toes searched for his lips. Sebastian wrapped his arms around her and kissed her with eagerness that ripped through his body like fierce lightning.

Arielle sighed deeply, "I love you, Sebastian!" she murmured into the kiss.

He framed her face and pierced through her eyes. "I'll never leave your side," he whispered. "That's a promise." They were very close to the house. They slipped their arms around each other and walked home.

Sebastian helped her out of her clothes first, shed his own quickly and led her into the shower. He turned on the warm water and let it run over them, comforting their anxieties. Arielle grasped the soap but he took it gently away from her and murmured. "I'll do that…" His silky soft voice sent waves rippling across her skin. He lathered his hands and with slow movements ran them over her curves.

Arielle quivered and leaned back against the steal wall of his chest. Sebastian's lungs locked at the feel of her warm skin. Desire flared like blistering fire but he maintained strict control of his wild cravings. His hands moved like velvet, methodically stroking her smooth skin. Ripples of excitement coursed across her muscles and she moaned blissfully. Sebastian groaned agonizingly as his hands wandered over the mounts of her breasts. He bit his lust back knowing he needed to get her out of the shower and take care of her injury. Her hair was his last challenge. He helped her wash and thoroughly rinse it.

"Thank you," she murmured, turning to face him. Leaning in she pressed her lips against his.

"It was my pleasure," he whispered into the kiss. He held her to that kiss for a long moment, refusing to let her go. Arielle pressed closer and the kiss deepened until they were breathless. Sebastian summoned his wits, broke away from the kiss and grabbed a towel. Arielle swayed in his arms, relaxed, still lost in the aftermath of the kiss. Holding the towel on each end, he spread his arms wide and wrapped her in it, pulling her into his embrace. He pat her body and hair dry, picked her up and set her on the end of the bed.

"I need to clean your shoulder, baby," he said softly. He retrieved a tube of antiseptic and a fresh bandage from the medicine cabinet, cleaned the abrasion and then bandaged it carefully.

"Thank you," she murmured again, looking into his eyes.

He leaned forward and pressed a kiss on top of her nose.

"It's my pleasure," he replied joyfully. "Just one more thing."

"What?" she asked inquisitively.

He went back to the bathroom and came back holding her necklace. "Can you please do me the favor of keeping this around your neck before I lose my sanity," he begged and snapped it safely around her neck.

Arielle smiled as she pulled him down for another kiss. "I do promise," she murmured.

"Thank you," he replied, pulled the bedcovers down, lifted her into his arms one more time, and sat her between the silk sheets.

Sebastian's lips curved as he looked down at her, his passion palpable. He got into bed, slid his arm under her back and pulled her to him. Arielle moaned softly and sank against his hard muscled body. Their lips met and quickly the rhythm changed to a more demanding, more ravishing, passionate kiss. Tongues intermingled, moans deepened and emotions flared rapidly like sparks of a scorching fire. They appeased their passion and eager desire lost in a haze of raw seduction as time stilled. Sebastian took her vigorously and she matched him every step of the way into that amazing dance of desire and passion until they shattered together, hearts and souls soaring to the peak of ecstasy. Their encounter was more than spectacular leaving them completely sated and in utter bliss. They'd never experienced fulfillment to this level in any of their prior encounters. Lying on their backs they exhaled simultaneously enjoying the aftermath. Arielle closed her eyes and chuckled. Sebastian turned to gaze at her beautiful face, his chest bursting with love. He rolled to his side, shifted Arielle so she settled against him with her wounded shoulder away from the bed. He leaned in and pressed a soft kiss on the side of her neck and she moaned.

"I can't understand how you can make each one of our encounters more mind-blowing than the one before," she murmured.

He chuckled blissfully. "It's my own personal secret recipe," he said and laughed aloud, making her laugh with him.

She snuggled eagerly, laying her cheek against her pillow as he spooned her, chest to back, buttocks to groin, legs intermingled. Sebastian wrapped his arm about her and rested it against her chest feeling the rhythm of her heartbeat. He held her closer, terrified at the thought of losing her again. Nuzzling her hair with his chin, he pressed his lips against her temple. Arielle felt the warmth of his embrace and, smiling in sheer bliss, she drifted off to sleep.

Sebastian thoughts surged powerfully through his mind. He smiled at the soft sound of her breathing that sent potent passions to his very core lifting him to a higher level of utopia. Looking down at her, his anxiety swelled for a moment as he recalled the night of her abduction, but then just as fast it poured out of him, leaving him with a warm sense of relief. Arielle had bewitched him body and soul and she was back in his arms sheltered from any harm. Three short weeks were left until she was to become his wife— *his*—to have and to love for eternity.

He looked at the clock on the nightstand. It was way past midnight and he was still wide-awake, overwhelmed with thoughts of the last three days. He drew a deep breath and gathered Arielle's warm body a little closer. He regretted exposing Arielle to a dangerous existence. His life seemed to be filled with people attempting to hurt him by hurting Arielle. The most important question still lingering in the air was how long would it take for Annabel to strike again.

Arielle's sudden sound of distress snapped Sebastian out of his deep thoughts. He felt her body shake uncontrollably, struggling to breathe. Sebastian relaxed his embrace as she sprang away from him and sat up on the bed arms suspended in midair.

"Get away from me!" she yelled frantically. Her arms were moving outward as if she was trying to push someone away. "Don't touch me!" she cried out, voice filled with anguish.

Sebastian's lungs locked in agony and he watched helplessly as Arielle was caught in a dreadful nightmare. He slowly sat up and moved approached her. He scanned her beautiful face that was now a display of sheer fright, lips twisted severely and eyes tightly shut.

He remained quiet as she stood still for a moment and then a soft sob escaped her lips only to be followed by a stronger one and then tears surged down her face. Her breathing became rough filled with fright. Sebastian knew she was having a shattering nightmare about the last three days with Gaston and he felt piercing agony coursing through his body. He decided to slip his arms about her gently and pulled her to him. Arielle gulped down a whimper as her body quivered wrenchingly. Sebastian leaned in and closed his arms around her pressing a soft kiss on her temple. Arielle's breath caught then she inhaled, pulled back and opened her eyes. Her pupils were dilated with astonishment as the dream broke and reality brought a palpable shock into her gut. Without a word she threw herself in Sebastian's arms. He held her tight as sobs and moans shook her.

"Sebastian!" she called out, as tears of relief ran down her face. Sebastian placed a soft kiss over each eyelid.

"It was just a bad dream, baby!" he murmured. She took a sharp breath and let it out slowly. She nodded, laid her head on the pillow and closed her eyes with relief. Sebastian pulled the covers over her and lingered over her making sure she was peaceful. His pulse beat worryingly as he lay slowly down and gathered her in his arms, pulling her tightly against him. He heard a sharp sniffle, and then silence; Arielle was deep in sleep once again. Sebastian blew out a sigh of relief and, closing his eyes, drifted off to sleep.

* * *

Arielle woke in the early morning. A streak of light was slipping through the curtain. She blinked sluggishly as her gaze fell on the picture on her nightstand. The most astonishing green eyes were looking right back at her. A warm overwhelming emotion enveloped her when she realized she was still trapped in his warm embrace and she didn't want to move. There was not a place in the world she would like to be right now but exactly where she was. She couldn't image her life without Sebastian. The memories of the last three days slammed back into her head and she recoiled. Her heart thudded anxiously and she bit her lower lip on a gulp. Sebastian's arm was resting on her chest and he felt the fast change in her heartbeat. He immediately lifted himself on one elbow and gazed down at her.

"What is it, baby?"

Arielle didn't reply. She rolled on her back; lips curved to a soft smile, enjoying the amazing sanctuary he provided.

"Good morning, Darcy," she murmured. Her arms moved about his neck, fingers clenched as she tugged softly and pulled him down to her. Sebastian's pulse picked up speed and he took her mouth eagerly as sensation soared along every muscle in his body down to his bones.

"Good morning, Lizzy," he murmured into the kiss. The kiss deepened and his arms closed around her tightly. She wiggled in his arms and he groaned in sheer excitement. His hands roamed over her satin flesh and she burned with desire. Her nerves rocketed with hunger and passion and she pulled away from the kiss gasping. Sebastian pierced through her eyes.

"Arielle, I don't think I can take much more of you being hurt," he said anxiously. Their lips met again in an agonizing kiss. Breaking the kiss this time he groaned in sheer frustration.

"I feel like I'm dying a little each time something happens to you," he said.

"I'm sorry," she whispered. "It's not my fault. All I want is to love you and that seems to bother a lot of crazy immortals from your past." She chuckled.

Her statement made him laugh and he pulled her closer. "You're an amazing girl, you know that, don't you?" he said, and she shrugged. "You're mine and I'll keep you with me for eternity," he said fiercely.

She was sure she would be with him for the rest of her life. As for the eternity part, that was still in question, but she didn't say anything.

"Did you sleep well?" he asked.

"I think I did, but for the nightmare. I slept better than I have in the last three days," she replied and pulled him back. Her breath burned full of emotion as she set her lips against the hollow of his throat.

Sebastian got lost again in the sensuality of the moment. "You'll be the death of me," he gasped, and she laughed blissfully.

This statement was one of her two favorite ones. The other was *miss me*. There wasn't a person on earth who could utter those two sentences better than Sebastian. There wasn't another man on the planet who could turn her world upside down.

"God! I love you so much," she murmured, "it actually hurts when I think about it."

Sebastian smiled wide at her words; he felt the same about her. He shifted, tipping her head back, and set his lips at her throat making her shuddered. Their breathing picked up and they groaned in blistering need. Arielle felt her lips go dry and she ran her tongue slowly over them. She closed her eyes and surrendered to his passion, to his built-up heat that slammed each and every muscle in her body with fierce force. Her need and fervor matched and surpassed his, leaving them exhausted, caught in the powerful magnificence of pleasure that washed over them. They were happy to be together again and ready to start working on their anxiously anticipated wedding day.

 *Chapter 19*

TEN DAYS LEFT until the wedding day, and Arielle was so excited she could hardly breathe. Every time she looked at Sebastian she thought she was living a dream. She couldn't believe this beautiful immortal man was soon to be her husband. There was a gleam of excitement in Sebastian's emerald eyes that filled her heart with warmth and anticipation. She was now even closer to taking this exhilarating yet frightening step toward his undying world.

The immortal group was back in town to celebrate Sebastian's bachelor party. They'd partied hard prior to Ian and Troy's weddings and were getting ready to party again, this time for Sebastian. They sure didn't party the same way human beings would. These guys could be on one side of the globe one night, and leap to the other side the next. So their kind of partying was a complete mystery to their mortal friends.

The invitations had been sent a few months prior, and everyone on the list, from family members to business associates and friends, had accepted. They were looking at a very large crowd and Arielle was thrilled. If it were possible, she would choose to share this astounding moment with every single person on earth.

Sebastian didn't want Arielle or her parents to worry about the wedding expenses. He'd tried long and hard to convince Arielle's father to let him cover the wedding expenses, but her father wouldn't hear of it. Sebastian would never tell Arielle that he'd used his immortal gift and compelled her father to finally accept. It would be an extraordinary wedding.

*   *   *

It was the night before Sebastian was to leave with his friends for his weeklong bachelor outing. Arielle wasn't happy that it would be a week before she set eyes on his beautiful face again, but quite excited that the night was not yet over.

It was bedtime and Sebastian was going to make sure that Arielle was loved the way she should be. It would be a week of torture before he'd have her in his bed again so he was going to make their encounter memorable.

Naked desire swirled in his eyes. The fragrance of freesia rose from her hair and sang deep into his bone marrow. His mouth came down on hers, his tongue parted her lips and dove into the sweetness of her mouth. The kiss seared her skin and the blood surged scorching hot, burning every vein in its wake. He kissed and suckled every inch of her body leaving a burning sensation that made her shudder.

"I don't think I can be away from you for a week," he breathed against her lips. "Will you miss me?" he asked, passion coating his voice.

"I think maybe a little," she giggled and sank deeper into his embrace, and his body enveloped her.

His hands moved slowly, cupping the swollen mounts of her breasts, kneading and teasing the nipples with his thumbs. Pleasure coursed through her and she moaned, drowning in passion. Sebastian's lips left her mouth and moved lower, grazing her silky skin with his tongue until he found a pebbled nipple and set his hot mouth on it, suckling and lapping with feverish desire.

Arielle wiggled beneath him and Sebastian flinched as their hips collided and he bit back a growl.

"You have to stop moving like that, because I'm not going to last long." He was breathless. His mouth returned to worship the other nipple and she nearly came off the bed. His hands shifted and slid around her pulling her even closer to his body. He lifted his head and stared into her eyes, lust emanating out of each pore of his body. He lowered his mouth to hers and the kiss became a wild, unleashed plunder.

Arielle's hand moved between them dragging her fingers slowly over his stomach and down his happy trail intensifying his hardness.

He let out a harsh hiss when her hand stopped over his arousal and her fingers closed tightly around it.

Sebastian lost control, consumed by strong desire that drove him to a sensuous meltdown. Her soft movements sent scorching flames across his skin and he became utterly incoherent. With a soft growl he moved fast, grabbed her hand, and pulled it away against her pleading protests.

"No, Arielle, no, I can't…" he trailed off, gasping for air. He shut his eyes against breathless desire, and rolled over, covering her body with his. With his knee he nudged her legs apart. He was beyond reasonable thinking, passion slumming hard and deep into his brain. He drove into her with savage hunger and she shuddered.

"Oh, God," she groaned and her eyes slammed shut.

He wanted to devour her, he could hardly hold back, she was his and she wanted only him. Their breaths mingled, their bodies flush against each other, their movements united in sensual dance. Sebastian struggled for control; with a slow dip of his head he took her mouth and plundered. His tongue moved inside the sweet like honey softness, with the same urgency that sent a rush of craving through Arielle, and she groaned into his mouth. His thrusts became stronger and a groan escaped her before she could hold it back. She arched beneath him, her fingers digging into the hard muscles of his back and his passion intensified. He rotated his hips and she rose to meet and match him until they were rocked into a powerful release. Sebastian covered her mouth in a passionate kiss, swallowing her scream of release. The powerful jolt shot them both to oblivion and slowly brought them back into blissful slumber.

For a long moment they didn't move, or speak, just held onto each other in silence. They were addicted to each other. He finally rolled onto his back taking her with him, keeping her tightly nestled against his side. She rested her cheek on his chest, an arm spread over his abdomen. With a soft moan he closed his eyes, his skin still on fire, trying to still his fast breathing.

She moaned and moved closer. His finger moved under her chin and lifted her face to his. He ran his tongue over her bottom lip, and groaned. God! She tasted so sweet. He'd never known passion like this. His voice came out in a husky rasp.

"Try to think about me, while I'm away."

She gasped and slanted her head up to look into his eyes. "Sebastian, all I can do is think about you."

"Thank God for that." He set his mouth on hers once again and sensation swept over him like a storm. "I don't think I can make it," he breathed against her mouth. He pressed his muscled hardness against her suggestively. "A week is way too long," he said on a breathy moan.

"Sebastian..." His name murmured past her lips. "I'll be right here, when you get back, my love."

He gazed at her peaceful face, a soft smile on her lips. He grinned, realizing that she was fast asleep. He wrapped her in his arms. Closing his eyes, a chuckle escaped him and he surrendered to sleep.

*   *   *

The nightly nightmares that'd plagued Arielle's sleep for over a half a month were more than just a worry for her. Her sensible and witty mind told her they were just that, *a nightmare,* and she shouldn't become as consumed over them as she was. However each night when time came for bed she would find herself anxious and terrified. It was a nightmare that left her powerless to end the hold it had on her.

Tonight wasn't any different than any other night. Arielle drifted into the same nightmare, reliving the same dreadful dream that played on fast-forward like a horror film over and over again.

*   *   *

She stood in the middle of a graveyard covered in thick fog. Her eyes darted left and right, back and forth; she heard steady footsteps approaching, and her muscles locked. She tried to run but she couldn't move. Why wasn't she able to move? Her hand came up and cupped her mouth trying to stop a scream from leaving her lips. The blood pounded her temples and her body shook like a leaf in a windstorm. There was nobody around to witness her distress or to help her out of this place. The footsteps were closing in and she held her breath, eyes wide open filled with terror.

A scream of relief left her when she recognized the man who came through the fog. It was Sebastian. She stared at the most compelling face on this earth and ran to fall into his arms.

Sebastian put his hands up and stopped her inches away from him. Arielle froze in place. The blood drained from her face and tears stung her eyes. It wasn't so much the rejection as it was the hardness of his face. Her heart sank. He didn't smile, he didn't speak, he just reached out and took her hand. Disappointment and heartache welled up.

Sebastian led her rapidly across a narrow path toward the other side of cemetery. The path ended at the entrance of a small church.

She tried to jerk her hand away, but Sebastian's hand was clamped tightly around her wrist. Silence descended between them registering the sullenness of their surroundings. He pulled her up the few stone steps and through the door with a quick motion. Arielle entered, and immediately she was enveloped in an icy cold air that lingered inside the church. Standing perfectly still, her eyes darted nervously from one dank corner of the building to the other. It was dusky inside the church; only a dim light streamed through the stained glass windows. Sebastian let go of her hand and without a second look at her he made his way toward the altar. Stunned, Arielle stared at his retreating back. She wanted to scream to call him back, but she couldn't speak. His footsteps rang heavily on the stone floor, and each step pounded like a sharp knife into her heart. Her eyes moved away from Sebastian and zeroed-in on the shape of a woman facing the altar, draped in a beautiful wedding dress. Icy fingers crawled up her spine, as she could only fear the worst. The woman turned slowly and Arielle gasped aloud.

Annabel's gaze was focused on Sebastian, a wide smile spread across her face. Silently and ever so quietly Sebastian strode toward Annabel, his eyes sparkling with mischief. Annabel reached for him and soon she was enveloped in his embrace. His mouth covered hers, and Arielle screamed and shook violently. She shut her eyes, trying to avoid the sight that was fracturing her heart to shreds.

Her eyes snapped open at the sound of strong, revolting laughter. Annabel was watching her with a victorious smile, eyes shooting painful daggers at Arielle, each one penetrating her heart, tearing it to shards. "He's mine! You miserable human, he's mine! You. Will. Never. Have him."

Arielle gasped at the venom in her voice, and soon the laughter would start again.

Sebastian stood next to Annabel, holding her close to his side, utterly indifferent to Arielle's anxiety, as if he didn't care how she felt, or how bad he was hurting her.

Arielle felt a stinging sensation at the back of her eyelids and soon tears poured down her face. She began to tremble uncontrollably, and her knees started to sag.

"I need to get out of here," she muttered. She gathered every last morsel of strength left in her body, turned and started walking toward the exit in complete hysteria. Her pulse pounded so powerful that she could hear the hammering bounce off her eardrums painfully. She tried to reach the exit but the distance to the door was becoming longer and longer. Pretty soon she broke into a run, trying to cross the threshold into the open air but no matter how fast she ran she was still inside that church hearing Annabel's horrible laughter piercing her ears. Her pulse beat faster and faster, breath heaving, sweat dripping; she felt she was going to pass out. A lump was rising to her throat, choking her windpipe...

* * *

Sebastian woke, startled to find Arielle on the other side of the bed, away from his embrace. He sat up and turned the light on. Arielle's face was damp, her body covered in sweat. She was tossing and turning, clasping at the sheets and moaning as if she was being tortured. He could feel that she was having a horrid nightmare and reached for her. He pulled her into his arms and gave her a soft shake. "Arielle, please, baby wake up!"

She was shaking like a leaf, tears rolling down her face. "Sebastian, please don't leave me, please come back," she was whimpering.

Sebastian frowned. These nightmares were becoming unbearable. Wretchedness seeped through him. How could he go away for a whole week knowing she'd be going through this alone? He cupped her face with his hand and stoked her bottom lip with his thumb. "I'm right here baby, I'm not going anywhere."

Her breathing hitched and she couldn't stop her strangled cry. He moved quickly and shook her awake. "Arielle...Arielle... Wake up baby."

Arielle woke in a panic. Pain lingered in her eyes. She was disoriented and completely unaware of Sebastian's presence. She sat up on the bed shaking her head to clear the fog of the dream. "Sebastian," she said softly sobbing.

"I'm right here, baby, I'm right here," he said again and pulled her tighter into his embrace.

Her eyes settled on his face and felt the weight of the nightmare crushing down on her. "You're here," she whispered.

"Yes, I'm here, I'm not going anywhere."

"Oh, this horrible dream," she whimpered. She shrugged away from his embrace and wiped her cheeks with the back of her hand. "You and Annabel," she said in an abrupt voice that left him utterly shocked.

He threaded his fingers through his hair, stared into her incredible blue eyes and lost his train of thought. He reached out and pulled her back into his arms. She clung to him, laying her wet cheek against his warm chest.

"Me and Annabel, what? Tell me," he insisted, his arms cradling her, his eyes searching hers to find the root of the dream.

She shook her head but said nothing.

"Arielle, every time you have these nightmares it tears me up inside. I hate to see you upset. Tell me about your dream, *please!*" he said, pain coating his voice.

Arielle regarded Sebastian hesitantly. Her emotions were in such turmoil. She straightened her shoulders with fortitude. It was time to finally tell him about the details of her dream.

"Every time I have this nightmare you leave me for Annabel. *She* is the bride waiting for you at the altar. *She* is the bride you run to, *not me.*" Her eyes filled with tears as the memories of the nightmare raced through her mind, crashing against each other, one worse that the other, and that evil laughter still ringing in her ears.

A sickening feeling enveloped Sebastian. How could she possibly believe he would leave her for Annabel? Jealousy and fear blinded Arielle's otherwise level thinking.

"My God, Arielle! It's just a dream!" he said wrapping his arms more firmly around her. "I hate the woman and everything she stands for. I want to hurt her in such a horrible way, the thought terrifies me. How could you ever let such a thought invade your mind?"

Arielle nodded slowly. She slipped her arms around his neck and leaned even closer. Sebastian let out a sigh of relief. He had his girl back.

"I love you, baby, I love you so much it actually hurts," he murmured against her ear. He held her gently soothing her as she sobbed against his chest.

"I'm having second thoughts about leaving you," he said.

Arielle tipped her head back to look into his emerald eyes. "You can't be serious," she said in utter shock. "You must...you have to...you just can't..." her voice trailed off. She was trying to finish the sentence but couldn't find the right words.

With his thumbs he gently wiped her tears off her cheeks, and brushed back the rich spill of her hair from her face. "I will do anything to keep you safe. You have absolutely no idea how I feel about you."

Arielle brought her hands to her cheeks and felt the moisture still lingering on her skin. She gave him a knowing smile, and nodded reluctantly. The nightmare was still in her thoughts, keeping her pulse throbbing. The reassurance she read in his eyes told her that even though the dream was repugnant and frightening, she had to let it go until she'd sorted out its meaning.

Sebastian lay back down and pulled her into his arms. He always enjoyed the feel of her soft body that fit his like a glove. The freesia fragrance was intoxicating and very sexy as he nuzzled her hair and moved his lips down her face until their lips met in a fiery kiss.

"I'm going to miss you," he breathed as he plundered the softness of her mouth and claimed what he knew was his.

Arielle groaned, surrendering to his intoxicating passion. She wrapped her arms around his neck and pulled him to her.

"Show me that you love only me," she gasped, her skin scorching with need for him. She needed reassurance that his desire was only for her, no other woman on this earth.

Sebastian's moved over her with unspoken hunger. "What do you want, baby?"

"I want you," she gasped. She couldn't hold back a growl as he thrust vigorously in and felt the hard length of fire deep inside leaving her breathless, struggling to keep her sanity for a little while longer. She wanted to make every last shattering pleasure to last for as long as possible.

Sebastian's muscles clenched at the sensation her body heat was spreading across every fiber of his body. She was his, body and soul and he plundered every inch of her body as if there was no tomorrow. Her body arched beneath him, matching him stroke for stroke with the same desire, the same passion until they sensed the thundering climax that was about to invade their senses and release them into the universe of oblivion.

Her name was on his lips, and his name on hers, as they rode the waves of ecstasy and the bliss of the aftermath.

Sebastian shifted, tugging the bedspread over them. He wrapped his arms around her, and pulled her protectively into his embrace. He closed his eyes and felt a sense of possession. Arielle pressed a kiss at the base of his throat. Sebastian growled with pleasure and nuzzled her hair.

"You're mine, Arielle. Sleep, my angel. I'm right here," he said, tightening his arms around her possessively.

Arielle smiled blissfully; she could still feel his gaze. She cushioned her cheek on his chest and sighed. Every bit of worry slipped away, leaving her warm and secure. She was sure he was ready to satisfy every craving she ever had and provide a perfect *sanctuary*. "And *you* are mine, Darcy," she murmured.

Sebastian cleared his throat. "Mmmm…yes, I am, my beautiful Lizzy," he whispered, his breath warm against her cheek. He gave her a soft squeeze, but she was already asleep.

Sebastian stayed awake a while longer just watching her in an undisturbed state of slumber, and soon surrendered to sleep.

* * *

Sebastian woke to daylight slipping through the window shutters and brushing across his face. Arielle was still asleep in his arms. Her hair spread like a silky waterfall across the pillow. Her lush lips pink and pouty asking to be kissed. He inhaled deeply the freesia fragrance that seeped through every pore in his body and left him spellbound. He decided he had to have her one more time before he left their bed.

He bent his head and brushed his lips over hers. Her breath was warm, alluring, and his body shifted closer.

Arielle's eyes flickered open and fell into his intense emerald gaze. "Good morning, Darcy," she murmured against his mouth.

"Good morning, my Lizzy," he breathed, his pulse pounding. "I know it's early, but I need you. I can't go away without showing you how much I love you."

"I'm not stopping you," she murmured and moved suggestively against the solid wall of muscles.

His lips curved, and a heated sensation made his pulse race. His fingers tangled in her hair and tilting her head back, he buried his face in the soft curve of her throat. A groan surged from his lips when he sensed the elevated pulse beneath her skin. He drew her even closer. The heat of her skin sent waves of scorching fire through his veins. The passion intensified and the desire for Arielle was mind-blowing. He wanted her like he'd never wanted another person in his long life through the centuries. His lips moved up the length of her throat, across her jaw and settled on her mouth. He plundered with a savage craving until sizzling pleasure spread and burned every inch of their bodies. Drawing back he gazed into the dark passion that burned inside the blue ocean of her eyes and was lost.

"Oh, God, Arielle, you have no idea what you do to me," his voice a low growl.

Arielle leaned in, her breasts softly pressing into his chest and he gasped. His hands moved over the curves of her body tracing the line of her hips and the inside of her thighs. He tilted his head and deepened the kiss stilling her breath away. Every stroke of his burning finger sent a sizzling sensation deep into the core of her bone marrow.

His hands slid slowly upward until he cupped her breasts. She gasped as he squeezed softly and let his thumbs brush over the hard nipples. Sensation slammed fast and hard into his brain and he growled. She arched her body and pushed herself against his hands. He squeezed harder, bringing waves of pleasure across her skin and settling below her belly.

His mesmerizing lips moved again and sliding down the bed he kissed and licked every spot along the length of her body. The taste of her silky skin drove him senseless, sending him to a suspended space of time. Reining in his wits he moved up her body until he reached her breast. He took one hard nipple into the heat of his mouth and suckled hard, bringing Arielle to a shuddering whimper.

Frantically he rolled taking her with him and pinned her beneath him. His erection was hard, pressing against the soft flesh of her abdomen. He wedged his knee between her thighs and pressed them apart. He lowered his head and set his mouth on hers, teeth nipping her bottom lip. The sensation was heady, intoxicating. His hands moved lower and gripped her thighs firmly, keeping her still. He moved fast and plunged deep and hard into her body, sending unfathomed pleasure crashing through her and she immediately fractured into a million shards. Her nails dug deep into his back and his name left her lips with a sob. Her body throbbed around him and Sebastian followed with a guttural growl of gratification falling off of the edge of ecstasy, propelling them both into oblivion.

He rolled onto his back and pulled her against his side and she snuggled into his embrace. He gave her a soft squeeze, nuzzled her hair and pressed a soft kiss on the top of her head. "I don't want to go," he murmured.

Arielle giggled a wicked glint in her eyes. "But you have to go, love. Your friends are in town for your bachelor party. In fact, they should be here in less than an hour," she said looking at the digital clock on the nightstand.

He groaned and, propping himself on one elbow, he lifted over her. He bent down and drew a nipple into his mouth and suckled hard. Arielle nearly came off the bed.

"Sebastian!" she gasped, "you need to get up." She set her hands flat on his chest and pushed gently. "Get up."

He lifted his head reluctantly and pouted. He looked like a little boy. Arielle burst out into a hearty laugh. "What are you, twelve?"

He just pinned her with his emerald gaze and shook his head with disappointment. "There's nothing funny about me leaving you for a whole week. I hate the thought of it." He leaned back down and pressed a soft kiss on her lips.

Arielle just stared back; she just didn't know what to say. He was acting like a small stubborn child.

"All right, all right, I am getting up." He flung the bedcovers back and jumped out of bed. "Are you sure you don't want to take a shower with me?" he called as he reached the bathroom door.

"No!" she yelled back chuckling. "Go take a shower, for God's sake."

"Just don't say I didn't give you a chance," he muttered amusement in his voice.

Soon she heard the water running. She rolled over, drew his pillow into her arms and buried her face in it. She inhaled deeply his sweet immortal scent and sighed.

 *Chapter 20*

HE EMERGED FROM the bathroom shirtless. His eyes fell on her perfect luscious body and a muscled ticked in his jaw. He didn't want to leave her.

Arielle pushed herself up on her elbow and focused on the man who'd turned her world upside down. The sight of his jeans low on his narrow hips showing perfectly defined muscles, created a wild pulsation on the nerves between her thighs. She bit back a groan. "Are you ready?"

"Almost." He approached the bed and bent over to kiss her. "Go to sleep and dream only about me."

She wrinkled her nose, her face heated as she recalled the last encounter. She pulled him down and deepened the kiss.

"Stop this," he growled against her mouth. "I'm already struggling with having to leave you for a whole week."

She released him immediately and flipped back on the pillows with a loud groan.

"You're not this making easy," he muttered, his eyes whirling with passion.

"Sorry, baby, I just can't get enough of you."

"You're using my words now," he chuckled and turned away from her bedside to retrieve a shirt from the closed.

"Don't you have to pack any clothes?"

"No, we manifest everything we need."

"Right. I don't even know why I asked such a stupid question." She buried her face once again in his pillow and inhaled deeply.

"What are you doing?" he asked curiously.

"I hug your pillow and pretend that you're here."

"Arielle, I don't think I can be without you for a whole week."

"You'll survive," she chuckled.

"I'm not sure about that. I may not."

Arielle giggled. "Well then I may have to find another gorgeous immortal to take your place."

Sebastian pouted. "Stop it, Arielle. I don't want you talking or looking at any other man while I'm gone. Is that clear?"

Arielle burst out into a hearty laugh. "Darcy, I don't want anyone else in my bed but you. Is that clear?"

Sebastian groaned at her words. "I love you."

"I love you, too."

He walked out of the bedroom feeling her eyes on him all the way until he turned at the end of the hallway.

It wasn't long before the immortals gathered in their study. She heard them laughing and having a good time. They were debating enthusiastically over which activity should come first, and which part of the planet they would visit today. The digital clock on her nightstand read 9:30.

Arielle palmed her face and breathed hard. She exhaled and something tightened in the pit of her stomach. She winced anxiously, knowing she would never be part of their world. She would never experience that sort of existence.

Immortality was so beyond her reality, she couldn't possibly grasp the meaning of it. She recoiled at the thought that Sebastian had been able to share that type of excitement with other women, but she wasn't one of them.

Unwanted thoughts invaded her mind. What if he met some of those women in their weeklong celebration? She bit her lower lip hard enough to make her jerk her head back in pain. She was truly happy for Sebastian and his friends, but she really didn't want to let him go.

She got out of bed and decided to start packing. She pulled out a small suitcase and placed it open on the bed. She was going to move back into her parent's home while Sebastian was away partying with his friends. She ran her fingers through her hair and shook her head, trying to clear her silly thoughts. She retrieved her iPod from the dresser, plugged in the earbuds and after choosing the music she wanted to listen to, she placed the iPod in her jean pocket to free her hands, and continued packing, singing along to an Adele tune.

She never heard Sebastian enter the room, and she didn't see him approach like a wild cat on prowl. She sensed him before he reached her, and whirling around, she fell into the magic emerald world in his eyes. Her breath held in her throat and she swallowed hard. The raw desire in his eyes took her breath away.

"What are you doing?" she asked, taking a step back.

His eyebrows shut up and his lips parted in a wide smile. He let silence be his reply, as he neared her.

"I know that look," she muttered, pointing at his face. "Remember your friends are here. And aren't you leaving anyway?" she asked, still backing up.

Arielle was babbling, captivated by his slow panther-like approach. Suddenly her back hit the dresser and she stopped moving. He stood in front of her and cradled her face, tilting it up to meet his gaze. He pulled the earbuds from her ears and let them fall. Then he took her mouth in a hot kiss and she stopped breathing. His hands left her face, and his arms snaked around her back, pulling her into his body. Her lips parted instantly, as if replying to Sebastian's silent comment, and her eyelids fell closed. His tongue slipped into the softness of her mouth, hot and demanding and plundered. Time stopped and sensation poured into her veins, making her knees buckle and her body sway. Before she could collect her wits that were scattered all over the floor, he pulled back; his heat was gone, leaving her empty and needing more, *much more*. "Mmm!" she groaned.

"I'm going to miss you," he murmured, his voice rasping. "I don't want to leave you," he added, and took her mouth one more time. "I want you to think of no one but me," he whispered against her lips.

"Sebastian, how can I do anything but think of you?" she snorted.

"Tell me you love me," he murmured.

"I love you," she replied. Still feeling the effect of his kiss, she gasped for air.

"One more week and you're going to be mine forever," he said simply.

"Sebastian, I'm already yours, in every possible way," she chuckled.

He smiled brilliantly, and she blinked. *God, he's beautiful!*

"I'm worried about you. Please don't let the same nightmare take over your thoughts. I love you, and only you," he said softly.

She was quiet for a moment. "I'll be all right, Sebastian," she replied quietly. "My parents will be there; I'll be fine." Her voice was firm, but not very convincing.

Sebastian discerned the small flicker that crossed her eyes. "But you're worried about something," he said, and his arms tightened around her. "What is it? I need to know before I go."

"I—I just have this terrible feeling that Annabel is going to try to disrupt our wedding," she murmured, quivering.

When his mouth returned to hers, the kiss scorched her. Arielle could feel the heat emanating from his body and she moaned, utterly intoxicated by his nearness. "Your friends are waiting," she groaned, pulling back from the kiss.

"Let me worry about my friends. Right now I want to make sure you won't worry. Annabel will not disrupt our wedding. Our friends will be in attendance, and they would like nothing better than to get the chance to destroy her," he said, firmly. Pulling her back in his arms his mouth returned to hers. "Trust in me, baby," he purred against her lips. He then moved his lips across her jaw line and down her throat. She tilted her head back, giving him access, and held her breath. He pressed a soft kiss right at bottom of her throat, lingering there for a short moment, enthralled with the feel of her pulse.

"Mmm…your heartbeat," he purred. "I love to feel your heartbeat," he repeated.

Arielle tried to pull back but he wouldn't budge. "Sebastian, you have to go," she said exasperated. "I can't think when you do that."

"Do what baby?" he asked softly, squeezing her tighter. She clutched onto his shirt as her knees buckled again. She heard his chuckle, and he loosened his embrace. "Tell me you love me, *only me*," he said, gazing into her eyes, but not releasing his dazzling power.

"I love *only* you," she whispered and giggled. *Like there's a chance in bloody hell I would be able to think, or even want to think of another guy,* she thought wittily.

Dropping a soft kiss on her forehead he turned and walked to the door. "I'll see you at the altar!" he called out joyfully. "You better show up!" he added laughing, and shut the door behind him.

She heard Sebastian and his friends leaving and soon stony silence spread throughout the house. Arielle exhaled a gentle laugh and shook her head. It was so easy for Sebastian to turn her world upside down, to make her knees buckle, to take her breath away, just by touching her. It was like time would stop each and every time she was in his arms. *God! How am I going to make it a whole week away from him?* The thought was depressing. Putting the earbuds back in, she searched through the music on her iPod and when she found what she wanted to listen to, she went on to finish packing. She was quickly drawn into the music and nearly forgot where she was until the words of the next song rang in her ears and she recoiled.

Now your nightmare comes to life
Peace of mind is less than never

She reached into her jean pocket, and fishing out her iPod, glanced down at it. *Nightmare* by the *Avenged Sevenfold* displayed on the screen. She winced and turned the music off. Her hands stumbled through her clothes and her eyes darted left to right as if she expected someone to come at her out of the bedroom walls. She stood there quietly and felt the floor quiver. She thought she caught a slight movement out of the corner of her eyes and bile rose in her throat. After what seemed to be an eternity she gather her wits and turned, but no one was there. She was alone. She finally shook her head and swallowed hard. *What in the world is wrong with me?*

Sebastian didn't want her to worry about the recurring nightmare, but she was consumed by the vivid images that sent a shock of fear through her and sank deep into her bones. She recalled waking up soaked in sweat, trembling like a leaf, and sobbing uncontrollably each night. What if it happened again? Who would be there to comfort her? The thought of being alone during one of those nightmares frightened her, but she didn't have a choice in the matter.

Letting out a shuddering breath, she regarded the silence for a moment and finally shook her head in frustration. *I shouldn't let Annabel consume every breath I take.* She let the thought soak deep into her bones.

Suddenly fury and rage replaced her fear. She refused to let Annabel lure her thoughts into chaos where they would linger and smolder until they consumed her completely. She pushed the fear deep down into the pit of her stomach, and just let the fury simmer and flow free into her veins to strengthen her determination to face her nightmare about Annabel. She stared down at the suitcase and continued packing. Her cell phone rang and she jumped. Sliding the arrow over to unlock the screen, she answered hesitantly. "Hello!"

"Arielle! What's wrong?" Eva said.

"Oh, hi, Eva. Nothing's wrong, I was just startled by the ring?"

"You sound upset," Eva said, hearing the anxiety in Arielle's voice across the wireless cell line.

Arielle stared at the wall, trying to decide what to say. She didn't want to talk about Annabel and her fears. Not now, not over the phone. "Oh, it's just that Sebastian just left, and I already miss him," she stated quietly.

"Well, I can understand that," Eva snorted. "I'm already missing Ian."

"Are we still going shopping?" Arielle asked.

"Yes, I haven't changed my mind, why?" Eva replied.

"Oh, nothing, I just wanted to make sure that nothing's changed," she said softly.

"Well, nothing's changed. I'm to pick up Gabby, before I come to your place," Eva stated.

"All right then, what time are you coming?"

"We're meeting Loren at the mall at 12:00, so Gabby and I will be at your place in about an hour. Is that okay?"

"Yes, I'm almost done."

"What are you doing?" Eva asked.

"I'm packing. I'm going to move in with my parents while Sebastian's away. Don't forget my mum invited all of you for dinner tonight," Arielle said.

"How could I forget," Eva chuckled.

"Eva, I know you and Loren don't like to eat but please do this for my parents' sake," Arielle pleaded.

"Oh, don't worry, Arielle, Loren and I will eat just as much as the rest of you," she snorted. "Maybe after dinner we can all go to see a film."

"Sure, I'd love to. Have you talked to Gabby about that?"

"No, but I've talked to Loren, and she said she and Paul want to see the new film *Blitz* after dinner, so she asked if you, Gabby and I would like to join them?"

"I'd love to go."

"All right then, we'll see you soon."

"See ya!" Arielle replied and ended the call.

Arielle finished packing, and jumped into the shower. She turned on the hot water, stood under the showerhead, and closed her eyes. The water *swooshed* and flowed over her hair, shoulders, down her back, and disappeared into the drain, releasing all the tension and discomfort out of her body. Fifteen minutes later, she stepped out of the shower, blow-dried her hair, and pulled on a pair of jean and a shirt. Looking at the clock again, she noticed it was 10:45.

She decided to read while waiting for Eva and Gabby. Reading was her weakness, and she wanted to do a great deal of it but with school, wedding preparations, and Sebastian, she didn't find enough spare time. She loved cuddling in bed with a romance novel in hand, but she never got very far into the story, because Sebastian would climb into bed.

She shivered as sensation washed over her spreading waves of pleasure through her body. Sebastian's seductive words crashed fast and hard into her memory, and she moaned uncontrollably. *Let's create our own romance novel*, he would murmur every night, and it would be enough to have her set the book aside, and fall into his arms. After that, everything would be a blur. His touch was always so hot and so exquisite that it would scatter her wits across the universe, stopping every thought from crossing her mind. She would remain lost in another world, a world of pleasure and passion and then they would glide into a peaceful sleep, utterly happy and sated. She couldn't believe all this wasn't just a dream, a figment of her imagination. This amazing, enchanting man would be her husband in a few days. She couldn't recognize the incredible changes that'd taken place in her life and the lives of her best friends.

She had settled into the large armchair with the book open in front of her but she hadn't read a single line. The doorbell snapped Arielle out of her thoughts. Opening the door, she saw Eva standing at the doorstep smiling and Gabby waiting in the car.

"Ready?" Eva asked.

"As ready as I'll ever be," Arielle replied, grabbed her purse, stepped outside and closed the door behind her.

The drive to the Lanes was filled with chitchat about the upcoming wedding, and wondering about where the guys were going, and what they were doing.

*   *   *

The parking lot at the Lanes was jammed. Eva, Arielle and Gabby stepped out of the car and strolled leisurely toward the mall chatting away. It was a beautiful warm day and Arielle ventured a swift look across the way searching for Loren. They were going to have lunch at their favorite spot, and do a little shopping; not that she needed anything after the wild shopping spree she had in Paris.

"Arielle!" Her eyes flicked toward the familiar voice and she saw Loren across the parking lot waving cheerfully trying to get their attention. Eva, Gabby and Arielle waved back and picked up their paces to reach her.

"Are the guys gone?" Loren asked.

"Yes, they left early this morning," Arielle replied.

"I wish Paul had the ability to follow them in their wild escapades," Loren said giggling.

"Do you know what they do on those outings?" Gabby asked curiously.

"What do you all think that they do?" she turned their question around.

"Well, we have our theories but what's really going on when the guys get together, only God knows," Arielle murmured.

"If you're worried about girls, you're completely wrong. I know for sure that for Ian, Sebastian, and Troy, you're the only girls they want, and the only ones they want to come home to. They just have fun being guys and doing things they like to do, and talk about things they love, mostly sports, and yes, maybe discuss hot girls," she said chuckling.

"I'm sure you know what they do, Loren. You've been part of their world for centuries. Eva is a newcomer to immortality, and as far as Gabby and I go, we're utterly clueless," Arielle said, pinning her with her gaze.

Loren turned and glanced between her friends and shrugged. "I'm not exactly sure, but I've heard that they do a lot of competitive sports."

"What do you mean?" Gabby asked.

"Well, they actually compete either against each other for money or take part in professional competitions."

"What type of sports?" Arielle's curiosity was peaked.

"I know they've taken part in horse races, sailing, golf, and polo. I was told they do all these in a big way," Loren said.

"Who told you?" Eva asked.

"Well, do you remember one of my friends, Marcus Bueller? He came to your birthday party, Arielle, last year."

Eva, Gabby and Arielle nodded in acknowledgment.

"Well. Marcus was the one who told me that they do all of those things in a big way."

"What do you mean by 'a big way'?" Arielle asked again.

"Well…they enter real races, not just among them."

"Are you joking?" Eva asked.

"Of course not. Sebastian and his friends used to be gone for weeks at a time doing exactly that. Entering some kind of real race with professional contenders. They raced cars, horses, they sailed yachts and entered, golf tournaments and polo tournaments."

"Oh, my…" Arielle's voice trailed off.

"I wouldn't worry about them being gone more than a week, Arielle." Loren assured her. "Not this time."

"That sounds so amazing," Gabby said. "Troy never mentioned that to me."

"Don't feel alone," Arielle said. "Sebastian never said a word. He's never gone anywhere since we met last year," she said quietly and winced.

"What's the matter?" Loren asked noticing her expression.

"I wonder if he's missed doing all those things. I sure don't want to be the person who keeps him away from the things he enjoys," she said pursing her lips.

"Oh, Arielle," Loren said kindly and put her arm around her. "Sebastian doesn't want to be anywhere without you. I'm sure about that. He did all these things because he was bored to death. Now he's happy."

Arielle looked at her and smiled. "Thanks Loren, I needed to hear that."

"Well, I'm sure they'll have fun!" Eva chuckled.

"I'm starving," Gabby complained. "Can we just sit down and have some lunch?"

Eva laughed at her best friend's whiny voice. "Well, here we are," she said.

They'd arrived at their favorite pub and chose a table outside. Arielle and Gabby each picked up a menu. Loren and Eva would have water, just for appearances.

Ten minutes after they sat down the waitress appeared. After taking their orders, she collected the menus and went back into the pub.

"Are we still coming to your parents' home for dinner tonight?" Gabby asked.

"Yes, my mum is expecting you all, and that includes Paul," Arielle said, glancing at Loren.

Loren smiled at the mention of Paul's name. "Are you all going to the movie with us after dinner?" she asked, moving her gaze from Arielle to Gabby, to Eva and then back to Arielle.

"Yes, I'd love to go," she said. "I love Statham," she added smirking.

"Tomorrow I thought we should go horseback riding," Loren said. "What do you all think?"

Gabby's eyes glittered with excitement, and she turned to look at Eva and Arielle. They were both pretty excited as well. They'd learned to love horses and horseback riding. Since Ian and Sebastian were both passionate about horses, the women had poured every ounce of strength and desire they could to become better riders, and now they loved their riding outings. They both had fought to rid themselves of their fear, and to bring into focus the happy moments they experienced while riding across open fields and on the beach. Just the look in Sebastian's eyes the first time Arielle rode beside him had been worth the agony and stress she'd endured to become better at the sport.

"That'll be awesome!" Gabby exclaimed. "Are we going to the club?" she asked.

"No. I thought we should go to my house and ride our horses. Some belong to Sebastian, and they're beautiful," Loren said.

That was a surprise to Arielle. She knew he had horses at the club, and at Saint Jean de Luz, but she didn't know he had horses at his parent's stables. She was excited to see them.

"We would love to do that," Arielle said, filled with excitement. Eva and Gabby agreed. And so it was set.

They enjoyed a great lunch and wonderful conversation. They walked around for about 3 hours and they all picked up a few things, mostly lingerie, and a couple pairs of shoes.

When they left Loren at her car, she agreed to meet them at Arielle's parents at 7:00 that evening with Paul.

In the car, Arielle asked Eva and Gabby if they wanted to spend the night with her, just as they used to do when they were younger. They both agreed without any hesitation. They dropped Arielle off at her house and left.

It was now 5:00 o'clock. She gathered her stuff and left for her parent's house. She was glad to be leaving the house because she didn't want to see Sebastian if he was to return for some reason or another before their wedding day. Eva and Gabby told her how excited they were to see their guys at the altar after not setting eyes on them for a whole week. The thought of being without him for a week was depressing, but she had to admit that the image of Sebastian waiting at the altar was exhilarating. She sank her teeth into her lower lip and shivered at the thought.

Her parents were thrilled to have Arielle home for a whole week. After their warm welcome, her mum went back to the kitchen to finish the wonderful dinner she was preparing, and her daddy went into his study and slipped back into the pages of one of his favorite books.

She excused herself, picked up her suitcase, and ascended the stairs in a rush. She stopped at the door of her childhood bedroom, and her heart thudded. She pushed the door open and stepped inside. She stood unmoved and stared in silence around the room, as tears began to burn the back of her eyes. Everything seemed to be where she'd left it the last day she moved her stuff out to the new house. She wasn't the same little girl who'd occupied this room not so long ago. As the door closed behind her, she heaved a deep sigh.

There was a quiet space of unspoken words, filled with love and warmth. What a unique and amazing feeling.

She unpacked and put her clothes away. Her throat tightened remembering the wonderful times she'd spent as a child in this room. The digital clock on the nightstand showed 6:30. This was going to be her home away from home for the next few days. The realization of becoming Mrs. Gaulle hit her with the force of a mallet. She bit back a groan at the thought of Sebastian and their earlier encounter. He was the most amazing man who'd ever lived, at least in her eyes. And now, this amazing man would become her husband. She took another quick look around and ran out the door. Her friends were waiting downstairs.

 *Chapter 21*

ON THE DAY OF her wedding, Arielle woke up late. The morning sunlight slipping through the sliver between the curtain and the window edge shot bright light on her face. Her eyes fluttered and opened slightly. How odd that she would oversleep on a day like this, but then not so odd after celebrating with her friends until the morning hours. Her head pounded and the effects of that tugged at her eyelids. She pulled the covers over her head. *One more minute!* She thought.

She finally flung the covers away and slowly sat up cross-legged in the middle of her huge bed. With a soft sigh she dropped her chin onto her hands, and closed her eyes. Her foggy mind instantly came alive. *I'm getting married today!* She giggled blissfully. Just the thought of Sebastian, and the very concept of marriage, made her body tense. She felt giddy, reeling from the warm sensation that erupted inside her. The sheer notion that tonight she would be sharing a bed with her *husband* sent delicious shivers down her spine. The word *husband* was a seductive murmur that rippled across her body and settled in the depths of her marrow.

Less than twenty minutes later she'd showered, dressed, and made her way downstairs to look for her parents. She entered the kitchen and found her mum preparing breakfast.

"Something smells good," she called joyfully.

"There you are," her mother said turning to face her. "Did you sleep good, darling?"

"Yes, thank you, Mum," she replied with a soft yawn. Closing the distance between them, she fell into her mother's open arms.

"Today's the big day!" her mother chuckled. "You'll be the prettiest bride ever," she choked tears as she held her tightly.

"I love you, mummy," Arielle whispered.

Her mum clear her throat, drew a tight breath unable to disguise her emotions. "Would you like something to eat?"

"Yes, please, I'm famished."

"How about some eggs and bacon?"

"Mmmm, that sounds wonderful," Arielle said. "Where's daddy?"

"He's in his study reading the newspaper. His breakfast will be ready shortly so please go and get him."

Arielle turned on her heels, walked across the hall and into her father's study. He was sprawled in his favorite chair, his face buried in the newspaper.

"Good morning, Daddy!" she called out happily.

Slowly he lowered the paper and looked at Arielle warmly. "Good morning, pumpkin." He scooted over in the big chair, and gestured with his hand for her to sit next to him. Her hesitation amused him. "Come on, you haven't grown *that* much. We can still fit in here just as we always did," he said and taking her hand, he drew her down on the chair with a chuckle.

Arielle squeezed in the big chair, falling into his embrace, and laid her head on his shoulder.

"I'm so proud of you, little girl," her father whispered, his voice breaking with emotion. "It'll be hard to give you up, but at least I know Sebastian is a good man, and he loves you very much."

Arielle watched the emotions swirl in her father's eyes and a lump rose to her throat. "Daddy, I'm not going anywhere. I'm still here, and you're still my number one guy."

Her father gave her a tight squeeze and she giggled. "You're marrying a wonderful man who loves you very much. I couldn't be any more proud of you," he said again. His eyes misted and he reached in his pocket for his handkerchief.

"I am a bit nervous, daddy," she murmured.

"There is nothing to be nervous about, pumpkin."

"I know, but..." her voice trailed. She sighed inwardly. "I can't believe I'm getting married."

"Breakfast!" her mother called before he had a chance to comment.

"We better go," her father chuckled. "You know your mother."

They rose and Arielle slipped her hand in her father's as they walked together to the breakfast room.

Five more hours before she would set her eyes on the man who'd turned her life into a wonderful, magical dream. Sebastian had text each and every day. Always the same text that made Arielle chuckle. "I love you, I can't wait to marry you, please miss me."

*   *   *

It was now 4:00, the house was a bustle of excitement, and her parents were blissful. The wedding was scheduled for 6:00. Arielle had arranged to meet Eva, Gabby, and Loren at the church at 4:30. They'd reserved a special room to get ready. The guys would be there a little earlier in a different part of the church so they wouldn't run into each other before the ceremony.

Sebastian entered first followed by Troy, Ian, and Paul. He heard swishing and soft whispering, but he didn't look at the guests. He took his place on the right hand side to the left of the altar. Troy, Ian and Paul stood next to him. He finally looked up. His gaze swept the front pew and saw all his immortal friends, including his mother and father. On the other side of the aisle he saw Arielle's mother, the Taylors, and Mrs. Winters.

The bridal music sounded and every eye in the church turned to look down the aisle. The silence was broken by happy whispers. Gabrielle walked in first, Arielle came in hanging on her proud father's arm and Eva and Loren borne the long train of her beautiful veil. Her father supported her as she walked nervously down the aisle. Arielle's mother started to cry at the sight of her daughter in her wedding dress. She looked absolutely stunning.

Her dress was of rich white satin trimmed with appliquéd flower blossoms. The bodice was fitted and strapless, trimmed with small diamonds around the edges. The pure white satin had been imported from the Far East and manufactured in Paris with a magnificent spray of brilliant stones all over the skirt. The design had been drawn expressly for her wedding and surpassed her expectations. The headdress was a gorgeous tiara trimmed with diamonds and the veil was of Honiton lace.

Gabrielle, Eva, and Loren wore emerald green brocade with satin trim and brilliant diamonds throughout the material, giving it a 16th century look. The color of their dresses had been Arielle's choice, to reflect the color of Sebastian's eyes.

Bouquets of freshly cut flowers adorned the aisles, filling the air with a breathtaking aroma.

Arielle's eyes fell on the man who'd made her dreams come true. A knot tightened in the pit of Arielle's stomach. He was stunningly beautiful. He looked so dignified, tall, with broad shoulders, long muscular legs and an aura of elegance and utter masculine beauty. She drank him in with her eyes.

At the sight of Arielle, Sebastian couldn't breathe or pull his gaze away from her. She was a vision to make any man lose control of his wits. Her veil covered her beautiful shoulder-length brown hair. Behind the veil, her sapphire eyes glowed with passion. He was lost in desire. He'd never seen another woman so utterly beautiful. And she was all his.

He drew a breath as she approached. He was aware that all eyes were on her. She was stunningly beautiful. Sebastian struggled to breathe as he vaguely heard the priest's voice.

"Who gives this woman away?"

"I do," her father replied and placed her hand into Sebastian's. Soft warm fingers gripped his hand and he looked down into her eyes. A dazzling smile painted her luscious lips and in a daze he smiled back.

They turned to face the priest and Sebastian kept her hand protectively in his. Shifting his grip he weaved their fingers.

Still in a haze he repeated after the priest the required phrases. Then Arielle took Sebastian's ring from Gabby and taking his hand in hers, slid the ring on his finger as she spoke her vows.

"I, Arielle, take you, Sebastian, to share my life, to be my husband, my lover and my friend in the presence of God, our families and friends. I offer you my heart, my soul and solemn vow to be faithful and be yours in joy as well as in sorrow. I promise to love you unconditionally, regardless of the obstacles we may face together, to support you, to honor you and respect

you, to comfort you. You have brought pure joy into my life and I can't be if you are not with me. You are the most wonderful, generous, and unselfish man and I'll love you for eternity."

Troy handed Sebastian Arielle's ring and he turned to her. She extended her hand and he closed his fingers about hers. He slid the ring on her finger. It was a perfect fit. He looked down into her eyes and their gazes locked. Passion scorched. He was now ready to vow his love and promise to her.

I, Sebastian, take you, Arielle, to be my wife, my best friend and my lover. My life didn't begin until I met you, the sun didn't shine until I looked in your eyes and the stars didn't come out at night until your smile appeared in front of me. I can't breathe if you are not with me and I can't imagine life without you. You're enchanting, funny, sensual and affectionate and you make the earth rotate, you bring the sunshine and the world feels right when you're next to me. I promise to love you, to protect you, to support your goals and to make you utterly happy with all the power I hold. I couldn't wait for this day and now here I stand in front of you ready to give you my very soul and I feel complete.

Their gazes remained locked and they stood unmoved as if time had stopped.

"And now, by the grace vested in me, I pronounce you man and wife." The priest's voice was loud enough for everyone at the church to hear, snapping Sebastian and Arielle out of their dazes. Both turned to face the altar.

The priest smiled kindly. "You many now kiss your bride."

Sebastian stepped closer, slid his hand about her waist, and drew her to him. Lifting her eyes she met his gaze. He raised her veil and drew her lips to his. It should've been a gentle kiss, after all they were standing in front of a crowded congregation, but it wasn't. It turned passionate and the weeklong separation made it powerful.

The priest cleared his throat, reminding them that they were still standing at the altar. Embarrassed, they pulled apart though everything inside them screamed against ending the kiss. Soft laughter and enthusiastic clapping filled the church as they turned to face the crowed.

Hand-in-hand, Sebastian and Arielle walked back up the aisle, smiling at the warm wishes from their friends and family.

Sebastian leaned close and murmured, "You look stunning. I missed you desperately and you're in deep trouble."

Arielle blushed at his words. "I missed you, too," she murmured.

He pulled her closer to his side. They were still breathless from the kiss.

At the reception hall, they greeted their guests as they came into the room. They had some of the most delightful moments with everyone before departing for their honeymoon.

Once in the back seat of the limo, Sebastian gave instructions to the driver. He then leaned back on the leather seat, pressed a button and closed the partition, separating the back seat from the driver. He then turned, pulled Arielle hard against him and, parting her lips with his tongue, plundered deep and hard. Their breathing increased, and her perfume of freesia dragged at his sense. His desire was barely restrained. He heard her soft sigh and drew a deep breath. Her warm breath brushed his skin, driving him crazy.

"I can't wait to take my wife to bed, and show her how much I love her," he chuckled.

Her gaze fell on the firm beautiful curve of his mouth and her breath hitched. "Oh! Is she waiting for you at the airport?"

With a low growl he leaned in and crushed his mouth on hers. "You're absolutely beautiful. I promise that I will take you to the moon and back, slowly and passionately," he breathed against her lips, shifting his hand to her thigh. "You're now mine, completely mine," he said a wicked smile on his face.

"We're going to the moon?" She feigned shock. "Don't tell me there's a spaceship at the airport, ready for the long journey." She was unable to wipe the grin off of her face.

Sebastian laughed out loud and dropped a kiss on her lips. "One thing I can promise you, it'll be a very long…and pleasurable journey for both of us," he murmured seductively.

"Oh, my!" she breathed, as she read the raw hunger in his emerald eyes. He held her in his arms all the way to the airport. His private jet was on the tarmac, the pilot standing by the steps waiting for the Limo to pull up. It wasn't long before the plane took off for their final destination. Sebastian unbuckled her seatbelt, pulled her up from her seat, and led her to the bedroom. Arielle's heart skipped several beats and her breath caught at the sizzling look in his eyes.

"Is this where you're going to take me on that long journey?" she giggled.

Sebastian rubbed his chin thoughtfully. "No, this is going to be a short stop before the long journey," he replied. He stood behind her and slowly unbuttoned her wedding gown. He pushed it off of her shoulders and let it pool on the floor. Arielle stepped out of the dress and into his warm embrace. He set his lips on her neck, nibbling and suckling until he reached the back of her ear. His tongue circled the soft earlobe and Arielle moved suggestively against him. A low growl left his lips. He unclipped her bra and his arms came around cupping her breasts in his hands, kneading, rubbing and squeezing. His thumbs brushed across the hard nipples and Arielle whimpered. Sebastian picked her up and set her in the middle of the bed. He removed his clothes feverishly and slipped beside her. His arms wrapped around her, cupped her breasts again and tortured them for a while, before his palms moved sluggishly over her abdomen and lower until he reached the very center of her world. He slipped one finger inside as his lips trailed hot kissed across her collarbone. Arielle squirmed with anticipation, and when a second finger slipped inside the intensity was toe-curling. She cried out his name, pleasure burning deep in her core.

"What do you want, love?" he whispered against her ear.

"I want you," she whimpered. "I missed you, Sebastian, and I need you now."

"Patience my love. This'll be a short journey, but not that short," he chuckled. He pushed her on her back, lowered his head and removing his fingers he claimed her center with his mouth. The pleasure was indescribable. His guttural groan set Arielle's body on fire. Passion burned as his tongue swirled spreading heat like wildfire across every nerve in her body. Her climax was powerful and shuddering. Her heart pounded, her body trembled and she held onto him, breathless. The sensual torture continued as he took her taut nipples between his thumbs and his forefingers and squeezed, sending liquid flames through her veins.

He lifted his head and slowly moved up, covering her perfect body, setting his hot mouth on one hard nipple. He laved at it, took it between his teeth and nibbled before drawing it entirely into his hot mouth as he worshiped the other breast with his hand. Arielle moaned. Sebastian claimed her mouth in a devouring kiss. Her nails scraped his muscled back and dug deep into the planes of his shoulders as he spread her thighs. With one powerful thrust he buried himself inside of her to the hilt. He felt a frenzied orgasm brewing as her muscles tightened around him. He stilled. He was hoping he could prolong this amazing encounter.

Arielle arched her back. "What're you doing?" she whimpered.

"Please, baby, stop moving." The expression on his face was a mix lust and torment.

"Why?"

"Because I want to prolong the pleasure for you. If you keep moving I won't be able to stop."

Panting, Sebastian drew a few deep breaths. He was insanely in love with her, and his desire was beyond anything he'd ever felt in his five hundred plus years on this planet. He took her mouth into a scorching kiss. His tongue slipped between her lush lips and plundered the softness of her mouth with unrestrained passion, tasting and exploring. He finally moved again and soon they caught the perfect rhythm. Arielle pushed her hips against his and soon his thrusts became stronger more powerful, pushing her higher and higher and Arielle cried out with a savage groan that sent them both over the edge and they shuddered into an explosive release. They remained in each other's arms until they reclaimed their senses. He rolled onto his back, taking her with him, resting his head on her chest.

"I love you, my Lizzy," he murmured.

"I love you too, Darcy," she mumbled, overtaken by exhaustion.

He set his mouth at the pulse throbbing at the base of her throat. This was his favorite spot of her body. His heart had stopped beating five hundred years ago, and her pulse had become his. She was his lifeline.

Arielle fell asleep in his warm embrace and he stayed awake watching her sleep. He was overwhelmed with passion and love. She was his wife, the woman he loved more than anything and anyone in this world. She was his to protect.

The captain's voice brought him back from his haze. They were nearing their destination. He shook Arielle lightly and dropped a kiss on her forehead.

"Wake up, baby," he murmured. "We're almost there."

Arielle blinked her eyes open. "Where is 'almost there'?"

"You better get up and dressed, if you don't want the captain to find us in bed," he chuckled.

She stretched and giggled blissfully. "I want to stay here in bed with you."

"I know, but we need to get up, love." He pressed a soft kiss on her lips. Arielle's arms came around his neck and she pulled him down to her, deepening the kiss. Sebastian moaned.

"What am I going to do with you?" he breathed against her lips.

"Anything you want." She giggled and rubbed against him suggestively.

"You're becoming insatiable!" He pulled the covers off of her and covered her naked body with his. "Are you ready for another round?"

"Do you think you can handle it?"

He groaned and took her one more time with wild hunger. He trailed kisses all over her face, her breasts, and caressed every spot of her silky skin.

"Is this what our lives are going to be like from now on?" she asked giggling.

"Yes, just a bit more intense."

"More than this?" she asked panting breathlessly.

"Trust me, much more than this. Now get up, Lazy Lizzy."

"But I don't want to. I want to stay here in bed with you. It is your plane after all, right?"

"This is *our* plane," he corrected and dropped a loud kiss on her lips. "And as much as I want to stay here in bed with you, we have to get to our honeymoon destination. And furthermore, save your strength, baby, there's more to come!" He threw his head back and laughed out loud.

"Mmmmm, I like the sound of that, Darcy."

"Get up, my lazy Lizzy," he repeated and jumping out of bed, lifted her in his arms and walked right into the shower.

She was insatiable, as she went for a third round leaving them utterly blissful and sated.

By the time they finished dressing the pilot announced that they'd been cleared to land. They walked into the cabin, took their seats and buckled in.

"Where are we, baby?" She asked looking out of the window.

"Turtle Island in Fiji."

"Fiji!" Arielle's face lit up like a Christmas tree and she clapped her hands with excitement.

Sebastian burst out in happy laughter. He loved surprising her and seeing her so ecstatic of the outcome.

 *Chapter 22*

THE HOTEL WAS NESTLED right in the middle of a tree-covered hillside, secluded from the rest of the world. Only a painter's hand could've brushed on canvas this piece of paradise with such warmth and skill. An ocean of flowers and exotic trees stretched for miles. The beaches were covered with soft white sand. The sun's rays spread across an ocean of transparent water in the deepest blue. The waterfalls were majestic, as the water leaped down the sharp slopes and broke into a mist of tiny dewdrops. The endless ocean seemed to blend with the horizon. It was hard to tell where the water ended and the sky began.

Sebastian had arranged for a private bungalow on a remote beach. This was a dream honeymoon any girl would die for. They made love for hours, in the room, on the beach, in the ocean. Arielle had never been loved the way Sebastian loved her. She wasn't sure what was so different about their encounters before they were married and now, but they'd changed. They were more powerful, more intent, and more breathtaking. She walked in a haze for days, bathed in love, sated like never before.

The place had the most amazing blue lagoons, hyper-romantic atmosphere that wrapped around you like a cloak, dark–leaved jungles and sky-blue waters kissing white sugar-sand beaches.

Horseback riding through the rolling surf provided the adventure preference for Sebastian and it'd become Arielle's as well. They spent hours upon hours walking hand-in-hand along the water and making love on the remote private silent beaches. They picnicked, as Sebastian was now familiar with the enjoyment of having a picnic by the ocean and swimming without a stitch of clothes on his body.

They swam together, explored the whole Island uncovering gorgeous and magnificent places completely hidden from the human eye.

It was in the second week of their honeymoon, and so far each day had been a magical fairytale, right out of a storybook. They were lying on the beach basking in the warmth of the sun, sated by another powerful encounter.

Sebastian lifted himself on one elbow and looked down, giving Arielle one of his smoldering glances, a smile etched on his gorgeous lips. "Have you ever seen anything so enchanting?" he murmured.

Arielle caught his gaze and chuckle. "Mmmm...I must say never." She never thought she could feel so utterly obsessive about one man.

"Baby, I don't mean me, I mean the place," he said, and waved his arm in the air in a circulate motion.

Arielle *humphed*. "All I can see is you."

Sebastian raised his brows, a predator's look in his eyes. Her eyes dropped to his lips and her breath held. Suddenly, she threw her arms around his neck and pulled him down to her setting her mouth on his. The sensual touch of her tongue on his lips set him on fire once again. She took his bottom lip between her teeth and sucked softly.

Sebastian groaned. The feeling was exquisite, the kiss deepened and lust poured over them once again.

"What am I going to do with you?" he breathed against her lips.

She giggled and provoked him with a suggestive wiggle. She felt his need hard and eager against her abdomen.

This was going to be a honeymoon he'd never let her forget. Sebastian's desire was stronger than anything he'd ever felt before. More powerful, more glorious than he'd ever imagined or expected to be now that she was his wife.

They watched the sunlight shimmering across the waves, slipping slowly but surely toward the end of the horizon.

It was late in afternoon when they returned to their room after spending an amazing day, swimming, chasing each other on the beach and making love. Completely overcome by a wave of exhaustion they fell asleep in each other's arms.

Sebastian came awake first. Arielle was still asleep in his arms. A wave of delight washed over him, knowing she was his and his alone. He smiled, propped on one elbow and looked down at her. He could gaze at her forever. Her soft breathing told him she was sound asleep. One finger gently stoked along her bottom lip and he planted a soft kiss on her temple. The jolt that shook him at the touch of her skin was that of pure exhilaration. He drew a shuddering breath and decided to get out of bed, take a shower and prepare the next day's itinerary.

*   *   *

Arielle woke with a start. Disoriented, she looked around. Deafening silence reached her. Her gaze flicked to where Sebastian should be sleeping, but he was nowhere to be seen. Her eyes roamed the room once again. There was just enough light to make out the furnishings in the room. *Where's Sebastian?* She couldn't shake the feeling that someone was watching her. She focused her attention to the balcony doors and gasped. Her thoughts came to a screeching halt. Fear gripped her like a metal vise and the hair stood on the back of her nape. Through the sheer curtains a woman's image stood. The blood drained from Arielle's face and her body started to shiver like a leaf. She sucked in a breath and closed her eyes. *Oh dear God, no! Please make it be a hallucination.* Holding her breath she opened her eyes slowly. The woman was gone.

Abruptly she came to her feet. The air in the room had thickened and she was hyperventilating. She grabbed Sebastian's shirt from the chair and threw it on her naked body. Moving slowly she approached the sliding doors and drew the curtains back. Mentally preparing to face whoever was outside, she opened the doors and stepped fully onto the balcony. A quick peek at the sky told her it was twilight. Her mind was on full alert. Her eyes scanned each shadowed corner, and leaning over the balcony, she tried to penetrate the darkness. She smelled the salty ocean, and heard the waves lapping the shore a short distance away. A branch breaking made her recoil and her head snapped in that direction. Her heart hammered her chest painfully. After a moment passed and nothing moved, she took a deep breath and let it out with a soft sigh.

Her mind was hesitant to accept the possibility of Annabel showing up to ruin their honeymoon. She shook off the sensation and stepped back into the room. She closed the doors behind her and leaned against them to steady her legs. She pressed her clammy hands against her thighs to stop them from trembling. *It had to be an illusion.* This was the honeymoon she'd dreamed about. Sebastian was hers to have, and to love for the rest of her mortal life. The thought of him moving through eternity without her made her heart ache. She knew there would be an end to her human life, but the thought of Annabel ending her life this soon, brought the unpleasant taste of bile into her mouth.

She lifted her head at the sound of a throat clearing to peer at Sebastian leaning against the bedroom doorway watching her intently. White-faced she stood frozen. She felt her heart thudding in her throat.

"What's wrong, love? You look like you've seen a ghost."

Arielle drew a shaky breath and cringed inwardly. She rubbed her clammy hands together and their gazes locked. The fear that lingered in her eyes sent powerful enough waves to unsettle him.

Sebastian looked around for a clue. "Something's terribly wrong; what is it?"

He didn't wait for a reply. Using his immortal speed he was in front of her in a nanosecond. His arms encircled her just as her legs gave way beneath her. His tight embrace prevented her from plunging to the floor. Her breathless gasping drove a chill down his spine.

"Arielle, you're shaking, baby. What's wrong?"

Arielle peered at him with clench teeth. She summoned her wits and let out a long shaky breath. "Sebastian, I think Annabel's here."

A wave of shock washed over Sebastian. Their gazes locked. He couldn't hide his disbelief. "Why would you think that?"

"I pray it's not true, but I'm pretty sure she was standing on the balcony watching me sleep."

Sebastian bit back an oath. "Is it possible you were dreaming?"

She shook her head vigorously, her eyes darting toward the balcony. "Sebastian, I was in a sleep haze, but I saw something out there," she said and waved her arm toward the sliding doors.

"Why didn't you call me? I was in the next room."

"I was too scared to think."

"Yet you went out there all alone to investigate. Oh, Arielle, what am I to do with you?" Sebastian pulled her into his arms and held her tightly. "Don't ever do that again. Call me first."

"So you believe it could be her?"

"I didn't say that. What I said is, I don't want you to get into trouble."

"Where were you?"

"I wanted to let you rest. I decided to take a shower and use the time to prepare an itinerary for tomorrow." Using his index finger he lifted her face to his and pressed a tender kiss on her lips. "I'm sure you had a nightmare and thought you saw something."

She was truly freaked out by the thought of Annabel on the same island, but masked her fear. "Maybe it *was* a dream," she muttered. She brought her gaze back up to his face, straightened her shoulders and narrowed her eyes. "Sebastian she can't have you. I won't allow it," she said firmly, pulling herself closer to his warmth. "You're mine forever," she whispered and buried her face against his chest.

"I'm yours baby. And don't forget, I'm also your husband," he chuckled.

"That's something I couldn't possibly forget for a minute even if I wanted to," she replied lovingly.

He turned her face up to his once again and his kiss was gentle. "And you don't want to."

He was so stunningly beautiful; Arielle had known that from the first time she saw him on that beach. She'd fallen in love with him desperately then and she was deeply in love with him now. For a moment she was lost in the wonderful memories of their life together.

"Anything wrong?" he asked.

"Should there be?"

He held her against him. "I've got you right here in my arms now, so how could there be anything wrong with that?" His reassuring words calmed her, and she clung to him.

She stood on tip-toes, threw her arms around his neck and pulled him down for a hot kiss. She needed him right now more than ever. His shirt barely covered her buttocks. His hands moved slowly and cupped her behind. Flames engulfed his body and set him on fire. He lifted her off the floor and moaned as she wrapped her legs around his hips. He could feel the intensity. He moved across the room with her still in his arms, lowered her gently down onto the bed and stood back to admire his new bride. She was perfect! He stared in awe with a devouring gaze at the vision that'd captured the core of his soul from the moment their eyes met. He gaped at the sexual image her luscious naked body offered. A sweet smile touched her lips, while fire churned in the depth of her sapphire eyes.

This was the perfect honeymoon he had promised Arielle. He wasn't going to let anything or anyone to destroy a single moment of their time together.

His eyes traveled slowly over every inch of her silky flesh. Her nipples had formed into taut buds and his control faltered. He'd never experienced this level of desire and passion, until Arielle. This was the ultimate gift from God in the five hundred years plus he'd roamed this earth.

He lay next to her and his arms locked about her. He took her mouth in a fervent kiss. His tongue parted her lips and plunged into the honey softness of her mouth tasting, exploring and ravishing her with love. Pulling back, he gazed into the deep blue pools of her eyes and smiled. Cupping her breasts, he ran his thumbs over the hard nipples and trailed soft wet kisses across the swollen mounds. Arielle whimpered as he set his mouth on a puckered nipple, laving with his tongue. He drew one nipple into the heat of his mouth and suckled while his hand worshiped her other breast. Arielle gasped and arched her back, pushing her breast deeper into his mouth.

Sebastian growled with savage, primal hunger and moved to suckle the other nipple, swirling the nub with his tongue. Sheer lust spread through his veins and his lungs locked. Pleasure beyond anything he'd ever known traveled like fire across his flesh and a growl escaped him.

Arielle drew a deep breath as his mouth moved again, trailing scorching open-mouth kisses downward over her tight abdomen, stopping at her center. She cried out his name with passion when he set his mouth there and spend a long torturous time giving her nothing less than pure pleasure. She wound her fingers into his sandy hair and pressed him harder against her. Waves of passion washed over her as he held her thighs firmly and continued the wonderful torture until her desire welled up and consumed her. She went over the peak and shuddered into oblivion, falling into the vortex of numbness and loss of awareness.

Sebastian licked his lips and drifted back up her body trailing kisses along every curve. He heard her whimpers and the small sobs that escaped her throat. He stopped and pressed his lips at the base of her throat savoring the thudding of her heart's pulse. Heat surged through his veins like fire and covering her body he pressed along the length of her, and instant combustion shook their very souls. Lifting his head he nuzzled her hair and breathed deep the intoxicating aroma of freesia.

Sebastian couldn't keep rein to his control any longer. He was aching with desire. He gazed deep into her eyes, green against blue. "I love you, baby," he said, his voice thick with desire. He pressed her legs apart, clasped her hips tightly and with a groan, sank slowly into her warm depths, savoring every moment until he was buried to the hilt. Her tight heat clenched tightly around him. Her hands moved down his muscled back and clasped his buttocks, pressing him harder against her. They moved in perfect rhythm, their souls connected. Arielle met each of his thrusts and his resolve quickly unraveled.

Sebastian felt the fragments of his control disintegrating. Although he tried to prolong this amazing sensation, he couldn't stop. The flames that washed through his veins penetrated his muddled mind. His mouth was hot and feverish against hers. Arielle swirl her hips against his. The thrusts increased in a powerful pounding rhythm. He growled as he thrust hard for the last time and sent both of them into a shuddering climax. He collapsed on top of her completely spent.

"You're taking my control with no effort at all," he whispered into her mouth. He rolled off her, bringing her with him, resting her head on his chest. He nuzzled her hair and pressed a soft kiss on her forehead.

"Do I please you, my love?" she asked softly.

His deep laughter echoed and bounced like a boomerang across the walls. He pulled her even closer and tilting her head up covered her mouth in a searing kiss. "Arielle, you have been the light that guides every step I take each and every day. You give my life true purpose to move on," he breathed into the kiss.

They spent long moments wrapped in each other's arms.

"Why don't we get dressed and I'll take you downstairs for dinner. You must be hungry," Sebastian said.

Her stomach growled in response and he laughed. "I guess you *are* hungry."

"Yes, I'm famished," she replied and got out of bed.

Soon they were on their way to the dining room hand in hand.

While waiting to be seated, she leaning close to Sebastian. "I guess dinner for one again," she whispered.

He looked down at her. His gaze roamed her face and settled on her lips. "I think tonight, I'll have a full meal," he replied, a crooked grin on his face.

Arielle's breath caught and she averted her gaze away from his intense eyes. "Don't do that," she murmured.

"Do what, love?"

"Look at me like you would like to devour me."

"I can't help that," he replied and squeezed her hand.

The host came to guide them to the private room that Sebastian had arranged for while Arielle was sleeping.

They enjoyed their meal chatting, laughing and kissing in between bites of food and conversation.

When the meal was over, Arielle stretched and heaved a deep sigh. "This has been a magical time Sebastian. I could've never imagined that our honeymoon would be this amazing."

He moved closer and his kiss was gentle at the beginning, but when her lips parted he felt the familiar lust and proceeded in devouring her mouth taking all she had to give. "It's been amazing for me as well," he breathed into her mouth. "But Arielle, our lives together are just starting. I plan to keep you this happy and sated every single day for the rest of our days." His deep-throated voice sent quivers of lust across her flesh.

"Oh, God! I hope I can live through it," she chuckled breathlessly.

Dragging his mouth away from her sweet lips, he gave her a sultry look. "Well I'll have to start on my promise as soon as we get to the room." Clasping her hand he rose to his feet pulling her up to him. "So let's go, baby."

How did this woman turn him on in such an outlandish way? This question had become one of the mysteries he hadn't been able to solve. He never seemed to get enough of Arielle. Astonishingly, his desire seemed to grow with each day they spent together.

Arielle giggled and soon they were on the way to their private bungalow, so full of love and passion they thought they would burst.

*   *   *

The time passed swiftly and they had only four days left on this picturesque island. Arielle wanted to explore the quaint villages, take photos of the incredible waterfalls, the fantastic vegetation and the magical beaches. Horseback riding, swimming, diving, and making love at every possible turn, were some of the items at the top of her list.

The thought of leaving this paradise made her unhappy. "I don't want to go home," she whispered when they woke the next morning nestled in each other's arms.

Sebastian tightened his hold and planted a gentle kiss on her lips. "We can stay as long as you want, baby," he said.

Arielle smiled wide and, throwing her hands around his neck, she pulled him back for a scorching kiss.

After a sizzling encounter, sanity slowly returned, and they decided to start their day with a nice breakfast in bed. Sebastian manifested a feast to fit a queen. Everything Arielle loved to eat in the morning was placed before her on a huge platter.

Arielle surveyed the huge meal, her mouth forming a perfect "O." She then turned to look at Sebastian, awestruck. "Oh, my, Sebastian. I can't help being astounded each time you do this," she said and pointed at the tray.

He heaved a small sigh. But before he could reply she put a hand out to stop him. "I know… I know… I know…another of your incredible immortal gifts. But it still shocks me to know that I'm eating manifested food."

Sebastian eyebrows furrowed. "I thought you would be used to this by now?'

Her shoulders rose a fraction and fell. "I should, but I'm not," she giggled.

"What do you want to do this morning?" Sebastian asked.

"I want to lay on the beach and soak up some rays."

"Okay, then that's exactly what we're going to do."

The soft ring of a phone startled them. They looked at each other utterly surprised. Who could be calling them on their honeymoon? Sebastian got out of bed and went to the next room to retrieve his mobile. Arielle flopped onto her stomach and hugged her pillow tightly. Sebastian glanced at the screen and saw Nathan's name. Sliding the arrow over, he unlocked it and answered briskly.

"Hello, Nathan?" he said into the phone.

"Sebastian, I'm really sorry for calling, but this couldn't wait."

"What is it?"

"I must have the numbers for the deal you're trying to close with the group in Australia. You didn't leave them with me before you left, and Madeline can't find the folder for that project."

"Are the Aussies already there?"

"Yes, they're in London and want to see the numbers by this afternoon, or they'll walk away from the deal. Again I'm sorry for calling."

"No, no it's all right, Nathan. I'm glad you called me. Hold on for a second."

Putting the phone in mute, he walked back into the bedroom. His gaze fell on Arielle's relaxed naked body sprawled across the white sheets and his muscles clenched. His eyes roamed hungrily up her long beautiful legs, and further up, to admire her breathtaking thighs, round perfect buttocks, small waist and lovely back. Her hair fell across her back, and spilled on the sheets and the pillow like a brown silk waterfall.

She felt him before she heard him and spun around to face him. A sexy smile touched her lips when she met his smoldering eyes. "Do you like what you see?"

He lowered his head and kissed her. His tongue slipped between her lips and tasted her. Arielle's eyes closed and a soft moan escaped her. Suddenly his warmth was gone. Her eyes snapped open to see a smirking Sebastian watching her.

"I love what I see and I want what I see, but not right now. Nathan's on the phone and I have to take the call. This deal is very important for our company," he said with a throaty voice.

"Okay," she replied a wide smile. She jumped out of bed, put her bathing suit on, grabbed a beach towel and strolled to the door. "I'll miss you!" she called out.

"Don't forget where we left off," he replied laughing.

Sebastian walked out to the balcony to continue his conversation to Nathan, while watching Arielle walked down the path that was surrounded by thick brush, heading toward their private cove. Soon she disappeared in the short distance and he walked back inside.

 *Chapter 23*

CLOSING THE DOOR behind her, Arielle leaned against it. She closed her eyes and chuckled blissfully. She ran her tongue over her lips to savor the taste of Sebastian's passionate kiss. This was the life she'd never dared to dream of. It was the closest you could get to a fairy-tale with an invisible line separating the dream from reality. She heaved a sigh.

Feeling happy, she climbed down the wooden steps and took the grassy path that led to their private cove by the ocean. The day was filled with sunny skies and warm temperatures. She hurried to the spot where she and Sebastian spent most of their time. A contented smile lingered on her lips.

She laid the beach towel on the sand, dug into her beach bag and she fished out her sunglasses. She kicked her sandals off and dug her toes into the cool, wet sand. Her heels sung deeper into the coolness and bliss engulfed. Dropping her beach bag on the towel she adjusted her sunglasses and walked into the warm waters that embraced her sending a delightful sensation through her as the warm waves stroked her body. She spent a short time swimming and floating on the waves in sheer pleasure.

When she emerged from the water, the cool breeze spread goosebumps across her skin and she shivered lightly. She ran her fingers through her long hair and shook her head in an attempt to dry it a bit more before she laid down. After toweling off, she reached into her bag and fished out her iPod and her book. She rubbed suntan lotion on every bare spot she could reach, while watching the waves lap against the shore. Pet Shop Boys' song "It's a Sin" blasted in her ears, and she hummed to the tune.

Lying on her stomach she placed the book on the beach towel and rested her chin on her hands. Fascinated by Anne Bronte, she was reading *Agnes Grey* once again.

She felt the sun's warmth on her back. She would need to be careful not to fall asleep and burn. That would not bring a happy ending to an amazing honeymoon.

Lost in the plot of the book, and the cruelty of Mrs. Bloomfield toward Agnes, she didn't notice that someone was standing right over her, blocking the sun.

A cool breeze blew across her skin and she realized that she'd lost the warmth of the sun. For some reason, a surge of panic went through her. Someone was blocking the sunlight but she was afraid to look up, unwilling to accept the gut feeling sending a surge of icy fear through every muscle in her body. She knew exactly whom she was going to find standing there; Annabel. Gathering her strength, she raised her eyes and peered at the woman who'd been drawn out of hell to become her worst nightmare. Her mind went blank and her breath caught. She swallowed the lump in her throat, and a shudder ran through her as her heart started to hammer her chest painfully.

She glanced around, wildly searching for Sebastian but he wasn't anywhere to be found. She couldn't move, she couldn't speak; at this point she was so scared all she could do was think that she was hallucinating. She shut her eyes and shook her head trying to get rid of the horrid image. *God please make this to be a dream!* She pleaded a silent prayer in sheer desperation.

Her eyes snapped open and the air thickened. Annabel was still standing there, arms crossed over her chest, cold fury in her eyes, an evil smile on her face.

There was something very eerie about her. Arielle tried to speak, to scream, to do something but she was completely paralyzed with fear. Setting her jaw, she pulled herself up slowly to face the other woman. The awful thing was that Arielle knew exactly why she was here. But whatever was to come, she wouldn't give up without a fight.

"What in bloody hell do you want?" she asked, her voice barely more than a whisper.

Annabel's smile broadened. "Now…now…is that any way to greet the woman who is going to end your miserable life?"

"Get out of here before Sebastian comes. He'll kill you," she muttered, not believing a word of it.

"You miserable human. Did you really think you will have a life with Sebastian?"

"We're married now and there's nothing you can do about it."

"Oh, but that's where you're wrong."

"What do you bloody mean?"

"Here is where it all ends for you, my dear."

Arielle gulped and mumbled something like, "I don't believe that." She turned to look toward the bungalow, praying that Sebastian was on his way.

"He's still on the phone, Arielle, I can hear him. He has no idea that I'm here and by the time he finds out, this will be over."

"What do you mean? This…" Terror was ripping through her and nausea churned in her stomach once again.

Annabel shot her a disgusted look and stepped closer. "I'm going to kill you and you have no choice in the matter. I just want to see you sweat for a while."

Arielle watched her, horrified. An icy sensation surged through her. "Annabel, why are you doing this? Sebastian will be here shortly," she managed to choke out.

"No he won't. But…I'm here because I'm keeping my promise to you and Sebastian. You didn't listen when I told you over and over again to walk away. And he didn't listen when I asked him to leave you alone. He belongs to me and no other woman will ever have him."

"He's never going to love you, Annabel."

"I don't care about that. I stopped caring about that centuries ago. The fact is, I made him an immortal to punish him, and punish him I will." Her laugh was ugly. "As much as I hate to say it, I know he loves you. There's nothing in this world that will hurt him more than finding you dead."

A wave of revulsion surged through her as she gazed into Annabel's evil eyes. Arielle's despondency was palpable. Reality struck her; Annabel was going to kill her. Nausea churned in her stomach and the bitter taste of bile filled her mouth. Fragments of Annabel's words reached her ears but didn't make any sense. Her world tilted and her mind screamed for her to run, but her legs wouldn't move. And even if she could, Annabel was faster than the wind; she'd never be able to get away. Her gaze drifted warily back. *But where is Sebastian?* she thought.

"I see you don't have that necklace on. How unfortunate for you," Annabel spat.

Arielle's hands moved of their own accord to her bare throat. A shudder ripped through her muscles and fear rushed icy fingers down her spine. She was going to die; she was never going to see Sebastian, her family, or friends. This is where the dream would end. She felt a wave of anger rush through her as she stared into Annabel's hateful glare. The pressure behind her eyelids forced tears to trickle down her face.

Annabel's blow came fast, taking Arielle by surprise. It caught her right in the middle of her face, sending her flying across the sand. The sheering pain threatened to choke her as the taste of blood filled her mouth. She cried out in shock and terror and everything became blurry. Her body quivered violently. *Oh God*, she whimpered, as she fully realize that Annabel was going to kill her. Despondency gripped her body like a steel vise. She tried to force her muscles into motion but the pain was unbearable. Before she had a chance to grasp her next thought Annabel was standing over her, one booted foot pressed against her throat. Arielle made a choking sound that barely found its way out of her mouth.

"You're going to die, you miserable human," Annabel spat, loathing laced through every word. She pulled her foot away, leaned down and grabbed Arielle by the throat, lifting her as if she was weightless. She squeezed brutally and her nails cut into Arielle's flesh, sending sheer waves of pain rippling through her body like blazing fire.

Tears mixed with blood drenched her face as darkness started to cloud her mind. She stared numbly at Annabel and tried to squirm away from her grip, but Annabel wouldn't budge. With a violent move, she pulled her free hand back and a punch ripped right through Arielle's chest leaving her breathless. The pain was so intense she grunted as panic washed over her. She tried to fight her way out of the deadly grip once again but to no avail. A silent scream pierced her mind and she started to lose consciousness. She clenched her jaw, shut her eyes tightly and waited for another hit to come with full force. Suddenly the grip loosened and she plunged onto her knees.

She swallowed the bitter taste of blood that made her cringe. Her hands began to tremble, and her breath was frozen in her lungs as her heart pounded against her chest, forcing more tears down her face.

"God, please don't let me die like this," she pleaded silently. She wanted to scream but the sound was lodged in her strangled throat.

Suddenly Annabel grabbed a handful of Arielle's hair and pulled her up to face her. "This isn't the way you're going to die. Open your eyes, you miserable human. I want to see the fear in your eyes when you take your last breath."

Arielle snapped her eyes open as the pain kept her close to the brink of unconsciousness. Her eyes widen in horror and her breath came in heavy gasps. A knife appeared in Annabel's free hand and it was but a flash before she leaned forward and plunged it right into Arielle's chest. The pain was excruciating as the blade delved deeper into her chest cavity and she screamed. Annabel twisted the knife once and pulled it upward, slicing through Arielle's ribcage. Pain ripped like fire across her muscles. She let go of Arielle's bloody body, and Arielle dropped to the sand, a guttural scream tearing from her lips. She was in agony, but tried to stay conscious, hoping Sebastian was near. She fumbled at her chest and blood spattered her hands. She stared at them in horror as her thoughts became dazed.

Annabel's laughter was profound and croaky but far away for Arielle's dying conscious. Anguish rippled through her and darkness was enveloping her. She could feel her heartbeat slowing and cold encasing her body. "Sebastian!" she muttered, "help me." She was dying, bleeding profusely, and she was alone. She was so very cold…

* * *

Sebastian's jaw clenched. A familiar scream tore right through him and drilled to the core of his soul. Terror surged and his lungs locked. "Arielle," he muttered. He dropped the phone and darted out the door, shouting Arielle's name. Moving in supersonic speed, he flew over the wooden steps, down through the path dense with growth that lead to the beach cove. As he came around the corner he collided with a hard body, stumbled back, but managed to keep his balance. Startled, he turned and came fact-to-face with Annabel.

He paled at the sight of her and a strange sensation crashed through him. His arms moved like whirlwind and grabbed her. Annabel looked stunned. She blinked at him in shock, but recovered quickly. She threw her head back and let an eerie sound escape her lips. A slow triumphant smile started to appear, but it was wiped off quickly by the rage burning in Sebastian's eyes.

He gave her a menacing look. "What have you done?" he hissed, shaking her violently. He froze at Annabel's next words.

"She's dead Sebastian, she's gone. Your beautiful human is gone," she spat venomously.

Fury poured through every pore of his body. "No!" he cried out, anger emanating from his eyes. He succumbed to seething rage. Annabel lunged at him. The fight erupted into a raw struggle of aggression. He caught Annabel with a hard blow on her side and she bowled over. Stunned, she struggled to rise, and leaped, lunging once again at Sebastian. She looked like a possessed demon, hair weaving in her face like a cyclone. She whirled and faced Sebastian, slashing a bloody knife through the air. Sebastian sucked in a breath and pulled back out of range of the blade. He raised a leg and slammed his foot in Annabel's midriff, sending her stomach colliding against her spine. She went airborne before crashing to the ground with a loud *thump*. She lost her grip on the knife and it disappeared somewhere in the distance. Annabel couldn't breathe. Before she had a chance to recover, Sebastian bent down, wrapped his hands around her neck and squeezed with every immortal ounce of strength, and fiber in his body. "I loathe you!" he screamed. His voice was a lash of madness.

Annabel recoiled and watched him through terrified eyes. She screamed as she squirmed, overcome by terror, and clawed against his chest. Her body thrashed on the ground as she tried to free herself from the deadly grip, but Sebastian wouldn't budge. It wasn't long before Annabel's eyes rolled back and the thrashing ceased as the last breath left her horrid body.

Sebastian spat on her in disgust, and separated her head from her body, making sure she was never coming back. He kicked her remains away, and shut his eyes tightly, hoping he was going to wake up and find that this was just some gruesome nightmare.

Complete silence fell around him. He had a hard time gathering his scattered thoughts. The uncertainty of what he was going to find at the beach weighed upon him as darkness shrouded his mind. He listened using his immortal ability and caught a soft gurgling sound that raised the hair on the back of his neck. He quickly located Arielle.

His eyes scanned her pale face and gave her body a quick inspection. Her clothes were soaked in blood and the ground around her was stained. Anguish surged through him like a tornado, ripping through his flesh, burning every muscle in his body. He swallowed, fighting the nausea gripping him. He dropped to his knees beside her and cradled her bloody body. She was dead weight. He took a deep shuddery breath, looked up to the sky and murmured a prayer. He remained unmoving, holding her against his chest, watching for any sign that she still lived. As if answer to his prayer a light movement of her lips left Sebastian breathless. He gasped, realizing that he'd reached her in time.

Moving in an immortal speed he scaled the wooden steps, burst through the door and laid her in the middle of the bed. His mind was filled with uncertainty. She'd accepted Eva and Ian's immortality, but how would she accept her own?

He swallowed hard at the thought, but he had no other solutions. She was dying and he wasn't going to go through eternity without her by his side. It was a promise he'd made to Arielle and he was going to keep it.

"Arielle...Arielle...I'm here, baby!" he murmured, his voice breaking. He touched his fingers to her throat. Her pulse was thready. He focused his thoughts on Arielle and felt the strength pulsing again in his veins. He rushed into the next room and came back with the Salve. He wasn't going to let her die...he wasn't going to let her die...She was the love of his life.

Lifting her head he tipped it back and quickly brought the edge of the bottle to her lips. "Drink, baby," he murmured even though he knew she couldn't hear him. He dripped a good amount of the immortal liquid into her mouth. He then laid her head back on the pillow, and standing, pinched the bridge of his nose, a sign of extreme stress for an immortal.

The day had seemed an eternity, and now he'd have to sit and wait for the next three days through Arielle's transformation, while drowning in mixed emotions. He visualized the terror she must've experienced at Annabel's hands, and it tore him apart. He hardly noticed the passage of time, lost in his thoughts.

He decided to use that time to get rid of Annabel's remains, clean up the stains from the bed sheets and change Arielle's bloody bathing suit.

He then called Troy and his shock was obvious.

"What in the world happened?" Troy asked.

"Annabel followed us and waited for the right moment to try and take Arielle's life. I was on the phone with Nathan and Arielle was waiting for me on the beach. I never thought this would happen, but it did. I got to her just in time and now she's going through the transformation."

"Good God..." Troy muttered.

"I know she's not ready to accept this change so I'm not sure what to do."

"Sebastian, Arielle was wonderful in supporting Eva and Ian through their transformations. I think she'll do fine."

"The issue I have is that Arielle is strong for others but never when it comes to her own self. I don't mind telling you that I'm terrified to tell her the truth. But, Troy, I couldn't let her die." His voice broke.

"Sebastian, it'll be okay. Trust me. Arielle is an amazing woman. She'll do fine."

"Thank, Troy. Please tell our friends. I want to avoid unexpected questions when we return home."

"What did you do with Annabel?"

"Nobody will ever find that despicable woman. The guys will be happy to know that they don't have to chase her around the world any longer."

When he hung up he felt much better. He was happy with his decision to keep the only woman he loved with him for eternity.

Her body rejuvenated and Arielle woke with a start. She opened her eyes slowly, lifted her hands and rubbed her temples. Her eyes darted around as if she was looking for someone or something and stopped when she met Sebastian's deep green gaze. She blinked rapidly and took deep breaths.

"Sebastian!" she said softly.

"Yes, baby."

"I had a horrible nightmare."

"Did you now?" he asked calmly.

Suddenly strange turmoil invaded her mind. Terror and panic crashed into her thoughts and her heartbeat elevated. She swallowed hard and let the silence envelope her for a moment.

Sebastian was watching her intently. Suddenly she moved swiftly to sit up, but his hands pressed softly against her chest keeping her still. She looked up to meet his gaze, her eyes glassy with horror, as if something ungodly lingered in her thoughts. But soon her mind stirred alert.

"Oh Sebastian, Annabel…" her shaken voice trailed. Her hands moved fast and grabbed her chest. Heart racing, eyes wide, she looked down and her mouth fell open. "I would swear it was real," she mumbled, perplexed. "She used a knife and dragged the blade upward," she breathed, making an upward motion with her hand. "I remember bleeding profusely and I couldn't call for help." Her hands moved feverishly now over her body. What she thought as a dream was so vivid. She stopped to recollect her thoughts and remembered putting on her bathing suit and walking to the beach. *Was it all a horrible nightmare?* She looked around again, her eyes darting from one piece of furniture to the other and stopped when she glanced at the nightstand.

"What are you looking for, my love?" he asked.

"Sebastian, where's my book?"

"What book, love?"

"The book that was right here," she said, and hit her fist on the small nightstand a couple of times.

"I'm not sure, baby, I haven't seen it."

"Sebastian, it was here this morning. And… I remember putting it in my beach bag, I remember reading on the beach…" Her gaze flickered to a chair across the room and her body tensed. "Where's my beach bag? It was on that chair," she said, pointing across the room. Abruptly she went still as a statue. Anxiety hovered in the air between them. Her hands moved quickly and touched her hair. It was in complete disarray. She always combed her hair before bed. Horror ripped through her body and the familiar nausea rose.

Sebastian tried to probe her mind but soon realized he couldn't do that any longer. She was now an immortal. Her body had rejuvenated to its perfect condition.

"How long have I been lying here?"

"Awhile."

"Awhile? How long is awhile?"

"Awhile," he repeated forcing himself to stay calm.

Her breathing elevated and she didn't look at him. "How did my hair get like this?"

There was a long silence. She finally lifted her head and stared at him intently and he had to say something.

"Arielle…"

"How?" she was now screaming hysterically.

"Arielle, baby, calm down please," he pleaded. "Do all these questions really matter? You're here now, and you're all right," he said, his voice breaking.

Instantaneous shock melted away her hysterics. Her fingers twined and her lips moved in a griping sound. "What in bloody hell do you mean I'm 'all right now'?"

"Arielle, we need to talk." The way he looked into her eyes spoke volumes, his warm loving eyes boring right into hers. He was sure reality hadn't caught up to her yet. She had no idea that she'd transcended from the human world.

But it didn't take long. Her lips started to tremble. She shut her eyes and pressed her hands against her temples one more time, and her expression dissolved into a frown. "It wasn't a dream, was it?" she asked without looking up.

He moved to sit on the bed and took her hands into his. "Look at me, baby," he demanded.

Arielle looked up and their gazes locked. "It wasn't a dream," he whispered. She remained utterly unmoved and he saw how deeply his words had sunk into her mind.

She shut her eyes tightly and took a few deep breaths. She then let a narrow strip of light slip through her eyelids and stared up at him through horror-stricken eyes. Her lips were still trembling, and her body shaking. She swatted his arm away and clamped her hand over her mouth. She was panic-stricken and he couldn't read her thoughts.

"But…" she mumbled. "If this wasn't a dream, then I should be dead."

"You're very much alive!" Sebastian said.

"Where's Annabel?"

"Annabel is dead."

Arielle jumped out of bed ready to run, but to where? She wasn't sure. Suddenly her legs buckled and she started to fall. Sebastian's arms moved like whirlwind and kept her upright.

She leaned against his muscled chest for a moment gathering her strength. She wasn't sure what to do next and she didn't know what questions to ask. She pulled away making her way to the balcony. Sebastian followed. Stepping outside chills prickled down her spine. She turned to face him. "Sebastian, I want to cry but I don't seem to be able to."

He nodded without saying a word.

"I'm not…" her voice trailed off. "Am I…"

He hung his head low, unable to look into her eyes. Silence enveloped them like a blanket. He finally looked up and reaching out pulled her back into his warm embrace.

Her eyes widened in disbelief. "What happened?" she asked.

"Oh God, Arielle, I thought I was going to lose my mind. I was sure that I'd finally created a safe haven far too steely for anyone to penetrate and hurt you. I failed you again. I can't remember any woman being such a huge part of my life until you. I was looking for you and one day I just turned around and there you were. I couldn't possibly let you go now."

He pulled back, took her face in his hands and brushed her cheeks softly with his thumbs. He then snaked his hands around her back and held her tight against him. "You scared the hell out of me. I thought I wouldn't get to you in time. I love you so much. I can't live without you, you're my whole world, the center of my universe."

She took in the seriousness of his voice, but couldn't reason with what Sebastian was trying to say. The anxiety was building up inside her and she felt she was suffocating. She couldn't breathe, still trying to process what was happening inside her body.

He watched her intently. "Please..." he started to say but she cut him off before he could finish his statement. She wanted badly to cry but how strange, no tears would form in her eyes. Her heart leaped into her throat, and she couldn't form a sound thought. *I can't cry.* The thought made her shiver.

"I'm not ready for this... I'm just not ready for this..." she muttered. She stepped back and scanned his face. "Sebastian, I'm scared," she murmured.

"Don't be scared, baby. Nothing can hurt you anymore."

"Oh God! I wish I could cry. I think I would feel better," she whimpered. "What am I to do now?"

"Arielle, please, love!" he begged. "You've been strong for everyone else, why can't you do that for you?"

"But I'm not ready," she stated inflexibly.

"It was either this or let you die. I thought you wanted to be with me forever. Have you changed your mind?"

She looked lost. "No, Sebastian, I haven't changed my mind, but this?"

"There was no other way. I'm sorry. I love you way too much and I wasn't going to let you slip out of my life. You'll continue to be *you*, only more powerful, utterly unbreakable. You will be mine for eternity and you'll never be afraid of anything or anyone. Arielle, you know everything about immortality. You've heard all the details from me in the last year plus and you helped Eva through her countless questions when she went through her transformation." He pressed her hand. "You have to do this Arielle, and I know you can."

She couldn't believe what she was hearing. She wasn't ready, she wanted to go back to how things were, but she knew there was no turning back now.

"I wonder how this is going to work when we get home."

"Arielle, it worked for Ian and Eva. No one but our friends sees them as being different. It'll be the same for you." His voice was calm and reassuring.

She watched him carefully as she considered what he was saying.

"Are you all right, baby?" He gazed into her sapphire eyes trying to see the answer he needed before she even said it. His devastatingly beautiful face was pleating for reassurance and his eyes were blazing with love and passion for her and her only. His hands came up and held her face gently, running his thump across her bottom lip.

"I love you, baby, and you're all mine now and forever."

"I love you, too," she replied gently. His lips were mere centimeters from hers.

His arms came around her and pulled her flush against him. His embrace felt warm and powerful as his muscles shifted and she moaned.

She stood on tip-toes and brushed his lips. Sebastian closed his eyes in a silent prayer and thanked God for making this transformation a little easier than he thought it would be.

Arielle wrapped her arms around his neck and drew him down to her. Sebastian's lips covered hers and fused them into a blistering kiss. The sensation was so much stronger than she remembered. Something was different; her knees nearly buckled.

Sebastian felt it and a smile tugged at his lips. "What is it, baby?"

"I'm not sure. It's a strange sensation."

"It's the immortal sensation," he replied, his voice amused. "Much more potent than that of a human."

Arielle skimmed her hands across his muscled shoulders and stepped even closer. "Now I understand what Eva was trying to tell me. Now I understand your unending desires."

Sebastian grinned. His gaze fell on her lips just as she ran the tip of her tongue over the bottom lip and he groaned. "How are you feeling?"

"I feel great, but I still don't understand how this can be."

"It'll take time." His voice was hushed.

"Am I going to need Salve from now on?"

He nodded as his mouth came down on hers once again and kissed her with unleashed passion. He felt her body respond and heard her soft moan. She drew back breathless and pinned him with her eyes. She needed a reply.

"Yes, you'll need Salve just like we all do, for strength, but you'll be able to enjoy human food just as you did before."

Her eyes widened in surprise. "Just as I did before?"

Sebastian pulled her back into his tight embrace. "Well, not just as before, but you'll be able to tolerate the food. It'll make it easy for you to function among humans." He was staring at her lips, eager to plunge back into the kiss.

She slipped away from his embrace. "I want to taste it."

Sebastian's eyebrows furrowed, but he walked into the other room and came back with a small glass filled with the special immortal nourishment.

She stared at the glass for a moment, and then took a small sip. She closed her eyes, letting the liquid trickle down her throat. Sebastian watched her intently. He saw no changes in her expression and waited eagerly to hear what she had to say.

Arielle stood, thoughtful. The liquid was sweet with a fruity kind of aftertaste. "I like it," she whispered into the glass and glanced at him over the brim.

He moved to take the glass away from her but she pulled back and smiled. "I'm going to finish it," she stated. "How long have I been going through the transformation?"

"It has been four days since..." he voice trailed. He didn't want to bring back bitter thoughts.

"I wonder what this new life will be like," she muttered into the glass.

"It will be amazing. You and me together forever."

She walked toward the bed, zillions of thoughts swirling in her head. This is what she'd envisioned from the moment she met Sebastian. *Why am I so worried about it now? Maybe I'm not ready for such a huge step, but ready or not I'm here now and there's no going back.* Her next thought was about the man she loved beyond any limits. He saved her life and she needed to make sure he knew that she was very much in love with him. What if he hadn't found her in time? The thought of Sebastian moving on through the centuries without her weighed her down. She didn't want to think about that any longer. She was now an immortal and they would be together for eternity.

He came around and stood in front of her. His hands cupped her face and his fingers caressed the curve of her jaw. "What are you thinking?"

She looked into his emerald eyes and smiled. "I told you before that my thoughts are always about you."

"As they should be," he said and his smile widened.

Suddenly Sebastian scooped her up into his arms, and carried her to bed. "Let me show you about immortal love," he said cradling her against his chest, his lips soft against hers, his love enfolding her like a warm blanket. He laid her on top of the sheets and their clothes came off with maddening speed. He let his gaze wander over her naked body and his breath held at the splendor of it. She was beautiful before, but immortality gave her a stunningly exquisite touch. He climbed on the bed and pulled her flush against his bare body. "You'll be mine always," he whispered against her lips.

She gasped at the feel of his skin against hers. His mouth came down on hers with unrestrained passion and his tongue plundered the softness of her mouth. Arielle moaned as blistering fire shot down her spine, curling her toes, leaving her breathless. His lips warm against her flesh moved down her throat, kissing and nipping her soft silky skin. His mouth moved lower and pressed further kisses along the curve of her breasts.

Arielle took a tremulous breath as his hand cupped and kneaded one breast while the tip of his tongue flicked over a taut nipple and then his hot mouth closed over it suckling fervently. A seductive quiver shot down her spine and she felt her body sinking into immeasurable pleasure. She made groaning sounds as his hands and his mouth moved down her body. His fingers stroked and teased every naked spot and his mouth kissed, suckled and tasted every part of her body. Her pulse rocketed and she melted into his touch when she felt his erection pushing against her thigh.

Sebastian moved over her body like a panther after his pray. He stretched on top of her and tilting his head, laid claim to her mouth. His tongue delved into its softness and he plundered hard pulling all the stops and sending waves of blistering fire across every single muscle of her body.

He slipped his hands around her hips, pressed her thighs wide and drew her up to him, jetting wild anticipation across her nerves. With one swift move and a loud groan he buried himself inside of her to the hilt. Arielle hissed a gush of air between her teeth. The filling was exquisite, the sense of fulfillment indescribable. Their encounters were always beyond anything she could ever imagine, but this was different; no mistake about it. The passion was glorious, overpowering, the strength was vast cloaked with primitive urge. He invaded her body and possessed her mind setting her flesh on fire.

Arielle slipped her arms around his neck pulled him down crashing his lips beneath hers. She shut her eyes, bowed her neck and pushed against him as he plunged into her body harder fusing them together like never before.

Sebastian had been watching the emotions cross Arielle's face and knew she was experiencing the supremacy of immortal sex. He was determined to show her the art of immortal sensuality. This was going to be a night she'd never forget.

Her hands moved helplessly across the muscled planes of his back and her nails scraped him seductively, sending his mind racing frantically. She wrapped her legs around his waist, pulling him even deeper into her body as urgency crashed into her. A guttural groan left his lips and he plunged into a ferocious kiss that left them both breathless, lost in waves of sensual pleasure. He took long strokes and she fell into the rhythm arching and shifting beneath him trying to get even closer.

The feeling was so startling that they wanted this to last longer, for eternity if possible. Arielle buried her face into his neck and clang to him as though this was going to be the last time.

Sebastian was bathed in bliss that only got stronger by the moment. The thought that he'd have her for eternity drove him into unrestrained hunger and intensity. Her muscles tensed around him as he drove harder and harder into her body.

She called out his name and her world exploded when she reached her release. She threw her head back and her body quivered clenching tightly around him bringing him over the edge. They'd never had an experience this remarkable. They were both speechless, drifting in an aftermath that was more overpowering and more consuming that ever before.

They lay holding onto each other possessively. Finally Sebastian drew a breath and rolled onto his back taking her with him. She rested her head in the crook of his neck and spread her hand lovingly over his chest. Sebastian held her close and pulled the covers over them. Soon they fell asleep utterly exhausted.

The next time Arielle opened her eyes the room was bright, bathed in the sunlight that was slipping through the balcony doors. She was still in Sebastian's arms and he was wide awake, watching her intently.

Their gaze locked and held. Wide smiles spread across their faces. She was now an immortal, more powerful than she'd ever dreamed she could be.

A new day had dawn for Arielle and Sebastian, and a new beginning in the immortal world as husband and wife.

Note to the Readers

Thank you to my fans. It is the most rewarding and surreal experience to receive your wonderful feedback after reading my books. To the future readers, thank you for loving books and making my book your choice. This is the eighth and final novel in my Immortal Rapture Series. I hope you will enjoy it.

.

Contact Information
My website: lilianroberts.com
My Twitter: @lilian3roberts
My Blog: lilianroberts.blogspot.com

ALSO BY LILIAN ROBERTS

Arielle Immortal Awakening
Arielle Immortal Seduction
Arielle Immortal Passion
Arielle Immortal Quickening
Arielle Immortal Journey
Arielle Immortal Fury
Arielle Immortal Struggle